Requited Harvest

Also by Charlsie Russell

The Devil's Bastard

Wolf Dawson

Epico Bayou

River's Bend

Camellia Creek

Honor's Banner

Requited Harvest

A Novel

Charlsie Russell

Loblolly Writer's House
Gulfport, Mississippi

Loblolly Writer's House
P.O. Box 7438
Gulfport, MS 39506-7438
Visit our website at www.charlsierussell.com (www.loblollylocker.com) and www.loblollywritershouse.com

First Edition: July 2018

This book is a work of fiction. Names, characters, and incidents are products of the author's imagination. Any resemblance to actual events or persons is coincidental. Any scenes depicting actual historical persons are fictitious.

Library of Congress Control Number: 2018903954
Russell, Charlsie.
    Requited Harvest: a novel

    ISBN 978-0-9894302-5-8
    1. Historical – Fiction

Book design by Lucretia Gibson
Copy editor, Nancy McDowell
Cover design by Lucretia Gibson

Printed and bound in the United States of America.

Guide to Characters

Markiston-King Clan

Tom Daws. Deceased. Eva Markiston's father.

Evangeline "Eva" Markiston. Matriarch of the family. Beautiful, powerful, ruthless. Adel Reed and Penelope (Penny) King's grandmother.

Clarissa Frederick. Adel Reed and Penny King's mother.

Stuart Frederick. Owner of King and Gibson Lumber. Clarissa's husband and Adel and Penny's stepfather.

Adelaide "Adel" Edmondson Reed. Jack Gibson's first love. Daughter of Clarissa Frederick and Ralph Edmondson. Penelope King's half sister. Mark Reed's wife. Eva Markiston's lieutenant.

Mark Reed. Newly graduated physician working with Dr. Hadrian Clark in Mississippi City, Mississippi. Married to Adel Reed.

Abner Lucian King. Deceased. Penny's grandfather. Father of Hugh King.

Hugh King. Deceased. Father of Penelope King. Founder of King and Gibson Lumber in Handsboro, Mississippi.

Penelope "Penny" King. Daughter of Hugh King and Clarissa Frederick. Grandchild of Eva Markiston.

Gibson Clan

James John "Jack" Gibson. Son of James Waymon Gibson.

James Waymon Gibson. Deceased. Original part owner of King and Gibson Lumber in Handsboro, Mississippi. Father of Jack Gibson. Executed seven years earlier for the murder of Hugh King.

Millicent James. Jack Gibson's maternal aunt in Lumberton, Mississippi.

Noble Clan

Alan Noble. Owner/CEO of Noble Corporation in Biloxi, Mississippi, with a branch in Mobile, Alabama.

Lorraine Noble. Deceased. First wife of Alan Noble. Mother of Harold Noble.

Harold Noble. Son of Alan and Lorraine Noble.

Florence Noble. Second wife of Alan Noble.

Jonathan "Jon" Noble. Head of Noble Shipping in Mobile, Alabama. Brother of Alan Noble.

Horace Noble. Deceased. Founder of Noble Corporation. Father to Alan and Jonathan Noble. Grandfather to Harold Noble.

(Abigail Fleet Knox. Deceased. Florence Noble's mother.)

Primary Support Characters in Alphabetical Order

Mars Bullock. Negro timberman who works for Jack Gibson.

Hadrian Clark. Markiston and Frederick family doctor.

Tobias Craig. Chief of police/town marshal in Biloxi, Mississippi.

Carrington Farrah. Markiston/Frederick attorney.

Clem Fletcher. Leader among Eva Markiston's henchmen.

Lucas Frazier. Jack's immediate subordinate at Humboldt's Biloxi River mill.

Deacon French. Deceased. Negro owner of the turpentine still sabotaged in Piotona, Mississippi.

Peter Fritz. Florence Noble's (the Noble family's) doctor. Coroner of Harrison County, Mississippi.

Thomas Gates. Administrative executive at Noble Corporation.

Robert Hays. Harrison County, Mississippi, deputy sheriff.

Humboldt Timber Company. Based in Chicago, Illinois. A large timber/lumber company owning and leasing large chunks of timberland in the Piney Woods of Mississippi. Jack Gibson's employer.

Lyle Jenkins. Harrison County, Mississippi, sheriff.

Angelina Ladner. Dowager socialite of Biloxi, Mississippi. An old friend of the King family.

Clive Morgan. Humboldt's attorney. Represents Jack Gibson.

Charlie Nixon. Policeman, Tobias Craig's immediate subordinate.

William Puknay. Local judge in Eva Markiston's pocket.

Nathan "Nate" Stephens. Jack's immediate supervisor in Piotona, Mississippi. Works for Humboldt Timber.

Peter Whithers. On the board of Noble Corporation.

Ralph Whithers. Peter's son. Assistant department head at Noble Shipping.

Chapter One

"Seduce him."

"Seduce him?" Adelaide repeated.

Eva Markiston looked at her granddaughter, a striking flaxen-haired beauty wearing a knowing smile, despite her feigned confusion. "Yes, sweetheart, seduce the fool. No hard order for you, and I have every confidence in your success."

Adel pushed away from the back of the settee and rounded the piece. There she sat and studied Eva, who stood in front of the plantation desk. "Grandmother," she said, "have you given any thought to Penny in this?"

"Lots of thought, little concern. I have bigger and better plans for Penelope than to wed her off to a man more easily manipulated by you."

"And what I want?"

"You want what I tell you you want, darling girl, and you're smart enough to know it."

"And Penny's not?"

"Penelope has been smitten with Mark since she was eight. She has no idea of the purpose of marriage."

Adelaide's eyes widened. "But you always considered theirs a wonderful match, as did Mark's parents. And the purpose of marriage in Penny and Mark's case, I believe, had to do with the canning industry."

"Canning is the Reeds' business, not mine, and that 'wonderful match' benefits them, not us. Besides, that entire prospectus

1

has been off track since Hugh's death. It's not like the loss will be a major setback for them." Eva turned to the commode against the wall and pulled out a cut-glass bottle filled with sherry. "No," she said, pouring them each a cordial, "my biggest concern at the moment is ensuring the 'match' does not include Penny. For all intents and purposes Mark has been away from our little girl for the past three years. No doubt he's grown up and perhaps having second thoughts."

"His letters do not indicate that."

"That serves to show the poor boy is backwards. Come to think of it, I've always thought so. Show him what heaven is like." She handed Adelaide the drink. "It's early yet, but who's to know?" She winked. "I want Penelope free of that obligation, Adel."

"Why?"

Eva held up her glass in a mock salute. "Because our Penny is fetching a much higher price elsewhere."

Chapter Two

The blast, two, maybe three miles away, woke Jack Gibson. Less than a minute later, three sharp blasts impaled the night. A steam whistle. The signal left him and the nine men bunked with him in the night-cooled railroad car staring into the darkness, their disembodied voices questioning one another as to what was wrong. Outside, dawn appeared to break to the southwest, and they were scrambling half an hour later, readying to leave for Piotona, when the rider came for Jack specifically. He and the others knew there was a fire. Not the cool, slow burning fire natural to the longleaf forest, but a conflagration that carried the scent, not of wood smoke, but of pine spirits.

His nostrils were stinging by the time he arrived at the still, the west wind driving the smoke into his face that last of three miles. Old Maggie French, her black eyes shimmering and her skin glowing orange in the midst of the burning building turned to him when he dismounted. "He be gone, Jimmy Jack," she said, her voice so soft he wouldn't have understood her had he not already been told. "Don't know what I'm gonna do now."

Sue Cotton stepped closer to Maggie's side and wrapped the woman in her arms. Silent, the girl laid her head on the old woman's shoulder, and Maggie rubbed the younger woman's enveloping arms.

"You don't have to worry about money, you know that, Miss Maggie."

In response, she hung her head lower and wept. Sue hugged

3

her tighter, clinging in support and for support. Sue Cotton couldn't find her man, Richard. Jack stared at the red glow above the eastern line of longleaf heralding dawn, then dipped his head to the mangled mass of glowing embers and twisted tin and the bulging shadow of the turpentine still, askew now, its platform collapsed beneath it. They'd found Deacon French, or what was left of him. Maggie had seen him run into the still house, and she saw the explosion immediately after. Even if they hadn't found remains, they knew he was gone.

On Jack's other side, his Aunt Millie touched his arm, then stepped around him to go to the two Negro women. "Let me try to get them back to the house," she told him. "There's nothin' more for Maggie to do. I hear she's been sick all week."

"What about Dick?" Maggie said to Aunt Millie moments later. "We ain't found Dickie yet."

"The men will come when they know something," was his aunt's soft reply, and he watched her rub Sue's shoulder.

The younger woman nodded. "Come on now," Sue said to Maggie. "Come on. We can wait at yo' house jes' as well."

Jack drew in a breath. Wood smoke laced with pine tar...and that sickly sweet stench of burned human flesh...attacked his nostrils, and he wished he'd thought before heaving in that breath of polluted air. To his left, a shadow emerged from the back of what had been the turpentine still, and it waved at him, a silent hail against the early dawn. Harvey Jones, the constable for this distant corner of Marion County, headed toward him. Despite his swollen gut's warning he not make a move without risking emptying his stomach, Jack started toward the man. God, Deacon French was dead. Jack had known him all his life.

Jones held out his hand, and Jack took it. "You got any enemies, Mr. Gibson?" The two men with Jones gathered close.

"I reckon I do. Why?"

"We found that young nigger worked for you. He's just inside the tree line yonder, back of the mill."

"He wasn't in the fire?" Jack wanted to feel relief, but the man's demeanor told him he shouldn't.

"Nope, but he's just as dead. Got a bullet in his head." Harvey Jones, owner of the biggest commissary in the dying Piotona, modest railroad investor, and deacon in his church, drew a handkerchief from his back pocket, then pushed his hat off his forehead. He wiped away sweat and soot. "Don't take a man of much sense to realize this fire was no accident."

*J*ack washed his face one more time. In a minute he'd go down to the creek and bathe. Aunt Millie had clean clothes for him. She would wash the ones he was wearing now, she told him, but he wondered if she could get the stench out of 'em.

Millicent James opened the door and stepped out on the back porch. "Wish you would come work for the Hintons. They're Southerners, at least."

"Folks at Humboldt are good to me."

"Yes"—she sighed—"and good to their people. You've told me. But I think your staying has more to do with Humboldt's refurbished mill on the Biloxi and the specter of King and Gibson looming over Bayou Bernard from your vantage point at Happy Hollow."

"Eva's way overextended," he said, taking the towel his aunt held out to him. "She's gonna destroy the company."

"And you're thinking you'll be able to pick up the pieces?"

"I'd like to try."

"Humboldt must be paying you better than I thought."

Jack made a sibilant sound. "Nah. Nathan says Humboldt's interested in it. Wants the mill over on the Wolf, so if I don't get the company...."

"You'll have the pleasure of working in it?"

"I'll have the pleasure of knowing she won't have it. That means a lot."

"It was more her people's than yours, anyway."

"Ain't so, and you know it. Daws lost his mills during the War. But for Hugh King's largess in helping old Tom after the court case, she'd have no say at all."

"Daws contributed a lot of timberland to King and Gibson."

5

"For which he retained ten percent of the company," Jack said, his voice bitter. "My daddy contributed a lot more. That ten percent Daws held on to got Daddy and Uncle Hugh killed, Aunt Millie."

Millie sighed. "You're probably right, but it was a good deal, your daddy always said so."

"It would have been had Tom Daws lived."

"A man can't live forever. He was already old when he sold to them. Neither Hugh nor your daddy could have anticipated the problems with Eva."

"Which wouldn't have happened had she not thrown her daughter into the mix. Hugh bought himself more than a longleaf forest with that deal. He bought his downfall."

His aunt touched his arm, and he met her eyes. "You think she was behind what happened tonight, don't you?" she asked.

"Not a bit of doubt in my mind." He wiped his neck, holding his chin high. "I'm not going to let her get away with this like she did Daddy."

She turned from him. "Come on in," she said. "I've got coffee made. You want breakfast?"

He tossed the towel next to the tin wash bowl and followed her inside the cookhouse. The kitchen was bright, and this would have been a cheery day, but for its start. "At the moment, I don't think I'll ever eat again."

"Harvey told Maggie he didn't want her to see Deacon's body. Thank goodness she listened to him."

At a rough-hewn little table, Jack pulled out a chair. Aunt Millie set a tin cup in front of him and placed another in front of the chair beside him, then sat herself. "It's possible someone was out to get Deacon, even Rick."

He looked at her. "Who, Aunt Millie? Who would have done it? Deacon would've been seventy-eight in July, and from what he's always told me about Rick, that boy didn't drink or gamble. Neither one of 'em had an enemy in the world."

"Maybe someone found out he owned the still."

"And who 'round here would have cared, really? That worry

was in Deacon's head. He was from here. Lived here his whole life. No one cared if he owned that still. Hell, half the folks round here secretly knew it. I know who did this, and she did it believing that still was mine." He sucked back a sob. "Deacon French worked his entire life in that turpentine still. He'd forgotten more about harvesting resin and making pine spirits than half this county will ever know. He was at Crombley Winters' side when we marched against Mexico, and he was already growin' old when he held Justin, dyin' in his arms, at Murfreesboro. Daddy said he had to pry Deacon loose from that boy's body. And that woman had him killed, him and Rick, for no other reason than to get even with me."

"Can we prove it?"

"'We,' Aunt Millie?"

"Can Harvey and the sheriff?"

"That she was behind it? I doubt it. I oughta do the world a favor and rid it of her."

Millicent James picked up her cup and took a sip of coffee. "My worse fear is that you'll hang for the likes of her."

"Which is the one reason I won't do it. Not until I'm sure I can get away with it."

She took another swallow. "You'll never get away with it. More importantly, you're not a murderer."

"She gets away with it."

"So far, but you're not like her. This family has already lost one man to her." Aunt Millie wiped her hands on her apron. "I can't understand her obsession. She pushed your daddy out, that's what she wanted. What's she—"

"King and Gibson pays shipping charges to use Humboldt's spur lines, this particular time to the Pearl." The coffee nauseated him, and he pushed the cup away. "Every time he increases the rate, she thinks I'm behind it."

"Are you?"

"Decisions like that are made at a higher level than me, and they're based on good business practices, not personal feuds. That's how she operates, and that's why she's in the straits she's in today. Humboldt wants the Wolf River mill, and she's gotten herself into hock to them working shipping on credit, and you can take it as gospel, those Yankee bastards were plenty generous with her at first. Offered her deals they'd never offer anyone else." He laughed shortly. "Unless, of course, that anyone else had something they wanted in return. Then they just sat back and let her dig herself into a hole. Now they're peering down at her from over the edge. She's stupid and has no one to blame but herself. She chooses to blame me." He shook his head. "I'm thinkin' I'll make a foray to the Coast."

"For what purpose, Jack?"

She sounded angry. He shouldn't have said anything to her, but he had. "What happened here last night was an act of retaliation. She's not thinkin' she's gonna persuade me to get Humboldt's policy changed. She did this to show me what she's capable of. I want to get closer to her home base, and Humboldt's having production problems with its mill on the Biloxi."

"You're a logger, not a lumberman. You never have liked working in a mill."

"War's..." *Hell*, he'd almost said, but caught himself. If Aunt Millie noticed, she didn't indicate.

"I can deal with it," he began again. "Once I've got a good crew in place, I'll be freed up to do other things."

"Other things?" She frowned. "Can Deputy Craig help you down there?"

"He hasn't been a Deputy Craig since he and Jenkins fell out over Uncle Hugh's murder investigation, and I doubt it. He's the marshal over in Biloxi now. Handsboro and Mississippi City are outside his jurisdiction."

"Still it's good to have an honest lawman close."

"It is, and one who dislikes Jenkins and Eva Markiston almost as much as I do."

Chapter Three

"She's getting desperate," Jack said and pushed the door wide. The finished one-room railcar with its plank walls and rough-hewn floor stood in the shade of the towering pines. It was the private office of Nathan Stephens, Humboldt Timber's regional field officer for its south Mississippi holdings. The car moved around. Right now it sat on wooden rails at the end of a half mile of tram that linked it to the New Orleans and Northeastern Railroad. The spot was four miles north of Piotona and was the car's third location in five years. In all those five years it had remained within a twenty-five mile radius of where it started. Humboldt had been cutting a lot of timber in this area and still had a lot to cut.

"She's threatening to file suit." Nate braced the door against the inside wall with a log, forcing it to remain open. "I'm already killing mosquitoes, but it's too hot in here with the door closed."

The converted railcar had a standard door, just like those cars converted into homes for the loggers and their families. The latter were subdivided into rooms, Nate's office wasn't. It was a wide, open space, typically a mess with broad tables spread with plat maps, railroad maps, and post road maps, many of which decorated the walls like pictures. And then there were the shelves of law books, bound plat books, and general forest information books and pamphlets and cubbies for more plat maps. Nate claimed he had it all organized, and to his credit, he always seemed to come up with whatever it was he needed.

9

The structure also had four windows, two on either side of the door and two opposite, on the back wall. They were glass, and they were screened. "I hear tell," Jack said, listening to him fuss, "that they're making exterior doors with screens to keep the bugs out."

Nate hung his hat on a peg beside the door and shrugged out of his jacket. How the man could stand to even put the thing on in this heat, Jack would never know.

"Any idea where I might find one?" Nate asked with polite interest...or was it sarcasm?

"Hell, Nate, I was thinking you could build one. All you'd need is a sturdy frame with screen stretched across it. Hardest thing would be coming up with enough wood."

Nate grinned. "Funny man." He pulled out his swivel chair and took his place behind the desk. "Hmmm..., mount it on the door frame?"

"Yeah. Have it hinged out."

"I'll set Tucker on it. He should be able to figure something out."

Shoot, Jack could concoct something, but Tucker was a good carpenter. He'd be able to build a solid frame, and that would be the hardest part of the project.

"Sit down," Nate said, "and tell me about your scheme to get even with the witch of Bayou Bernard."

Jack grabbed the closest seat, such as it was, an unpainted ladder-back chair with a cowhide bottom Nate had scrounged up from somewhere. He'd been dragging it around with him for the past five years that Jack had worked for him.

"I've spent the good part of two days coming up with an alternative to ten miles of rail, all for the express purpose of saving my employer time and money."

"And depriving Eva Markiston of a dummy line within proximity of her cut parcel."

"Dammit, Nate, if she can't afford freight on that dummy to Piotona, she's not gonna pay it to a new site on the Pearl either. And I'll freely admit that in addition to conserving resources, my design also serves in aiding and abetting you Carpetbaggers' lust for King and Gibson's Wolf River mill."

"And for that you deserve to be hanged."

"I look at it as screwing a thieving Scalawag."

"And all this time I thought you were a Scalawag."

"I'm not, and that should make you appreciate how strongly I feel about that woman."

"I know what drives you, Jack, and I know what happened a few nights ago in Piotona has got you riled. Mr. Humboldt can take risks based on his own emotions. He doesn't need to be taking them based on his employees'."

"I've been reconsidering the value of that tram to the Pearl for the last two weeks, well before the turpentine still."

"Give me the details."

"We'll move our timber down the Crooked to Clear Creek. The Clear empties into the Pearl less than two miles above the county line. There's a bend in the river there. With high water, the transition should be smooth. It's a lot faster and cheaper floating 'em down to Nicholson than building a dummy line to the railroad."

"For it to work, you've got to get that section cut before the spring rains. If you miss the rains, and you don't have a tram built, you've lost a lot of time. Time enough to get you and me both fired. Can you manage it?"

Hell, Jack wasn't prescient, and he wasn't Mother Nature. All he could base the decision on was what had happened in the past and what was happening now. "If I didn't think so, I wouldn't have suggested it."

"All right. I'll give you the benefit of the doubt, but only because I like the idea of not having to build that tram. That'll save money. Humboldt's gonna like that." Nate drew in a long breath, then leaned back in his chair. "You do realize, Jack, that if Humboldt gets that Wolf River mill we're gonna hold on to it?"

Till the longleaf was gone, Jack thought, but he shrugged. "It's lost to me anyway. You're not her only creditor. You're just the one to whom she's most beholden."

"You know, when Humboldt was first scoutin' out this area eight or nine years ago, we considered King and Gibson a force to be reckoned with. We knew it already had a chunk of the domestic market, but it being a small outfit, we figured we'd eventually eliminate it from the competition. But we've hardly had to do a thing. She's done it to herself. Funny thing is, she blames you and sues us." He snorted softly and shook his head. "When she lost Hugh King and your daddy, she lost all sense of sound business practice."

Evangeline Markiston hadn't *lost* those men. They weren't hers to lose. They founded the company, and she bought her way in.

"What she lost," Jack said, "or eliminated, were the impediments to her concept of progress. I'm surprised King and Gibson has lasted as long as it has. But if she files suit over the price hike, she could tie us up in court. I don't think Humboldt will like it, but you'd be a better judge of that than me."

Nate pursed his lips and nodded.

"But if we don't build another rail," Jack said, "she'll have no basis for the suit. The state of Mississippi isn't going to expect Humboldt to build rail just to accommodate her. Let her build her own rail to Piotona or, better yet, float 'em down Crooked Creek to the Clear like I plan for us to do. And that northern section she's now got layin' on the ground has easy access to Black Creek once the freshets start. Guarantee you her granddaddy made good use of swollen creeks, and Stuart Frederick certainly is aware. She won't listen to anybody." Jack pointed an index finger at Nate. "And I've got one more suggestion. Buy Blake Shipping."

"Why do you say that?"

"She's looking for someone to ship her lumber. I've heard she's making overtures to them."

"And you're getting this information from where?"

"Last week one of their department heads boarded a few days with Kate over in Happy Hallow. She overheard him talking about it at dinner."

Nate narrowed his eyes. "You've been to the Coast recently?"

Jack smiled. "She writes when she hears something I might be interested in."

"Ah, so Miss Kate's your spy?"

"Just an old family friend. Most of what she tells me is gossip. Rarely do I get something valuable like this."

"Well, that little tidbit is interesting." Nate leaned back in his chair, then crossed his ankles atop the desk. "You think Eva's planning to ship overseas?"

"Blake does business with Brazil primarily, and it's possible."

"According to my sources, she doesn't have the capital or inventory to pull that off."

Jack grimaced. "Nate, this is Eva Markiston we're talking about here. She should have been curbing her activities two years ago and concentrating on ingress and egress out of the Piney Woods. Instead she depended on big rail and Humboldt, and now you're about to bury her. If she's got plans to sell on the international market, you can bet she's gambling freightage against future profits. She's planning to cut a deal with Blake Shipping. I guarantee it."

"Noble Corporation does business with Europe."

"What does that have to do with anything?"

"I was talking to George Blake's brother-in-law when I was in Biloxi a week ago. Seems Noble Corporation has made an offer to buy Blake out. George is seventy-two and he's seriously considering it."

Unease washed over Jack, though he wasn't sure why it should. Eva was painting herself into an ever-shrinking circle. "Has Noble Corporation ever exported lumber?"

"No, but as you know, Blake Shipping does. Look Jack, don't make too much of this. Noble Corporation's shipping branch is in Mobile, but the senior man, Alan Noble, has pretty much moved the corporate headquarters to Biloxi since the War. Blake is speculating that they want some subsidiary shipping out of Pascagoula. I just thought your reference to Eva and Blake Shipping was interesting when weighed with what I heard."

13

"Any chance Humboldt would counter Noble's offer?"

Nate Stephens laughed, then dropped his feet and sat straight in his chair. "Sorry, Jack, but Humboldt doesn't need the Wolf River mill bad enough to justify the purchase of Blake Shipping. We don't need it, and as soon as Mississippi has done something about Eva's bogus lawsuit, we intend to demand payment."

"If she gets her lumber to market, she could make enough to get herself out of hock."

Nate was already shaking his head. "No, she can't. We're not taking partial payments this year, and as you said yourself, we're not her only creditors. We intend to accept the Wolf River mill for payment in full, and we'll give her enough additional to equal the true value of the mill. That will be enough to pay off her other creditors. She won't refuse."

That was something. One of King and Gibson's most valuable assets would be transferred from a hated rival to the progeny of Carpetbaggers.

"There's something else I need."

Nate snorted.

"I gotta get down to the Coast for a day or two. Anything you want me to check on down there? Still having problems at that mill on the Biloxi?"

"Hell yeah, I'm having problems with it," he bellowed. "I'm having problems trying to get a section of timber cleared here in Marion County, too, for movement to Nicholson. How the hell are you gonna get it finished if you're playing lumberman in Biloxi?"

"After the freshets."

Nate snorted. "I wanted you to go a month ago. You had too much to do, remember? Had to get that timber cut, you said, and you were hell-bent then to build a damn tram and get those logs to the railroad. Now you're wanting to go the opposite direction and float 'em down the river. And no sooner do you sell me on that, then you're talking about leaving before the project's finished. What's up?"

"I said, *after* the freshets, Nate. I don't plan on heading down

14

in the morning. Eva is causing me problems about some of my personal property, which she's trying to tie to Daddy's forfeited estate."

"Your granddaddy's farm?"

"Yep."

"Seems like that would best be handled at Columbia."

"I've been to the courthouse. I'm good as far as Marion County is concerned. I just need to run some paperwork by Harrison County, that's where the forfeiture was ruled."

"Do you have time to wait on the freshets?"

"That section will be cut by the end of the week. The rains will be here by then. Less than a week, I should be able to make my way on down. Shoot, I might even honcho the float. I haven't rafted logs to a mill since I was a kid."

Nate was staring at him in disbelief, his mouth open. "How, *old* man, do you know it'll be raining by the end of the week? More important yet, raining enough to move timber on those creeks?"

Jack grinned. "I know."

He didn't. The main thing was that the rains hold off till the timber was cut.

"Never mind the Biloxi mill just now. Put Pat in charge of the crew, and you get on down to the Coast and back up here. I'll give you two days."

Chapter Four

"Oh god."

Jack felt Adel stretch beside him, and when she raised her bare arms above her head, he rose to hover over her, to feast his eyes on her long limbs, the gentle swell of her belly and the golden cleft peeking from her coyly crossed thighs. Dipping his head, he ran the tip of his tongue the length of her arm from right above the elbow to the soft tuft of golden down at her arm pit. Adel gasped, and he growled, then found a breast. She arched her back, offering more of herself than the nipple he teased with his tongue. He laughed, collapsed, and rolled back onto the prickly hay.

"If I'm to make you happy one more time, you're going to have to let me rest."

She raised herself on an elbow. "I don't know if we have time to waste."

He smiled at the hay tangled in her disheveled curls, and when he felt her hand roam over his stomach to his pelvis, he found her eyes, watching him. "Perhaps I can help," she said.

He caught her hand and raised his head to gauge the sunlight piercing the cracks and old knot holes of her family's barn. He sat up. "Honey, that might have to keep you this time around."

A laugh escaped her throat, and she fell back, face up, deliciously naked and wet and ready and waiting, and good lord, he wished he did have the stamina to love her again. And the time. He reached for his pants.

16

"You're leaving so soon?"

A smile moved over his lips at the implied jest in her voice. "Soon, my ass," he said and stood to pull the britches over his buttocks. "The Frederick manse might rise late," he said dryly, "but we're getting way past early here." He eyed her askance, still on her back, still naked and exposed. She touched her upper lip with the tip of her tongue, then with a grin, moved her legs.

He watched her antics a moment, then sat back down and reached for a boot. "I do have business here."

She pushed herself up at the waist, then reached out and touched his shoulder. He kissed her fingertips and reached for his other boot.

"I don't believe Grandmother is expecting you."

"She's not. I'm gonna be a surprise."

"Hmmm. For me, a delicious one, but I'm sure she'll find you quite distasteful." She touched his chin with her index finger. "Wouldn't you rather take your grievance up with me?"

He pulled his boot on with a grunt. "She's claiming Grand-daddy's farm was part of Daddy's estate."

"And part of the forfeiture," she said matter-of-factly.

He eyed her askance. "That farm never was Daddy's, and she knows it. So do you. She's doing this knowing it costs me money to secure a lawyer and fight it. Well, I don't have to fight this one. Harrison County and Marion County are in complete agreement. Daddy preceded Granddaddy in death. That farm is mine."

"Yes, well, you know what's driving her? She says Humboldt raised freightage on her timber three cents a foot."

"I know what her true motivation is." He finished adjusting his britches over the top of his boots and looked at her. "How come you are aware of all this?"

She traced his lips with that inquisitive finger. "I overhear her and Stuart talking."

He turned on her suddenly and crushed her into the prickly hay. She squealed.

"You're full of cow shit, Adel. You participate in their conversations."

She drew up close to him when he kissed her. "Yes, I'm privy to their evil plots. Make me happy, and I'll tell you whatever you want to know."

His chest was still naked, her body still warm and soft. But a third time in less than an hour and a half? "Baby, I've been up half the night and haven't eaten since noon yester—"

"Sodomize me," she said, clipping her words and sucking in hard breaths. She was like this sometimes, burning with need and desire, making demands no normal human male could meet. Her hand stroked his chest, a thumb his nipple. "Please, Jack, it won't take long, I promise." She caught his shoulders and pushed him, urging him on, but he used his hand instead. She cried out within seconds, and he, ready now, sat up on his knees and reached for the buttons on his...

"Oh, sweet heaven, Jack, you made my wedding night something to remember."

He chilled. She'd covered her mouth with the back of her hand. She was watching him, gauging his reaction. He breathed in her musky scent, strong from their repeated lovemaking, and thought he might throw up.

She sat up slightly and reached for his waistband. "Take me now. I know you want to."

He twisted away from her awkward reach. "What did you say?"

"I said to take—"

"Before that. What did you say about a wedding night?"

She shrugged, then wrapped an arm around her legs and drew her body tight. "I said you were the highlight of my wedding night."

He rose slowly to tower over her. "You're married?"

"Since last evening." She shrugged. "I thought you needed to know before you see Grandmother."

Jack swallowed the saliva forming in his mouth and stepped away from her to retrieve his shirt, wadded up in the hay where she'd thrown it less than two hours ago.

"Who?" he asked quietly.

"Mark Reed."

"I passed him at the gate as I was coming in. I thought that odd. Actually wondered if maybe he and Penny had married and I hadn't heard."

"He left early to break the news to his parents. I came out with him to bid him adieu." She smirked. "And wish him good luck."

"Well, that explains your wandering around the barn in your nightdress." Jack straightened and pushed a fisted hand through a cotton sleeve. "I actually thought you saw me coming from your bedroom window like in the old days." He rammed his other arm into its sleeve, then jerked the shirt shut. He started buttoning. At the same time, he shook his head in disbelief. "You married your little sister's intended."

"I did."

"Had they called off their pending engagement?"

"How quaintly put. Well, if one must do such a thing, he had."

Jack forced himself to look at her. "When?"

The sheepish grin curving her lips faded, and she looked away. "Yesterday morning."

"When you married him?" he said loudly.

Her face snapped back around to him. "When he made love to me. We wed yesterday afternoon in Mobile."

"Penny waited patiently for three years for him to get out of medical school. Hell, I didn't even hear anything about a coming-out party, and he's back...what, a month...and you steal him from her?" Jack stuffed the tail of his shirt into his waistband. He grinned, and he hoped he looked as hateful to her as she now appeared to him. "You screwed the bastard, and the idiot felt he had to do the honorable thing and marry you."

She smiled. Obviously his hateful grin had not adequately conveyed his true feelings. "On the contrary," she said, "he wanted to marry me. I took him places he's never been."

"I wonder if he realizes all the places you've been."

"He never heard about me and you, I guess."

"Everyone knows about you and me. That's what compelled

you to wish your groom good luck as he was leaving to tell his mother he'd just wed the Whore of Babylon. Do you remember that?"

"I do, and I will find great satisfaction in learning that horrid woman suffered an attack of the vapors upon hearing the news."

Jack twisted, his gaze sweeping the stall behind him. He needed his belt, and he found it. He looked down at her, watching him, and he saw her eyes rove the length of the leather.

"Go ahead. Beat me."

"You'd probably enjoy it." He'd like to beat her. Leave cruel welts all over her beautiful, treacherous body. Her buttocks and her breasts. Like to listen to her explain that to the fickle dog who'd married her.

"I did what I had to do."

"Don't try to feed me that, Adel. Not any longer. You could have come with me years ago." He threaded the belt through a loop. He had to get out of here.

She reached up and grasped the hands hooking his belt. "We—"

He knocked her hand aside, then grabbed her nightgown— "Get dressed"—and threw it at her.

She scrambled to her feet, and he turned away, sickened now by the sight of her body.

From the corner of his eye, he saw the hem of the gown drop to the ground, and he tossed her the matching silk robe.

When he stepped toward the barn door, she grabbed his arm. "My being married means nothing."

He narrowed his eyes on her.

"There's no reason our relationship can't continue as—"

He shook off her hold and sought the door. Two more steps and she was on him again, blocking his exit. "It's all we would have ever had, Jack. What difference does it make?" Eyes glistening, nostrils flared, her lips curved into a smile. "I could have your baby now, your blood would get the mill back."

He shoved her. She stumbled, but righted herself and held her place. "That's exactly what I want, Adel, my son bearing

Mark Reed's name at the head of a company that will never be anyone's but who your grandmother decides, and you, honey, as well as your progeny, are a ways down the list of prospective heirs. Now get out of my way."

She folded her arms over her breasts and stood her ground, staring at him. Again, he started to move, but she stepped slightly sideways to put herself between him and the broad barn door. "You'll not walk out on me for long, Jack Gibson, I heat your blood."

"Standing here looking at you, sweetheart, you've got your work cut out for you, because my blood is running ice cold." He grabbed her arm and yanked her aside, then tore off the brace on the door. With a quick move, he drove his shoulder into the panel. It swung open, and he stepped out, then cursed beneath his breath. A stone's throw away, Penny King looked up from where she sat on the backyard swing, which hung from an ancient live oak. She was dressed in light blue. Her daddy always loved her in blue. The color matched her eyes, he said. Jack's own mother always said, too, that the color complimented the child's copper curls.

Child? She must be seventeen now, but a child no longer, and from the look on her face, she knew it. Knew the young man she'd pledged her heart and soul to from the time she was eight had betrayed her for her own sister. Jack watched Penny's gaze travel behind him. Expressionless, the girl rose from the swing. Slowly she walked from beneath the shade-mottled yard, across the dirt drive, to stop in front of him, a question in her eyes. Jack glanced over his shoulder. Adel was there, within his reach, her eyes fixed on her little sister. Adel raised her chin, then glanced at Jack. Instinctively he knew she'd followed Penny's gaze back to him.

"I didn't know," he told Penny.

He saw her chin pucker, and she looked at Adel.

"I did," Adel said.

"You stole Mark, then came out here this morning to whore yourself with Jack?"

21

"I've always whored myself with Jack, Penny. You've repeatedly told me so."

"Why?"

Jack sensed Adel move closer to him. She touched his arm. Annoyance shot through him, and he pulled away.

"Jack is a better lover."

Christ! He'd always known her to wear a callous mask. Once he'd deluded himself into believing it was all a cool façade, hiding a warmer, more beautiful woman. Over the past several years, from time to time, he'd accepted the possibility that he might be wrong in his regard for her, but he'd held out hope. Hope for them. Now he realized her cold, calculating actions were real and they penetrated to her marrow.

"I swear to you, Penny," he said, "I did not know."

"And would it have mattered if you had?"

"Yes, it would have mattered."

Adel snorted, but he kept his eyes on Penny. "But it won't ever matter again." Penny wasn't the only one who'd lost her dreams this morning. No matter how much his own might have paled over the past few years, an hour ago he'd held out renewed hope.

"Tell what you've seen here, Copper Lee"—her eyes flashed at the nickname—"pretty Doc Mark can annul the marriage, and you can have him."

"And why, pray tell, Jimmy Jack, would I still want him?"

He gave her a long study. Why indeed? He turned to Adel. "Tell that whore mother I got her message at Piotona, and I understand what she meant, and that all she's accomplished is to strengthen my resolve. Tell her, too, that my father's alleged debt to King and Gibson was paid in full seven years ago. My granddaddy's farm was never part of the equation and Harrison County knows it. Tell her if Humboldt raised freightage on King and Gibson, he did it on every other timber company using his rail in the Piney Woods. I had nothing to do with it. State's attorney is already looking at the injunction, and the Marion County sheriff has no intention of taking action."

Chapter Five

<u>Biloxi, Mississippi, April 1889</u>

"You're a son of bitch, Alan." Jonathan Noble sat down hard in the wing chair in front of his brother's desk.

"I would have never thought to speak of your mother in such a manner," the older Noble said without looking up from his paperwork.

"That's because you loved my mother."

"Indeed I did, and you never knew mine."

"I apologize," Jon said sarcastically. "That was Harold's mother I was speaking of. He, too, is the son of a whore."

"She was many things, but she wasn't that." Alan signed a document, then looked around Jon to the closed office door. "I take it you've just gotten back from Mississippi City?"

"Where I discovered you have displaced me in the affection of my new ex-best friends."

Alan tossed his pen atop the papers he was perusing, leaned back in his swivel chair, and laced his fingers atop his stout belly. "Yes, well, I doubt affection had anything to do with your displacement. Greed, I believe drove those people's decision. Mrs. Markiston insisted I better your offer before she'd renege on the two of you's unwritten agreement. So I did."

"You consider offering Harold as a husband for the girl a better offer?"

"Do you refer to manhood or potential status?"

Jon glared at Alan. "So you bribed Harold to take the girl?"

That made Alan laugh. "Harold's assumed rise within Noble

23

Corporation is not what I'm referring to. It's your proposal involving Blake Shipping that has the Markiston woman salivating. She'd sell that girl to an Arab if she thought it would improve her lot. My only question regarding the ploy—actually, as it turns out, it's the most interesting question in this whole convoluted mess you've created—is why you want that particular child bride to begin with?"

Jon clenched his jaw. "Why were you over there, Alan? I discussed the Blake Shipping deal with my people. They saw the advantage."

"The ships you mean? Yes, nice sleight of hand, that."

"Those ships were on the sales block. I offered them to Blake Shipping. My department conducts transactions like that all the time."

"Pshaw! The board knows nothing of it."

"This is routine, Alan. I don't have to clear transactions of this level with the board. It knows the ships have been written off the inventory. All I need to do is report any profit from the sale, then write off the losses."

"Yes, but what the board won't be aware of when it gives its obligatory nod to the sale is Eva Markiston. I, however, have recently made a direct correlation between Eva Markiston, her granddaughter, and Blake Shipping. You intended to sell Blake Shipping those old carcasses, which I happen to know have a minimum of five good years' service left on them, for the single purpose of accommodating King and Gibson exclusively. Even more significant, I suspect you intended to buy Blake Shipping, replete with its new fleet. It's a small outfit. You figured you could purchase it underneath your rather extravagant threshold, didn't you? You wouldn't even have to inform the board. In fact, it's already rumored over at Blake that Noble Shipping plans to make a bid. Now tell me, was it your idea to buy or the charming Mrs. Markiston's?"

Alan could ask her that himself, assuming she hadn't already told him. "If I were you, I'd snap it right up, because if you plan to keep up with that woman, you're going to need it," Jon said.

"I've already decided to set my head of shipping on it."

"He might not be able to get around to it anytime soon."

Alan smirked, then swiveled to the credenza behind him. A crystal decanter half full of Kentucky Bourbon sat there along with several matching tumblers. He turned two of them right side up and pulled the top from the decanter, then poured them each a drink. Holding one glass in his left hand, he pushed the other to the front edge of his desk and motioned for Jon to take it. Jon didn't.

"I don't think that should be a problem for you, Jon. I realized Blake Shipping's value the moment I reviewed the prospectus you never submitted. That long-hoped-for railroad from Mobile to Memphis is in trouble in all three state legislatures, Mississippi most of all, since that's where most of the track will be laid. Because of that, I've been toying with an expansion of our river fleet for the past year."

"You never brought that up with me."

"Some members of the board, as well as me, were thinking of a new department."

"It belongs in shipping."

Alan wrinkled his nose. "Something less autonomous is what we're striving for. Noble Shipping is focused on international import-export. We were thinking you might be able to expand timber exports. That market seems to be growing by the month. With Blake Shipping, we could free up more of your domestic assets for the international trade, help out small, ambitious companies such as King and Gibson. Now let's get on with it, shall we? Just carry through on your misbegotten offer. George Blake is chomping at the bit to retire to Brazil."

"Why did you interfere with my pursuit of Penny King?"

"Why did you want her to begin with?"

"I'm ready to settle down."

"She's not your type." Alan studied him and after a moment, he sighed. "In answer to your question, she was part of the package. You made that so, not me."

"Only because I asked for her."

25

"A point I didn't miss." Alan rocked back, and again folded his hands over his paunch. "I fear it may be lost on her rather obtuse grandmother, though."

Jon had tensed with Alan's *point not missed*. How much did he know, or was he bluffing? When Jon didn't say anything, Alan nodded.

"Florence gave you away on the girl," he said with an apologetic smile. "In fact," he added, waving his hand to take in the room, "her distress over the thought of you actually marrying another is what brought this entire matter to my attention."

"I'd already concluded that."

Alan chuckled. "You need to be careful what you tell her."

"I concluded that, too, a long time ago."

"Then it's hard to sympathize with you. Have you seen her this morning?"

"I did ask upon my arrival. I was told she was out."

"Yes, neither of us expected you today. She's having brunch with Angelina Ladner, her first outing in a week. Her ulcer has been acting up. Anxiety, you know. Your intent to wed upset her. That, or she's anxious about how you're going to react to her discussing it with me?"

Jon anticipated Alan's saying more, finally bringing his and Florence's relationship out in the open. He thought about that happening every time he and his brother had one of these little tête-à-têtes.

"Florence suggested Harold would be a far better match for a seventeen-year-old than you. She further suggested that whatever value you saw in the young woman would remain in the family."

"I'm certain you didn't tear my playhouse up to please Florence."

Alan chuckled. "Actually, Florence brought her crisis to me at an opportune moment. There's a nice spot for a quay and warehouses over in Jackson County, which is perfect for the proposed expansion of our Brazilian trade. It's about two miles up the Escatawpa. Gates discovered it last December. When he checked

26

into buying it, he discovered it was owned by a Miss Penny King, the granddaughter of Eva Markiston in Mississippi City. The property is tied up in the girl's inheritance, one of two properties left to her in her father's will seven years ago. The family property will remain as part of her estate until she reaches her majority at twenty-six, but that Escatawpa River site will become hers outright upon her marriage."

"Her father's precaution to ensure her grandmother had little or no influence over her."

"I figured you'd done some research, little brother, and I already know that Hugh King intended the Escatawpa property to go to his daughter and proposed son-in-law, the youngest son of the Biloxi Reeds, owners of the Back Bay Seafood Cannery."

Jon forced himself to relax, then shot his brother a contemptuous smile. "Found that out, did you?"

"I didn't. I just tapped into the same investigator you did." Alan shrugged. "He'd already done the work, but was happy to get paid twice."

Alan always found humor in outbidding Jon's lackeys...and his lovers.

"From what your man told me, for a price, of course, is that the animosities prevalent in the King household at the time of Hugh King's death are still common knowledge among the servants in Mississippi City."

"And everyone else, considering the trial that followed his murder."

"You could have saved yourself the cost of an investigator and talked to the servants themselves. Probably would have resulted in more discretion, too."

"I doubt that would have outfoxed you, Alan."

With a smirk, Alan swiveled around and reached for the decanter behind him. He poured himself another drink, looked at Jon's glass still full at the desk's edge, then placed the stopper back into the bottle, and drank.

"The evolution of that group over there makes an interesting story in its own right," Alan said, "though I guess we all do. King bought that Escatawpa property more than twenty years ago while he was still in a court battle for his own sawmill, which was stolen from him by a cousin during the War. The thief claimed King was dead, laid claim to the deceased grandfather's old mill, then sold it to Eva Markiston's ailing grandfather, who was trying to re-establish his own lumber fortunes lost during the War. King won the suit against that man's son. Tom Daws, I believe his name was."

"And had the misfortune of acquiring Eva Markiston along with the victory."

"And who are we, Jon, with our rather odd assortment of family members, to cast stones? Daws offered up the balance of his properties in return for ten percent interest, presumably to ensure an income for his remaining family. Eva Markiston threw in a daughter to boot. In the interim, that Escatawpa River property has just sat there. Tom Gates also discovered that in more recent years, John Reed of Back Bay Canning approached King with an offer for that land, but King was still deciding what to do with it. His partner wanted to add another sawmill over that way, giving them better access to Pascagoula, but Eva Markiston, with her ten percent, was opposed. I know this because I asked John Reed when I had the occasion to meet him at a Mardi Gras fundraiser last January. It seems he and King became good friends after King refused Reed's offer. According to Reed, King was showing some interest in diversifying into canning himself at the time of his death. Also, Miss Penny, then just a little girl, and John Reed's son, also a child, had developed a passion for each other. The families thought it 'cute,' but during the intervening years, their infatuation apparently turned to love, a romance recently soured when the boy ran off with his sweetheart's older sister." Alan smirked at Jonathan. "Did you have anything to do with that?"

Jon casually turned to the floor-to-ceiling window on one side of Alan's desk and gazed out. "I was not privy to Eva Markiston's solution for freeing Miss King up."

"But your offer precipitated it."

It was a statement, not a question, and required no response.

"Was your plan to go into the canning industry, Jon, or was it timber? Or is there something else?"

Jon shifted his gaze from the sunny window to his brother. "My intent was to get out from under your thumb."

"Well, whatever you intended has resulted in our now being in the business of exporting lumber."

"And is the board aware of that?"

"Is it any of the board's business?"

So Jon had interpreted that last cryptic "our" correctly. "You've made that woman a private loan, haven't you?"

Alan finished his shot and placed the tumbler on the polished surface of his desk. Jon narrowed his eyes on his brother.

"In return for what, Alan?"

"A grandson."

"Have you lost your mind? I sure in hell hope you got something solid in the way of collateral, because I doubt your 'boy' will live up to his end of the bargain."

"I believe I've made a good bargain. I always do, and as far as Harold's living up to his end, that's Eva Markiston's problem. But with all due respect to my son, I believe he will make an effort to be a good daddy and husband in return for what he considers his 'rightful place on his grandfather's board'." Alan held up an index finger and pointed it at Jon. "All I need is one grandson out of his bride to ensure the name and company will go on."

"To ensure I'll never get it, you mean."

"Our father already made sure of that."

"Which begs the question, why didn't you simply let me move on?"

"Because you don't plan to move on, you plan to take over."

"You just said I couldn't."

"And we both know that there is *always* a way. Sneaking in through the back door, for example."

"I wouldn't have to if I had the resources available to me that you have."

He'd caught Alan's eye with that, but to his credit, his brother didn't flinch. After a moment, Alan smiled and said softly, "I own the place."

"Less and less of it every year."

Alan shifted his weight and brought his body forward, then locked his eyes on Jon's. "Actually, I wish you would move on, so I could stop worrying with your attempted diversification into regions where I do not wish to venture."

"Or do you mean regions where you shouldn't venture, Alan?"

As decisively as he'd come forward, Alan fell back into the chair. "Drink your drink."

Sure he was now calm enough not to throw it in his brother's face, Jon leaned forward and picked up the tumbler. "And you've got yourself into a real mess now, Alan." Jon downed the whiskey. It burned his throat, then swelled his stomach with heat and nausea.

"While you were doing your research on Eva Markiston, did you glean anything from the fate of the men who associate with her and hers?"

"I always do my research, Jonathan, so you should thank me for diverting you from certain disaster."

Chapter Six

Jonathan Noble turned from the mirror when the parlor door opened behind him.

Florence stopped short. "Alan thought you'd gone back to Mobile," she said momentarily.

Alan thought no such thing. In fact, Florence's discomfort amused Alan. No doubt, he hoped Jon's presence would prove an unpleasant surprise.

Florence glanced at Harold, who'd risen from the settee when she entered. "How did he say things went?" Harold asked her.

She closed the paneled door, secluding the three of them inside the room. "He says that he, Stuart Frederick, and the Markiston woman reached an agreement earlier this morning." Her eyes darted to Jon, who now turned to Harold.

"Before I arrived Mississippi City," Jon said dryly.

Florence moved decisively toward Jonathan. She'd regained the poise lost upon finding him in the room. "Things have gone marvelously for us, to hear Alan tell it." Her eyes were fixed on Jon, but she addressed Harold. "I'm surprised your uncle didn't tell you."

"I didn't even feel like greeting him," Jon said, "much less carrying on a conversation."

She stopped in front of Jon and raised her chin in defiance, then smirked and turned her beautiful face to Harold. "Miss King has agreed to the marriage."

"Great," Harold said with a decided lack of enthusiasm.

Jon wondered if Eva Markiston had even broached the subject of marriage with the girl. He had met her, a pretty little redhead with freckles and, from what he'd been able to gather, a

31

mind of her own. Still, marriage to the assumed heir to Noble Corporation was a good match, so her agreeing to it would not be extraordinary.

"She really was an odd choice for you, Jonathan," Florence said.

He wanted to slap her. His gaze moved from the haughty Florence to Harold, who grinned.

"She's too young for you, Uncle."

"She's too young for either of you, but certainly Harold is the better choice for her."

"Certainly," Jon mimicked, "for her grandmother. Why settle for the head of Noble Shipping when one can snag the whole corporation?" He looked at Harold. "And I'd advise you to wipe that grin off your face before I knock it off."

Harold's grin widened.

"Don't blame this on Harold. I'm not ashamed to say it was my idea, not his."

"I know it was, and I'm equally certain you take pride in your perfidy."

Florence turned to Harold. "Could you leave us, dear. Things are about to get personal."

"Under those conditions, gladly." He turned to Jon. "And I'll take my triumphant grin with me."

Florence waited a moment, holding up her palm to discourage Jonathan from speaking, should he feel the need to, which he didn't. She walked to the door, surveyed the hall, then closed the door and turned to him. "I really don't trust him."

"You trusted him enough to help the sod bastard steal my prospective bride."

"Oh, really, Jon, did you think I was going to sit back and do nothing while you married a seventeen-year-old girl?"

She'd been furious when he told her his plan, as he'd suspected she would be. Obviously, he'd been premature in gloating. He'd never considered her stooping to this, though, not given what she'd already done to him, not after years of tearful requests for forgiveness and repeated confessions of sorrow over her own choice of husbands, followed by passionate compensation freely offered in her bed. Of course, those had all been for her benefit, not his, and he'd always known that. He knew her too well to have made this tactical error now.

"You and I have each other, darling," she coaxed softly.

"Not quite, *darling*. Alan sleeps in between."

"I haven't slept with that sadist in months and rarely before that, and you know it. We certainly don't need to put yet another person in our bed after coming this far."

"Go to the devil, Florence." He turned his back on her and walked to the delicate Queen Anne secretary where she kept a flask for him. The whisky burned, and he burned with the satisfaction of it. "What you're afraid of," he said, "is that I'll crawl out of your bed altogether."

"I'll admit that was part of it."

He snorted. "How did you get Harold to agree to this?"

She started around the settee after him. "I suggested he dicker with his daddy for the company. In return, Harold would agree to wed and produce a grandson. Of the two of them, Harold took the most convincing, but he seems resolved, even excited now."

"Alan's goals stem beyond the girl, and Harold is the soft spot in your plan. Do you really think he can produce a child on anything designed to give birth?"

"It doesn't matter what I think. The important thing is Alan thinks he can."

"What does Harold think?"

She shrugged. "Why shouldn't he be able to?"

"That's another thing I've only begun to appreciate in you, this odd influence you have over your stepson." He glanced over his shoulder. She had reached him, and he turned to her. "It's particularly noteworthy, being that you are female and frightening to boot."

"That's because I've always supported him despite his perversions."

"I am supportive, Florence. You are, at best, forgiving."

"Really? How much did he confide in you while his mother was still alive? And even now, I take his side against his father in most things. You have no idea how difficult Alan can be in dealing with his son."

Jonathan laughed at that. "*I* have no idea how difficult Alan is?"

"It's not the same."

"There are almost enough years between me and Alan for me to be his damn son. I'm very aware of Alan's manner of dealing with his 'son.' Nor is their father-son relationship particularly unusual. Alan isn't any rougher on his son than many fathers, especially when you consider what Alan has to deal with. I'm amazed he hasn't killed him. No, what Harold is to you is a useful tool. That is the reason you take his side." Jon waved the flask in an indiscriminate circle in front of him. "Such as in this particular instance."

She watched his movement, and when he stilled, she nodded to the flask he held. "I do love the taste of whisky on your lips."

"And I wish you'd restrict your tongue to kissing and quit wagging it." He took a swig, then circling her waist with his free arm crushed her to him, assuaging his anger with her grunt. Leaving her no time to recover, he kissed her hard.

She raised her arms and tangled them behind his neck, and when he was done, she licked the whiskey from her lips, then his with the tip of her very talented tongue. He suppressed a groan.

"And do you find me a useful tool, my love?" she asked.

"As you do me."

Her lips still close to his, she said, "I know what you wanted from her, and with Harold as your partner in crime you can have your cake and eat it, too."

He prayed she hadn't felt his tensing with her words. "Like you, Florence, have your cake and eat it, too? Oh wait, for me to indulge in such sweet decadence, I'd need a spouse." He shoved her away. She looked at him in surprise, then narrowed her eyes.

"Something I will move heaven and earth to prevent!" she spat.

Ah, she was angry now. Good, because he had been boiling for the past three hours since he'd walked into the King House on Texas Street in Mississippi City, and Eva Markiston told him she'd cancelled their tentative agreement in return for a better deal from his older brother. He'd attempted to counter, but she'd rejected him. He didn't know what Alan had offered her, other than Harold as a replacement for Penny King's groom. He had suspected a loan, and Alan confirmed that a short while ago. Jon had informed the Markiston woman of Harold's shortcomings, but she hadn't cared. He knew then he didn't have the resources to beat Alan. Not on this field anyway. His heartbeat quickened, and he glared at Florence.

"Selfish, don't you think? And I don't want Harold as my partner in crime. He's cast his lot with his father." He took another swig. "What's Alan thinking about me in all this?"

"He thinks, as always, you're trying to better your position within the company. He was particularly interested in your motivation in choosing that particular girl."

"And what is his speculation on that?"

She didn't answer.

"Come, Florence, you must have asked him what he thought I saw in her, a lovely young woman, virginal, smart? Someone a man ready to settle down might start a family with?" He had forced his voice calm, but his gut churned, and not just from the whiskey.

"Smart? How do you know she's smart? You chose a girl you'd never met, more than half your age, and promised to another? Ha! I knew whatever flamed your desire was not the girl herself."

Florence stalked back to him, seemingly as defiant in her own right as he was in his. She flattened a manicured hand on his chest, then moved it up beneath the lapel of his jacket, her face turned up to his, her lips gently parted.

Jon seized her wrist, stopping her movement. "Why does Alan think I wanted Penny King?"

She strained against his hold, and he squeezed tighter.

"Tell me," he said.

Her breath caught, then she spat out between labored breaths, "You should have never told me your plans to marry Penny King. You thought to torment me, but I knew there was something more."

"I really would like to know what you and he assume was driving me."

"Let me go!"

He sneered, twisting her right wrist. This time she cried out. He relented slightly. "Tell me, or I will break it, I swear."

She blinked at him in disbelief, then breathed out, "The property on the Escatawpa River."

He stared at her and prayed his frustration didn't show. She must have seen something amiss in his eyes, because she added, "He said you were trying to foil him by getting your hands on it."

Jon racked his brains, trying to recall Alan's ever bringing up that property with him before this morning. He didn't recall any such disclosure. Shit. Alan no more believed he'd gone after that girl for a mosquito-infested piece of real estate than he believed the moon was made of green cheese. But whatever his brother thought, he hadn't confided it to Florence.

He let go of her, and she scrambled back, staring at him with wide, indignant eyes and rubbing her wrists. "What has gotten into you?"

He had never been physically rough with her, not even when she had told him she intended to forsake their promise to each other and wed Alan. He reached for her. She startled, but he was quick, and her mild resistance was quieted with a gentle touch. He chuckled.

"It amazes me, Florence, how resourceful you are," he said soothingly. Resourceful maybe, but not bright. She relaxed in his embrace. "You told Harold about my plan to marry the girl?"

"As soon as you told me. He agreed you were up to something."

Gently he took her shoulders and pushed her back far enough so that he could look her in the eye. "That's when you suggested he approach his father?"

She swallowed. "Yes. At my urging, he approached his father with a sudden passion for Penny King. Given Alan's prior interest in the property, of which I was unaware at the time, Alan was favorable to the idea."

"Who told Alan it was my idea, not Harold's, to marry the girl?"

She was quiet.

"Come now, darling, he must have put two and two together, Harold's sudden desire for a young woman who just happened to be key to a property he lusted for."

"It was me, and Alan informed Harold about the property. I didn't even know about it."

Foiled by a jealous fool.

"My plan was simply to stop your marriage, but at the same time draw your precious asset, whatever it was, under Noble ownership. I figured you and Harold could then work together to thwart Alan, since it's usually the other way around. I didn't know Alan had been looking at that property these past few months." She touched his cheek. "Truly, I was trying to help."

"Help whom?"

"To help us, you and me. I knew you couldn't possibly want to wed that girl. I thought to mitigate my intervention—"

"Meddling."

She made a soft sound, then continued, "By tying her to the family for you and Harold."

"Where exactly do you see me fitting into this, Florence?"

She laid her head on his chest, and he rubbed her back. Throttling her would be so satisfying at that moment.

"I know you can manipulate Harold," she murmured. "He thinks so much of you."

Yes, well, he'd just proved that, hadn't he? Of course, Jon knew better than to trust Harold for even an instant. Where Jon had made his mistake was in assuming fealty from a woman who'd already betrayed him once.

"I understand you've been ill," he said.

"My ulcer has been disagreeing with me."

"Guilty conscience, perhaps?"

"Perhaps."

"Well, you can stop worrying about this now. The deed is done and everything is out in the open." He brought his hand beneath her chin and raised her lips to his. "We'll find a way to make the best of it."

"You've forgiven me then?"

"Sweetheart, I've little choice. You remain a useful, if reckless, tool in your own right."

Chapter Seven

"**I** can't do this."

Harold Noble set Penny aside, then turned to the cold fireplace that provided a touch of winter romance to the Carrollton's bridal suite. Harold, his back to her, braced himself with one arm against the marble mantel and looked down at the clean-swept hearth. He hadn't been rough, quite gentle in fact in his rebuff, but the rejection, instead of the anticipated kiss, was disheartening nonetheless.

He was so handsome, her new husband, his white shirt taut across his broad back, his suspenders hanging from the waist of his trousers to dangle beside both thighs in a state of relaxed undress. It had been a long day for both of them. A short service at the Presbyterian Church in Handsboro, followed by a barbecue at her home on Texas Street. Not many were present, mostly family from both sides. Adel and Mark were there. She had actually held a short conversation with Adel. Two hours later at the Louisville and Nashville station platform, Penny, by then dressed in a baby blue spring ensemble of cotton sateen, accompanied by an attentive Harold in a dark frock suit, which a man of his coloring and build could wear imperiously, had received a kiss on the cheek and best wishes from her sister. Mark had not been present at their sendoff, apparently having taken Penny's mute response to his attempts at conversation after the ceremony as a hint. Penny had been anxious and excited at their departure, even considered herself happy. Harold had seemed in good

39

spirits, too; however, he'd become reticent after they debarked the tram, which took them from the train station at Canal Street up St. Charles to the Carrollton Station. From there he took her hand, hailed a porter to gather their luggage, then crossed St. Charles to the Carrollton Resort. There, they were greeted by a smiling and indulgent staff, heavy with congratulations and ready to fill every anticipatory need for the newly-weds' two-night stay. After a light supper, they explored the resort's famed gardens and walked among the china ball trees adorning the levee at Riverbend overlooking the Mississippi. It was a beautiful, warm evening, and though Harold was mostly quiet, he held possessively to her hand, and when the gaslights were lit, they retired to their suite.

And now came his unanticipated confession.

Penny's hopes rose anew as she watched her husband of eight hours turn back to her. But he simply stood there, watching her as if waiting for her to react.

"What's the matter?" she finally asked, sure there must be something wrong with her.

"Did you want this marriage, Penny?"

The knots in her stomach tightened. Days ago, after agreeing to the proposed marriage to Harold Noble, she'd begun to thaw from the cold numbness she'd felt in the wake of Mark and Adel's betrayal.

"I agreed to it, so yes."

"Why?"

Duty? Hope? Her grandmother had convinced her Harold Noble was a splendid catch and that uniting their up-and-coming lumber business with the Coast's import-export giant would prove a boon for King and Gibson Lumber. In addition, Penny's mother had been ecstatic about Harold, the handsome heir to Alan Noble's "fortune." Penny thought the hackneyed hyperbole sounded New England in character... and value, but Clarissa Frederick was given to New South rhetoric no matter how unapt.

"I understood you were agreeable, too," she said to Harold.

"And I still am." He shrugged and stepped from the hearth.

Her heart quickened, and she hoped her response, meek as it was, had placated his misgivings and they would continue their wedding night.

"Consummation of the marriage is where my difficulty lies," he said. "I thought I could deal with this, but I realize now that I can't."

Beneath her breast, Penny's heart sank, and she frowned, genuinely confused.

"I'm impotent with women," he said.

"Oh?"

He laughed at that. "You don't understand what I'm talking about, do you?"

"I don't think I do."

He tilted his face up. "Sweet Jesus, help me," he said to the ceiling, an action she found belittling. "To put it simply," he continued, "my sexual partners have always been male. Well, except for one time, but that did not work out."

"Male, as in men?"

"Precisely. Surely you've heard of such things, Penny?"

She opened her mouth. Closed it. Then said. "The Greeks. But I thought that was out of necessity."

He furrowed his brow. "I can't imagine why such a thing would have been 'necessary,' as you put it."

"The absence of women? The prevention of pregnancy?"

"Ah." Then he smirked. "I don't think either was the case way back then. No, my dear, it wasn't necessity that drove the beast. Just a simple matter of taste."

An unexpected chill swept her body, and Penny bit her lip to quell her chattering teeth. She hugged herself. An hour earlier, as she prepared her bath and toilet to make herself desirable for her groom, her stomach had quaked in anticipation of being with him. Harold had not been the man of her choice. That had been Mark, but as it turned out, Mark had outgrown her and their juvenile romance—his words, not hers. And he didn't say them until two days after his elopement with her sister, when he finally garnered the nerve to face her. She had not responded to Mark's

41

cutting words, but turned her back on him and left the room.

Harold Noble, with his sleek black hair and blue eyes, handsome to the point of being pretty, seemed a suitable choice for a heartsick girl to wed and share a bed with. A man to make her a grownup, too. Now, she waited for him to say something to lessen the blow of his revelation. There had to be more. Something to set this right. He was joking, of course, and in a minute he'd laugh and say he'd made it all up. But he didn't.

"Why didn't you tell me this before you married me?"

"I didn't want you to get away, and in my defense, I thought I'd be able to perform my conjugal duties."

Duties? Well, yes, his and hers. She always understood their union was starting out as a business arrangement.

He sighed when she didn't respond, and with that soft expulsion of breath, his eyes softened. "Your parents talked to you, didn't they?"

"Not about this."

"About the nature of our marriage, I meant."

"I did ask why a man with all your positive virtues wanted to marry a woman he didn't even know. Grandmother said your father was particularly keen on your settling down and starting a family, but that you'd proven difficult. Then apparently, when you heard my relationship with Mark Reed had ended, you expressed a desire to marry me. I actually toyed with the thought that you pitied me, which I found degrading enough, but now I see that what you needed was a naïve fool."

"You said that, not me, and I would have never put it that way. What I really needed was a woman of good family whom my father would be willing to sanction."

Since her mother repeatedly made reference to both Adel and Penny's "scandalous antecedents," Penny doubted Alan Noble found much to sanction in the Markiston-King clan, nor did she believe he had really been searching for such.

"We need to annul this marriage, Harold. I might be naïve, but I am not so big a fool as to remain in a union where I am not desired."

Harold studied her for a long moment, then swallowed, and held out his hand. "Come," he said, "let's you and I have a talk."

He guided her to the resplendent Louis XIV bed with its silk sheets and lace counterpane turned back in welcome anticipation of conjugal bliss. There he helped her onto its foot, then sat beside her. Not long before, she'd imagined Harold carrying her to the bed in his arms, then laying down beside her. What a romantic little twit she was.

"Listen to me," he started. "What you heard about my relationship with my father is true. I am his only son. I am almost twenty-seven and my father demands conditions from me in return for inheriting my grandfather's company. He insists I marry and produce a family to carry on not only Noble Corporation, but the family name. He went so far as to tell me he will consider retirement once I've learned the ropes. I do not think that will happen short of his death. He can be a demanding tyrant when it comes to the company and the family. I can't see him turning over the reins to anyone as long as he's alive."

"And he opposes your 'preference'?"

"Only because he credits it for my reticence to marry."

"And your mother? How did she feel about your—"

"She despised me," he said sharply and with such force that he startled her. Shamefaced, he looked away, then after a moment, patted her hand. "Let's not talk about her, Penny. We've enough to sort out."

"All right, let's talk about you and me and this deception you have perpetrated on both me and your father."

Harold groaned, then said, "I sense you intend to be difficult about this." He didn't sound as if he were angry, nor even annoyed. Perhaps he was amused. Certainly he intended to be patient, some consolation in the wake of his outburst when she mentioned his mother. "I've told you what I finagled out of the deal, now what did you get?"

"You."

He laughed. "Who at present you consider a dud. No, sweet Penny. Even though you do not realize it, there is more."

43

"A good match, a stable family, and a de facto merger between our families' companies."

"And there you've hit upon your recompense."

"What do you mean by that?"

"My father has made your stepfather and grandmother a loan."

"Grandmother did hint at such a transaction. She's having trouble with one of the larger companies shipping her lumber to the Coast."

"Humboldt, and she is deeply in debt to them. Now she'll be able to get out from under them and, she hopes, get her timber to the mill. From there, I understand, she intends to expand her market."

"How much was the loan for?"

"Ten thousand dollars."

Penny stifled a gasp. How much of that did her grandmother owe Humboldt...and for that matter, other shippers who hadn't been paid?

"And the terms?"

"My father insisted on collateral for a loan that large."

"What did she put up?"

"A large tract of timber in Perry County, the largest, I believe, she can still lay claim to—"

"Does your father intend to go into the timber business, because that's the only value to that property?"

"In answer to your question, no, but if it came down to it, he can sell the land and timber. Look, this is not a conventional business agreement. It's a transaction between family members. And it gets worse. The most valuable collateral is King and Gibson itself."

Eyes wide, she stared at him. "She doesn't own—"

"Your mother and Stuart Frederick do."

"What are they thinking?" she whispered.

"My impression of your grandmother is that she thinks narrowly and gambles recklessly."

"The interest on the loan?"

"None. My father was very generous with her."

That relieved her until she caught Harold's wary eye, and it occurred to her he was wondering how much of this she understood.

"When is the principal due?"

"The first of November."

"Of this year?"

"I am afraid so."

Penny placed her hand over her stomach. "Well, she'll just have to return the money to Noble Corporation, that's all there is to it. You and I can't continue—"

"The money is owed to my father, not Noble Corporation. Despite the abbreviated time period, this would have been considered a bad investment by his conservative board members. He never approached them."

"Then we'll return it to your father."

"There is one more clause in the agreement, which under the circumstances I'm embarrassed to bring up."

"What is it?"

"The loan will be forgiven if you are pregnant by the first of November."

"Forgiven?" she repeated, and he smiled.

Penny wasn't believing this, not for an instant. "My grandmother and Stuart Frederick agreed to that?"

"They did. So, you see, your grandmother isn't quite as insane as she appears. She's taking a big gamble, but for an equally big pot."

"She's playing against a stacked deck. How is that to happen, Harold, if you won't even touch me? And there's no guarantee, under any conditions, that I would have been pregnant by then."

He held up a palm, but she slapped it away. "This is about stealing King and Gibson, isn't it? It was all a confidence game." She jumped from the bed. "What I can't understand is what you intend to do with me. I want this marriage annulled. My family will take this flimflam to court. You people will not get away with it."

45

He reached out and clasped one of her wildly gyrating hands to his breast. "No. Stop"—he laughed at her—"I truly intended to consummate our marriage, I swear I did. I had no idea I would be unable to have relations with you."

Her heart was slamming against her chest. "Please, Harold, we need to annul this marriage."

"We can't. Neither one of us can afford to, and your grand-mother is desperate for that money. She's not going to give it up."

Penny freed the hand he held captive, and he sighed.

"The contract between my father and Stuart Frederick and Eva Markiston is in writing, Penny. If you renege on this agree-ment, Alan Noble will foreclose, I'll see to it."

"*Who* is reneging, sir, and why would you do such a thing? You couldn't possibly want me."

"Shhh," he said gently. "What I want is what my father of-fered me. I can't get that without you. You do see that, don't you?"

She sucked in a stuttered breath. "But what about our family, Harold, yours and mine?"

"Actually, neither of us can get what we want without a child. He retook her hand. "Let's give this time. All we need is a preg-nant Penny."

"Oh, good lord." She tried to pull her hand away again, but this time he held firm. "I will not whore myself for you, Harold. I'm not a twelfth-century princess trying to produce an heir to the throne."

"Give me time. Come home with me as my wife." He brushed his thumb over her knuckles. "You'll be happy in the Noble house-hold. Florence has entertaining projects for the new Mistress Noble. Social obligations, pet philanthropic clubs and artistic endeavors she enjoys supporting for the city of Biloxi. She's excited to introduce you to her friends. They do bake sales and book readings, and"—he laughed—"palm readings and séances, and all sorts of silly, fun things. And father is ecstatic that I've finally wed and agreed to have a family. You'll live like that twelfth-century princess you so disdain. They needn't know I'm having difficulty carrying out my end of the bargain." He brought her fingers to his lips. "Stay married to me, Penny. You'll not regret it."

Chapter Eight

Jack finished his beer and pushed the empty mug to the edge of the table. "One more," he said to fifteen-year-old Del, Remy Taloose's eldest. Remy made the best damn beer on the Coast, dark with lots of froth. Despite the mood that had settled over him, Jack loved this place. Remy had the best crawdaddies and étouffé, too. And the coffee, he mustn't forget the coffee. Nate Stephens, who'd just left him, claimed he came down to the Coast for Remy's coffee alone, strong with the taste of chicory. Jack had planned to top his meal with cobbler and coffee, then some poker in the back room. Given the sudden turn in his luck, he decided to forego the poker. What he really wanted now was to meander back to Happy Hollow, and Kate's, and finish off his recently purchased jug of moonshine.

"Jack Gibson?"

Jack jerked in the direction of a shadow that had snuck up beside him. The shadow stepped around and became a man, solid, but still dark in the dim interior of the rustic watering hole on Biloxi's Back Bay. The stranger stuck out his hand. "Jonathan Noble." Jack rose and took it.

He was a nice lookin' fella, this Jonathan Noble. Dark-haired and dark-eyed in the poor light. Late thirties, early forties, Jack guessed. He had a good, strong shake, perfected to impress.

"A Noble Corporation Noble?"

If anything, the name impressed, and the fact the man was here, seeking him out, engaged Jack even more.

48

"Noble Shipping, I'm out of Mobile, but Noble Shipping is a subsidiary of the whole." The man looked around the nearly empty room. It was mid-afternoon and the lunch crowd of cannery employees, dock workers, and fishermen had pretty much cleared out. "Got time to talk?" Noble said.

Jack motioned the man into the chair across from him, then sat. Delgado Taloose set the beer in front of Jack and turned to Noble. "Bring another, Del." The boy nodded and disappeared. "You would drink a beer, wouldn't you?" Jack asked.

"Sure," he said and eyed Jack. "Look, I've recently become saddled with an obligation wanting to ship lumber. To put it mildly, I'm unhappy with the arrangement. I'm looking for an ally and my obligation just happens to have your name attached to it."

"King and Gibson," Jack said matter-of-factly.

"Not a hard guess."

"Eva Markiston is better described as a usurper, not an obligation."

"She speaks even more highly of you."

Jack snorted.

"My immediate problem stems from my nephew's recent marriage into that family. I understand you are intimately familiar with the entire lot of them."

"Well unless the black widow killed off Adel Reed's new husband"—and Adel is where Jack's intimacy, literally speaking, resided—"your nephew has wed Penny King."

"Late yesterday morning. A hastily arranged, but mutually agreeable union from all other accounts, made particularly reprehensible to me in that it was a double betrayal."

Jack thought the man might explain that, but he didn't.

"Unfortunately, as part of my nephew's 'dowry'," Noble said with no small degree of sarcasm, "my brother Alan and Eva Markiston agreed to a shipping obligation that will place a strain on my assets. I've been with my brother and Mrs. Markiston all morning 'finalizing' an ad hoc agreement, mutually agreeable to them, but not to me."

Well, hell, this must explain Nate's bad news. "Two days

ago," Jack said, "my supervisor was informed by Chicago that Eva Markiston paid off her debt to Humboldt Timber."

Noble, his mug halfway to his mouth, nodded. "Nullifying Humboldt's offer to accept her Wolf River mill in payment for the outstanding balance. I assume that means Humboldt will start moving her timber again."

"No reason not to."

Noble pursed his lips, then maneuvered his chair closer to the table. "I understand you have some influence on Humboldt's local operations."

"You got that understanding from Eva Markiston because she chooses to believe it's my efforts to sabotage her that created the financial bind she got herself into, rather than admit it was her own reckless greed."

"Do you have influence on local operations, Mr. Gibson?"

"Not much, but I can tell you that Humboldt is extremely disappointed over the loss of that mill on the Wolf."

"Humboldt had her where they wanted her, did they? Then I will assume that Mrs. Markiston's windfall is a disappointment to both you and your employer. What I'm asking, Mr. Gibson, is whether or not you'd be willing to use your influence with your seniors at Humboldt to, shall we say, hinder Mrs. Markiston's getting her timber to the mill?"

Jack waited, but when Noble didn't elaborate further, he asked, "In return for what?"

"Why, for what you've been striving for all along." He frowned as if not sure of his footing. "As for you and Humboldt's local lieutenants, I'm in a position to offer moderate compensation for your efforts."

Jack studied the man, who, to his credit, didn't waver. Finally Jack said, "What else did Noble Corporation get in return for Penny King?"

"You're fishing, Gibson. Don't."

"The hell I won't. You approached me, Mr. Noble. Eva Markiston's balancing her rather large bill with Humboldt comes as a real shock to me, not to mention a disappointment. Now either there's something really special about Miss Penny I'm unaware of—and I've known that little red-headed mite all her life—or there's a loan involved. Eva Markiston needed capital and you people have provided it, which doesn't endear me to you at the moment. Now you're asking me to approach my bosses and ask them not to provide rail service to the woman. That's gonna cause problems with the state, especially considering hers is a Southern company and those denying her are greedy Northerners. They're gonna ask me why they should do it, and I don't know that you can offer my immediate supervisor enough money to offset what he'll lose when Humboldt fires his ass."

Jon Noble leaned back and rubbed his chin. Then suddenly he sat forward. "All right, there was money involved, a gift with terms favorable to Noble. My brother wants a grandson, and he was willing to bail Eva Markiston out in return for her grand-daughter."

"Eva owed Humboldt a lot of money. I know how much, and I also know they weren't her only creditors. I know how much she owed them, too, because that was going to be part of Humboldt's offer when they officially addressed the sale of that Wolf River mill, so forgive me for not buying your bull. A sub-stantial gift in return for Penny doesn't sound like favorable terms to me."

Noble leaned back in his chair and shot Jack a toothy grin. "You're smarter than I thought."

Jack said nothing.

"Look, Gibson, I know the history between you and Eva Markiston. I know what happened to Penny's father and who hanged for his death. I know you don't believe it happened the way authorities claim."

Jack scoffed. "Humboldt had Eva in a hole. They were about ready to start tossing in dirt. I had the satisfaction of her thinking I was responsible instead of her own stupidity. Now you've hauled her up and out, and you're offering me a chance at vengeance?"

"You might think you're the only one unhappy about this, but

51

you're wrong. She most assuredly does blame you personally for her recent setbacks. Her vitriol in response to your name is why I'm here. I, too, have had the pleasure of being screwed by her. I was well underway to cutting a deal with her—and I'll be up front with you since you feel so strongly about it—I'd have bailed the bitch out if my brother hadn't, but when push came to shove, he had more to offer, and she dropped me like Lincoln dropped McClellan. I could have dealt with that, but her double-dealing in favor of my brother has left me at the mercy of a two-edged sword. He is compelling me to commit to an endeavor he knows will ruin me and lead to my removal from my own department. In my place, he will set my nefarious nephew, who is equally culpable in this treachery. My anger at Eva Markiston does not even begin to compare to the malice I hold for my brother or the hurt resulting from my nephew's compliance with his father's wishes. I just want her to fail in this insane delusion to ship lumber to Europe."

Jack closed his eyes and gave his head a little shake. Europe.

"I don't think she realizes I can't do this with the assets I have available, but neither does she care that Alan's real objective is to eliminate me from the family business. I offered to get her out of debt. Alan offered her that and exclusivity to my shipping department."

"She's going to pay for her shipping from the capital included in the loan."

"You might call it an investment."

Jack squinted at him.

"You were right when you implied there was more than just a bride for Harold included in the terms. Eva Markiston put up a thousand acres of longleaf up in Perry County and the company itself as collateral."

"She put up King and Gibson, and Stuart Frederick agreed to it?"

"I think he put up a weak fight, but he was the one who signed the agreement as chairmen of King and Gibson's little bitty board."

"Probably under duress. In truth, it's a board of one and the primary stockholders are irrelevant."

"I don't know what she has over Frederick, but she rules that company, Jack."

With the use of his given name, Jack eyed Jon Noble, who grinned. "Call me Jon." From inside his frock coat, this man, with whom Jack was apparently now on a first-name basis, pulled out a couple of cigars. He offered Jack one, but Jack shook his head. He didn't dip snuff, he didn't chew, and he didn't smoke a pipe. On rare occasions he might smoke a cigarette, but he couldn't afford cigars, so he'd always steered clear of the things.

"So she's thinking she's gonna make a killing in Europe?"

Noble, cutting the tip of his cigar, looked up. "And if she wouldn't ruin me before she realized her downfall, I'd happily get her lumber there and watch her fail trying to force her way into an established market. But I'll have run into so many broken contracts before she can set sail, I'll have been removed from the board and Harold will be set in my place to save Noble Corporation's shipping department."

"Could he do it?"

"Sure, if his daddy provides the assets to do it with, a courtesy he won't provide his baby brother. It's a plot, you understand."

Well, maybe he did, and maybe he only saw what Jon Noble wanted him to see. The one thing Jack was relatively sure of was that for whatever reason, this man wanted to hurt Eva Markiston. "How important is it to your brother that he fulfills his obligation to Eva?"

Noble puffed on the cigar. "Not very."

"Is he looking to go into the timber business?"

Now the man grinned around the cigar held between his teeth. "I don't think so, but he could always sell it to Humboldt...or an up-and-coming entrepreneur, should he end up saddled with it."

"So you don't think he's trying to get King and Gibson?"

"No. My brother is pleased with the union between Harold and Penny, and even more so at the possibility of getting rid of me. But if Eva and her cohorts don't fulfill their end of the bargain, he will foreclose, if only out of contrariness for her failure to ruin me."

"And what about the son, Harold? His new wife has emotional ties to King and Gibson."

"Does she? I was led to believe her father left her set to enter the canning industry."

Jack laughed shortly. "You're talking about that land on the Escatawpa. One could argue that was a consideration. Hugh King and old man Reed, of Back Bay Canning here in Biloxi, were friends. Reed wanted that property. The Reeds had a son, Mark. And from the time they were very small, it appeared all Penny King and Mark Reed wanted were each other. It was Mr. Reed who suggested Hugh make it Penny's dowry. It was a joke. My dad wanted to build another mill there. It's true Hugh was looking to diversify. Too little capital and too much finagling of the public domain after the War he always said. Legal access to large tracks of timberland was unavailable to small outfits like King and Gibson. But Uncle Hugh never considered canning in that swamp on the Escatawpa. Truth is, I think he hoped to draw the Reed boy into timber. Reed had capital. Uncle Hugh and my dad had a good domestic market. My dad was a timberman. He had ideas when it came to regeneration of the forest, but his was a lifetime commitment to place. Hugh King was more a businessman, but he shared my dad's sense of place. They wanted something they could grow and rejuvenate here. It doesn't matter either way. They both died before anything was done with that property." Jack eyed Jon Noble. "So what happens to it now that it's a Noble asset?"

"I don't give a damn. The only thing I care about is not shipping Eva Markiston's lumber, and you know what I want from you."

"I'll talk to my boss, but Humboldt isn't the only company with dummy lines in the Piney Woods. They were just the ones who offered the best rates until they had her deep in their debt."

"They're still the only one with rail close enough to do her any good." Jon Noble pulled an envelope out of his pocket and pushed it across the table to Jack. "Here's a little something on the side."

Jack looked at it. "How much?"

"A hundred dollars in U.S. bank notes."

"Lotta money for what's gonna turn out to be a useless talk with my boss."

"You tell your boss, if Noble ends up with King and Gibson, I'll guarantee Humboldt gets first dibs on the Wolf River mill." Jon nodded at the envelope. "You consider that a retainer. I might come up with other suggestions as I grow more desperate."

Jack contemplated the ominous price of being bought. He thought of Deacon French and Rick Cotton. He thought of Hugh King. He thought of his father. He pushed the envelope back across to Noble.

"I'll take suggestions on a case-by-case basis."

Noble picked the envelope up and put it back inside his jacket. "I thought I might like you, Jack. Guess we're clear, then?"

"I'm clear on Jack Gibson. Are you?"

Jon Noble slapped his thigh, snuffed the cigar in his empty mug, rose, and stuck out his hand. "I'm clear I have one thing which I've been sorely lacking and that's an ally in my struggle."

Jack, who had risen with him, took his hand, then watched Jon Noble retreat. For a moment the restaurant was scorched with heat and sunshine. It darkened with the closing of the door. Jack retook his seat and sipped his beer.

More likely what Jon Noble thought he had was a scapegoat.

Chapter Nine

Eva Markiston glared at her son-in-law, Stuart Frederick. "Alan told me personally he would happily extend payment should Harold and Penny's relationship prosper, whether she's in the family way or not."

"What constitutes a prospering relationship, Eva? And did he tell you about Harold's sexual proclivities, too?"

"He did not."

Stuart rose from the settee where he was sitting beside Penny. "No, I guess that was a stupid question, but I bet I know who did tell you. Why did you keep it from me?"

"You were already opposed, and my source was prejudiced and not to be trusted. I chose to discount it rather than endure more of your opposition."

"Damn you, Eva."

"Harold Noble is hardly unique. Many men with his peculiar tastes marry and have families. I see no reason for him not to do likewise."

Stuart turned suddenly on Penny. "Did he consummate the marriage?"

"Enough, Stuart. Penny's acquiescence was based on sound business sense."

"No, Grandmother," Penny said. Her voice sounded resolute to her ears, surprising because she considered herself anything but resolved. "I agreed to marry Harold because you said it would be *good* for King and Gibson, because Harold was handsome and and wealthy and he wanted me. I knew that last part couldn't possibly be true. I should have listened to myself. I agreed because the plan looked promising, and I thought for certain I had nothing left to lose." Penny rolled her lips together. "And you knew that when you approached me with that too-good-to-be-true bargain." She looked from her grandmother to stepfather. "Both of you knew it, so stop talking around me as if I'm not here or am incapable of thinking." Or feeling. She refocused on her grandmother. "Why didn't you tell me about the size and terms of the loan? Harold says it's in writing." Again she turned to Stuart. "Did Mr. Farrah see the thing?"

"He did," Stuart said, "and he advised against our signing it."

"Oh, for Christ's sakes, Stuart!"

Stuart, face taut, hands clenched, turned from Penny to Eva as if he were about to spring across the polished surface of Hugh King's magnificent plantation desk and throttle her. He pivoted suddenly and stalked to the French doors overlooking the shaded brick patio at the back of the house. "They're up to no good."

"Don't be absurd," Eva said.

Stuart, calmer, turned from the window and looked at Penny. "Did he consummate the marriage?"

Eva turned to her now, too. They'd been talking around her again as if she weren't there. She was angry and frightened and frustrated. She said nothing.

"This is important, Penelope," Eva said.

"He did not."

"Why not?"

Stuart spun and placed himself between the desk and Penny. "How would she know, Eva? She doesn't know anything about sodomites."

"Then you explain it to me, Stuart?" Eva said sweetly.

"Why don't you explain it to the both of us? I know nothing about the sexual appetites of deviant males and even less about Harold Noble. The power of sex is your strong point, but on the subject of Harold Noble, you obviously didn't put enough study into the subject."

"The deal was too good to pass up."

"We've been bamboozled."

"Alan doesn't want a lumber mill, he wants a grandson."

"Quit worrying about what Alan wants and start thinking about what Harold wants, because obviously he's not much interested in siring one. One might conclude that he *is* interested in the timber business."

Penny sprung from her place on the settee. "Excuse me!" Amazingly, they both looked at her. "I accused Harold of the same thing two nights ago. He says that's not the case at all. He wants me to stay married to him."

"Did he tell you the terms for vacating the loan completely?" Eva asked.

"Yes. He says that he'll try"—Penny felt her cheeks warm— "well..., he implied he'll try to be a better husband."

Stuart cursed under his breath, then looked at Eva. "Adel is better suited for this task."

The words stung. Stuart must have noticed because he added quickly, "That is not a reflection on you, Penny, and I apologize if you took it as such, but your sister would have no qualms at seducing a reluctant male."

Eva chuckled. "No, she wouldn't. It is a pity you're not more like her, Penny."

"It doesn't matter. I'm not like her, nor am I convinced she would have any more success than I've had. This is all too risky for King and Gibson. You'll need to return the money. I intend to annul the marriage."

"Whoa," Stuart said at the same time Eva interjected a crisp, "You'll do no such thing."

Penny startled. "It's the only thing that makes sense at this point."

"Your returning to your husband's house and sleeping with him is the only 'sensible' thing to do."

"I don't want to stay married to the man. He has no interest in me, and even though his liaisons might be with members of his own sex, it's still infidelity."

"Oh, don't be foolish. Do you think he'd be more faithful if his taste ran to women? Now,"—her grandmother raised clasped hands to the desk—"your and Harold's marriage is a business arrangement, and we knew that going into it."

Penny's gut tightened. "Admittedly, I wasn't in love with Harold, but I did like the man. I had hoped love might come. Just because Mark jilted me doesn't mean I can't be happy, but now I fear staying with Harold will end all chance of that."

"You said Harold wants you to stay married to him. Is he going to agree to an annulment?" Stuart asked.

"He made an agreement with his father in return for marrying. If I leave him, the agreement is void." Penny frowned. "He says he'll see to it his father forecloses on the loan. That's why you must return the money now."

Eva glanced at Stuart, who had assumed a concerned demeanor.

"We don't have the money," Stuart said.

Penny widened her eyes and looked at her grandmother, who said, "I want you to go home to the Nobles' house."

Penny whipped her attention back to Stuart. "You don't have the money?"

Eva threw her arms into the air.

"The money was obligated, honey," Stuart said. "At least part of it. If not for Alan Noble's loan, Humboldt would have taken the Wolf River mill a month ago."

She jerked back to her grandmother. "A month ago? How—"

"Alan approached us immediately after Mark wed Adel."

"There were rumors we were in trouble," Stuart said. "We had something Alan wanted...you as a wife for his son."

"The lumber business is booming. I thought—"

"It's booming for those willing to take risks," Eva said, her voice loud.

"Those willing to gamble have capital to risk."

"And that's how they got their capital."

"They came here with capital, Eva," Stuart said, "backed, by a corrupt central government."

"And we need to be taking our fair share of it."

"Your fair share has already been earmarked for them. That's why they're here, and it also begs the question, where have you been for the past twenty-five years?"

"I remember Daddy used to tell you the same thing," Penny said.

"They get away with it because we let them."

"Eva, where were you in the spring of '65?"

"Oh, bah. Quit blaming everything on the damn War. My recent problems were Humboldt's doing, and we know who was behind that."

"Humboldt, Humboldt. Umm, where are they located...oh yes,"—Stuart snapped his fingers—"Chicago. I remember now."

Eva's nostrils flared, and she returned her gaze to Penny.

"I'm sorry that handsome devil you married hasn't worked out as you'd hoped, but it's truly irrelevant. You're married, and as a result, Alan Noble has, for all intents and purposes, invested in the company."

"He owns the company, Grandmother."

Stuart sat hard on the settee. "We're worse off now than we were with Humboldt."

Eva looked on him with disgust. "How have I managed, my entire life, to surround myself with spineless men?"

"The ones who have kept you in silks and brocades, you mean?"

"You didn't know me growing up."

Stuart wanted to say something more, Penny knew, but the glint in Eva Markiston's eye must have dissuaded him. Eyes still locked on him, Eva added, "We now have that one last item we needed in order to expand."

"Your timber is still in the Piney Woods, and you'd be a sight better off using it to build your own damn fleet."

Noble Shipping in Mobile, Penny thought. That's what they are referring to.

"Perhaps I will one day."

Stuart looked away, and Eva caught Penny's eye.

"I need you to go home to your husband and make me a great-grandbaby."

"And how am I to accomplish that with a man who refuses to touch me?"

Eva leaned forward, over the desk. "Convince him to touch you, my dear. Ask Adel to teach you how."

There was flippancy in her grandmother's voice, and Penny stung with the hatefulness of it. "If you're depending on that happening, Grandmother, you'd best resolve now to lose the company."

The woman opened her mouth, but Stuart said dryly, "You'd best change tack, Eva dear."

Penny took a quick step toward her stepfather. "What is going on?" When Stuart didn't immediately answer, she spun back on her grandmother. "Harold mentioned an expansion. What have you done with the borrowed money? Why is King and Gibson in trouble?"

"What's this sudden interest in the company, Penny?" her grandmother said softly. "I must say I'm surprised."

Strictly speaking, King and Gibson belonged to her mother, or more accurately, her stepfather, but Eva Markiston had a familial tie to the company's history and she'd never let anyone forget it, including Penny's father. Hugh King had dealt with the woman more tactfully than he had other nuisances. Stuart, however, had no such advantage, the result of a prenuptial agreement between Penny's mother and Stuart, an agreement framed by Eva. Penny had never thought about why Stuart had agreed to subordinate his role in favor of Eva's, but management of the company had long ago devolved into Eva's hands. Now, seven years after Hugh King's death, she controlled both family and company with an iron fist. Penny had, for all intents and purposes, been spared her grandmother's machinations, but this morning she confirmed what she'd suspected since her wedding night. She'd been manipulated, even ill-used.

"Yes, I am interested."

When Eva didn't answer, Penny bridled. "I am a favored

daughter-in-law of your primary investor, Grandmother. A man who's in a position to take control of my daddy's company. If you expect, even for a moment, that I will remain in this sham of a marriage without good reason, then you are wrong."

Eva studied her with feigned amusement, but the glint in her eyes suggested something less benign. Penny steeled herself and said, "It's Europe, isn't it? You've put everything at risk for the European market?"

Chapter Ten

Dr. Hadrian Clark brushed the dark spot on the inside of Penny's left arm. A hematoma, he'd told her yesterday. "You're certain that's the only one?"

"I haven't seen or felt any more."

"The jaundice concerns me. The two are indicative of a liver disorder. When is the last time you threw up?"

"Last night."

"There have been several cases of yellow fever reported in Mobile. Do you remember what you ate while you were there? Your mother-in-law does not."

Penny worried her bottom lip. "Sea flounder at lunch, at a place on the wharf. Florence suggested the —"

"McQueen's," the man said. "She remembered where, but not what."

"We ate at the Battle House both nights and returned home the third day, but I was feeling poorly before we left."

"Your husband insists the sickness started four nights ago."

"He's talking about the vomiting, but I've been tired and lacked an appetite for the past month."

"Did you mention this to Harold?"

"No, he might have ruined our plans." Penny didn't really believe that, but what did it hurt to make her husband sound attentive? "And Florence had been planning the trip since the fourth of July."

More to the point, Penny's mother had wanted Penny to go

on a shopping jaunt to Memphis with her and Adel. As an excuse to forego that trip, Penny had committed to Florence Noble before she'd started feeling poorly. More than the lesser of two evils, the Mobile trip had been a reprieve.

Dr. Clark pulled her hand from beneath the spread on her bed and patted it. "Despite the yellow tinge to those angel kisses across your nose, you're much better today than the sick girl I saw yesterday. Let's assume a distemper of the stomach." He waved an index finger under her nose. "And quit drinking so much of Alan Noble's chocolate. I told you before it's not good for you."

"I haven't had any since day before yesterday."

He glanced to the delicate cup and saucer on her nightstand. "And what, young woman, is that?"

"Florence sent it up earlier." She leaned forward. "I'll tell you a secret, Dr. Clark, if you promise not to tell." She nodded to the potted plant beneath the window next to her bed. "I pour it out."

"Why don't you simply tell Florence you don't like it?"

"But I love it." She smiled. "I'm merely following my doctor's instructions, but these things must be handled delicately. Chocolate is one of Alan's leading imports. It's very expensive."

"So you routinely pour one of his luxury items into the potted plant."

"That's better than hurting his feelings, don't you think?"

The doctor laughed. "Hurting his feelings? And I thought you feared angering him, which you might do if he finds out you're wasting it." He leaned toward her pretentiously as if to preserve her aura of conspiracy. "I'd be willing to bet he doesn't drink the stuff."

"He drinks coffee, wine on special occasions, and a brandy after supper every night." She laid back onto her pillows. "And does chocolate ail the liver?"

"Not that I've heard."

"What does?"

"An inflammation of the liver, yellow fever...." He met her eyes. "When did you last see your mother?"

"She and Adel returned from Memphis yesterday. I hope to meet Mama for lunch tomorrow." Penny sighed. "I take this turn in conversation to mean alcohol consumption is on the list of ailments."

"Excessive consumption, and yes, your mother needs to quit. You've not taken to imbibing, have you, gal?"

"Never."

"Have you taken any medications I am unaware of?"

"I'd never take anything unless you gave it to me, and per your instructions, I don't use snuff nor smoke cigars, and I do not drink fruit fizzes." She shrugged when he frowned at her. "Well, an occasional fizz."

He held up a finger. "Be careful with those. They've cocaine in them. Things should be outlawed."

She fell back on the pillow and draped the back of her hand over her forehead theatrically. "How will I ever endure my life here, denied my vices?"

Dr. Hadrian Clark looked out the east-facing window, near Penny's head. A breeze caressed the drapes and caused them to billow.

"Even with the drapes open this room is dim, isn't it, gal?"

"It's bright in the morning, and I'm told quite warm in winter."

"When the sun's shining, you mean?"

She twisted around on her pillow. Out a corner of the glass she caught a glimpse of blue sky. "It's a nice room. It belonged to Harold's mother before she died. The way the oaks surround this house, every one of its rooms are dark at least part of the day."

"All the more reason to get you out of this bed and on the veranda. It is a lovely day. So much so I looked forward to the trip over here. Trip back will be hot. When did you eat last?"

"Grace brought me chicken broth at lunch. I've kept it down."

"Well," he said, "four days of intermittent nausea and no fever. The lack of fever is key. I think I can report to the health department we won't be needing that quarantine after all. Authorities will breathe easier. I feared you were about to ruin our lovely Coast's near spotless record this year."

He closed the medical bag at his feet. "And you're sure we're not expecting a little Noble after Easter?"

He'd asked her that yesterday when Florence had finally sent for him. Today, Penny looked him in the eye.

"I ask this in strictest confidence, Dr. Clark, and with only some degree of humor, but mustn't I have had intimate relations with a member of the male gender for that to happen?"

Chapter Eleven

Penny King Noble stopped at the entrance to the Gulf View Hotel's dining room. Halfway to the back of the sunlit room, Clarissa Frederick bounced in her seat, and Penny groaned. Her mother's exuberance testified to early-morning imbibing. Worse, Adel was with her.

She pointed to their table when the maitre d' started toward her, and the man nodded, then led her there and pulled out her chair.

"I'm sorry I'm late," she said, bending to kiss her mother's cheek before sitting. The scent of gin tickled her nostrils. She glanced at Adel, golden and beautiful in a tailored red satin frock trimmed in gold braid and lace collar. Her mother was similarly overdressed, and Penny chafed at her own lack of sophistication. "The trip did you good. You both look wonderful." She fidgeted with her modified bustle and sat. "New hats?"

"Oh," her mother cried, too loudly, and touched the brim of hers, a pretty ecru-colored thing embellished with salmon and yellow ostrich feathers and ribbons. Adel's was brown velvet with red plumes and gold ribbons. "We brought you one, too," Clarissa slurred, looking at the little straw bonnet Penny wore. She handed her a smart blue and white lacquered box. "I do wish you had come with us. Open it."

Hers was the same fashion as Adel's only of ecru velvet trimmed with navy blue feathers and looped ribbon. "It's lovely, thank you, Mama."

"Adel picked it."

Penny smiled and dutifully thanked Adel.

"And I found a dress pattern for you." Her mother gushed. "I wish I'd thought to bring it, but we'll take it to Ilene together. She is forever asking about you. Anyway, the dress has puff sleeves with wide cuffs and a pointed bodice"—she'd pushed back from the table and smoothed her palms over her belly and waist to demonstrate, then raised a hand and crisscrossed the air beneath her chin—"with a scooped neck. I thought navy blue for the fall to match the ribbon in the hat." She went silent, then said, "Your grandmother says you've been ill."

Penny blinked at her mother. "How did she—"

"Mark, of course," Adel said, with a barely perceptible nod, then gazed for a moment at a portly gentleman at the next table. Penny turned to her mother.

"Then Dr. Clark told him. I certainly haven't seen Mark."

"Oh, dear, I didn't mean to upset you."

"I am not upset, but my medical condition is not a subject for common discussion."

"It was hardly a common discussion, Penny. Mark is your brother-in-law and Hadrian's assistant. It's my understanding that for a day or so Hadrian feared you'd contracted yellow fever. He told Mark to let the family know."

Sweet Jesus. Penny rubbed her temple, then kicked Adel's ankle. "We are over this way," Penny hissed at her now attentive sister. "You've ordered?"

Adel graced Penny with a smug smile. "Mama ordered you and her the red fish. Our waiter said it was excellent. I ordered oysters."

"For your libido, no doubt."

"Precisely," Adel said, and placed her hands on the table in front of her so she focused fully on Penny. "And who told you that little tidbit about the potency of oysters? The handsome devil you married or your father-in-law?"

"Florence."

The tray-laden waiter arrived at that moment, and Clarissa reached for her napkin. "Doris Worth tells me her cousin and her husband will arrive from Chicago next week. They have a home in Pass Christian. Doris says the woman is fascinated by the occult, so much so that Richard refuses to visit them while they're here and doesn't like Doris to, either. This couple has had a house over there for years. Penny, we must get the woman together with Florence."

Her poor mother grasped at any opportunity to hobnob with Florence Noble, but Penny doubted Florence would be interested in meeting the woman if she had to do so through Clarissa. When it came to the Markiston-Frederick clan of Mississippi City, Florence was a proven snob. Clarissa Frederick's oft-noted preoccupation with another manner of spirits made Florence even less inclined toward friendship. Florence genuinely seemed to enjoy Penny's company, though, and Penny had become a confidante and even a trusted secretary for Florence's social agenda, which Penny didn't mind. The effort kept her busy and her mind off her own failures at 'being a Noble.' Penny met the expectant eyes of her beaming mother.

"Who is this woman coming to Pass Christian, Mama?"

"Her name is Pickering."

Penny did not know the name, but that wouldn't rule out Florence's potential interest in the woman. Florence knew more about Coast society than she, and that included the annual snowbirds in the Pass.

"Have you sat through another séance since your last?" Adel asked.

"Next month." Penny glanced at her expectant mother. "Florence has sent her invitations, but I'll mention the Pickering woman to her." Penny took a bite of fish. Gracious, it was good.

Clarissa took another sip of wine. "If God wanted us communicating with the dead, He wouldn't have killed them." Then she giggled at herself.

"Or He'd kill us."

Again, Clarissa tittered. "Oh, Adel, the things you say."

"Well, Mama, it would make things easier, don't you think?" Adel squirmed forward on her seat, then rested her chin in her palm. "I sat through one with Mark's cousin Estelle last week."

"Estelle hosted a séance?"

"Gladys Malin. Estelle didn't want to go alone, and since I had a little sister enraptured by the spirit world, I told her I'd go with her."

"I'm hardly enraptured," Penny said. She looked down at her plate and cut another piece of fish with her fork. After a moment, Adel sat back and picked up her water goblet.

"Well, what happened?" Clarissa asked.

"The wild-eyed medium supposedly conjured up the ghost of a Spanish soldier who died of diphtheria in Biloxi in 1804."

"Madam Vernal," Penny said and returned to her plate.

"The Spanish soldier?"

Penny ignored the juest. "The medium."

Adel pursed her lips. "Yes," she said, "I do believe that was her name."

"Florence has spoken of her, but some in her circle consider the woman a fake."

Adel laughed that lovely laugh of hers and said, "Do tell? And are there some they consider are not fakes?"

"Was the Spanish soldier related to anyone present and did he speak to you all in Spanish?"

"Edith 'Aguirre' North's great-granduncle, and it's funny you should ask that, because I asked her about that after. Edith knew him as a little girl. She speaks and understands Spanish, and they spoke Spanish to one another in life."

"So one would assume he would have communicated with her in Spanish," Penny said.

Clarissa widened her eyes. "Why, Penny, don't you know the dead can do things the living can't?"

The response wouldn't have been so ludicrous, if her mother had been teasing, but Penny believed Clarissa was serious. Adel chuckled. "Frightening things would be my guess. Things to make one's blood freeze, and those would not include spouting off in an unfamiliar language. And as far as Madam Vernal and her hoax, the living can still learn Spanish, and for the sake of her livelihood, it might behoove her to do so if she plans to persist with Spanish ghosts."

"Well, we don't really know he didn't speak English, now do we?" Clarissa said.

"I think he would have spoken Spanish whether or not he knew English. Certainly he should have spoken his English with a Spanish accent." Penny looked at Adel. "Did he?"

Adel laughed. "You two are unbelievable." She stopped suddenly, grasped Penny's arm, and said with faux seriousness, "Have you taken to drinking?"

Penny looked at Adel's hand, then found her eyes. Her sister smirked and removed her hand. "Sorry, I couldn't resist. Try to get over your contempt of me. We had fun together once."

Penny glanced at the portly man at the table next to theirs. Early forties, if she were to guess. He seemed to be ignoring them now, but she knew he was all too aware of, and interested in, the beauty who had been flirting with him. No doubt Adel knew him, or of him. The man was probably wealthy, and maybe influential. He wore a wedding band. That made him safe. Harold, a terrible gossip, had told Penny some of her sister's indiscretions.

"Adel, I understand what Mark saw in you. What I don't understand is what you saw in him."

"Oh dear," Clarissa said, "don't start this, Penny."

"What did you see in him, little sister?"

"I honestly no longer know."

"Then it no longer matters, does it? But since we're on the subject of men, how well do you know Jon Noble?"

"Have you cast your eyes on him, now?"

Adel smirked. "I've only spoken to him twice, and since you ask, he is pleasant to look at." She plopped an oyster in her mouth, then pursed her lips. "I ask because Grandmother is interested in the interaction between the Noble brothers. Apparently Jon is giving big brother Alan some difficulties about shipping her lumber."

"Oh," Penny answered and returned to her fish. "You can tell Grandmother that he and Alan are always at loggerheads over one thing or another. I gather Alan has completely subordinated the shipping department to Noble Corporation, but Jon thinks of

himself as more a partner in the organization than a mere department head."

Penny watched Adel drop her gaze to her plate and skewer
another oyster. She didn't believe for a moment her grandmother
wasn't already aware of that.

"How does he act toward you?" Adel asked.

"Jonathan or Alan?"

"Jonathan, of course."

And why the "of course"? "He's quite charming, actually, as
if he likes me."

"Mmm," Adel said. "Does he look at you the way men look at
me?"

"Lustfully?"

Clarissa leaned over her plate. "Girls, please."

Adel waved her fork in front of her mother — "It's all right,
Mama" — then turned to Penny. "If you must be vulgar, yes."

"Why would you ask me such a thing?"

Adel shrugged and returned to her plate. "Grandmother may
need your assistance in subduing the savage."

Good lord, why had she asked? "On the two occasions you
happened to meet, how did he look at you, Adel?"

Adel's face split into a grin. "Not like the man sitting next to
us, I can tell you that."

The words had bubbled up her throat and out her mouth,
frank truth filled with amusement and irony that Penny had once
so admired and envied in her sister, back when she had loved her.
Now she only envied — and then only some things. Penny glanced
back at her fish. Her appetite was gone. She set her fork down.
"I can't imagine Grandmother suggesting I attempt such a thing."

"Penny, for Saint Peter's sake, she didn't. That was me teasing you. I think she's trying to get a feel for whether he likes you,
because he doesn't like her."

"On account of the shipping thing, you mean?"

Adel shrugged. "I think there's more to it than that, but all
that concerns Grandmother at the moment is the shipping."

Chapter Twelve

Jack stopped work and wiped the sweat from his forehead before it ran into his eye. The man he'd noted on the train platform fifty yards away waved at him, then Jon Noble started his way. Jack stuffed the red bandanna into his back pocket. As of mid-September, summer in Mississippi remained undaunted by the threat of impending fall, but then summer here had never been prone to turn tail and run. Jack turned away and pushed the sack of coffee deeper into the bed of the wagon.

"Yo, boss," Buck Bolee, his colored hand, hollered at him from the shaded porch of the Humboldt commissary. Jack nodded, then grunted when the man tossed him a fifty-pound sack of flour. He didn't really catch it, just stopped its forward motion before letting it drop to the floor of the wagon.

"Let's take a break," he called to Buck, then jumped from the wagon bed. Jack started toward Noble, and Buck climbed adeptly over the side of the wagon and began to organize their supplies.

"Something must be up to drag you this far into the Piney Woods," Jack said, taking Jon Noble's outstretched hand.

Noble laughed. "Sure never thought it would be this easy finding you up here."

Jack figured that was bull. Either he'd done a lot of searching to track Jack down or this meeting was an accident. He led Noble onto the porch of the store, a whistle stop two miles north of the dying community of Piotona on the New Orleans and Northeastern Railroad. Surrounded by a sea of longleaf pine, the fully functional general store didn't have occasion to see many shipping magnates, not of the sea-going variety anyway. Jon wore dress shoes, dusty now, and tan trousers. His long-sleeved shirt, so white it hurt to look at it in the noonday sun, was soaked in sweat. He'd draped his frock coat over one arm.

Jack stepped around a rocking chair to the water barrel next to the door of the building. He took a drink of cold spring water, closed his eyes with satisfaction, then took another. He passed the dipper to Noble.

"How are things in Mobile?"

Done, Jon handed the dipper back. "Well, I tell ya. I have two assistant department heads, one for import and one for export. Two of my largest transports recently returned from South America, both stacked to their main decks with goodies for the domestic market. My import head is happy.

"Now, that said, we normally retain half the goods on board for further shipping to Europe. Those are exclusively Noble goods. Then we refill the balance of the hold with about fifty percent Noble products purchased here"—he waved a hand—"or hereabouts, on the domestic market, and the balance with the goods of clients who have their own established European accounts. These two particular ships, however, I have earmarked for King and Gibson lumber." He grinned broadly. "It gave me the opportunity just yesterday to reject transport for an old and steady client. My export head is not happy. What's particularly special about this fella is that his father sits on the Noble Corporation board."

"Why don't you just tell the board the bind your brother has you in?"

"It's a long story, one mired in the profligacy of my youth, an absolutely *perfect* older brother, and the unfortunate circumstance that Alan has been acquainted with that bunch of bastards since I was still in a ruffled dress.

"My maternal grandfather founded Hampton Shipping, now Noble Shipping. It had a board of its own, a board composed of men who were, as you might guess, as ancient as my grandfather. My father's marriage to my mother nominally established an ideal merchant and shipping enterprise, but make no mistake, they were two different companies. The marriage was followed all too soon by the demise of my maternal grandfather. My mother was his sole remaining child. My father, and to a lesser extent, Alan, adroitly managed to consolidate the two companies and their individual boards. Only two members of the original Hampton Shipping board remain. Both are now truly ancient, but one of them just happens to be the aforementioned father of my export assistant, whose decision I overrode when I told that favored client we wouldn't be able to ship his goods before November. That got the export head's attention. When he asked me what the hell was going on, I told him to ask his father." Jon met Jack's eye. "Of course, the father isn't going to have the answer. He probably has never heard of King and Gibson, and he's certainly unaware of a private agreement between my brother and Noble Corporation's shipping department to accommodate Eva's lumber. At that point I hope to receive a summons."

"And if your brother receives the summons?"

"Which will probably be the case, and he will blame the entire fiasco on my poor management."

Then what was the point of this game? But Jack didn't ask.

"Eva has about thirty days to get her timber to the Coast, cut, loaded and shipped to Pascagoula. What's her status?"

"She's only got half of what she's cut to her mills on the Coast, or moving that way. She's dependent on Humboldt's dummy lines to get the stuff to the main rail, but those dummies are all queued up. She's gonna be delayed, no conspiracy needed."

"No conspiracy needed in her impending failure to get the lumber to Pascagoula, either. Blake Shipping is contracted to move almost a million board feet of Jason Brothers' lumber from Humboldt's Biloxi River mill to Brazil in two weeks." Jon chuckled. "That should come as an unpleasant surprise to Alan."

That had been a trade-off between Jason Brothers and Humboldt, the former cutting Humboldt's timber at one of its interior mills for shipment north in exchange for Humboldt cutting Jason's requisition to Brazil. Humboldt had played no role in contracting Jason Brothers subsequent shipping arrangements to South America, but Jon Noble had obviously figured it out.

"Another delay," Jack said. "Who'd have thought it?"

Jon grinned. "That contract didn't cause my new head of domestic shipping a qualm, but he did wonder why the verbal agreement made with King and Gibson in June didn't go through."

"Blake himself?"

"Nah, his nephew. Blake's retired. Things are working out real well with that asset." Jon smiled, more to himself, Jack thought, than at Jack. "I have Alan to thank for that. You can bet he's gonna want my head when he hears of the Jason Brothers contract."

Jack pushed back with his heel and looked across the shaded road to the towering forest, vast, pristine, and carpeted with clean, sweet-scented straw, manicured with God's own hand. Over there and down a little ways stood a one-room dispensary, its door and windows open. Nothing stirred. No foresters were sick or injured at the moment, nor were any of their dependents. It was siesta time. Even Buck had taken a break, as instructed. Jack rocked forward, setting his feet firmly on the wooden planks of the porch.

"If Eva were to get the lumber to you in time to meet your schedule, would you still have a problem with her?"

"Just acquiesce, ship her lumber at hurtful rates, and keep sailing along, you mean?"

"Actually, I'm wondering where you're coming from. From my point of view, shipping her lumber is to your advantage. The only person helped by her failure to ship is your brother, who stands to gain a lumber mill."

"I don't..." Jon Noble swallowed his response, a demeaning one, no doubt. It wasn't the first time in their four-month association that Noble had subtly told Jack that he didn't care to explain his motives to the hired help, but he was more careful now in dealing with Jack, who'd reminded him on one such occasion he hadn't been hired and was, in reality, a partner in some sort of alleged crime.

"Alan wants to remove me from the company completely.

He owns over forty percent of the stock in Noble Corporation proper. I own only fifteen percent, but that is the bulk of what was once Hampton Shipping. With my father's consolidation after the death of my grandfather, that was all watered down. A pity, because the private ownership of our shipping was at the heart of Noble's expansion after the War."

Since Jon Noble first approached him back in May, Jack had made a point of finding out why the Noble patriarch had marginalized his younger son's position within the company. Young Jon had been neither dependable nor trustworthy. Alan, on the other hand, had been his father's right arm and today was considered the company's backbone. According to what Nate Stephens discreetly uncovered on Jack's behalf, Jon finally grew up and was now doing a commendable job as head of Noble Corporation's shipping department, but how much of his success was attributable to his own turnaround and how much to the leadership of the older brother, no one knew. From what Jack gathered from his conversations with Jon, Alan unjustifiably gave credit to himself.

"I still don't get how your brother's confronting the board and placing the blame on you is going to help your cause."

"It won't, but I have another ace up my sleeve regarding my perfect brother."

"And other than my confirming for you what you already knew, what brings you to me today?"

*N*othing, as it turned out.

"Did you get that extra coffee?" Jack asked Buck, when they were about done loading.

"Got it."

Oh, something brought Jon Noble to the Piney Woods, all right, but it wasn't a need to talk to Jack. Noble's long, rambling conversation, though interesting, conveyed nothing critical in regards to time or resources. It could have waited or never taken place at all. The man's finding Jack at the commissary at Piotona had been inadvertent and, having been seen, Noble's "visit" was nothing more than a veiled subterfuge masking why he'd really been up this way. And the fact that Jon Noble felt a need to disguise his visit was the only thing that made the bizarre meeting interesting at all.

Chapter Thirteen

Penny took a seat at Florence's Queen Anne desk at the same time Gracie pulled back the heavy curtains, letting in enough morning light to almost render the coal-oil lamp unnecessary. Almost. With just one window overlooking the house's wrap-around veranda, Florence's south-facing parlor was a gloomy place, cluttered with heavy, upholstered furniture, a huge coal-gas chandelier, which Florence rarely used, and two walls covered with gilt-framed portraits and mirrors. A third wall was reserved for a bookshelf filled with tomes that Penny loved to peruse. Florence confessed she'd never opened the first one. The books had belonged to Lorraine, the first Mrs. Noble, and this room had been her personal office.

Penny laid the list Gracie had given her on the desk.

Flour, salt, beans, cornmeal...striknine. *Strychnine*.

That meant a rat.

Adel was a rat.

Alan would prefer a cat rather than poison for getting rid of the rat. Penny closed her eyes and imagined herself a cat, while Gracie adeptly tied back the heavy velvet drapes. Truth was Adel was the cat and Penny a pathetic little mouse.

She corrected the spelling of *strychnine* on the grocery list and gave Gracie, now standing beside her, a questioning look.

"Roland say he seen one in da barn. Miz Florence tol' me when I lef' las' evenin' to add poison to da lis'."

The vicious things would be in the house if they didn't do something. Roland had complained of them in the barn all summer.

"Mr. Noble's not going to like it," Penny said, somewhat

79

relieved Florence was finally taking a stand. "The poison, I mean. We've already used arsenic. He's right about a cat."

"Missus say get it. Won't 'av no cat. Hates 'em."

Penny added toothpowder to the list. "She doesn't hate them, I don't think. They make her sick."

"Roland ain't seen a rat in 'is bunkroom since he got Alcorn."

Alcorn was his cat. Penny initialed the list so Florence would know she'd seen it. "We'll name our rat Adelaide, what do you think?"

"Too pretty fo' a rat."

"Some rats are pretty."

"You evah seen a pretty rat?"

Three days ago, but it would have been much longer if only her mother would quit trying to mend the divide between her daughters, sloughing off Penny's broken heart as a childish disappointment she should have outgrown by now. But Adel had betrayed her. Not for love nor hate. Not for any reason that Penny could ascertain. She took Mark because she could, and she didn't even want him. Penny hadn't mattered at all.

"Dem ladies call up da dead heah las' night, didn't dey?"

Five silly women, and she counted herself among them, their hands linked and eyes fixed on Madam Natasha's globe. The woman used no surname best Penny knew. Three of the ladies, including Madam Natasha, were past sixty, their wrinkled faces and sunken eyes ghoulish in the muted light. The spell was broken early into the sitting when a violent wrench of the table upset the globe and left the room in total darkness, but for the low glow of the pilots belonging to the three wall sconces. By the time Penny reached the closest one and brightened the room, Margie Ashton was hysterical. She'd rushed out with wild eyes and cries that icy fingers had touched her neck. Florence, the long anticipated evening forced to end early, was livid, not so much with the timid Margie, but with the highly touted Madam Natasha, who had gone, Florence accused, a bit overboard with her rendition of spiritual contact.

"I, madam, am not a charlatan," the woman had countered in

a deep and heavily accented voice that Penny figured was as phony as the fog-filled globe that the woman inadvertently smashed on Florence's oriental carpet. Surely she hadn't meant to do that? "You opened a portal here tonight and something entered this house. Something angry." She'd waved a bony finger under Florence's nose. "Take care it finds its way back to the realm where it belongs."

Realm, indeed. Florence all but rolled her eyes with that, but two of the guests had lingered and heard the medium's words, and oh how they'd tittered when the door closed behind Madam Natasha. The dire warning, for all intents and purposes, salvaged the entire evening. Certainly Florence had hosted the most exciting séance of the summer here on the Coast, and she ended up going to bed quite pleased with the evening's entertainment. This morning, she concluded that the "novice" Margie Ashton was not a novice at all, but a culprit in league with the renowned Madam Natasha. Penny figured that the more sensible of the guests would conclude it was all a hoax perpetrated by Florence herself.

Penny looked at a pensive Gracie. Still, just the thought that something from the other side might have actually been in this room with them left Penny suddenly uneasy.

"It's great fun, actually. Madam Natasha claimed—"

Florence Noble's office door flew open. Gracie jumped, and Penny twisted around to see.

"Penny, dearest," Florence said, "would you be kind enough to substitute for me at the Coast Arts luncheon today?"

Penny glanced at the bonnet on Florence's head. "You're going out?"

"An emergency." She started to turn, but Penny held out Gracie's grocery list.

"Something has come up I must take care of," the woman added hastily and took the paper from Penny's hand. Immediately she flashed Gracie a smile. "The shopping list? I'd forgotten." She handed it back to Penny. "I should let you run the house, and I play all day. You are simply too efficient."

That wasn't so, but Penny would happily take the compliment. "Where —"

"Angelina Ladner's." Finding herself in the mirror, Florence licked her fingers, then plastered a gilt curl in front of her ear. Momentarily, she twisted her head this way and that, admiring the effect, then settled on Penny's reflection, watching, behind her. "Does it make me look younger," she asked.

"You are young," Penny said.

Florence laughed and again played with the curl. "Not as young as you."

"That's because I was born years later."

Still admiring her own reflection, Florence Noble recited, "Magic mirror on my wall, who's the fairest in this hall?"

She turned quickly to face Penny, who responded, "You are."

"Ah, you are a sweet and tactful child. However, I don't believe Prince Charming would agree any longer."

Penny rose and stood beside her in front of the mirror. "There is no Prince Charming, only the mirror."

"And the mirror never lies," Florence said with mock sadness, then tapped Penny on the nose, "though you are still looking a bit peaked." Florence started to turn, then stopped abruptly. Reaching out, she touched the mirror. "Oh, dear." Abruptly she turned on Gracie. "How did that happen?"

"Weren't theah yesta'day, Miz Florence.

Penny positioned herself to see what Florence was looking at. A crack, a good six inches long, ran vertically along the mirror's lower right side.

"Odd," Florence said, somewhat distracted. "I wonder" — she turned to Penny — "perhaps it happened last night when the globe broke."

"I guess it's possible." Penny perused the area around the mirror, but saw nothing on the floor which might have damaged the mirror. Still, Jane might have removed whatever it was last night when she cleaned up.

Florence threw her arms into the air and laughed. "Oh, well." She looked at Penny, any expectations of further explanation apparently forgotten. "Angelina will be tickled to have you there. I intended to bring you along anyway. She does so consider you a delight. Noon sharp, you need to change."

"Did you have anything to bring up at the meeting?"

"No, no, no. All you need to do is sit there and look pretty. Thank you, dear, and thank you, Gracie. I'm sure you've done an excellent job with the grocery list." She disappeared into the dark hall. A moment later the front door slammed.

Penny handed Gracie the list. "I corrected the spelling of *strychnine*, if you want to look at it."

"I saw. Thank you."

"You did do a fine job with the list. I wonder why we bother to approve it anymore."

"The mister, he—"

"Alan. I know. I'll be leaving in half an hour." Penny pushed the chair beneath the writing table on the secretary.

"'A delight,'" Gracie said. Penny, her hand still on the chair, looked at her, and Gracie granted her a rare smile. "She say Miz Ladner thinks you a delight and she was gonna bring you wif 'er. Makes you sound like dessert."

Chapter Fourteen

The ladies at the Coast Arts Association didn't gobble her up, but the charming and influential dowager Angelina Ladner did have a penchant for making Penny feel a celebrity of sorts. As a young woman, Angelina had known Abner Lucian King, Penny's grandfather, and thought highly of the man. What the true relationship was between a once beautiful woman and a reputedly very handsome young man, Penny didn't know, but several of the women that made up Florence Noble's inner circle, including Florence herself, did their fair share of speculating. Penny secretly believed it was Angelina's high regard for A.L. King that had ensured Penny's acceptance as a bride for Harold.

Dorothea Bonneville, pleased to find Penny present, insisted on an update to Florence's initiative to bring a national play troupe to Biloxi. Penny muddled through as best she could, mentally berating Florence all the while. Sit and look pretty, indeed.

Alan offered Penny the perfect opportunity to get even at dinner that night when he asked Florence pointblank how the luncheon with the Coast Art Association went, and without even a glance at Penny, the woman responded the lunch was delicious and the company charming, if boring.

"They want more money?"

"I want more money, darling. Your support puts me in good stead with the diminished old wealth of this city. I take it your lunch did not go well or Jonathan would be joining us tonight."

"It was his decision to stay at the hotel, and that's fine with me. I'm sure my supper will sit better on my stomach than my lunch has."

"You fought, then?" Florence asked.

"We managed to keep things cordial. I wanted to discuss the loan for that tract of land up in Perry County."

"You've rethought it then?" Harold asked.

"I considered doing so, briefly."

"I thought you kept things cordial."

Alan thrust a forkful of rice into his mouth, chewed, and swallowed, then drew his napkin from his lap. He dabbed at the corner of his mouth and settled his gaze on Harold at the opposite end of the table. "I haven't told him I do not intend to loan him the money."

"You're trying to persuade him not to approach the board tomorrow by giving him false hope you might actually support him with that land deal?"

"Hardly. The board does not sympathize with his complaint."

"Peter Whithers does, and I know for a fact there are others."

"Which others, son?" Alan snapped. "Peter was listening to his son whose complaint is that Jon overstepped him by refusing to accept Dorsey's shipment this fall. Hell, Dorsey had cancelled a shipment on us in April. We needed the space, so we rightfully presumed not to rely on the man's business. Jon was absolutely correct in the way he handled the situation. I've told Jon that, and I've explained it to Peter. He's in agreement." Alan placed his forearm on the table and leaned forward, eyes wide. "Now who else do you have?"

Harold's eyes dropped back to his plate, and he speared a piece of chicken. "You're draining his assets, Father, and you know it. It was you, after all, who drew us into the timber business and inadvertently dragged Noble Corporation along with us. Why not allow Uncle Jon to reap some of the benefits?"

"Us, son, *we*? *I* am in the timber business, not 'us' and not Noble Corporation. Jon is extorting me to provide him a loan by threatening to draw Noble Corporation into, not the timber business, but my private contract. And who among us"—he waved his fork over the table to take in all present—"is the primary benefactor of my dabbling in timber?" He nodded curtly at Harold. "Yes, you'd best take that into account, son."

85

Alan dropped his napkin on the table. Penny had never seen him so agitated, and she shot Florence a wary look. Florence smiled and took a bite of her supper.

Harold sighed. "He's threatening to expose King and Gibson exclusivity, for which you are responsible. The imbalance between his imports and exports will look bad on the department's year-end reports. That's what bothers Ralph Whithers—"

"Bah. What bothered Ralph was Jon's daring to usurp what he considers his sole authority, him being the progeny of one of Hampton Shipping's original board members. There's nothing more to good ole Ralph than that, and his esteemed father has smoothed his feathers."

"Uncle Jon says that Dorsey knows members of the board, and he knows that those ships should have left Mobile four days ago. Jon fears—"

"He brought no such fears up to me today."

When Harold didn't respond, Alan continued. "He implied to you that I'm doing this on purpose, didn't he?"

"You are."

"It's my asset."

"It's *our* asset, Dad, including Uncle Jon's, and there are separate inves—"

"Enough! Peter Whithers is not going to bring it up at the board meeting in the morning and neither is Jon. In fact, Jon isn't even supposed to be present, and should he go back on his word, he will not have Peter's support."

"Because you led him to believe you'll give him the loan for that timberland?"

"I told him the prospectus looked good and I favored the idea."

"You purposefully misled him?"

"I told him the truth, but I'll probably hold on to my capital at present."

Harold snorted and returned to his meal. "I support him regarding the shipping, and I believe the land deal is a good investment. He is your brother."

"Your support is noted, and regarding any vote on shipping, should it come up, you've received yet another reprieve regarding your loyalty, which, I may add, I expect to be given to me." Alan's eyes darted to Penny. "That was a gentleman's agreement within the family."

Penny nodded. She didn't think she was expected to say anything, but she was never certain.

"That land will be worth a fortune," Harold said.

"When? In twenty years? We need the capital now. He's not buying enough timber there to make a significant payback. Besides," Alan said, pointing his fork toward Harold, "I'm not so sure he doesn't intend to go into the timber business himself."

"Like you?" Harold said.

Alan glowered. "That was a loan, not an investment."

"So is this. Blood is thicker than water."

"Jonathan is up to something, and I'm not so sure you don't know what it is. But I expect you to support me, not your uncle, should it come to that."

"I'll give you my support if you'll give him the loan. In the end, the unfettered success of Noble Shipping is sound for the company."

Alan dropped his eyes and began cutting the meat from a chicken thigh. "You, son, need to be looking out for your own welfare. I am."

"Are we certain Noble Corporation doesn't wish to become involved with lumber?" Florence asked.

"Of—"

"No," Alan said, "it does not, not beyond shipping it, anyway."

"The board might consider it," Harold said.

Alan chuckled. "My anticipation of the board's opposition is why I made Eva Markiston a personal loan." Alan took a sip from his water glass and nodded at Harold. "And you may rest assured that under no circumstance does Jon want to share with the board this bamboozle he's concocted."

"That timberland is a sure bet."

"Until the next recession or the next timber glut."

"Why should you care? Lend him the money. When he fails, you can force him out of Noble Shipping."

"The hell I can. I'll be out twenty-five thousand dollars and that's all I'll get from his latest scheme. Twenty-five thousand dollars, son. That's a lot of money. Five dollars an acre for land still selling at a dollar twenty-five."

"It's a sound investment, what with Humboldt's interest."

"Humboldt?" Alan asked.

Harold looked up at his father, started to speak, then shut his mouth.

"What about Humboldt?"

"He said nothing to you about Humboldt's interest?"

Alan eyed his son suspiciously. "He did not."

Harold released a much-put-upon sigh and returned to his plate.

"Well?"

Harold raised his head and grinned sheepishly. "Well, I guess the cat's out of the bag. Uncle Jon obviously didn't want you to know. I must wonder why?"

"What," Alan said firmly, "about Humboldt?"

"He didn't choose that parcel willy-nilly. The owner of that land is Louise Adcock. She's in Pennsylvania. She—"

"I know, I know. The daughter of a Yankee land speculator who purchased it in 1878. Jonathan told me today. How do you know Humboldt is after it?"

"Uncle Jon told me."

"Did he tell you how he came by this knowledge?"

Harold shrugged. "A friend who works for Humboldt. They are looking at rail, of course. Within a few years that land will be selling for as high as twenty-five dollars an acre."

"I don't have a few years."

Harold shrugged. "Neither does Uncle Jon. He doesn't believe Humboldt is gonna wait around until it brings top dollar. I think he plans to buy at the five Adcock is asking, then turn around and offer it to Humboldt for ten. Maybe start at fifteen.

For sure he plans to turn that twenty-five thousand into fifty fast."

"And is Louise Adcock aware of Humboldt's interest?"

"Not yet."

Alan pursed his lips. "If Humboldt wants it, why haven't they approached her?"

"They recently finished clearing a parcel, the Dillison tract, I think. They're selling the cut-back land in lots. They need those profits to make an offer."

"See what I mean? Risky, even for the big mills." Thoughtfully, Alan wet his lips. "For him to know that, Jon's friend must be a high-placed representative of Humboldt."

Harold shrugged.

"Did he tell you who?"

"He did not, nor did I ask. I knew he wouldn't tell me. He doesn't trust me with you anymore than you trust me with him."

Penny considered that Jon was right in his reticence to confide in either of these two.

"Why does Humboldt want it, outside the timber, that is?"

Harold flexed his jaw, then returned his attention to his plate. "Maybe they don't want to compete with a railroad for it."

"I'll need to see the plat," Alan said more to himself than the rest of them. "At least now I know for sure that Jonathan is up to something."

"You'll support him then?"

Alan laughed. "Hardly. I intend to beat him at his own game, my son."

Harold's eyes narrowed on his father. "You intend to buy the land from under him?"

"Like I said, I need capital now, and a diversion for a quick return might prove a lifesaver at the moment." Alan waved his fork over the table. "I'll check that plat, first. I find land speculation much easier to swallow than timber. So much more in keeping with Jon's character." He sobered suddenly, gave his wife a passing glance, then settled his gaze on Harold. "I assume I have your discretion?"

Penny, her stomach sick in anticipation of the treachery she was about to commit, said, "I think it's a terrible thing to do to your brother, Alan."

He gave her that conciliatory smile of his, as he always did when he wished to console her, without telling her outright that her opinion didn't matter. Then he patted her hand. She looked at it, her little mousy paw. "One must be ruthless in business if one is to survive, sweet child." He turned to Harold and barked, "Do I?"

"I think it's a terrible thing to do also." Harold smiled. "But I can live with myself."

"And can you, my dear," Alan said to Florence.

She smiled. "I, too, have lived with worse betrayals, darling, as you well know."

"Why does he treat him that way?" Penny asked her husband later.

Harold grimaced, turning his head in an awkward manner, then buttoning the collar of his shirt beneath the chin. Done, he found her in the mirror. "Uncle Jon is not without fault in this. He hasn't been forthright in divulging his purpose for the loan. Despite what I said at dinner, Jon should be offering dad at least sixty percent of the profit. It is, after all, his money."

"That sounds more like offering him a partnership."

"Where the other partner puts up nothing?" Harold laughed.

"That's my point. Jon asked for a loan, which he'd pay back, I assume with interest."

"Dad isn't a bank, which would, by the way, want collateral for the loan."

"That would be the land."

He stared at her in the mirror. "My father is technically an investor, who should enjoy a percentage of the profits on the investment, except Uncle Jon has falsely presented his purchase as a long-term investment in timberland in anticipation of a later demand for the lumber." Harold walked to the foot of his bed, picked up his frock coat and leaned forward to kiss Penny on the top of her head. "The ploy is unethical at best. Uncle Jonnie squandered his capital account years ago and has never made any effort to rebuild it."

"But doesn't he get —"

"He heads the department at Noble Shipping, yes, but from what Dad and Uncle Jonnie, and even Florence, have told me, I'm amazed Jonathan Noble got a piece of the business at all. Dad says it was because the old man was very fond of Jonathan's young mother." Harold placed his bowler atop his head and tapped the narrow brim with two fingers.

"Why did you betray your uncle's trust?"

"That was inadvertent, Penny, you heard the conversation. But I'm not real bothered by it. Alan Noble is my father."

"Yes, he is. You'll be gone all night?"

"I plan to be."

Penny half-slid, half-jumped from where she sat at the foot of Harold's bed.

"How are you feeling?" he asked.

"Much better."

"Then whatever was wrong is passing. You ate well tonight."

"Dinner was exceptionally good tonight."

"Exceptionally."

Penny started for the door joining their two bedrooms. "I seem to amuse you, Harold. Pity I cannot keep you amused."

He started for the hallway door. "I think you are charming. That's one reason I agreed to marry you."

She turned at her threshold and looked at his departing back. "And what are the others?"

He looked over his shoulder. "The others?"

"The other reasons."

"You're pretty."

She laughed at that. "Supposing that were true, what would my being pretty matter to you?"

Now, he turned to face her, mock disbelief etched on his face. "Why, I get to show you off, dear girl. That pleases my father."

"Take care tonight, Harold."

"And how much fun would that be?" he said and stepped into the upstairs hall.

Penny shut the door joining their rooms, and with some regret, she poured the cup of chocolate Jane had left for her into the plant next to the drape-shrouded window. She was feeling too good now to risk the heartburn that always seemed to accompany Alan Noble's number-one selling import.

In front of the mirror, she began pulling pins from her hair, and after cleaning strands of red hair from her brush, she started brushing. Harold had called her pretty, but he himself was beautiful. What lovely children he could sire, if only he would try.

Chapter Fifteen

"You stayin' in Handsboro?" Lucas Frazier asked Jack.

"Happy Hollow."

"Kate's?"

"Yep."

Lucas cocked his head and studied him. "You takin' over management of the mill?"

Jack grinned. "I hear the doubt in your voice. I grew up in a sawmill."

"When I first met you, you said you grew up in the woods."

"Both."

"And ain't you a valuable fella." Lucas shook his head. "Either way, I'm glad Humboldt has finally done somethin'. I was about ready to walk out myself."

"Nate Stephens has wanted me to come down for a while. Just so you know, I volunteered. I have some other business to take care of. And as far as Cranston is concerned, you shouldn't have let it go on like it did." Jack looked past the day supervisor to three other men, two white, one black, who'd gathered upon his arrival. Jack brought with him a new edging machine for which he'd diverted to its delivery point in New Orleans. He turned back to Lucas. "Stephens is gonna listen to you."

Another black man, crowbar in hand, sidled up to the wagon. He handed the tool to a man already inspecting the crate.

"Cranston has been working for Humboldt since before the War," Lucas said. "Me and Duke was sure he was handpicked, and we didn't figure we could oust him, no matter what. You know damn well us goin' over his head wouldn't have looked good."

"Well, he hasn't been working for Stephens since before the War. Production at this mill has been steadily declining all summer, but that quarter drop last month jumped right out and smacked him in the nose. Now he's the one looking bad. We've got to get that Jason Brothers' lumber cut and moved out. Got a load of our own comin' in."

"Can't get any work done without workers," Lucas said.

"An' dat damn fool didn't know nuffin' 'bout dat carriage feed neitha. Say da chain be weak, dat's wha' cause it to break. Went 'n fired ol' Floyd Humphrey when he argued wif 'im."

Jack nodded at Polly Thom. "Do you think we can get Floyd back here now that Cranston's gone?"

Old Polly pulled a kerchief out of his back pocket and wiped his forehead. "Well, don't know now, Masta Jack. Know fo' a fact he's done gone an' took—"

"We can get him back," Lucas Frazier said, "now that you're here."

Jack glanced at Lucas, then back to the old darkie in front of him. "You wouldn't be tryin' to bullshit me, would you, Polly?"

The man's teeth lit his dark face. "Well, don't know dat you really gonna need 'im. Me an' Floyd, we bo'f know 'bout da carriage, an' me, I ain't gone nowheres, so I don't know dat you—"

"I'll need the both of you and more to maintain these saws." Jack's eyes glanced to the three white men gathered on his left. "We're going to twenty-four-hour operations within the next two weeks. Let your buddies know that Humboldt is hirin' and Cranston is gone. We've got a lot of timber to move and lumber to cut. Y'all might be wishin' him back before we're done."

Lucas blew out a breath. "Doubt that."

"Doubt that sho' nuff. Dat man reminded me of a nigga driber heah on Pine Hill befo' da Wah. Meanest nigga you evah seen. Always whippin' dem darkies till sometimes dey couldn't eben wawk."

"Pine Hill?" Lucas asked.

"That's what this place was called," Jack answered. "Pine Hill Plantation. Cattle, sheep, and timber. Ranchers and ranching are gone. Before the War, it had an absentee owner named Ponce Ridgely, a cotton planter over in Greene County, Alabama. The mill stayed in the family till old man Ridgely's son died about three years ago. Heirs sold it to Humboldt. The Ridgelys managed to keep it somewhat updated, but this mill is ancient. That gang saw Ridgely designed, however, is unique."

Jack turned and started walking toward the carriage feed for one of the mill's two headsaws. Except for three men still on the wagon trying to uncrate the new equipment, the others followed. "My daddy told me you belonged to John Snow, Polly. Didn't realize you were part of Pine Hill way back then."

"I did belong to John Snow, but Massa Johnny used to cut a few trees each yeah jes' fo' a little extra. Me an' him's boys was playmates. Ole Massa John and da olda boys, dey did da cuttin'. Me an' da two younga ones handled da oxen an' ran da logs down stream. Dem was good times den. He'ped heah at Pine Hill, too, when I gots olda. Massa John would hire me out."

"I'm surprised you wanted to be here if that driver was so mean."

"He'd a nevah whipped me, Massa Johnny wouldn't 'low it but he was gone by den anyways. Massa Po came down from Al'bama an' seen what he was doin'. Fahr'd da ovahseer an' sen' dat driber back ta Al'bama to pick cotton."

"Anyways, dat's when I learned da carriages and da saws. Massa Johnny dickered fo' my pay. Kept a nickel fo' evah two bits I earned. Mama, she ask Massa Johnny to save da res'. He let me buy my freedom when I was eighteen an' I come back heah to wawk fulltime wif a wage." Polly laughed. "Massa John dickered a good wage fo' me den, too. Him and ole Massa Po, dey be good frien's. Massa Johnny was a good, good man." Polly gave his head a firm shake. "Anyways, I tell you all dis so you know you don't need ole Floyd. Ain't nobody, an' I mean nobody, know d'ese saws better'n me."

Jack couldn't quite squelch his smile. He'd known Polly Thom for some time. This was the first time he'd ever heard him bring up being on Pine Hill. Still, he had the names right and the

95

man knew the saws, there was no question about that. Other than keep Floyd out of the equation, there was no reason for him to make anything up, other than he was a notorious bullshitter.

"What is it between you and Floyd, Polly?"

Polly clamped his teeth together and sucked in a breath with a grotesque grimace. "Ah, he be such a damn ole know evah-thin'."

"And I could use a couple of 'know-everythings' when it comes to these old saws."

Chapter Sixteen

Penny had one hand on the ribbon beneath her chin, the other on the doorknob to Florence's parlor, when she caught sight of the pretty Negress Jane, hands waving, hurrying down the hall toward her. She'd been too late registering the girl's intent, Penny realized a heartbeat later, when she pushed the panel open, and Florence whirled in surprise out of Jonathan Noble's embrace. Penny, feeling the blood drain from her face, gathered then that Jane had been trying to intercept her.

"Penny, darling," Florence said, "I thought you'd gone to visit your mother."

Penny drew in a breath, nodded to Jonathan, who smiled in response before turning to the room's single window.

"I'm sorry," Penny said to Florence. "I expected to find you in here, and yes, I was on my way to Mama's, but at the depot the telegram operator recognized me and gave me this." Deflated now, Penny held up the piece of yellow paper. "It's from New York. I'd hoped the news was good, and I wanted to be the one to deliver it to you."

"Oh, sweetheart," the woman said, stepping forward and hugging Penny to her. "Such child-like enthusiasm. Thank you for your loyalty to me."

Penny noted an emphasis on "loyalty," then Florence pushed her to arm's length. "Let me guess. Phillip Baker has agreed to come."

"He likes the idea and wishes you to follow up by letter." Penny pointed to the telegram. "He's asked some questions."

"Excellent."

Florence shifted her gaze behind Penny, and Penny looked

over her shoulder to Jane, waiting with lowered eyes. "You may go, Jane," Florence said.

Jane nodded stiffly and walked out the door, which she pulled shut behind her.

"I should go too," Jonathan said, "before we have any more surprises." He took Penny's hand and kissed it. "The next one might not be as pleasant as this one." He pushed back as if to take in the whole of her. "Nor as beautiful. I hear you've been ill?"

"Yes."

"I can see it in your eyes...and your color."

"Jaundice. Dr. Clark feared yellow fever for a while. But I'm better now."

"Something you ate?" Jonathan persisted, not taking his eyes off Penny's, nor did he surrender her hand despite her gentle tug.

"Perhaps."

Gently, he rubbed her knuckles with the inside of his thumb, then turned to Florence, bringing her into the conversation. "Has he given you any idea what?"

"No," Florence said, "nor do I believe he intends to pursue the matter. She's much better now." Florence looked at Penny's hand in Jonathan's, then back at him. "You should go. Penny and I need to talk. You can see yourself out?"

Reluctantly, it seemed, he dropped Penny's hand. "I know the way, and don't be too hard on Jane."

She laughed. "I could hardly afford that, could I?"

With the soft click of the door, Florence drew Penny to the settee. "It was foolish for Jonathan to come here. He came to wait on Alan. You remember our dinner discussion last week?"

"Yes, his hopes for a tract of land in Perry County."

"He returned to Mobile confident Alan was going to loan him the money in return for his not approaching the board regarding the abuse of Noble Shipping. He learned only yesterday that Alan had bought the land out from under him."

"And he's returned here in a huff?"

"Regrettably. I'm afraid he's quite angry at Alan and Harold, too, in whom he'd confided."

98

"Surely he considered Harold wouldn't go against his father?"

Florence bit her bottom lip. "Things have passed between Harold and Alan, as I'm sure you can imagine, given Harold's sexual perversity."

"They seem to get along—"

"Only since Harold agreed to marry you, my dear. You have no idea of the tension in this house before you came. Your union creates a proper front for Alan's friends and associates, and he does hope for grandchildren."

Penny looked away, and Florence patted her hand. "Yes, I know. Harold confides much to me. Rest assured his lack of interest is not your fault. Jon, who is more liberal-minded, has always been closer to Harold than his father. Needless to say, Jonathan was hurt by Harold's betrayal. He came here to confront Alan. I don't believe he has anything to say to Harold at all. Look at me."

Penny did.

"I've managed to dissuade Jonathan from a fight." Florence squeezed Penny's fingers. "I doubt you will approve my tack, but I hold, if I might be so frank, a great deal of influence over Jonathan, if you understand my meaning."

"I believe I do."

"Over the course of my marriage to Alan, I have managed to maintain a truce of sorts between my husband and his brother. I'd like to continue to do so."

Penny wanted to clench the hand Florence held, but didn't dare. "If you think I will tell Alan what I saw here today, I promise you I will not."

"Thank you." Florence rose and started to her desk.

"Do you love him?"

Florence turned.

"Jonathan, I mean."

Florence's gaze drifted away, and she continued to her desk. "Jonathan and I had promised ourselves to each other. Then Alan, who had been recently widowed, took an interest in me.

Jon had a reputation, and his position within Noble Corporation was not clear. Alan was the head of the company." She sighed. "Suffice it to say my parents decided I should wed Alan."

"Did they know you loved Jonathan?"

"I was young. They had never approved of my promise to Jonathan. I believed they knew best."

Florence turned at the desk so that she faced Penny. She laughed. "How sordid you must think me, but I never stopped loving Jon."

"I don't think you sordid." But she did, actually, just a bit. "I'm simply...surprised."

"You're shocked, and I'm sorry you found out. Jane was supposed to be guarding the door."

"Does Jane know about you two?"

"The coloreds know everything. They did in the old days, too."

"And you trust her?"

"I pay her and Gracie well. They're loyal to me, and there's no sentimentality involved."

"In my case, you'll have to rely on sentimentality."

"I'm very grateful, my dear."

Chapter Seventeen

"**I**s my room empty?" Jack asked simultaneously with his opening of the back door. Kate Peele whirled.

"Jack," she said and added a heartfelt smile before stepping around the dining room table and giving him a hug. She pushed back and held him at arm's length. "I made biscuits and gravy for my boarders this morning. Made me think of you. And yes, I keep it empty," she said. "Humboldt pays too well."

"Good. I was worried. Heard there'd been an influx of lumbermen. Afraid you'd given it away with me not being around."

"Influx?" She eyed him. "I think you've been smelling too much in the way of pine spirits up there in those woods." She sucked in a breath. "I'm sorry, I wasn't thinking. Anything more on the explosion?"

"Nope, and it's been months. Reckon the only kind of justice I'll find for Deacon will be of the Southern persuasion."

He might have heard a sigh, he wasn't sure. She nodded her head, indicating he follow. When she opened the door at the end of the upstairs hall, light from the sun-soaked room flooded the passage where they stood. "I stripped the bed. I'll send Angel up to make it."

"I can do it."

"You'll make a mess of it."

He could make a fine bed. His mother taught him and made him do it from the time he was eight, but he sure didn't mind Angel doing it.

"Are the authorities even still working the murders?"

Jack tossed his bag on the unmade mattress. The room was hot. "Got their ears open, that's about it."

101

He set his flop hat on top of the bag, then looked at the round clock face by the bed. It showed seven o'clock. He didn't know the exact time, but he knew the time was closer to noon. "I'm in time for dinner?"

"You are." She picked up the clock, set it, then started winding. "How long will you be here this time?"

"I'll be in and out for the next couple of months. They've put me in charge of the Biloxi mill."

"You hate working in a mill."

"Nate made me a deal. He wanted me to take over until he can find another experienced supervisor. Had to fire Cranston, a veteran from Humboldt's mills in the Midwest. He treated the crew like they were dumb mules. Those were the white ones. Treated the coloreds worse. The horse's rear-end was always bad-mouthing yellow pine and the South. He made it to sergeant with the 8th Illinois. Lost a brother at Shiloh, and he was proud to let everybody know it, as if we didn't know what loss was. He's fired a good quarter of the crew and another half have left on their own accord. Nate was afraid what was left of 'em was gonna lay the good sergeant out on the carriage feed one night and somebody'd come in to find him sawed in half."

Kate pushed a loose strand of graying brown hair behind her ear, then walked over and opened a window. "We need to get fresh air in here. Prettiest view in the whole house, your daddy always said so." She looked over the steel-gray waters of Bernard Bayou glinting in the noon-day sun, then pointed with her chin. "He liked to look at the mill from here, too."

Jack moved around the bed to stand behind her. There it was, its massive twin structures that were the saw mill and kiln, imposing above the trees growing between them and the water.

"This was where he wanted our house to be," she said, and Jack felt a twinge of empathy for the woman. He wondered if his daddy would have ever wed her, less a reflection on Kate than the feelings the man had retained for Jack's mother.

King and Gibson had one other mill, on the east shore of the Wolf River just north of the Bay of St. Louis. His daddy had always been real partial to that one on the Bay. Hugh King was the one who liked life on Bayou Bernard.

Jack laughed, determined to lighten the mood. "You'd have probably ended up in that swamp over on the Escatawpa."

"That would have been all right, too."

Kate moved around him, then picked up the pitcher from the washbowl. "From what I hear, there's more potential for the company over on the Pascagoula. I wonder if Hugh would have ever built a mill over that way, given Eva's opposition?"

At the door, Kate stopped. "If it were all your and your daddy's now, as it should have been, would you build a mill over that way?"

"Oh, yeah."

She held up the porcelain pitcher. "I'll send Angel back up with water and a bar of soap. Crews will be coming in any minute. Some of your friends are here. They'll be glad to see you." She pursed her lips. "So what do you want?"

"Fried chicken."

"Catfish is on the menu, but I meant for your future."

"Granddaddy's cabin in the woods with the longleaf still standin'."

She snorted softly and glanced out the window. "Got peach cobbler, though."

At least once a week she had peach cobbler, his favorite.

Kate pulled the door shut behind her, and he turned to stare across the water. He could see both their names, the red monogrammed letters faded by time. One had the know-how, one had the vision, and together they'd made a team to be reckoned with in Mississippi's post-War Piney Woods. He'd stopped them though, dead in their tracks. Literally. He'd destroyed them, by default sure, but he'd been responsible all the same.

Yes, Jack knew what he wanted and so did Kate, and it wasn't that cabin in the woods with the trees still standing. That he already had. He wanted to destroy Eva Markiston and he wanted his daddy's company back, and he couldn't accomplish the one without sacrificing the other.

Chapter Eighteen

Penny lifted the queen of diamonds from the stack in the middle of the table, then glanced at the backs of the ten cards Harold held in his hand. He grinned at her. "It's big, isn't it?" he asked. He hadn't laid down the first card, and he had a bad habit of going out on her and leaving her with a handful of face cards, high pointers she liked to collect. She laid down three kings and the four, five, and six of spades to be safe.

"Chicken," he said. She discarded the deuce of clubs. He picked it up, laid down ten cards, and discarded the jack of diamonds. "Rummy," he said.

"I do believe I hate playing gin with you," she said and started adding up the hodge-podge face cards (because she'd picked up half the discard pile three tricks ago) and the nine of clubs, but he rose.

"Don't bother counting them. I won. You lost, and I'm leaving."

"To meet David at the club?" Florence said from her wing chair across the room. She wasn't looking at Harold, but at Alan coming through the pocket door with a tray and two china cups. "I enjoy imagining your father's reaction should you ever bring David to the Merchant's Club."

Alan's face hardened, and Penny reckoned his mood darkened with it. He'd been quiet at dinner, contemplative, a mood unusual for him, and because the man seemed to like her, Penny hated for his wife's teasing, good-natured though it might be, to further dampen what apparently had been a trying day.

Florence rose from her seat near the cold hearth. "I'm sorry, darling, that was in poor taste."

"Poor timing fits your remark better, not to mention the per-fidy of it."

"If you hadn't been coming through the door, I wouldn't have said it."

"Father is in one of his moods," Harold said and stepped around Alan.

"Not so much as to diminish his consideration for his women-folk," Florence said, peeking at the contents of the tray. "Chocolate, I see."

"I found Jane in the kitchen preparing to bring it. I told her I'd save her the trip." He held out the tray to Florence. "She insisted this cup is yours and this one is for Penny, the sweeter one."

Florence brought the cup to her lips. "Are you referring to the chocolate or your women, dear?" She took a swallow.

"Both," he answered and watched her drink, then lowered the tray to Penny. Harold took her cup before she could reach for it and set it beside her on the table. "Florence shouldn't drink the stuff at all," he said to his father.

"You tell her. I am done attempting to prevent the folly of women."

"I allow myself one cup a week. This is it, and behind every woman's folly is a man."

"Most women never realize that," Alan said. "And I'd be willing to bet, despite your overt wisdom, I can count you in that majority."

Harold cleared his throat. "Speaking of folly, Dad, play gin rummy with Penny. She's reckless tonight."

"Still holding handfuls, eh?"

Harold looked her in the eye and smiled. "Seems she'll never learn."

"You'd think I never win a game to hear you two tell it, and you both know I've overwhelmed you any number of times."

"We humor you," Alan said, "because we love you so, but I'm not in a gaming mood tonight." He leveled a disapproving eye on Harold. "You're going out, I take it?"

"And I'll be late."

"I'd prefer not to have my breakfast ruined."

"I'll try to beat the sun in the morning." Harold started for the door. When he disappeared into the hall, Alan straightened in front of Florence and blessed her with a nasty look.

She cocked a brow and took another sip of chocolate. "You're his father."

"You condone his behavior."

"Oh, good god, Alan, there's nothing to be done about it. He is the way he is."

"Bah," Alan said.

"Why don't you ever blame Penny? She's his wife."

Penny picked up the deck of cards. This was the second time in two weeks Florence had insinuated her into this argument.

"Penny is an innocent bystander," Alan said.

Florence winked at Penny, who noted, not for the first time, that the wife was much more a beautiful woman, than the husband a handsome man. Alan was shorter, a physical shortcoming all too obvious with the two of them standing face to face, him sneering at her, and her smirking at him. But in Alan's defense, Florence was a very tall woman, lithe and graceful, her tawny hair streaked with gold. Alan bore the shape of a tortoise with its shell on backward. Gray speckled his dark hair and neatly-trimmed mutton chops. As a rule, Penny disliked any form of facial hair on men. Still, neither those nor his stout body put him out of place with numerous middle-aged men she knew, and as a member of the Noble household of Biloxi, she now knew a number of them, Alan's friends and business associates and the husbands of Florence's social circle. Few of those men had wives as attractive as Florence Noble.

Penny knew nothing of Harold's personal friends.

Before taking Harold's vacated chair, Alan asked if Florence cared to join them.

"Rummy for three?"

"We could play poker," Penny said.

"I prefer my magazine to poker with a hostile opponent,"

Florence answered and started toward her plush chair on the opposite side of the room. "Besides, if I won, Penny dear, my victory would put him in an even fouler mood." She stopped, as she often did in this room, and admired herself in the gilt mirror on the wall above the fireplace.

"But consider your losing would improve my mood considerably."

Florence looked at him.

His chair creaked when he sat, then he maneuvered it noiselessly on the thick oriental carpet so that he sat facing Penny at the game table. "Pity she can't glimpse her soul in that looking glass. She'd look in it less."

"I beg your pardon?" Florence said.

"You do realize, dear wife, that when the mirror spoke it was referring to the queen's soul."

"Ridiculous, Alan," she said, fidgeting with a curl. "If it had been, Snow White's queen would have never been in competition for fairest in the kingdom, and I'm not sure what has stirred your ire at me this evening, but I assure you the queen not once knew remorse."

"Until she ate the poison apple and died."

"Snow White ate..."

Alan spun in the chair. "I know."

"You do?"

"Snow White was the one who ate the apple. But tell me this, dear, why was the queen jealous?"

Florence squinted, as if to see him better. "You're being absurd."

"What did she have to be jealous of?"

He turned back around in his chair so that again he faced Penny. Florence contemplated her husband's back. Then, catching Penny's eye, she shrugged and returned to her chair in front of the fireplace.

Chapter Nineteen

Penny stopped at the threshold when Alan looked up. He was in his spot at the dining room table. Morning waned. She'd been late getting downstairs and was a tad surprised to find her father-in-law still here. Florence was worse than she thought.

"I've sent Roland for Dr. Fritz," he said and pushed aside his edition of *The Daily Herald*, still folded. Nothing else was on the table. No coffee cup, no dirty plate waiting to be removed by Jane. On those mornings when Penny made it to breakfast before Alan left for the office, she found him hid behind either the day-old *Picayune* or Biloxi's *Daily Herald*, his coffee growing cold in front of him. Penny, usually an early riser herself, felt honored to get a grunt in greeting out of him until he folded up the paper, smiled, and actually spoke on his way out the back door.

"I passed Jane on the stairs. She says Florence has been sick all night."

"Since about two. She's vomiting blood. Her ulcers." He tightened his lips. "I have warned her repeatedly about her selfish indulgences. She doesn't listen. This time she has done herself in, and you, my dear, are the root cause."

"Me?" Penny smoothed her cotton skirt and sat carefully in the dining room chair next to him.

"She kept the stuff in the house, did she not? And she did so to fill you with it. But it didn't appear quite right unless she drank it, too, now did it? Not to mention, it was a luxury she enjoyed. But the chocolate itself has proven as bad for her as your mix has for you. I am almost certain that the source of your corruption

108

these past two months is in the chocolate. Many doctors will tell you the stuff is not good for you, even under the best of circumstances. How are you this morning?"

The panic rising from what Penny initially feared was an accusation subsided. "I feel fine."

"And if I remember, you did not drink your chocolate last night."

"It hasn't sat well on my stomach since I got so sick a few weeks ago."

"And I would wager it, not infection, is the source of your illness."

"It's your most popular import."

"Yes, but like everything, it should be consumed in moderation and without too many additives. You, for instance, enjoy an excessive amount of sugar."

"It's bitter."

"True, and sugar masks the bitterness. Sugar rots one's teeth, and chocolate is bad for one's stomach, sweetened or not. It is particularly bad for a stomach that is already diseased, which Florence's doctor has repeatedly told her." He started to unfold his unread paper, then refolded it. "Jane let slip yesterday that Jonathan was at the house last week, but I didn't see him."

When Penny said nothing, Alan sighed. "When I asked if she knew why, she suggested I ask you."

"May I get some coffee?"

"Or do you need a shot of whisky?"

"Coffee will be fine." Penny rose and walked to the buffet on which sat two covered chafing dishes, one containing grits, the second scrambled eggs. Shimmering silver serving spoons, both clean, lay on the buffet beside them. The normally ravenous Alan hadn't eaten.

"Have you talked to Florence?" she asked, pouring herself a cup of coffee from the porcelain pot.

"The relationship between Florence and my brother goes way back, farther than the relationship between Florence and me."

"She told me. Let me fix you a plate, Alan."

"So, he was here to see her? And, no, I have no appetite."

"Coffee then?"

"Nothing. Come over here, Penny, I want to talk to you."

He was angry, or getting there, she could hear it in his voice. He'd usually devoured half the breakfast offerings by now, so he was off his feed.

Penny returned to the table with only her coffee. "Florence told me he was here to see you," she said. "He was angry because you purchased the land out from under him. She says she hoped to prevent discord between the two of you and wanted to get him out of here before you returned. She succeeded in dissuading him from waiting on you and asked me not to betray her trust. I saw no harm."

"Noble on her part, no pun intended." Alan leaned across the table. "Jonathan knew I was going to buy the land before I purchased it."

Penny blinked at him. "She told him?"

Instead of answering, Alan waved his hand in the air. "Do you know the land I purchased?"

"No."

"It's in Perry County. Does that have any significance, do you think?"

"I"—she narrowed her eyes—"have land in Perry County."

"The land I recently purchased abuts yours on the northwest, about twenty-six miles due south of Ellisville and seventy-five miles southeast of Jackson as the crow flies."

"And you—"

"Do you know if your grandmother has ever dealt directly with my son?" he said sharply.

Penny shook her head.

"More recently with my brother?"

She hesitated, then said, "No."

"Don't lie to me, Penny."

"I wouldn't lie to you. I'm not a liar. To the best of my knowledge Harold has never dealt directly with my grandmother. And other than knowing Jon heads your shipping over in Mobile, I have no idea what he does. Adel did recently ask me how I stood in Jonathan's regard. Grandmother apparently put her up to that, because she anticipated Jonathan giving you trouble regarding the shipment of her lumber, and you are already aware of that."

He slapped the paper on the table. "That or he's already approached her and she's trying to figure out how far she can trust him, and given what she did to him, she should know, not very."

Penny opened her mouth to ask what her grandmother had done to anger Jon, but Alan said, "What did you tell your sister?"

"I told her he's always been charming to me."

Alan sucked in a breath between clenched teeth. "Have you talked to Harold about children recently?"

"I bring the subject up from time to time."

"After I've suggested that perhaps you should?"

"I don't need your encouragement to try and improve my married life," she rejoined.

"And has he indicated any desire to give you a child?" Alan asked as if he hadn't noted her shortness.

Desire was a ludicrous term to use regarding how Harold reacted to her.

"I didn't think so," Alan said. "Once I would have suggested a change in tactics, or whatever it is you use" — Penny warmed with shame — "but it has occurred to me of late that your relationship is exactly what Harold intended it to be from the start."

Penny looked at her cup of cooling coffee and picked it up. She'd realized soon after agreeing to stay married to Harold he had no plans to be a husband to her. Florence knew it. She and her mother-in-law had even recently discussed it. Penny was for show, a discretionary ploy to keep the rumormongers at bay. That, Florence told her, would keep Alan happy. Penny watched him now, sitting across from her in the dining room's golden morning light. He wasn't looking at her, but appeared deep in thought, and Penny was certain he was anything but happy.

"He wasn't always a fairy, you know?"

Penny's heart skipped a beat. According to Harold that was not so.

"Why would any young man prefer to be with a man instead of a lovely young woman?"

Because he preferred a man to a woman, but Penny didn't say that to Alan.

"He took a wife, but for what?" He resettled his gaze on Penny, sighed, then said, "I need you to talk to your grand-mother."

"About?"

"The loan. The note is due in forty days. She expects me to offer new terms. I told her I would, and that not so long ago." His lips tightened. "I'm not going to now. Tell her I will be paid on the due date or I will be forced to foreclose."

Penny's heartbeat quickened. "You'd become a timberman?"

Alan stared at her, then he narrowed his eyes as if he sud-denly understood what she'd said. "That's irrelevant," he barked. "Your grandmother has started cutting that tract of hers up in Perry County. It abuts your land on the southeast, and that par-cel is collateral on the loan. I wouldn't be concerned if she weren't being so risky with it, but she's determined to remain focused on the European market, or so she says, her only snag being lack of a shipper. She hoped, from the beginning of our joint venture, that would be Noble Shipping."

"So, you don't think it's a good plan to expand into Europe either?"

"It's an idiotic plan, I've always thought so. King and Gibson is too small to compete there, but I wasn't going to argue with her, either. At the time she had no broker and even with one it takes time to work one's way into that market. Believe me, I've dealt with Europe for decades. Maybe she assumed I'd manage it for her, but truth is she's given too little thought to the overall requirements." He laughed mirthlessly. "You'd have thought Frederick would have guided her better."

"Stuart opposed the plan."

"She can't even get the timber to the mill."

Penny was beginning to feel ill. This matter had Alan extremely agitated. He'd never spoken so in-depth with her about business matters. Of course, his brief reference to Jonathan knowing he was going to buy the land...and Florence's being so ill? Penny wasn't sure, exactly, from where her father-in-law's agitation stemmed.

"Now I've been led to believe she's already signed a contract. If that's so, it'll prove disastrous." He glared at her. "She's going to end up sued in a damn Prussian court. Where's my collateral then?"

"You fear Jonathan will go to your board and blame—"

"Jonathan has already assumed responsibility for Eva's shipment by disregarding his own export division head." Alan rose so quickly the chair scooted noisily across the floor and almost toppled backwards. "Goddamit!" he bellowed, and slapped the rolled newspaper on the table, making a horrific racket. Penny jumped. "I suspected a rat. I should have known, but I was so wrapped up...." He looked down at Penny. "At this point, she'd be better off selling that timber on the domestic market and getting out of hock to me, but if she's signed a contract with some Prussian, I don't think she'll be able to. At best, he'll hold her to some penalty for late delivery. That's at *best*." He blinked, then calmly turned around and found his dislodged chair, pulled it back into place, and sat.

"You talk to her. Today. You tell her that her bonus option for my forgiving the debt appears to be another lost cause. You understand my meaning?"

Penny nodded, then mustered the courage to say, "She'll claim you purposefully made an offer you had no intention of fulfilling."

His ensuing smile was contemptuous. "And though I suspect you are in no way at fault, my dear, I will claim the fault lies with her granddaughter. Eva Markiston hasn't a leg to stand on."

Penny tightened her lips and prudently said nothing.

"As far as any contracts are concerned, you tell her I want to review them ahead of time from here on out, not that our business arrangement has much time left on it. And if she's signed an agreement with any European firm with anything in the way of a deadline, she'd better find a way to get that timber to the mill, and I don't care if she has to lug each log herself. I will take King and Gibson away from her and make this right, and I will bury her if she's in cahoots with Jonathan or Harold, either one. And you remember that in your own dealings with me."

Chapter Twenty

"**I** have a broker in Mobile." Eva rose in indignation from her desk, interrupting Penny's reiteration of Alan Noble's dire warning. "And Prussia's demand for yellow pine is insatiable!"

A reliable broker, her grandmother claimed, who has contacts with agents in Prussia. Eva Markiston had been quite pleased with herself up till now. Stuart, sitting on the settee, had said little, but seemed less positive. His focus, Penny figured and rightly so, was on Alan Noble's growing impatience.

"He's concerned about the terms, Grandmother. In fact, he's going to be disheartened you've already signed a contract."

"It's not his concern."

"He believes it is. You're cutting away part of his collateral on that Perry County—"

"He knew I intended to do that," she screeched. "It was a gamble, but one worth taking. He agreed."

Trusting to an agreeable Alan Noble, Penny figured, was risky in its own right. "How much lumber did you contract for? Can you get it cut and shipped in time, because time is something you're running out of? And what is the penalty for late delivery?"

"I beg your pardon, young woman?"

"Don't shoot the messenger, Eva," Stuart said calmly. "Those are Alan's questions not Penny's."

Eva's glare switched from Penny to Stuart, then back to Penny. "He's threatening me with foreclosure?"

"He says he will foreclose on the first of November."

"When I talked to him last week, he agreed to extend the loan, despite your failure to reign in your deviant spouse."

Penny bridled with that and raised her chin. "He referred to that conversation, then said specifically he now will not agree to an extension."

Slowly, Eva Markiston sank back into her swivel chair. The woman's silver hair was perfectly coiffed, her nails manicured. Eva Markiston smelled like a flower garden, and the entire room smelled like her. Her lavender morning dress settled over her like angel hair. Angelic, however, was not the look in her eye.

"He hinted that he might be more agreeable if you will refrain from this Prussian initiative."

"And how the hell am I to do that? As noted, I've already signed a contract."

Penny looked away. "He didn't know that for sure." Penny looked at Stuart. "Can you get enough lumber cut to fill the Prussian order on time?"

"Maybe, if there are no more setbacks. We —"

"Two-thirds of what we need for the Prussian shipment is already being cut at the Wolf River mill. The Handsboro mill will have the balance of the shipment by the end of this week."

Stuart looked at Eva, said nothing, then rose and walked to the French doors overlooking the garden, now resplendent with colorful peonies. Penny had come to realize, and this just over the last few weeks, that he did that to move himself out of striking distance. She'd seen him repeat the action for years, but until recently, hadn't contemplated the reason why.

He said, "I qualified my answer to your question, Penny, as dependent upon there being no more setbacks."

Eva sat back in her chair with a heavy sigh. Penny ignored her.

"Jon Noble," Stuart continued, his face now turned halfway between the door and her, "has three ships that must sail in order to meet deadlines at Liverpool and Bordeaux on the 10th and 18th of October respectively. Rotterdam in the Netherlands, which is where our timber for Prussia will be offloaded, hasn't been factored in. Those three merchant ships are half empty. Jon is scrambling to fill them with other merchants' goods, a standard business practice that has been, under normal conditions, already completed this late in the year. This year, however, Noble Shipping did not contract with other merchants in anticipation of shipping King and Gibson lumber as, he now knows, to Prussia."

"So he claims," Eva said.

Stuart glanced at her. Whatever he might have said, Penny preempted. "You're dealing with Jon Noble directly on this?"

"Yes," Stuart said. "The other problem is our anticipated shipper to Mobile, who has provided our shipping to other domestic markets here on the Gulf and to South America, Blake Shipping, is now a Noble Shipping asset. You would immediately think that is not a problem. However, Blake was contracted to move a load of Jason Brothers lumber to Parangua, Brazil, at the time of the sale. Fulfillment of prior contracts was included as terms of the sale. Blake Shipping...or rather Noble Shipping...can make our shipment for reloading at Mobile, but not until the 8th of October, which puts Jon Noble's British and French shipments in jeopardy."

"To meet his deadline only."

"His deadline severely impacts your deadline, Eva. And don't forget, he'll have penalties to pay too, and that reflects badly on him before the Noble Corporation board."

"Which pleases Alan," Eva snapped.

Penny sat back and drew in a breath. That was probably true.

"Dammit, Stuart, he's toying with you. Noble Shipping has never indicated doubts about its ability to move our Prussian order."

"Jon Noble told you about the diversion of the Blake Shipping assets a week ago."

"And he implied to me they'd be back in time."

"Yes, well, who benefits if they aren't?"

And that was key, wasn't it? Who did benefit or who was worst hit? Alan and Jon, from where Penny sat, both indicated this entire evolution was hurting them, Jon from the start and Alan just recently. Was the issue more between Alan and Jon with King and Gibson a mere pawn in their cutthroat battle over Noble Corporation?

"Grandmother, I fear that you're caught up in their family squabble, and you're vulnerable. You are grossly overextended and even a novice like me can see it." She looked quickly at Stuart. "What would be the penalty for breaking the contract with the Prussian merchant?"

"I would have to—"

"We're not breaking a contract I worked like a dog to get," Eva said.

"Grandmother, listen to me, you can move the timber to the Handsboro mill and sell it on the domestic mar—"

"Enough of this," Eva snapped. "You marry into the Nobles and suddenly think you are an expert in business dealings."

"I've seen how treacherous they can be."

Stuart turned back to the garden. "Something's not right over there," he said to Eva. "It's obvious to me that Alan Noble needs cold hard cash *now*. He doesn't want to be saddled with two out-dated lumber mills. I doubt they'd fetch the face value of the loan, much less the interest."

"I don't think he cares," Penny said. "He's worked up over something. I think I can dissuade him from foreclosure, if you'll take the conservative route."

"That fever you suffered through recently must have dam-aged your brain," Eva said. "I'm moving timber and cutting lum-ber. I've got my shipper—"

"Have you been listening to us? Alan sent Penny over here with advice."

"Advice to cover himself. I've ascertained that much, too. He's gotten himself into a bind somewhere else and now he's try-ing to rush us. We have until the first of November."

"You are dependent on him to make back that money. Don't you understand that?"

"Jonathan," she countered.

"You've more a friend in Alan than you have in Jonathan!" Stuart yelled.

Eva glowered at him. "I've signed a contract with a Prussian firm to deliver."

"No money has changed hands. Penny made a good point. We need to—"

"I don't want out of it." Eva focused on Penny and folded her arms over her breasts. "King and Gibson will continue its pursuit of the Prussian market. The only thing you need concern yourself with, young lady, is securing an extension on the loan, should the need arise."

Stuart turned suddenly to the office door. Penny's gaze followed. In the hallway, the young Negress, Edwina, was calling for "Mr. Stuart" above the persistent clop of boots coming down the hall. Stuart started for the door.

"Yes, Frederick," a male voice boomed, "you'd best get into the Queen of Pine's office. You've got a..."

The door flew open, and Jack Gibson stepped through, almost colliding with Stuart. Jack stopped short. "...crisis," Jack finished.

"I'm sorry, Miz Eva," Edwina stuttered. "He asked if you wuz heah, and when I told him you wuz, he come bustin' on—"

"Don't blame the servant. There was no way any of you could have stopped me. Besides," he said to Stuart, "you need to know what I'm about to tell you."

"It's all right, Edwina," Stuart said, ushering the girl out. He closed the door. "What do you want?" he said to Jack, stepping back to be closer to Eva.

Jack looked him over, then cast Penny a glance. "Ah," he said and swept the slouch hat from his head. "The younger Mrs. Noble. I haven't seen you in a month of Sundays. You look as peaked now as you did then. Times still tough, or are your losses mounting?"

Penny glared at him and conquered the urge to retake her seat.

"I'm about to have you tossed out on your ear, mister," her grandmother said. "State your business and get out."

Jack opened his jacket and pulled a folded paper from an inside pocket. He set it on the desk in front of Eva. Calmly she retook her seat. Stuart picked up the paper. To Penny's right, the office door opened and Adel, dressed in rose lawn, her blond hair pulled up in an elegant chignon, floated through the door and closed it. Jack turned an interested eye on her, and she leaned back against the door and smiled. "I heard handsome Jack had come to visit."

"Hardly a social call," Stuart said and passed the paper to Eva.

Her grandmother's change in demeanor was subtle, but telling. After a moment, she looked Jack in the eye. "If he delays my shipping, I'll sue."

"Go ahead, we've got time. The lumber from your new lease is already piling up in the woods. How much time do you have?"

"Does Humboldt even know about this?" Stuart asked.

"Probably not, and I doubt he cares. He's in Chicago, protected by the same cutthroat staff that spearheaded the demise of the North's white pine. I doubt they care either. Might try the federals. Some of the less corrupt among them claim to be trying to make some headway against big business." Jack shrugged. "I figure they're just waiting for a bigger cut, and they'll probably be prepared to take him on in a few months when he doesn't pay it."

"Jack doesn't have the power to do this, Stuart. Nathan Stephens has to be behind—"

"I was born and raised in those woods, Eva, like most every man working for Humboldt out there right now. We know one another. We like one another. We do things for one another, but the truth of the matter is your requirements fall way down the list of priorities."

Jack turned to the door. Penny glanced at Adel watching him. He looked at Adel, turned to Penny, then back to Eva. "You know, I've done some research figurin' out how you finagled that acreage up in Perry County last spring. Since I knew you'd run my daddy's company into the ground, I figured you had to find some rich fool to make you a loan. Not a bank around was gonna cover you. Right now I figure you've got close to a hundred thousand board feet of raw timber piled up in remote Perry County, and your money is no good, no matter how much you got for Penny. Build your own tram to a shipping point on the North Eastern. And buy oxen. They're cheaper than a rod engine."

"Twenty miles away?"

He shrugged. "Black Creek's only five. Move your timber east to..." His mouth dropped open in mock realization, and he snapped his fingers in front of her face. "Oh, that's right. You don't have a mill on the Escatawpa, do you? That was somebody else's vision, wasn't it? And you didn't like it. And when you couldn't stop it, you butchered the visionaries."

Eva rose again from her seat. "You are a bastard."

"Figuratively speaking and darn proud of it. You know where you stand with me, Mrs. Markiston. No skulking around in the middle of the night blowing up turpentine stills and murdering the old and innocent in acts of petty vengeance. Does your financier know he's bankrolling murder?" He looked at Adel, made a sibilant sound and settled his gaze on Penny. "And that, honey, explains your big sister's sudden interest in your intended this past spring. Your grandmother needed to free you up. Though I don't know why Adel wouldn't have worked perfectly well to make a man out of Harold Noble."

He reached for the door. Adel moved out of his way. He nodded at her, spoke her name, then was gone.

*J*ack stepped into the dark central hall of the Mississippi City Victorian Hugh King had built for his wife, stepdaughter, and later his own daughter almost twenty years ago. He knew this house as if it were his own. His heart echoed in his pounding head, and it amazed him he'd carried his message through without charging across that desk and throttling Eva Markiston. He thought of the beautiful Adel. His loins hadn't heated at the sight of her, at her scent.

Preoccupied, or over her?

He started to the left and the back of the house, planning to let himself out the same way he'd barged in, but attracted by voices in the front room, he turned again. From Eva's office, he heard Penny talking and Eva's calm, if loud, response. He moved in the direction of the front door with its beautiful cut-glass window and peeked inside the parlor. Here he lingered, unnoticed by Clarissa Frederick and her son-in-law, Mark Reed.

"But she is better now. Dr. Clark doesn't think there's reason to worry any longer."

"And the vomiting has stopped completely?"

"A while back, I believe."

"I had so hoped she was in the family way."

Reed shook his head. "The vomiting went with the ailment. She was cramping terribly, and apparently this had been off and on for several weeks. A few days ago, Dr. Clark gave her ginger to calm the cramping and had planned to check on her this morning. He was drawn away around nine by a difficult labor, one of his older patients, who he is very concerned about, and asked if I'd go see Penny. I knew that wasn't a good idea, but I agreed.

"Peter Fritz was there when I arrived. I initially thought Penny had taken a bad turn, but he was there for Florence Noble, who, as it turns out, is gravely ill." Reed leaned closer to where Clarissa sat next to him on the settee. "He told me, confidentially, that he is in fear for her life."

"Oh, no. Penny is terribly fond of her. What's wrong?"

"She has ulcers. They are bleeding, the result of some sort of attack on her stomach. He was pleased to confer with me, since I had studied so recently with Dr. Tomkins in Boston."

Clarissa squeezed Reed's hand, lying casually by his thigh, and he smiled.

"We concluded it might be the same ailment that attacked Penny, but exacerbated by the senior Mrs. Noble's ulcers."

"Penny's skin still looks dingy to me."

"It does. Still, Dr. Clark says it's better than it was a month ago. I don't believe she's fully recovered. She insisted that she would come despite my advising against it. Alan Noble wanted her to talk to Eva. So I brought her, at Mr. Noble's direction I should add."

"Ah, she didn't want to accompany you?"

"Certainly not. She simply can't accept the unrequited love I felt for Adel is real, and that when I returned from school, I couldn't deny it any longer. It was best for all our sakes."

Clarissa opened her mouth to speak, but Jack, his heart back in his chest, knocked loudly on the doorframe. Clarissa looked up, and that horse's butt Reed spun his head around. He rose when Jack approached him. Jack thrust out his hand. "Been awhile, Mark."

Mark Reed, his mouth agape, looked at Jack's hand as if he suspected some sort of trick. Ill at ease or challenged or just plain embarrassed, Jack couldn't tell. For sure, it wasn't anger in the man's dark eyes. Reed knew the history between Adel and him, everyone did, the Reed family better than most, given their relationship with the Kings. Jack dropped his unshaken hand and smiled broadly. "Haven't had a chance to congratulate you on your marriage. Surprised me, actually. I remember you at barbecues following little Penny around like a lost puppy. I think your unrequited love for Adel came as a shock to everyone."

Reed stepped back. "I'll forgive that, Gibson, under the circumstances. You'll have to accept that the best man won."

He'd been flippant when he said that, as if he expected Jack to take it in good humor, and Jack wondered how much of that good humor would remain if the man knew his bride had given herself to Jack just hours after they'd wed. "Won out, and I must agree. Nobody knows better than me what a lucky bastard you are. I'm happy for you, no joke, but that's mainly because I'm the one who got lucky."

Jack saw the man's face cloud, but Clarissa Frederick stepped between them. "Jack, I didn't know you were here."

"Snuck in the back door," he said, then bent to kiss her cheek. She didn't hug him; once she would have. It was eleven in the morning. Already, he could smell gin on her breath. "Had some business to discuss with your mother and husband."

She frowned at him.

"They're all in Uncle Hugh's office" — oh, how he loved saying that — "had the pleasure of seeing Penny and Adel, too. Haven't

123

seen 'em since the morning following Adel's marriage." He looked over Clarissa's head at Mark. "Penny does look a little sickly, but Adel is as beautiful as ever." He turned his back on them and started out the door. Clarissa followed him, then looked back down the dim hall to the closed office door.

"Don't worry," he said to her, "they were all alive when I left them."

Mark had followed her into the hall. Again, Jack started down it, then did an about-face when the office door opened. He left by the front.

*P*enny kept her eyes on the door through which Jack disappeared, but only until she heard it click. The diarrhea she thought had passed threatened now, a physical response to Jack's veiled reference to her grandmother's role in the death of her father, something he and Uncle Jimmy had always maintained, and now, apparently, more recent violence. But mostly it was his brutal revelation, all too clear suddenly, as to why Mark had jilted her. She turned to her grandmother.

"Jack's right, isn't he? Alan's hope that Harold and I wed wasn't something that happened after Mark and Adel wed. He and I were still promised to one another, weren't we? You planned to make good on Alan's request, but first you had to get Mark out of the way."

"Alan approached me at Harold's request."

"Harold's request?" Alan had implied that too, but Harold always said his father—

"That's what Alan told me. Now, we've got more pressing matters to contend with than your mooning over Mark."

"I'm not mooning over Mark." She looked at her sister. "I'm merely questioning Adel's motive for marrying him."

"I did you a favor," Adel said. "Taking him away from you was so easy. You deserve better than that, baby."

"I deserve a better sister. You went after Mark because Grandmother told you to, didn't you?"

"Yes," Eva snapped. "She did. You were in demand by the

Nobles. As for your sister, she was merely being cooperative and will be justly rewarded for her duty to the family. She knows this. You might consider doing the same."

"I've done everything you've asked so far."

Eva retook her seat and motioned for Penny to take hers. "I'll stand," Penny said.

"I'll sit," said Adel, moving quickly to the settee. "This promises to be interesting."

Stuart briefly closed his eyes, then retreated back to the window and his view of the garden.

Eva flattened her palms against the gleaming surface of the desk. "I'm going to take a precious moment and explain this to you, Penelope, simply so we can move on to what we need to be doing right now. What I did was strategic planning."

"Power-mongering," Penny countered.

"Or, in my case," Adel said, "pandering."

Stuart turned from the window and stared at the back of Adel's head. "Upper-class prostitution," he said.

Adel turned. "Are you referring to me and Mark or you and Mother, Stuart darling?"

Hands behind his back, he turned back to the window. "I simply like upper-class prostitute in reference to you."

Disgust settled over Penny, and her eyes locked on Eva Markiston.

"No one put stock in your childhood infatuation with Mark Reed," her grandmother said.

"The Reeds did, Daddy did, I did."

Eva's eyes hardened. "Obviously Mark didn't."

Penny refused to flinch. "You were overextended more than you admit."

"'More than I admit?' Ha, I don't need to deny anything. I admit I needed money. Given the Nobles' sudden interest in you, I knew Alan would help."

"I'm glad I proved so valuable. And where is the profit?"

Eva slammed her palm down on the desk. "I'm on the brink of my efforts paying off."

"You can't even get the rest of your timber to the mill," Penny said, carefully enunciating each word, "much less lumber to Prussia."

"Because I'm hostage to that son of a murdering bastard who just walked out the door!"

"As of five minutes ago you became hostage to him. But the first of November is only weeks away. Even with Humboldt's cooperation, you'd have never made back that money in time, and that's true if you were doing something reasonable, like selling to the domestic market."

"Oh, pish," Eva said and pulled her swivel chair into the kneehole. "I intend to ask Alan to extend payment on the loan."

Penny drew in a breath. "He will foreclose."

"Alan Noble doesn't want a lumber mill."

"Humboldt does." Penny looked at Stuart. "The Wolf River mill I believe you specified." She refocused on her grandmother. "Alan already has a buyer, and you can bet he knows it." Penny didn't know that for sure, but she felt powerful saying it.

"I wouldn't have to worry about foreclosure if you'd done your job and screwed your husband."

"You've risked the company and never once bothered to confide in me regarding your twisted schemes."

"I'm warning you I won't let this happen, Penny."

Penny began pulling on her gloves. "You play with people's lives as if you believe yourself God. You destroyed mine and Mark's future and my relationship with my sister, then married me off as a store-front mannequin to a man who has no more use for a wife than a dog has for a cat, all for a pot of money, which having won, you turned around and squandered."

"He is not to call in that loan, do you understand me?"

"Then pay him by the first of November."

"Sit down."

Penny flexed her gloved hand and picked up her reticule. "Grandmother, I am not the one with the problem here." She started for the door, and Eva rose.

"Don't you dare leave this house!"

Penny seized the knob and opened the door. "I hope you find a way to move that timber to the mill"—she rolled her eyes—"and the lumber back out again, but even now, I fear it's too late."

She pulled the door shut behind her and was besieged by her mother in the dark coolness of the hallway. Yes, she felt better, or had until just now, and no, she couldn't stay for lunch. Florence was very sick, and yes, her business for Alan was finished. Lucy had chicken broth in the cookhouse, her mother said. She'd get a jar. Penny could take some home for Florence.

Mark took Clarissa Frederick's place and a chill wracked Penny's body. He had comprised her young world, particularly following her father's death. He'd been her future. Now he was Adel's cuckold and the callous butt of tasteless jokes.

"Why do you and Adel live here," she asked him, "and not with your parents? I wonder about that."

"Why do you care?"

"For the satisfaction of knowing I guessed right." She moved around him. "I should stop in and see them. I haven't seen them since my wedding."

"I'm sure they would enjoy that. Are you ready to go?"

"I'm going to walk to the depot. I'll take the train back."

"I brought you, I'll take—"

"Your presence pains me, Mark. Stay home. I wish to be alone."

Stern-faced, he held the front door for her, and she went out on the porch to wait for her mother and the broth for Florence. A familiar plank groaned beneath her weight, and before her, the Gulf disappeared beyond the horizon, its expanse broken only by the dark silhouette of Ship Island. Today was the first day of fall. The air, fanned by a sea breeze smelling of salt and ocean, was cool beneath the shade of the live oaks in the yard. Behind her, the door clicked shut.

Chapter Twenty-one

"You're a glutton for rejection, or did your grandmother send you?" Jack started to ease out the door to his room at Kate's boarding house and into the hall, but Adel placed a manicured hand against his belly and stayed him.

"Grandmother sent me. We need to talk. Inside your room."

He graced her with a lopsided grin. "Most everyone's at work, sweetheart."

She cocked her pretty head, only inches below his, and smiled. "You're not." She tried to move around him. He wouldn't let her. "Afraid?" she asked.

"Honey, you'd be as dangerous here in the hall as inside. Or in a crowd even, if I still allowed you to get to me."

"I'll always get to you, baby, but you've got too much pride to admit it."

He stepped aside and let her in, then followed and closed the door behind him. The screened windows were open, and the room in late morning was pleasantly cool.

"So, this is where you call home these days?" She was tugging on the fingers of her gray suede gloves. The peach silk of her dress hummed when she moved. She got the gloves off and laid them on the bed.

"It is."

"Is this where you bring your girlfriends?"

"Kate doesn't allow such carrying on." He picked up yesterday's work britches and tossed them on top of the bed, then sat in the rocker they'd occupied. "She'd toss you out by your hair."

Adel's gaze lingered on the bed. "If she knew I was here, which she doesn't, seems you'd be the one she should toss out."

128

"I can't believe you got up here unnoticed. But she won't send me packing. She likes me."

"Hmmm. Do you like her?"

He studied her, but did not respond.

She sat on the bed. "As much as you like me?"

"I don't like you."

She smoothed the quilted counterpane with her hand. Not looking at him, she said, "Yes, you do."

"What do you want, Adel?

"Do you remember what it's like to be naked next to me, baby?" She twisted her head and found his eyes. "Do you remember what my skin feels like?"

"I remember."

She started pulling pins from her hat. A preposterous thing, marked by broad curves and covered in flowers and satin ribbon and bows. Given the size of that hat, he found it a wonder she could walk steady with it on her head and again couldn't believe she arrived unnoticed.

"Where did you leave your driver?"

She placed the hat on his bed and fussed with one of the faux flowers. "I drove myself. Left my carriage at the livery in Handsboro. We have all the time we want."

"Do you do that often?"

She raised an eyebrow.

"Drive yourself when you go to visit men?"

Her laugh was melodious, as beautiful as she was. "A necessity, wouldn't you say?" She fiddled with wisps of hair, spun gold in the waxing sunlight that pierced the windows of his room.

"Grandmother needs to move that timber in Perry County."

"And she thinks you can convince me to change the policy?"

Adel chuckled. "She's hoping."

"That you'll screw me...figuratively speaking."

"And I'm hoping you'll screw me, literally speaking."

"That way you both get what you want."

She wet her upper lip with a pink tongue. A very talented pink tongue, he knew. She was using it for effect now.

"When you get back downstairs," he said, "check with Auntie Ruth, Kate's cook. She's baking pecan pies this morning. You need to pick one up for your husband's dessert tonight."

"Dear sweet Mark eats whatever our cook makes for him." She looked at Jack and smiled. "And I'm not the cook."

"You didn't make Aunt Ruth's pie, either, so I don't see any conflict."

She squirmed, trying to get comfortable atop an elaborate bustle. "Let's talk about conflict, Jack."

Let's talk business, she meant. It occurred to him how much like her grandmother she was becoming. An accomplished whore who realized, in the course of growing up and marrying well, the benefits of power and the value of sex in gaining it. But power didn't mean business acumen, and when the black widow of King and Gibson Lumber had eliminated the obstinate males standing in the way of her total control of the company, sex had proven a meager substitute for their brains and experience. He wasn't sure Eva realized that, even now, though she had managed to acquire a cadre of replacement mates for her daughter and granddaughters. He wondered if those men realized what danger their lives were in, and he stifled a smile. Adel watched him with sultry eyes and pouty lips.

"Let's do talk conflict, Adel."

"She wants to know what you are ultimately up to."

"She knows what I'm up to. What she wants is for you to stop me."

Adel knitted her brow. "But I know I can't do that."

"Something you probably should not have admitted to me." Adel was savvy, and she was dangerous. "All she has to do is admit her role in the deaths of Deacon French and Richard Cotton, and I'll be satisfied." That, of course, was a lie. He would not be satisfied and it would make absolutely no difference to Humboldt's shipping policies, but Adel's being here was pretense, after all.

Adel frowned.

"The men who died in that turpentine still outside Piotona."

130

"You think she had something to do with that?"

"She had everything to do with it."

"You're asking her to admit to murder."

"I'd be asking the impossible. Unless I find the killers, and I doubt I ever will, I won't be able to prove she hired them, and I'm smart enough to realize it. So I intend to destroy her."

"You'll be destroying King and Gibson."

"She destroyed Hugh King and my father, both of them. Now she's destroying their company. My one consolation is that I'm going to do my best to make sure she's destroyed with it."

"She's going to file suit."

"Any suit she files will have no grounds. She's on Humboldt's schedule, just not as soon as she'd like."

"She says she can prove she requested shipment three weeks ago. Humboldt will fire you and Nathan Stephens."

"I doubt it. Humboldt doesn't consider an outfit the size of King and Gibson much of a concern. The worst thing that could possibly happen to me is that the board will move her up in the queue, then we'll have suits from every other outfit forced into line behind her. The best thing that will happen is Humboldt will say it's his damn dummy line and he'll decide who uses it and when. It's a matter of principle. He enjoys fighting with the federals. Should have been a Southerner. But of course, these are a brand new breed of federals, the ones the Yankees built, so they're really fighting their own Frankensteins." He leaned forward in his chair. "Tell her extortion, from her neck of the woods, is not going to work."

Adel rose from the bed. "I'll pass it along." She reached for the top button on her bodice. "Now that all that boring business talk is over, would you like to see what I have beneath my dress?"

"A weapon to kill me with?"

"Certainly one potent enough to bring you to your knees. Or perhaps you'd prefer me on mine."

Chapter Twenty-two

"Your mother says you were out all afternoon," Mark said. He closed their bedroom door.

Adel turned from him and pulled the hat pins from the lavish hat atop her head. "Do you like my new hat?"

"It's appalling."

She twisted her golden head around, a silent "O" on her lips. "Nasty, darling." She shaped that mouth into something between a smile and a sneer. "Once you approved of everything I did."

He hid his clenched fists behind his back. Once he'd been a fool. Adel was making a man out of him in the worse ways imaginable. "My guess is you spent all of two minutes at Lopez's picking out that hat."

She sauntered close, her body's movement as sleek and smooth as the rich peach silk covering it. "I spent an hour, and I haven't stepped foot in Lopez's Mercantile since I married you. I bought this hat at Madelyn's." She stopped in front of him and flattened her hands on the lapels of his jacket. "Mother gushed over it."

"Give it to her."

Adel laughed and leaned into him. She smelled of jasmine and soap and the hint of sex. He hardened the same moment his gut crashed.

"Who have you been with?" But being a fool, he touched her, drawing her to him, and she laid her head on his chest. He breathed in the familiar scent of her hair. Blond wisps tickled his chin, and he surrendered.

"I met Grandmother and Stuart for lunch at the Gulf View," she answered. "Mother is peeved at us all, I imagine, so she tattled on me."

"Where was she?"

"Sleeping one off. She and Stuart are fighting."

"Over?"

"Stuart has another girlfriend." Her hand trailed past his navel, lower, and with the back of it, she brushed the bulge in his pants. She chuckled. "I see your concern for my whereabouts now, darling."

He trembled in anticipation. "You haven't seen anything yet."

She cupped him, then raised her skirt and maneuvered herself onto her knees, and he watched her unbutton his pants. A moment later he closed his eyes and hissed in a breath as the touch of her hand, then her lips and adept tongue castrated the man he tried to be. He should strip that expensive silk from her body, force her into bed, and explore her treacherous woman-hood for evidence of another man. He swallowed with the increasing pleasure, then locked his jaw tight. But it was a hell of a lot easier to endure the degradation then to learn the truth and lose this—white light exploded behind his closed lids, and he threw back his head with a small cry—forever.

"All better now, baby?"

He looked at her, watching him through half-closed lids. "What about you?"

She smirked and moved toward the door, leading from their bedroom. "I'm going to take a bath before dinner."

He turned on his heel. "You don't need me at all, do you?"

She graced him with a sympathetic look, and self-disgust washed away the comfort he had gained from her attention. "I'm tired, Mark. Dinner is in less than an hour, and lastly"—she smiled and glanced between his legs—"you're hardly in condition to satisfy me now." She winked. "Later tonight."

Chapter Twenty-three

Penny was attending a morning meeting of the Biloxi Chapter of the Women's Christian Temperance Union. Not her first meeting. Florence had dragged her to several, but she determined this would be her last. Earlier she'd squeezed in an impromptu meeting with Father O'Herlihy regarding the Father Peter O'Hara's Boys Home. The boys' home she would enjoy working with, but the women comprising the Temperance Union she flagged in descending degree from self-righteous shrews to misguided do-gooders, who believed they were qualified to dictate mores to those they judged in need of their unique guidance. Such social contaminants were residual from the War and Reconstruction. They had New England written all over them. The meeting left her stomach churning in disbelief and a grudging respect for her maternal grandmother who despised progressives in every form. Invoking a heretofore non-existent government sanction to force a prudish minority's will on the majority went against everything Penny, in her near eighteen years, believed in. She reminded herself there were many disadvantages to being a grown woman, but she wasn't sure yet that she would allow another's sense of social obligation to be one of hers. And Penny did not understand why Florence participated. The Noble household was a far cry from a teetotaling one. For Florence, of course, membership was required for social status, and what was best for the wayward, lower, and new immigrant classes and what was good for the Nobles and those of their status were two different things.

After the meeting, Penny went to the public library. She'd left there fifteen minutes ago and now stood just off the north end of

Main Street, looking up three steps to the side entry of Biloxi's town hall. This side of the old building housed Biloxi's police department consisting of a city marshal and one officer.

Despite the three-quarter sleeves on her light blue poplin walking dress, she was hot, and the Tuscan bonnet on her head had given her a headache. Her hair pulled up and covered with a hat always gave her a headache. She remained a bit under the weather from what Hadrian Clark was now calling a stomach distemper, and she should probably go home, for her sake as well as Florence's. But she was conveniently downtown, and she wanted to settle a question that had been weighing on her mind since hearing Jack Gibson's words to her grandmother two days ago.

It was cool inside the Police Department's airy front room. At a desk facing the door, a young man looked up.

"I'm looking for Marshal Craig," she said.

The man rose, but before he could speak a large man with dark hair and a magnificent handlebar mustache appeared in a door set in the back wall of the spacious room. "I'm Chief Craig."

From the corner of her eye, she saw the younger man retake his seat, and she moved toward Craig as he moved toward her. "Mr. Phillips at the library suggested I speak to you."

Chief Craig raised a brow. He was broad and tall. Penny guessed him to be around the age of her father...or the age her father would have been. And, she realized, the man was familiar to her. She had seen him years ago.

"The librarian?" Craig asked.

"Yes. I went there this morning to search old newspapers. I'm looking for information on the destruction of a turpentine still in Marion County this past spring. But there are no relevant papers. I did find a couple of sentences in *The Herald* referencing an explosion, but no details."

"There was an incident up at Piotona in March. Jack Gibson's still. Two men were killed in the explosion. Both Negro. You're Hugh King's daughter, aren't you?"

Hugh King's daughter, not Eva Markiston's granddaughter. "I do apologize." She held out a hand. "I am Penelope King."

135

"Noble," he said and took her hand. "And your interest in the explosion?"

Despite everything, she wasn't about to implicate her grandmother for arson on Jack Gibson's suspicions. "Curiosity."

"Curiosity?"

"Jack Gibson's father and mine used—"

"To be partners. Hence, King and Gibson Lumber. I'm aware of that, Mrs. Noble."

"Then you know Unc..., Mr. Gibson killed my father."

"I know he hanged for his murder, yes ma'am."

Penny swallowed, then raised her chin. "Can you satisfy my curiosity about how the men in Piotona died, Chief Craig?"

"An elderly man died in the fire. He ran into the still house looking for his nephew. He was inside when the building blew up."

"Was the nephew the other man who died?"

"He was, but not inside the burning building. He was found out back of the building with a bullet in his head."

𝒥obias Craig took two steps toward the door through which Penny Noble left. He folded his arms over his chest, then looked at his single subordinate, sitting to his right and watching him.

"Charlie," Toby started, "I wonder why she's looking for information about those killings up there?"

Charlie shrugged. "Because she knows something, and that something has made her suspicious."

Toby pursed his lips. "You're a smartass, Charlie. Now I wonder what has made her suspicious."

"And I, Chief, am wondering why we care?"

"Because, Charlie, that little gal is Eva Markiston's granddaughter. Seven years ago now, Mrs. Markiston used her influence to have my corrupt boss remove me from the murder investigation of that gal's daddy. As a result, an innocent man hanged. That innocent man was James Gibson, the father of the man who owned that destroyed still."

"Hmmpf," Charlie said. "Smells like somethin just might be cookin', don't it, boss?"

Chapter Twenty-four

The evening was balmy, pleasantly cool, one of those wonderful nights that harbingered fall and kissed summer a sweet goodnight. Jack lay in the grass beneath an ancient live oak on a small rise overlooking Bayou Bernard. He was no more than a body length from the marsh grass, then water, which together stretched 400 yards and ended in tangled forest, above which hung the southern wall of King and Gibson's Handsboro mill. He held a jug of whiskey in his right hand.

"Are you drunk yet?" Kate said.

He looked around. She had surprised him. "Just enough to welcome company."

"That young woman in your room this morning was either a very expensive whore or the infamous Adelaide."

He turned back to the rippling bayou. "Correct on both counts. I knew there was no way she could have got past you. Why did you let her come up?"

"Ah," she said, and pulled her cotton dress tight over her buttocks and sat beside him. "I recognized her, and you're a big boy now. I figured it best not to interfere." She held out an empty glass, and he poured a shot of the fiery brew into it. "She's even more beautiful now than she was seven years ago."

"The difference between a woman and a girl." He sat up and took another sip of whiskey. "I paid for a 'very expensive whore' in Jackson about a month ago." He glanced at her. "I'm drunk enough to speak when I shouldn't, Kate. Tell me if I offend."

She raised her glass and took a swig. "I'm a big girl, too. I'll try not to blush." She stretched out and kicked his booted foot with hers. "Go ahead."

137

"She was older than me. Still pretty. I picked a woman with dark hair and eyes." He blew out a breath. "But I still saw Adel's face when I took her."

"You'll see her face until you find someone you care about more than her."

He laughed, a sharp sound, more cough than laugh. "Care about more?"

"They say hate and love are closely connected, Jack."

"I don't hate her."

"This morning?"

"God," he said and lay back on his elbow. "I don't want to think about that. The thought of touching her left me..."—he grinned at Kate—"limp. So why her face?"

"She hurt you, but you're not over her, no matter what you try to tell yourself. Let's hope one day you'll find someone to break the hold she has on you."

He looked at the water. "You'd think she would have already managed that on her own. The price I paid for her was too high to gain nothing."

"Are you talking about the whore in Jackson, or Adel?"

"Adel, all those years ago."

"So, that's what this is about. You're feeling guilty?

The quiet bayou was suddenly oppressive, his mood as dark as its water. The possibility he'd been seduced and used pressed on his heart and tensed his gut.

"What happened was not your fault," Kate continued. "You know your father didn't kill Hugh King. Neither of them considered your relationship with Adel an insurmountable problem."

"The law said they did."

"The law was fed a lie. Hugh King was dead and couldn't contradict it."

"A lie that couldn't have been offered up if I hadn't been involved with Adel."

"Lyle Jenkins allowed Eva to frame your father. I'd bet a month's worth of rentals that fat pig knew all the time she was behind it."

Jack corked the jug and laid it between them. "Finish it," he said, but Kate shook her head.

"My boys are cleanin' the kitchen, I can't let them see me stagger up to bed."

Jack smiled. "I think I'll stagger on up myself."

Chapter Twenty-five

Penny bathed right after supper. The household schedule was off with Florence ill and Alan spending an inordinate amount of time at the office. He had eaten out more often than not this week, happy, he said, to forego Dot's heavy plantation meals.

Harold was home this evening, though. She heard him moving about in his room next to hers, opening and closing drawers, rustling paper. He was working at his desk tonight, not dressing for an evening out. The stage appropriately set and her dressed in what she considered a lovely sheer nightgown of delicate blue, she knocked softly before opening the door joining their rooms.

In Penny's mind, she could not possibly make herself more desirable, but when Harold turned and looked at her, his face stilled, then clouded with anger followed by disdain. He turned back to his desk.

"I heard you'd been out," he said. "Went over to see Grandmamma, I assume, and she's sent you home with firm orders."

Penny pulled his door shut behind her with a quiet click. "I'm taking no direction from Grandmother, but I had hoped—"

He yanked open the top drawer to his desk, then snatched up the paper he'd been studying and rolled it up. "I'd hoped to get some work done tonight, but you have effectively put an end to that."

"Harold, can't we talk?"

He slammed the drawer shut and spun on her, taking in her entire being with a quick bob of his head. "You didn't come to talk, Penny. You came to demand action."

She blinked. "No, I—"

"Get out!"

140

She startled. He had never, ever reacted to her like this. "There's no need —"

Fists clenched at his side, he lunged toward her, one arm raised. She stepped back and covered her head with her arms.

The blow did not come. Instead he squeezed talon-like finger-tips into her shoulders before giving her a mighty shove. Her head walloped the door panels. He grabbed her by one forearm and yanked her toward him pushing the door wide, then shoved her through it. She twisted an ankle and stumbled ungracefully onto the Aubusson carpet, landing on one hip, a confusion of arms and legs swathed in blue.

"And stay out!" he bellowed, his words echoed by the slamming of the door.

"*F*ather fired the cook," Harold told Penny when she entered the dining room the next morning.

She stopped in the threshold and stared at him, surprised not by what he said, which would have been surprising enough under any domestic circumstance, but by the fact he spoke to her as if last evening had never happened. Her head still hurt and one place in the very back was tender to the touch. She'd had difficulty raising her right arm to brush her hair this morning, and her ankle ached to walk on. She frowned at Harold, and he quickly rose. "Look, I apologize for my boorish behavior last night."

Boorish? He'd been wild with rage. Brutal was the correct word.

"I wasn't looking at the matter from your point of view," he continued. "I know you are being pressed by your grandmother and step —"

"Don't concern yourself, Harold. I've stopped worrying about my family's self-accommodating goals. I think that my attempt to woo you last night was to reassure myself of my feminine wiles. Do not fret. There will be no more attempts."

"I am...." He stopped abruptly when Alan entered the room, and Penny, anxious to change the subject, turned to him.

"You think Florence's illness is because of Dot's cooking?"

141

"My son seems to think so, and don't concern yourself with the woman. I awarded her significant severance pay. I can prove nothing, and both your Dr. Clark and Peter Fritz say food poisoning would have affected everyone who ate her meals, but as Harold pointed out, we cannot help but be concerned when two people in the house develop a gastric ailment."

Penny frowned at Harold. "You were behind this?"

"I didn't tell Father to fire her. He did that on his own. He doesn't like her." Harold looked at his father. "He never has."

"Florence gave her too much leeway."

"Too mouthy," Harold said, his eyes on Penny.

"Jane can fry eggs," Alan said. "I just talked to her.

Penny wished he'd talked to her first.

"Jane needs to be helping with Florence's laundry, not cooking," Penny said. "I'll check on her, then go up and spell Gracie until Amanda Pettigrew gets here."

Alan snorted.

"She's Florence's friend, and it's good of her to help."

"Let Jane help."

"On top of her cooking duties, you mean?" Penny said.

"Florence abhors Jane for some reason," Harold said, then looked his father in the eye. "It's probably best for Florence that Jane stay away from her right now."

Alan held Harold's gaze for a moment, then shrugged. "Well, that Pettigrew woman drives me to distraction."

"Then stay out of the sick room," Penny said. "Really, Alan, you couldn't have picked a worse time to leave us shorthanded."

$\mathcal{P}$enny was with Florence when Harold escorted Dr. Peter Fritz into the sickroom. Florence's bloody diarrhea had worsened.

"Jonathan?" Penny heard Florence ask her stepson.

"I've sent for him," he responded. Florence nodded and threw up again. Harold left the room.

Hadrian Clark arrived mid-afternoon to check on Penny. She looked tired even to her own eyes, not having slept well after her encounter with Harold. After a quick check and an admonition that she herself would relapse if she didn't rest, he went to Florence's sickroom to offer assistance to the worried Peter Fritz. After a short time Penny followed him back in. The stench of vomit and human defecation assaulted her at the threshold.

Peter Fritz and Hadrian Clark had known each other for years and could claim over sixty years of medical experience between them. Respectively, they were residents of the two-hundred-year-old Biloxi and the younger Mississippi City farther west, joined by a common beach, by rail, and by five unbroken miles of the Biloxi-Pass Christian Road paralleling the Gulf of Mexico.

The two doctors stood on the other side of Florence's bed from Penny. They stopped talking when she entered, and she wondered what ominous premonitions they'd been discussing for her presence to cause silence. She was about to ask if they wished her to leave when Peter Fritz sighed heavily and stepped closer to his patient.

"I can only assume Florence's stomach ulcers have caused the bleeding."

"And the bloody diarrhea?" Dr. Clark asked. "Did she suffer from intestinal ulcers?"

"None that I know of. That's why I wished to consult with you regarding the younger Mrs. Noble's case." Dr. Fritz glanced her way. "There was no internal hemorrhaging?"

"None, nor fever. As you can see from the fatigue around Penny's eyes, she's not fully recovered."

"Indeed, but I fear we are looking at two unrelated illnesses."

Again Penny relieved Gracie of the rocking chair near the sleeping patient's head. Florence's sallow skin clung to hollow cheeks and sunken eye sockets. Florence was more cadaver than living person with scarcely a hint of her beauty remaining.

"Don't you suspect the intestinal bleeding to have originated in the stomach, the result of her ulcers?"

"I do agree." Dr. Fritz stepped closer to Florence and raised her arm. "Her heart rate is extremely fast."

143

"Penny's was, too, but you know, Peter, we can attribute that to the dehydration."

"Understood, but now I fear the kidneys are beginning to fail."

"And the jaundice clearly indicates liver failure."

"Which could also explain the intestinal bleeding and bloody vomit." Hadrian Clark met Peter Fritz's eyes, and a silent communication passed between the two men.

"I don't think," Dr. Fritz said, "she has the strength to last the day."

Penny felt the blood drain from her face.

Dr. Clark took the wrist Peter Fritz held, then said, "I fear you are correct."

"Have you any suggestions?"

"We could put her on intravenous fluids. Certainly trying to keep her hydrated could help"—he cursed—"but for the kidney failure. Still, it's worth a try. If nothing else, it might make her more comfortable."

Penny rose to ask them if...

A soft knock and the door opened. Alan stepped in. "I received word she'd taken a turn for the worse."

Roland had run to fetch Alan more than two hours ago. Peter Fritz motioned Alan back into the hall. When the door closed, Penny looked at Hadrian Clark. "You believe," she started, but Dr. Clark held a finger to his lips and came close to where Penny sat. "You believe she is going to die?"

"She's gravely, ill, Penny. If indeed she has, or ever had, what ails you, her ulcers have exacerbated it. Her illness is acute. What ails you appears to be more chronic."

"Then you no longer believe my sickness has passed?"

"You have not fully recovered."

"That's only"—she waved a hand over Florence's sleeping body—"because I've not been able to rest."

"And all the more reason for your continued monitoring."

Penny sat back and took Florence's clammy hand. "If I end up like this, would you just shoot me?"

"I would hang, child." He squeezed her shoulder. "Where there is life, there is hope, which is why we will not shoot the senior Mrs. Noble. But each passing moment, the damage to her internal organs grows. Some things are irreversible. Neither myself nor Dr. Fritz have any way of knowing how much damage has been done or how long she may live."

"You'll attempt, what was it?"

"Intravenous fluids. It's a rather new technique, whereby we hydrate, or get fluid to, the dying organs by bypassing the stomach, which is rejecting everything put in it. I'll assist Dr. Fritz as soon as he's done informing Mr. Noble that his wife is in dire straits."

They weren't able to do the intravenous procedure. Florence Noble's veins collapsed with every attempt, so Penny kept to Florence's side. Once, when Penny was attempting to give her tepid tea, Florence cried out, swatting the air and striking the cup, upending the tea. The move was violent, displaying strength Penny couldn't believe remained in the wasted body. It was as if Florence were striking at something unseen, or perhaps it was simply an unwillingness to drink the tea.

Later Florence fought Alan, too, who managed to force the tea down his wife's throat. Obviously the woman did not want the tea, but Alan insisted she take it if she were to have any chance of survival at all. She tried to spit it back out, but the effort made her choke, and he held her up as she swallowed it, then laid her back on the pillows from where she glared at him with a morbid face and sparkling eyes. Penny told Alan he could go and she would watch over Florence, certain Alan's presence was causing the suffering woman more harm than good.

Penny couldn't make out what Florence was saying, and Florence motioned her closer. Her mother-in-law's brief periods of cognizance filled Penny with hope the woman might yet survive. She stood and brought her ear to the woman's lips.

"Was it you who told Alan that Jon had been here?" The

pressure from the bony fingers that bit into Penny's forearm was surprisingly strong and painful.

"No, but he knows. Alan approached me, and I confirmed he had been, but I told him nothing of what I'd seen —"

"It was Jane. She said it was you." Florence closed her eyes. "But I didn't believe her."

"I told Alan your discretion was to prevent a row."

"Such a sweet little fool you are, Penny."

The words hurt despite the gentleness of Florence's admonition. "Jane is a bitch. Alan knows. He's always known. His knowing about that particular day is what mattered."

Penny opened her mouth to ask...

Florence pulled Penny closer and glanced to a dark corner across the room. "Lorraine is here." Penny turned quickly, then back with Florence's gentle tug. "I've been trying to ignore her all morning, but she just stands there and glares at me. Waiting."

Penny glanced again to the empty corner, and her heartbeat quickened despite the vacant space. "Harold's mother?" Penny asked.

"Yes. She's been coming in here for days." Again Florence tugged her dress sleeve. "Sit on the bed beside me. She frightens me. She always did."

Penny rose and sat on the edge of the bed. "You knew her?" She took Florence's hand.

"Our families socialized. That's how I met Jon. What that horrible, sick woman did to Harold is —"

Suddenly Florence was struggling to sit up. "Get away! No, don't you come closer."

Penny was on her feet, leaning over Florence trying to calm her, force her back onto the bed, but Florence was flailing now, her arms waving violently, her residual strength shocking. She screamed, then kicked at the covers and finally hit Penny in the jaw, causing Penny to step back. Florence continued to flail, then collapsed back, her eyes fixed on something hovering over her. "You deserved it," Florence hissed at something Penny did not see. "You deserved what happened...deserved it...! Yes," she forced out, her eyes wide, her face twisted in what Penny thought must be either terror or hate. "You got exactly what was coming to you."

Florence let out a bloodcurdling scream, her breath foggy in a room, Penny realized, that had inexplicably become frigid, the cold permeating her bones to the marrow. Penny turned and lurched for the door. She grabbed the knob. Outside she could hear the thud of shoes running down the carpeted hall, behind her, an agonized gurgle, then all was quiet. She released the knob as Harold pushed the door open. No longer alone, she looked back at the bed.

Florence lay there, her lifeless eyes staring up. Knees weak, Penny came back to the bed and studied the skull-like face tightly sheathed in yellowed flesh. Steeling herself, she reached out a shaking hand and closed Florence Noble's eyes. She felt Harold's hands on her shoulders. Gently he pulled her back and maneuvered her into the rocker.

"What in the world...?"

Alan was there now. "Why is she..." then stopped, silent.

Peter Fritz rushed in and around to the other side of the bed. He held Florence's wrist, then checked her breath....

"She's gone," Penny heard herself say.

Harold leaned over her shoulder. "Why was she screaming at you like that? What did you say to her?"

Penny shook her head. "She wasn't screaming at me."

He stepped around and squatted beside her. "Who then?"

Penny looked at him. "Your mother, Lorraine."

*J*onathan Noble arrived at dusk. Within moments, his shock upon learning Florence had died turned to bitterness, then anger. In turn, Harold was angry at him for his delay. Harold had, after all, sent for him the day before, and Mobile was only a short train ride away.

For his part, Alan took one look at Jonathan, then sequestered himself in his office. He did not protest when Harold put his uncle in one of the spare bedrooms. Later, Jonathan was cordial to Penny, who accompanied Jane into his room with fresh linens and a pitcher of water. With a heavy spirit, he told her he was pleased to find her, at least, in better health.

Chapter Twenty-six

The one thing Penny was certain she loved about being a Noble, and perhaps it was the only thing, was attending the Episcopal Church of the Redeemer downtown on Howard Street and the thrill of seeing Jeff and Varina Davis on Sundays. That's where Harold made the funeral arrangements. Penny, exhausted by the end of the death spiral, assisted when asked, and it was she who coordinated with the ladies from the church in organizing the wake at the house. In the interim, she, Gracie, and Jane prepared the house for mourning...and for grieving guests. Several of Florence's friends and cousins from Mobile had trekked over to say their goodbyes. Florence was interred at the Old French Cemetery in Biloxi.

Penny knew Alan and Florence had not loved each other. Still, during the five months Penny had lived beneath their roof, they had interacted, put on an excellent social front, and even appeared to enjoy each other's company in the absence of other distractions. Penny assumed that had been the case for all the years of their marriage. Florence's death would prove a formidable change for Alan Noble.

Now, sandwiched between Alan and Harold, Penny departed the cemetery on a mercifully cool, gray-shrouded September morning, the three of them dressed in black. Alan took her hand, and she thrust her tear-soaked handkerchief inside her dress pocket before reaching for Harold's. He squeezed her fingers, then fell back to walk with his uncle, two steps behind.

"What will it be like, do you think, taking on all Florence's responsibilities?"

Penny hoped Jon Noble didn't perceive her jump. She hadn't noticed him to her left when she opened the door to Florence's parlor. After a quick look his way, she returned to her task of drawing the heavy drapes against the coming night. His presence explained the well-lit room. She should have guessed the moment she opened the door and sought solitude elsewhere. The relentless army of family, friends, and fellow mourners were gone. Done with the drapes, she turned. Except, of course, for Jon Noble, who stood in front of a portrait of Florence's mother.

"Abigail Fleet Knox," he said. "Florence favored her. Sweet, mercenary Abigail liked me. She always had concerns about me, my youthful past, you understand, but she'd about come around to accepting me as Florence's suitor until my father's death, followed conveniently by that of my brother's wife."

"And Florence's father?" Penny asked, moving toward Jon.

"He was much older than Abigail. He never regarded me as suitable for Florence."

Penny stood beside him and studied the painting of Abigail Fleet. "And Florence submitted to her parents' wishes."

He laughed softly. "Florence agreed with their assessment."

"She told me —"

"She lied." He placed his hands behind his back and stepped away from the portrait. Penny pivoted with him.

"You loved her."

"Not since the day she told me she was marrying Alan. I knew then what she was after. What she'd always been after, even as I wooed her." He stopped and looked at Penny. "Not Alan, Penny. Money and power. I was merely sufficient as head of Noble Shipping. Alan proved a much bigger catch. Suffice it to say my feelings for her, which did indeed run deep, were relegated to carnal. We used each other."

"Oh." She thought she understood what he meant, but then she thought Florence's feelings for Jonathan had been different. Perhaps she, in her naiveté, had been wrong.

"What did you tell Alan about what you saw that day in this room?"

"Nothing."

He studied her hard, then flexed his jaw and looked away. "Her sickness was sudden."

"I'd been sick, too."

"I know."

"The doctors originally thought—"

"I know what the doctors are saying. What they're thinking is a different matter. But it's best to leave sleeping dogs lie at this point, wouldn't you say?"

Penny's heartbeat quickened, and she frowned at Jonathan. "I would not say so, no."

"Are you sure?" He smiled when she said nothing. "I think for all our sakes it's best to leave our dead buried."

"Then why have you implied what you have?"

"I wanted your opinion on the matter before I leave is all."

"You're going back to Mobile?"

"Tomorrow or the day after. Florence, I believe, once pointed out to you she was the peacekeeper. What welcome I ever had in this house passed away with her."

"And Harold?"

"Is not to be counted on. I believe you realize that by now."

"I thought you and Harold were closer."

"Like you thought there was more between Florence and me? Oh, there's plenty between us Nobles, Penny. At the moment there is a business gamble, but I am no longer needed." He took her hand and kissed her knuckles. "It was I who planned to bring you into the family, you know?"

Penny's mouth went dry. "I was promised to another. Did you know that?"

"You should understand that such promises instill little confidence in me, but I merely informed my lover of your, how should I say it, appropriateness as a wife. She was the one who approached Harold, then Alan. I am not responsible for anything beyond that, but I must agree with Adel"—Penny pondered that association—"you deserve a better man than Mark Reed. You deserve a better Noble, too. Harold bungled this."

He turned to the door. She stopped him with a touch on the arm. "Speaking of Harold and the dead, how did his mother die?"

"Ah, the harpy, Lorraine. Has Harold not told you?"

"He refuses to speak of her, becomes quite rude regarding the subject, as a matter of fact."

Jon stepped around her and walked to the settee. He sat and patted the place at his side. She joined him.

"She took a tumble down the main stairwell and landed most ungracefully on the entry floor. The coroner confirmed her neck broken."

"Are you sure it was an accident?"

"Are you implying she was pushed?"

"Like you imply Florence was poisoned? Yes, that's what I'm asking. Could someone have pushed her?"

"I think any number of people would have pushed her if they thought they could get away with it. But with pushes down stairs, one doesn't know that the fall is going to kill the victim until after she lands. If the ploy fails, then what's the failed murderer to do?"

"So you don't think she was pushed?"

"I know she wasn't. There were several witnesses, myself included. Lorraine was a raving lunatic, chasing her distraught seventeen-year-old son down the stairs when she lost her footing. It was early morning. He'd snuck out during the night and was in the process of sneaking back in. He decided to forego the admonition, and the beating, to which she routinely subjected him. Her harangue brought both Alan and me from the dining room and Gracie, Lorraine's new hire, from an upstairs room she was making up. She can confirm all this for you if you wish validation. Lorraine was halfway down the stairs. Harold had reached the bottom and was gaining distance when the witch..." The gaslight flickered, and Jon hesitated, looked around, then smiled at Penny and said, "The *witch* began to choke on her screeches. She let go the handrail and did two somersaults down the stairs. What I remember most about that moment was the sudden hush that echoed the crack of Lorraine's head on the floor. The sad part is we all, I believe, relished it."

The light continued to flicker, causing Penny to look at it. She felt Jonathan touch her hand. "There's air in the line, that's all."

Easier, she looked at him. He let go of her hand.

"I wouldn't say Alan hated her, but I'm not sure he didn't. For the most part he ignored her, but he should have paid more attention to how she dealt with their son, who did, I assure you, hate her passionately, and not without cause, if you can ever justify hating a parent." Jon stood, then offered his hand and pulled Penny to her feet. "As for it being a case of murder, I guess one would have to ask, what caused her to choke and lose her footing?"

And the gaslight blinked out completely.

Chapter Twenty-seven

For the first two days after Florence's funeral, Alan worked late and retired early. He didn't come home for dinner and didn't join them for supper. Though Penny considered grief the reason for her father-in-law's withdrawal, Harold attributed it to Jon's presence and told his uncle the time had come for him to go. Jonathan apparently agreed. Truth was both brother and son vexed Alan. Penny felt a degree of vexation of her own toward Jon, knowing now it was he who put in motion the plan to bring her under the Noble roof. Alan was right, Jon had sidled up to the Frederick-Markiston clan, but she didn't know how long ago or what his full purpose was in doing so.

Penny set her book on the Queen Anne table when she heard the back door open and looked at the mantel clock. Harold had taken Jon to the depot almost an hour ago—a long time for a short trip, but she figured he hadn't wanted to leave Jon waiting for the train alone, and the thing was sometimes late.

Moments later Harold stuck his head inside the front room. "There you are. I won't be here for supper, and I doubt Father will be either. You should go ahead and eat."

She rose from where she'd been reading. "Could I talk to you about something before you go?"

He'd turned to go. Now he stopped. "What?"

His short response, rare for him, indicated he was bothered. She made her way to the entry and stood next to him.

"Those last few days, did Florence say anything to you about seeing...?" She shot him a furtive glance.

"My mother?" he snapped.

With no small degree of relief, she said, "Yes."

"Is that why you asked Uncle Jon about how she died, because in her delirium Florence hallucinated Mother's hellish soul from beneath the floorboards?" Inexplicably he laughed. "And that's where the true demon lurks, you know, beneath the floorboards in this house."

Penny swallowed. Harold spoke as if they'd buried her here, underneath the floors inside this house, and Penny shuddered. But she'd seen Lorraine's grave in the family plot at the Old French Cemetery. "Florence said nothing to you then?"

"No one brings her up to me. No one." He started to turn away, but pivoted back. "Jon said you asked if her death could have been murder. Did you think I killed her?"

"I thought no such thing," she said, "and obviously Jon has little compunction about bringing her up to you."

He bent down and brought his face close to hers. "Shut up."

She closed her eyes, drew in a breath, and released it. "Florence asked me if I told Alan about Jonathan's visit last week. She was worried Alan knew Jonathan was here. I think she thought I might have betrayed her. Jon questioned me, too."

He'd tensed when she started speaking again, and for a moment, she feared he might slap her. Then he pulled back, more relaxed. "And what did you tell them?"

"I told Jon nothing, but I told Florence I confirmed what Alan already knew. I'd have been caught in a lie otherwise."

"And do you know how he knew?"

She shrugged.

"Of course you do, you little fool. Jane told him. Do you think you're protecting her from me?"

She warmed at the insult. Was she a fool? Well, that went without saying. Of course she was or she wouldn't be here married to him, but did it necessarily follow she was a fool in the context of this bizarre relationship between the elder Nobles?

"Since you already know," she said, "why did she tell him? Did she tell you that?"

"She was coerced, I imagine."

"By whom?"

"The intricacies of human interaction in this house are complicated, Penny."

"Jane is sleeping with your father?"

"I hope not." He started moving toward the stairs, and she hurried after him.

"The main point is..."

"Is what, Penny? That Uncle Jon and Florence were lovers and you walked into her parlor and caught them in a compromising situation." He narrowed his eyes on her. "It wasn't about Jon and Florence, Penny. Father has always known about them. Florence flattered herself for thinking she actually mattered. The two men shared a tacit agreement never to broach the subject. She was nothing more than a beautiful tool, one of several they use in all the games they play from sex to business." Again, he started to move away.

"Well, if the matter wasn't about Florence, then it's about the land." He stopped dead in his tracks and looked at her.

"The Perry County property you and Jon and Florence duped your father into buying."

He flexed his jaw, and she had the satisfaction of thinking he might be considering her not such a fool after all.

"Yes," he said finally. "It's about the land." He turned on his heel.

"Wait," she cried, "I'm not done."

His spine stiffened, she saw it. Impatience radiated from him. He threw his head back in supposed exasperation, his face towards the ceiling. "I've got a dinner engagement, then an important meeting. What is it?"

"Do you believe your father could have killed Florence?"

He pivoted. "You were with her when she died."

"He forced her to drink tea. I think she, at least, thought he was poisoning her."

"By then everyone was forcing her to drink. She wouldn't do it on her own. If he were going to poison her, he'd have done it a long time ago. So, in answer to your question, yes, he could have, and no, I don't believe he did."

"But..." She followed as he again started away, and she touched his arm. He whipped around.

She braced at his response and searched his face. He stood towering over her, then suddenly he softened. "Look, I've got to change. I'm in a hurry."

"Do you want me to help?"

"Come up to your room. I'll call you when I'm ready for the tie."

She joined him on the stairs. "You're seeing David?"

"David has grown tedious of late. He gets demanding from time to time, and I have no desire to perform for anyone tonight."

Chapter Twenty-eight

"Alan?" Penny said.

He turned from where he sat in his wing-back chair near the cold fireplace and looked to where she stood, just inside the open pocket door to the front room. He'd been staring into space before she spoke. She didn't want to disturb him, but she was worried about him and didn't want to leave him down here alone if he were in need of a friend.

"Harold is out?" he asked.

"Yes," she said and slipped into the room. "Did you get anything to eat?"

"Cold chicken. It was quite good. I apologize for skipping supper, but I didn't want to risk seeing my son."

She stopped at the game table. "Would you enjoy a game of rummy?"

"Not tonight." He glanced at the parlor commode that held his whiskey and brandy. "Perhaps another drink."

"I'll get you a brandy," she said.

"Ah, and here's Jane with your chocolate."

Penny turned as she poured the brandy and gave the girl a smile. "Set it there," she said and nodded to the game table.

"That will be all, Jane," Alan said in dismissal, and he rose, teetering just a bit. Penny handed him his brandy, and he looked at her chocolate. "You don't want it, do you?"

A sigh escaped her lips, but she was already reaching for the fine china cup. He'd been drinking, which explained his morose demeanor, and she cursed herself for disturbing him. Plaintive drunks could be tedious, and she was in no mood to deal with him.

"I don't think you'll offend Jane. She'd probably be thankful for less work."

"It's you I fear offending."

He shook his head, and bent in closer, the smell of whiskey all too strong now. "You can't offend me, not over that."

And how might she offend him, she wondered, thinking back on his doubts and veiled accusations during the days before Florence died.

"I buy the stuff to turn a profit, not because I think I'm doing the world a favor." His voice had warmed. "Here, give it to me. I'll drink yours and you drink mine. I should have asked you to pour me a whisky tonight." He laughed. "Had a few before I came home."

Dutifully she took his snifter and surrendered her delicate cup.

"Egads! So sweet."

She laughed good-naturedly, then threw back her head and drained the small portion of brandy. Nausea threatened, but she forced it back. "Not sweet."

"And not the way brandy was meant to be enjoyed," he said.

"I don't care for brandy and wanted to be done with it."

He chuckled. "My sentiments exactly." He drained her cup. "Now, fix us a whiskey, and we'll drink to the rift between my son and brother whatever the hell it might be."

She had wondered about that...the barely perceptible rift...and considered she might learn something. But she didn't want the whiskey.

"Please," he coaxed when she protested. "I don't want to drink alone. In fact, I insist. Just one little drink. Yes," he continued, "let's you and me have a little drink." He looked her up and down. "Time for a new game, little brother." He chuckled. "Big brother shall regain the upper hand yet."

Penny frowned.

He turned back. "Drink up, my dear."

The brandy she drank had soured her stomach. She'd drink the whiskey slow. She had no intention of getting drunk with him now, and the last thing she wanted was a row. Some drunks were all too easily riled. For her, Alan was an unknown entity in that regard.

He blinked and turned away, perhaps aware he was making her uncomfortable. "Stuart came to my office today," he said. "Wants me to extend the loan. Apparently you told them you wouldn't ask."

"I did."

"Good, because they are all working together behind my back."

"Stuart and Grandmother?"

"And Harold and Jon. Even Florence was. They duped me about the land, you know? All three of them."

Quiet, she uncorked the whiskey bottle and poured them each two fingers. He watched her approach, then took the glass. "You didn't have anything to do with it, did you?"

"I promise you I had nothing to do with that land sale. If you recall, at dinner that night I told you I thought it terrible to steal that land out from under your brother."

"So did they all, but in your case, I believe you were probably the only one being honest." He threw back his head, drank the shot, then hissed, before pointing at her with his empty glass. "It was me they were after in regard to the money, but you're the key nonetheless. You don't realize it, but you are."

"How?"

He stepped around her without answering and poured himself more whiskey. "You need to be...."

"I need to be what?" she asked when he didn't continue.

He smirked and again allowed his eyes to roam over her before taking another swig from his glass. "You need to consider a new alliance, my dear."

He was more intoxicated than she thought. He cast her another appreciative glance, then had another shot of whiskey.

"It's time I confronted Harold myself." He nodded to her glass. "Are you going to finish that one quickly or do you intend to relish it?"

"You are drunk, Alan. I'm going to bed. We can talk in the morning." She left her glass on the game table on her way out.

Chapter Twenty-nine

The room was so painfully bright Penny could no longer open her eyes. Alan said he'd wanted to see her, see everything. She was sweating and sick. Her breast ached. She felt the liquid on it, heard him laugh, then felt his tongue move over the injury, lapping up the champagne all the while groaning with sadistic pleasure and smacking his lips. She twisted her torso, filled with disgust and determined to escape him, his probing, his filthy innuendo, his cruelty, but he had her weighted down, his leg across her thighs. She felt his hand on her right shoulder, sensed the delicate fabric of her gown being forced down her arm. She sensed it tear.

"Now for the other one."

She screamed, and twisted. He grunted, then slapped her, and pushing an arm under Penny's head he forced her into a half sitting position. "You didn't drink enough," he said.

Her head lolled on her shoulders. She opened her eyes in time to see him raise the champagne bottle. She felt its mouth forced between her lips, then his tilting it up and back. Liquid poured over her chin and down her neck, into her ears, and yes, down her throat. She coughed, and twisted her torso to one side, spewing champagne and vomit across the bed covers. He didn't appear to care. He was off the bed, yanking her night gown over her feet. He tugged once, and she fell flat on her back. She closed her eyes. and let her body spin with the room.

"There now," she heard him say, "That's much better." He was moving about. He'd removed his dressing gown, his thick body and huge paunch covered with dark and graying hair. She closed her legs and twisted away. Her breast burned. She lay in

162

vomit, its stench making her sicker still. He seized her hips and roughly forced her off her side and onto her back. She felt him crawl upon the bed, felt his manhood touch her thigh. He reached down to spread her legs, and she struck out to ward him off...

The door to the bedroom crashed open in tandem with an otherworldly wail, shredding what was left of her ebbing sanity. She felt the cold, sensed Alan rise, heard his subsequent gurgle, then heard him choke. The room was frigid, like a cold January day in Perry County. Alan loomed over her, not looking at her, but in the direction of the door. Another wail rent the air.

Alan cried out at the same time his body went limp and crashed down, crushing her, right before pain and an explosion of light blew her brain apart and thrust her into blackness.

Chapter Thirty

Charlie Nixon hurried back into the room and slammed the door. Toby Craig looked up in question.

"Sheriff's here. He's gonna take this one away from you."

Toby cursed. The bastard could try. "Who notified him?"

"Wasn't me."

"Charlie, I didn't think it was, but someone did. How many people know about the killing?"

Charlie kneeled next to the body. "Clerk. Stuart Frederick. Mr. Frederick was here to meet him, he says. Got here shortly after we did. Clerk didn't say anything about sending for the sheriff, but I'll ask him."

Toby pulled a pocket watch out of his vest pocket. Nearly twelve thirty. He had been awakened roughly forty-five minutes ago. "Jugular?"

"Yep." Charlie placed two fingers beneath Harold Noble's chin and exposed the neck. "No ceiling below us. Blood just started pouring through the cracks into the lobby."

"Clerk recall what time he sent for us?"

"Little after eleven."

"Say twenty minutes to get us up and movin'?"

Charlie shrugged. "Give or take."

"Frederick was fast on your heels, you say?"

"Yep."

"I'd say it was probably him who sent for the sheriff. Still, it would have taken another forty-five minutes, at least, to notify Lyle and add forty-five minutes for him to get here from Handsboro. He shouldn't be here yet. How'd he get here so fast, Charlie?"

Charlie looked up at him. "Don't know, boss."

The door flew open, and Lyle Jenkins blustered inside. Toby rocked back on his heels, and the sheriff gave him a hard look. "Whatcha got?" Jenkins asked.

"One Harold Noble with a cut throat."

Jenkins swaggered full into the room. Deputy Robert Hays followed. Much less the swaggerer or braggart was Bob Hays, and Toby could almost bring himself to like the man, except for his boss. Then again, once Toby had worked for Jenkins, too.

Jenkins stopped near the body of Harold Noble, lying on the floor in a pool of blood. "Who did the clerk say he came up here with?"

"He came up alone."

Irritated, Toby twisted to squint at Frederick, who'd snuck in behind Hayes.

"And before you ask, he didn't see anyone follow him up here either," Frederick said.

Jenkins shot the man a wary glance. "Is that so?"

"Unfortunately," Frederick responded under his breath.

Toby rose. "Gone into law enforcement have you, Mr. Frederick?" Toby had known the man since the Gibson trial. He considered him a liar.

"I was supposed to meet him here. As far as I know it was a private meeting between me and Mr. Noble. I asked the clerk out of curiosity."

"Interesting it was you meeting him here tonight."

"Don't get cute, Craig. We had timber and shipping business to discuss. We were keeping it private for discretionary reasons, nothing more."

Jenkins cleared his throat. "We need to find Pascal then."

Toby jerked around and looked at the man. "Who?"

"David Pascal. Noble's boyfriend. They've been fightin'. Seems Noble liked variety in his assholes. Pascal considered Noble's cock his personal"—Jenkins gave Toby an ugly grin—"plunger." Jenkins looked at Stuart Frederick and snickered. Frederick countered with a look of disgust, and Jenkins shut up.

Charlie Nixon looked at the sheriff. "Clerk says Noble had permanent dibs on this room. Was here a couple of hours, at least, three nights a week. He gave me some names. Pascal's was not one of them."

"According to my sources," Jenkins said, "Pascal has a home, and that's where those two entertained each other."

Toby looked around the room with its worn wallpaper, greasy, unwashed windows, and undusted surfaces. A shabby hostelry on Biloxi's Back Bay, west of the city proper, but close enough to the action. The mattress on the tarnished brass bed was sunken in the middle and lumpy in several places. Definitely not a spot for a good night's rest, but then, that's not what the clientele used it for. A cheap whorehouse catering to male whores. Toby was well aware of the place. At first glance it would have been hard to figure why a man as wealthy as Harold Noble met his lovers here, but it made sense given that Harold Noble was known to be generous with his affections.

"That would seem to rule Pascal out," Toby said.

"Not if he followed Noble here expecting to catch him with another man." Jenkins shuffled across the worn wood floor to a small pine wardrobe next to the door. The whole damn wardrobe moved when the man yanked it open. It was small, Jenkins was large, and the thing was empty. "Pascal probably confronted him, they argued, and Pascal killed him."

Toby looked at Frederick. "If that theory is correct," he said dryly, "looks like it was lucky you were late."

Jenkins turned to the dresser near the bed.

Toby rose from his squat. "This is my jurisdiction, Lyle."

The man graced him with a jaundiced eye, scraped at the stubble on his chin, then pulled the top drawer open. "Your jurisdiction ended one block east, and there's gonna be some important folks interested in this pretty boy's death." He slammed the drawer shut. "Gonna have to relieve you of it."

"You seem well-versed in the habits of Harold Noble."

The sloppy son of a bitch slammed the middle drawer shut, then the bottom.

"There's been some interest in him lately."

Toby glanced at Stuart Frederick, who caught the look. "From whom?" Toby asked.

Jenkins ignored him. "Might ask for some help from you, though."

Jaw tight, Toby watched the man turn to him in the center of the room.

"You find anything in this hole?"

"A dead body."

Jenkins' lips tightened. "Weapon?"

"Nope."

Jenkins squatted and moved Noble's head from side to side, then he looked up at Bob Hays. "You get Sams and get over to Pascal's place. We need to lock him up."

"You don't need to find Sams. Take Charlie."

Charlie frowned, but with his chin, Toby pointed to Robert Hays, already retreating out the door. Charlie followed.

Jenkins rose, clearly displeased.

Eyes fixed on Lyle Jenkins, Toby said, "I intend to lend you as much support as I can."

Chapter Thirty-one

From where he had stopped at the opposite end of the dark alley, Jack could see Jon Noble's silhouette against the light cast through the dirty windows of the shabby boarding house on the other side of Reynoir Street, roughly fifty feet from where Reynoir entered Back Bay Road. There was activity over there now, and Jack figured Jon was waiting for Jack to be escorted out under arrest. Double-dealing son of a bitch.

His mind now made up as to the sequence of events, Jack started toward the lurking shadow, and when he was almost upon the man, he scraped his boot against the brick. Jon spun on his heel at the same time he reached inside his coat.

"Don't," Jack said, striking a match to highlight his face, then immediately shaking it out. "It's just me." Neither of them wanted to be seen here now, not after what had happened across the street.

Jack could see enough of Noble to know if the bastard resumed his reach for what Jack suspected was a gun...or a knife. Jon didn't move, nor did he speak. The silence was downright awkward.

"Harold Noble is dead," Jack said finally. "That is my reason for being here, right?"

"Did anyone see you?"

Jack smiled in the dark. "Sorry to disappoint you, but not a soul."

Jon leaned a shoulder against the wall of the alley. "Who found the body?"

"Clerk. Stuart Frederick showed up a bit ago, too. Was he supposed to meet you, too, or just find me?"

"Maybe he was meeting Harold."

And maybe Jon Noble had prior knowledge of that meeting...then again, maybe not.

Jack saw the glint of Jon Noble's teeth that accompanied his smile. "Well, I guess we know where we stand with each other, don't we?"

"I believe we do. You can go, Mr. Noble. The deed is done, and nothing more is gonna happen now, at least not in regards to me."

Chapter Thirty-two

The frog nearby stopped its croaking. It never ceased to amaze Jack how one could sound like a multitude. It was near three in the morning and the night was quiet, but for the gentle laps of river water against the hull of the flat-bottomed boat. Anticipation churned his gut, like the skiff churned the shallow river water when the kid guided it onto dry land. He did a good job landing, and Jack told him so.

"You still got 'em?" Jack asked Lucas Frazier, waiting for him on the moon-lit bank.

"Yep."

A mosquito buzzed near Jack's ear, and he swatted at it, then he turned to the twelve-year-old Negro boy Lucas had rousted sometime after one to retrieve him. Jack hadn't even undressed from his foray into Biloxi earlier in the evening. He flipped the boy two bits, silver he'd won in the poker game in a Biloxi back-room before the Harold Noble business. "You go on back to bed. I might be awhile."

"You be needin' somebody to ferry you back, Mista' Jack?"

"I'll get one of the men to do it. They'll be freed up by then. Git on home."

Jack turned to Lucas, five steps in front of him on the well-worn path to Humboldt's Biloxi River mill. Forty minutes had passed since Kate brought the boy to his room. At least two hours had passed since Lucas had started the boy on his way.

"How much damage was done?" he asked the day foreman.

"They've put that special gang saw out of commission."

Shit!

"How many of them were there?"

170

"Three."

"Where was the night watchman?"

"Knocked him out. Only reason we caught 'em was 'cause Bobby's wife is expectin' their first real soon, and he asked Mike Friedo if someone could relieve him an hour early so he could spell his mother who wanted to be home before midnight. Her man is sick."

"Mike walked in on 'em?"

"Julio Simms did. That's who Mike sent to relieve Bobby. Julio had just left Henry and Peters shootin' dice at Daddy Joe's two minutes away, so he knew where to find help. Surprised 'em."

"How's Bobby?"

"Conscious now, think he'll be okay."

The lighted mill loomed in front of them. Jack stopped well outside the building and looked behind him. The Negro boy was close on their heels. "Can you see to find your way home?" Jack asked him.

The boy grinned at him as if Jack were an idiot. "Sho, I can."

"Good, get on home to your mama, and you stay put. I don't want you hangin' round here tryin' to find out what's goin' on. You can't get nothin' but hurt."

"Yes, suh," he said with a wave and disappeared around the long side of the mill.

"Where's his house?"

"'Bout a quarter mile up the road. His mama's Miss Edna, she does some of our lunch pails."

"Check 'im."

Lucas moved to the side of the building and looked around the corner. The area around the mill was bright enough given the lights inside and Jack saw Lucas turn to him and nod. Jack grabbed a discarded piece of two-by-four lying on the ground. Lucas fell into step beside him as they crossed the threshold of the open mill doors. Across the expanse of the interior, Mike Friedo, a shotgun against his shoulder, turned their way, as did Nick Henry and Jason Peters. Friedo was a white man, the other two were Negro. On the ground, three men sat. They were all white. One, a man Jack recognized as Clem Fletcher, a long-time employee of King and Gibson Lumber, started to get up, Peters moved to stop him, but Jack motioned it was okay.

Clem grinned. "Well, well, it's handsome scrappin' Jack, hapless Jim Gibson's prodigal son."

"What do ya know about a turpentine still explosion up near Lumberton, Clem?" Jack called above his clamoring heart. Halfway to them now, Lucas at his side, he was swinging that two-by-four like a club.

"Heard two niggers got kilt workin' for ya." He sneered at the men on either side of him. "Maybe others will think better about who they cast their lot with." Clem eyed the two-by-four and snorted. "You tryin' to scare me, scrappin' Jack? I don't scare easy."

Jack caught Peters' eye. "Hold 'im," Jack said sharply. "You, too, Nick."

They moved so fast Clem didn't have time to react. He struggled a moment, then looked Jack in the eye. The smile had disappeared, but now a snotty grin took its place. "Murder ain't your way, I know that." He grinned. "That's your daddy's way, ain't it, boy?"

"Lucas, stretch out his right arm and roll that elbow over. Mike, keep your eye on the other two."

Lucas did as he was told, and Mike stepped out of the way, lowering his rifle, his eyes on the two prisoners still on the ground. One was bloodied around the ear, and Jack didn't figure he'd be a problem now, even if he wanted to be.

Jack raised the two-by-four, and the three men holding Clem braced against the man's sudden lurch. He'd probably already dislocated the elbow on his own before the two-by-four met it with a sickening crunch. Clem's scream echoed through the quiet mill and the prisoner in the best shape said, "Goddamn."

"Did you set that turpentine still on fire?" Jack railed. He stepped forward, the two-by-four high, and Clem, mumbling oh god, oh god over and over, fell back against Nick and Jason, who now struggled to keep him upright. Lucas, quiet, had let go of Clem's hand. Again Jack lunged at him. "Did you?"

Clem, struggling to hold his limp arm with his other, now turned his tear-streaked face to Jack. "You go to hell!" the man raged and managed to thrust his body toward Jack, who hit the injured arm with the two-by-four again, though not with great force. That would only cause the bastard to pass out, and that Jack didn't want. Clem howled and fell to his knees. The un-injured prisoner said, "For the love of god, man," but Jack ignored him. He didn't look into the faces of his own men for that matter, but lowered his own to glare into Clem's eyes. "Did you set that fire in Piotona?"

Clem glared at him, and Jack reached toward Mike.

"Give me that rifle."

Mike handed it over. "Buckshot."

"Between the eyes. Won't matter at this range."

"Oh, Jesus," the uninjured prisoner whispered.

"Murder and mayhem can be costly," Jack said to the man, but he never took his eyes off Clem. "If I kill one of you, I'm gonna have to kill you all."

"We was just supposed to damage your saws," the man yelled. "Ain't no cause to kill nobody."

Jack pointed the rifle at Clem, whose back was now supported by Peters' legs. Jason Peters stepped out of the way, and Clem toppled over on his broken arm and writhed on the ground.

"You three have sabotaged Humboldt's mill," Jack ground out. "Probably set him back weeks. Obviously, y'all have forgotten what motivates Yankees to kill." Jack settled the rifle against his shoulder. "Hell, they might kill me. I'm the one responsible. For sure I'm gonna lose my job on top of bein' dragged out of my warm bed in the wee hours of the mornin'. That is, of course, if I don't make this right."

"Clem hired me," the other man cried, "but he said he reckoned we was doin' this for Mrs. Markiston."

"Shut up, Arly," Clem managed. He made some effort to rise, but rolled back. "Goddamn it, shut your mouth."

"You reckoned, Clem?" Jack said to the injured man. He cocked the rifle. "You didn't talk to her direct?"

Clem rolled on the ground. He was pale, clammy-looking, and sweat had broken out on his forehead and upper lip.

"No," Arly cried, scooting closer to Jack. "It was another fella."

Now Jack shifted his focus to Arly. "Did you see him?"

"Naw, it was Clem said it was somebody else."

"Stuart Frederick?" Jack asked Clem.

Clem said nothing. Jack steadied the rifle.

"For sure it was him," Arly cried.

"Shut your mouth, Arly."

Jack looked at Arly.

"You were at that turpentine still?"

The man glanced at Clem, then back to Jack. "I—"

"Shut up, you idiot," Clem yelled, then forced himself up with his left arm and made to lunge at Arly. "He ain't gonna kill you over a goddamn saw, but he will over them two niggers." Peters' boot slammed Clem's right shoulder into the sawdust covering the floor. Clem screamed.

"Clem shot that boy out back," Arly said quickly. "I didn't have nothin' to do with any of it. I stood guard, that's all."

Clem, still writhing, started laughing, giddy. "The hell you did."

"That's all I did," the man cried and jumped to his feet. Nick knocked Arly back down. Arly pushed away from Jack with the heel of his shoe. "I didn't kill nobody."

"He set the fire," Clem said.

"Okay, I set the fire, but only 'cause Clem told me to. Weren't anybody in the still house when I did. Old man ran in after."

Clem had managed to sit up again. He looked at Jack and laughed. "It was the explosion killed that old man, weren't it, scrappin' Jack?"

Jack looked at the third man, the bloody-headed one. He stared sullenly at Jack, bent over, and threw up, then he leaned the back of his head against the wall. "I wasn't there, and that's the honest truth. And believe me, at this point I'd tell you any-thing you wanted to know."

"How about that night?" Jack asked Arly. "Other fella hon-choed it, too?"

"Clem said it was the boss lady. Didn't say nothin' about any-body else."

Jack, heart pounding and mouth dry, turned to Clem, who said, "I ain't sellin' out Eva Markiston. You can break my other arm and both legs, but I ain't doin' it."

Jack nodded. He still held the rifle ready, and Clem paled. Then he lowered it. "I'll get her in my own way. In the meantime, there's still the matter of my turpentine still."

Clem snorted. "Ain't nobody gonna care about what hap-pened there."

"Funny thing about old Deacon French. Folks round where he lived thought a lot of 'im."

"Yeah? What did the sheriff think?"

"Only know of 'im, but Sheriff Thornton impresses me as an honest man." Jack glanced at Arly. "That's why I'm deliverin' you to him for murder and arson."

"The hell you say. What about Clem?"

Jack turned back to Clem, who was studying him with glassy eyes. "Him and bloody-head there I'm turning over to Lyle Jenkins for the destruction of private property."

"That ain't fair!"

Clem said nothing, but Jack knew the bastard's mind was working.

"Tryin' to figure me out, Clem? Well, I tell ya, I'm thinkin' Eva Markiston will have you out within hours, and I'm bettin' she's not gonna be pleased at how bad you've bungled this."

Chapter Thirty-three

Penny's head throbbed, and her breast hurt, an indefinable pain between a burn and a sting. She lay face down on her thick carpet, her cheek damp and her nostrils burning with the acid stench of vomit. Vaguely she remembered fighting herself awake after being knocked out. She'd been sick to her stomach, and it had been the very real terror of drowning in her own vomit that had given her the strength to force Alan's deadweight off her and onto the floor. She'd rolled over to retch where she lay, then tried to get up, clean herself up, but she'd passed out again, this time on the Aubusson carpet.

Her heart started to pound, and she pushed her torso up on her arms. The room was bright. He'd turned up her lights, she remembered now.

She was on all fours. Her gut quaked and her head exploded and vomit splattered the fingers she'd splayed on the floor. Alan? She turned. He was behind her, also on the floor, on his back, naked, his silk robe a few feet away where he'd dropped it hours ago. At least she thought it had been hours. She sat back on her naked butt. The room spun, and her stomach reeled, but she forced the sickness back and faced the beast, staring at nothing with dark, glassy eyes fixed in a twisted face. She rose, but too dizzy to keep upright, she returned to the floor and, assuming a posture on all fours, crawled the distance to the hall door. She rose to her knees and reached for the knob. The door was locked. She locked it last night when she came to bed. How then...? She twisted and put her back to the door, then slid down to a sitting position. She cradled her now throbbing breast and wept.

※

Someone was pounding on the front door. Penny folded the torn nightgown down its rent middle and tossed it over the back of the wing chair near the window. The mantel clock said four thirty a.m. She'd been shivering for the past twenty minutes, despite the warmth of the room and the sweat and sickness. That was in part due to the cold water she'd poured into the basin and used to clean herself up before donning new nightclothes.

The entry's gaslight blazed, and Jane, in her robe and night-gown, was at the door by the time Penny reached the bottom step. The young Negress, her eyes widening with Penny's approach, moved back, and Penny, her heart clamoring in her ears, took note of Tobias Craig on the dark front porch. "How did you know?" she choked out.

He blinked at her. "Beg your pardon, ma'am?"

How could he know? Of course he couldn't. She sucked in a breath. "What has happened?" she forced out.

Craig removed his hat when he stepped inside.

"It's about your husband, Mrs. Noble. Is the senior Mr. Noble available?"

She shook her head, then started to cry. "No." She wiped her eyes and her nose with a kerchief she retrieved from a pocket of her robe. "What has happened to Harold?"

Craig glanced at Jane. Immediately Penny turned to her also. "Could you make coffee, please." The young woman nodded, then started down the hall. "Jane?"

She turned.

"Wake Rodney. Send him for Dr. Fritz."

Jane cast a furtive glance at Chief Craig. "Go on. It's Mr. Noble."

"Mr. Noble's ill?" Craig said.

"Mr. Noble is dead."

The man stared at her. Barely able to maintain her composure, Penny waved her hand in front of him and motioned him into the front room. "What's happened to Harold?" she said, her voice so altered she could scarcely understand her own words.

"I'm afraid he's dead, too.

She covered her mouth with her hand, then drew a breath into her nostrils. "How?" she croaked out.

They were still near the room's entry, and Chief Craig took her arm. "Why don't you sit?"

She nodded dumbly, and he led her to the settee in the middle of the room. She felt the cushion beneath her, then the couch give as Craig sat down beside her. "Someone cut his throat."

"Who?" Her stomach quivered as did her voice. She looked the man in the eye. "Why?"

"Sheriff Jenkins plans to arrest a man named David Pascal."

"David.... But he wasn't supposed to be with David," she blurted out.

"Do you know who he was supposed to be with?"

"No, I only know that it specifically wasn't David because"— Penny felt her face heat—"David had become tedious. Harold said his meeting last night was business-related."

"Did you know where your husband was going?"

She shook her aching head. "He left about five yesterday afternoon. I don't know where he went other than he was supposed to have dinner, then go to a business meeting."

"He was in a rundown hotel in west Biloxi. A hotel where, I am told, he rented a room on a routine basis."

"He never told me where he went to meet his...associates. I was aware he had a friend named David and that David sometimes grew boring, so I assume he had other friends, but last night he specifically told me he didn't wish...well, that he didn't intend to be involved with anyone. His meeting was related to business."

"Mrs. Noble, he might have lied—"

"There was no reason for him to lie to me, not about his relationships with men. I knew. He told me. He didn't keep it a secret, at least, not after we wed."

"I take that to mean you were unaware of his perversity when you married him."

Penny closed her eyes tight, shutting out the police chief's scrutiny. "Our marriage was a business arrangement. My grandmother hoped to utilize Noble Shipping to transport lumber to Europe."

"And what did Noble Shipping get in return?"

Penny frowned. The evening and the waking nightmare had beat her stupid. For certain it made no sense. She looked at the chief. "Me," she said. "Noble Corporation got me."

"And I'm sure it has proven a good trade, Mrs. Noble."

Penny listened for sarcasm in his words, but for the life of her she didn't detect any.

"Can you think of anyone who might have wanted your husband dead?"

Wanted him dead? "No, but I know very little about my husband's personal life outside this house."

Craig's intense study continued, him watching her with dark, steady eyes as if he were trying to detect a falsehood in her words. Finally he nodded. "I can tell you that one person he was supposed to meet last night was your stepfather, Stuart Frederick."

Penny blinked. "Oh?"

"He was at the scene. Mr. Frederick says he was meeting your husband to discuss business. Does that sound plausible?"

Why hadn't Stuart come along with Chief Craig to break the news about Harold? Befuddled, Penny nodded. "Yes, I imagine it had to do with the shipping of the lumber. It is plausible, Chief Craig."

"At such a time and in a place like that?"

She rubbed her aching temples. "That is odd, I agree."

This was all very odd, but she didn't want to say anything about the family squabbles until she talked to Stuart.

"If you come up with anything else that might prove useful about your husband's plans last night, will you let me know?

"Of course."

Thank goodness Craig didn't press, because she wasn't thinking straight and doubted her ability to successfully fend him off with anything less than the truth.

"Now, tell me what has happened to your father-in-law?"

Chapter Thirty-four

Toby Craig watched the just-arrived Charlie Nixon squat by the shrouded body of Alan Noble. This whole damn wee-morning had been spent squatting next to dead Nobles. Now sunlight streamed through the window.

Charlie pulled the sheet over the elder Noble's head. "Wish I could find a sweet young thing like her to warm my bed."

"He's not in his bed, not even in hers. He's on the floor, and the verdict is still out as to how sweet she is."

"I bet the doc's saying his heart gave out, isn't he?" Charlie asked.

"Dr. Fritz says it looks like it could have been a stroke. It would have been a helluva lot more interesting if it'd been a butcher knife through his back."

"And simpler, too."

"How did Pascal's arrest go?"

"Roused that pitiful fella out of bed and hauled him off to jail. You think they're railroading him, don't you?"

"I have a strong suspicion that's what's happening. Did you happen to note the looks being passed back and forth between Lyle and Frederick back at the hotel?"

"Like they expected someone to have seen Pascal?"

"Like they'd planned it that way, yeah. Did Pascal have any-thing to say?"

Charlie rose from his squat. "Pascal, to my eyes, appeared moved by the news Noble was dead and confused at being accused of the crime."

"Did Jenkins disclose any evidence against him while you were there?"

180

"Nope. Just locked the fella up."

"Pascal is a convenience. Whoever's behind Harold Noble's murder wants the case closed quickly. I don't think Pascal will ever see trial. Did he come right out and say he was innocent?"

"Repeatedly. Broke down and cried."

"Did Hays and Sams ask him anything?"

"I don't think they wanted to know anything."

"Did you get a chance to question him?"

"We hadn't been in Mississippi City five minutes when that colored you sent after me walked through the door. How'd Mrs. Noble take the news of her husband's death?"

Toby coughed into his fist. "I'm not sure which death has her more upset, but on the subject of her husband's murder, she did say he wasn't supposed to be with Pascal last night." Another point supporting Toby's assumption of subterfuge. If Lyle Jenkins were really interested in investigating Harold Noble's death, he'd have been chomping at the bit to talk to Penny Noble himself. Instead, he'd left the Biloxi police to inform the woman of her husband's death.

"It smells like the morning after a drunken binge in here. Did you get anything out of her about what was going on between her and Alan Noble?" Charlie asked.

"She says he knocked on the door joining hers and her husband's rooms last night around nine. She was already in bed, reading, but she got up. She says he'd been drinking, been drinking all evening. She feared he was sick."

Charlie picked up a man's silk smoking jacket from the floor at the foot of the bed. "Are we to assume he entered dressed in this?"

"We can assume it, yes, not that it means much. Obviously he shed it pretty quick. And look at this," Toby continued, stepping through the door that joined the younger Mr. and Mrs. Noble's rooms. From the desk against the opposite wall, he picked up two crystal flutes, both containing traces of liquid, which a quick sniff readily identified as alcoholic. Charlie reached into a trash basket next to the desk and retrieved an empty bottle of champagne.

181

"From the smell and looks of things" — Toby began to meander back toward the death scene, Charlie by his side — "they had a party in the missus' bedroom. The liquor's in the carpet and on the bed sheets along with the puke."

Toby stopped short of Alan Noble's body, looked back at the door, then at the bed. "Now, she says he fell after she let him in, and when she tried to catch him, they both toppled. She hit her head on the bed frame and was knocked out. When she came to, not too long before I got here, apparently, Alan Noble was as you see him."

"Well, he looks like he's been dead since about nine. Are you believin' anything beyond that?"

"Doc Fritz says she's got a good knot on her noggin. I'm just not sure how it got there, because it's not on the back of her head where it should be if she hit the way she says. It's on her forehead above the left temple..."

"Maybe," Charlie said, taking in the bed, then Alan Noble's body, "if she twisted a bit to her left. But I think Mr. Noble is laid out wrong for it to be the way I'm imagining it."

"And without a doubt more went on between the time she opened her bedroom door and her being knocked out than she implies."

"How specific was she?"

"Not very. She's not talking much now. Says she doesn't know what happened or what he did after she hit her head. As far as she knows, she says...he was alive when they fell."

Charlie blew out a breath. "Well, she should have tried to get that silk jacket back on him if she expected us to believe that hokum." Charlie looked at him. "Will she inherit everything now?"

Toby frowned at him.

"Everything that was the Nobles, I mean?"

"I don't know, but *that*, Mr. Nixon, is a very good question."

"You know, I asked Hays how Jenkins learned about the killing so fast. He said the clerk sent for him at the same time he sent for me, but that's not true, 'cause I went back and asked the clerk."

"It'll probably be true when we ask him next time. My guess is that Lyle was already in Biloxi, but it don't matter none. We know all we need to know. Whoever brought the sheriff in on our heels probably didn't even expect us to be there, and that is the person behind the murder."

Toby looked down at the shrouded corpse. God, he hoped when his time came he went with more dignity.

"Hasn't been a good night for the young Mrs. Noble, has it?" Charlie said.

"Better than the one Harold and Alan Noble experienced. And think about this, Florence Noble died Sunday. She was buried Tuesday. Doc Fritz says she died from internal bleeding, her condition aggravated by dehydration." Toby waved a hand over Noble's body. "Now, given the presence of a naked Alan Noble, dead, on the floor of his daughter-in-law's bedroom, Doc Fritz thinks we need to consider an exhumation and autopsy."

"He's thinking the senior Mrs. Noble was poisoned?"

"Or given something that would have a detrimental effect on her ulcers. If we assume Alan Noble wished to dispose of his wife, we need to consider how much the younger Mrs. Noble knew of his intent?"

Charlie snorted softly, then prodded the body with the toe of his brogan. "Some poisons can cause a stroke."

"You're implying she killed them both," Toby said, matter-of-factly.

"I am implying *someone* may have killed them both."

Toby flexed his jaw, then smiled at Charlie. "And then there's Stuart Frederick, of all people, at the scene of Harold Noble's murder. You know, this has the foul smell of a Markiston plot."

"Can't rule it out, boss."

"And that's the first thing we need to do, rule out murder in the case of Alan Noble. An autopsy might do that, but even if we confirm Alan Noble died a natural death, that don't mean his wife did. An exhumation is gonna be harder."

Toby watched Charlie turn slowly on his heel and scan the room. Toby was lucky to have a subordinate, especially one as talented as Charles Nixon. Charlie stopped his perusal at the chair near the bedroom window, then stepped toward it and picked up the white nightgown draped over its back. "Well, well," he said, holding the garment by its shoulders and nodding to a ragged tear on the bodice. He looked Toby in the eye. "Perhaps we're being too quick to judge."

"I asked her about that. She says he grabbed the neck of the gown when he fell. It was an accident."

"You think that's true?"

Toby shrugged. "All we have is her word, but if he raped her, I can see her wanting to cover it up. Where is the 'sweet young thing' right now?"

A fist rapped on the door leading from the hall, and Peter Fritz stepped in. Charlie glanced at him, then focused on Toby. "She's downstairs, waiting for her mother. She instructed that fella you sent after me to stop by the Frederick house in Mississippi City and break the news about Alan Noble's death. I went with him."

Toby cursed. "That means we can expect Eva Markiston to swoop in on her broomstick any minute now to protect the family interest." He looked at the door. "Come on in, Doc."

Charlie tossed the gown in the seat of the chair and started back to the body. "Speaking of witches, Dr. Fritz, there's something that struck me about Mr. Noble." He squatted and motioned Peter Fritz forward while at the same time raising the sheet covering Alan Noble's face. "Look at his eyes."

The doctor looked. Toby did too. There was something peculiar about the entire, twisted death mask, not just the glassy eyes. Toby looked at Charlie, who was watching Peter Fritz expectantly.

"What are you thinking?" the doctor asked.

Charlie immediately turned to Toby. "This man looks, to me, as if he were scared to death."

Peter Fritz scowled "Evidence of a stroke."

Chapter Thirty-five

$\mathcal{J}$ane had just finished helping Penny button the back of her satin mourning dress when a soft knock drew Penny's attention to her bedroom door. Careful of her injured breast, Penny turned as the door opened, and Clarissa Frederick, concern rife on her face, peeked into the room.

Her mother's clear eyes, a rare occurrence for most of Penny's memory, welled tears at seeing her daughter, and Clarissa threw the door wide and rushed to Penny, folding her in her arms. "Oh, my poor, poor darling. Are you all right?"

"What do you mean by 'all right,' Mama?"

The woman placed her palms on either side of Penny's face and forced her to look at her. "You cared for him? Oh, my poor sweetness." Her mother sobbed, and now Penny sobbed, too, because she was tired and sick, and her world had turned upside down. Clarissa held her tighter, rubbing her back and forcing Penny's cheek against the taffeta of her jacket, and despite the pain in her left breast, Penny ignored the urge to pull herself from her mother's embrace."

Clarissa pushed Penny to arm's length. "Roland said Alan died last night, too, but the officer with him said Harold was murdered." She frowned. "Are they both really dead or is there some confusion?"

Penny shook her head. "Both are dead."

"Were they together?"

"Harold was out, Alan here. Is Stuart with you?"

"He's downstairs."

Thank goodness. She freed her arms from her mother's hold, eager to talk to her stepfather about not only his meeting Harold last night, but her predicament regarding Alan. She looked around, then grabbed the wadded handkerchief on her dressing table. Her eyes had been dry for the past half hour, but her mother's sympathy had changed that.

"Thank you," she told Jane, "you've been a dear all morning." Penny dabbed at her nose, then looked at her mother. "Have you eaten?"

"Stuart and Mother did, very early. I'm not hungry, but you must eat, Penny." Clarissa glanced around the sunlit room, then leaned closer to Penny and said, as if she feared waking him, "Is Alan in his room?"

Penny closed her eyes and drew in a breath. "The county coroner has taken Alan's body. They want to do an autopsy."

Clarissa Frederick's eyes widened. "Dear god, why?"

"To determine what killed him, Mama," Penny said and started out the door after Jane. "I need to talk to Stuart."

"He's in Alan's office."

Penny stopped and turned to her mother. She almost asked why, but realized the question was best asked directly. She hastened down the stairs, her questions regarding Stuart's alleged meeting with Harold, and her need of counsel now overshadowed by what Eva Markiston's right hand was up to in Alan's office.

"What are you looking for, Stuart?"

The picture behind Alan's desk, the one that covered the safe, had been removed and was on the floor against the wall. Stuart had removed it, she knew, because he was in the process of rifling Alan's desk. She would have taken him completely by surprise, if not for her mother jabbering at her heels.

Stuart sat back in Alan's swivel chair and studied her. She had stopped in the doorway, but now came in, followed by her mother.

"Quite a lot happened last night," Stuart said.

"Yes."

"Noble Corporation has lost its head."

"Both heads it would seem, but how does that concern you?"

186

"The loan..."

Penny shrugged. "That was a private loan, if I understand it, and will be the concern of Alan's heir."

Stuart set his mouth in a tight line. "We know Harold was murdered, Penny, but what happened to Alan?"

"Dr. Fritz thinks he had a stroke."

"When he learned Harold was dead?" her mother breathed out.

"He died before word came."

Clarissa took two quick steps toward Stuart. "They are going to do an autopsy," she told him.

Stuart said nothing, but watched Penny. Her head was splitting, and nausea burned her stomach. She didn't want to deal with this now. She wanted to sit on the settee, where three hours earlier she and Chief Craig had discussed Harold's death, but to do so would mean looking up at Stuart. She wasn't going to do that. The desk wasn't even his.

"Where's the key to Alan's safe?" he asked.

Ah, now we're getting to it. "Probably still in his suit pocket at the coroner's office." She didn't avert her eyes until Gracie came in with a coffee service. "I need to inform Noble Corporation what has happened, then I'll stop by the coroner's office and retrieve it."

Stuart rose. "I'll get it this morning, and Jonathan Noble is on his way to inform Thomas Gates of Alan's and Harold's deaths."

The heavy heart that had weighted Penny's chest since Toby Craig told her Harold was dead crashed to her gut.

"Jonathan returned to Mobile last—"

Stuart shrugged. "Maybe he did, but I found him here when we arrived this morning."

"Where?" Penny asked.

"Here, in this office," Stuart answered. "I assumed at that time you'd already talked to him, or someone had, and he knew about Alan. As it turned out he didn't know. Seems Alan is an early riser...." He cocked a questioning eyebrow at Penny, who confirmed with a nod. "Well, Jon said he had some questions

187

about Florence's death, but Harold was hindering Jon's talking to his father. Jon wanted to get to Alan before Harold rose."

"So he didn't know about Harold either?"

Stuart started, then said, "No, he didn't. I told him."

He said nothing more, didn't volunteer that he'd actually been at the murder scene. She wanted to confront him then and there, but the very fact he didn't bring it up meant something, though she wasn't sure yet what that something was. "Do you know anything of the row between Harold and his uncle, Stuart?"

He narrowed his eyes. "You'd know more about that than me. You say Jon returned to Mobile last night?"

"I was led to believe he had. And if he learned from you this morning that his brother and nephew were dead, why didn't he wait and speak to me? It's not Jonathan's place to address anyone at Noble Corporation."

Stuart opened his hands wide. "He's the family's senior surviving male."

"He's not a member of the board. His father was very specific about that. His purview is limited to Noble Shipping."

"Which makes him the logical choice to break the news. I can't understand why'd you'd question that, Penny."

Good lord, was she overreacting?

"I'm sure he means no harm."

"I fear, Stuart, that he means to usurp Noble Corporation if he's allowed, and I am concerned about this relationship between him, you, and my grandmother. Would you care to explain that?"

"Penny!"

Penny turned to her wide-eyed mother. "I can guess what Grandmother's up to, Mother, and I will not let it happen."

"She's not up to anything, honey," Stuart said, his voice calm. "She's been working with Jonathan directly concerning shipping the timber. Alan was aware of it."

Of more interest to her now was the relationship between Stuart, which implied her grandmother, and her dead husband, the possibility of which had greatly concerned Alan.

Penny heaved in a breath, and said, more calmly. "Is that so?"

"She is only looking out for the interests of King and Gibson." He smiled at her. "Sit down. She's only recently realized your interest in this matter."

Penny rubbed her right temple. The knot on her head was hidden beneath her hairline. "Please, I thank you both for coming, but I have two funerals to prepare."

Clarissa clenched her hands together beneath her chin. "Adel and I will help, of course, darling. We could hold one service?"

"I don't" — Penny closed her eyes — "I don't even know where Harold's body is."

Plumed hat still on her head, Clarissa smiled a painful little smile. "You want to rest? I'll stay with you."

"No, Mama. I do want to rest a bit, but I don't want to tie you up. I'll send Roland when I've decided about the funerals. Right now I'm at the mercy of the authorities."

"I'll find the bodies." Stuart stepped around the desk. "But I wouldn't count on your grandmother waiting for a summons."

Penny heard the front door close behind them. She stepped into the empty hall. Her breast ached from being trussed up in her whalebone stays, but she had more pressing things to worry about — more important than funerals for that matter. She started up the stairs. She'd begin with the suit Alan Noble wore yesterday, which was still in his room.

Chapter Thirty-six

"**I** told them to wait an hour before delivering Clem and Tompkins to Jenkins," Jack told Nathan Stephens. He dragged a chair out from the wall of Humboldt's one-room office in Piotona and motioned for Mike Friedo to sit. "Mike and I brought the skiff up the Biloxi to the landing at Perkiston, then overland and up Red Creek. After we got to Lumberton, we took the spur to Columbia. Delivered him to Sheriff Thornton yesterday afternoon. It was the shortest route I could devise."

The early morning sun shone through the open front windows, effusing the room and the three men in amber light. Nate glanced at Mike, then back to Jack. "So now it's been a day and a half. What's your rationale in delivering Clem to Jenkins and this other fella—"

"Arly Putman," Jack said.

"...to Thornton," Nate finished. "That's not getting that saw fixed."

"Well, it sure wouldn't get fixed any faster if I was there. Mike neither. Lucas is getting the saw fixed, and he's the best man for managing that job. And as far as getting Putman to Columbia, I don't think the time was wasted." Jack took another ladder-back chair and placed it in front of Nate's desk, then sat himself. "Clem's the leader on both jobs, but Eva will post his bail. She'd have posted Putman's, too, but with him locked up for murder in Marion County, I'm hopin' she can't get him out."

"You think a judge will keep him in for killin' a colored?"

"You Northerners are real bad about believing your own propaganda, Nate. Lotsa folks liked Deacon and Rick, and most of 'em are white."

"And once this fella Clem is out?"

"Arly is gonna be blamin' him and Eva for the killings. He's not going to willingly take the blame."

Nate narrowed his eyes. "You're thinking Thornton will issue a warrant for Clem?"

Jack blew out a breath. "I'm hopin', and if he's got enough evidence, which he won't have unless Clem sells her out, he'll issue one for Eva, too." Jack grinned. "She's not gonna risk that happenin'."

"And you're thinkin' what?

"I'm thinkin' she'll have good ol' Clem eliminated almost as soon as he's out of the Harrison County Jail."

"Which means he won't testify against Eva Markiston."

"He never would have," Jack said, "but one of the killers will be dead, and I won't be on the run for having killed him."

Nate snorted, but Mike Friedo straightened his shoulders and said, "I don't think he would have talked either, Mr. Stephens. If you'd seen what Jack did to that bastard's arm, you'd know what I mean. Hell, if it'd been me, I'd have been makin' up whatever Jack wanted me to say."

"Nevertheless, I can't believe he'd go to the gallows for her."

"It would have never gotten that far, Nate. I know Eva's lawyer. It was a matter of criminals accusing her. All hearsay."

"Then why do you think Eva will kill him?"

"Because Clem's stupid. He told Arly the orders came from Eva. She's not gonna like that."

Nate looked Jack in the eye. "It's kind of a convoluted path to justice, don't you think? And if you're wrong about her doin' him in, justice isn't served."

Then he'd get him, but instead, Jack said, "I want Clem dead for what he did in Piotona, but Clem's not who I'm after. Eva is."

"And I want my saw fixed, and sorry, Jack, your vengeance isn't accomplishing that." Nate leaned back and drew in a breath. "Speaking of King and Gibson's fortunes, my shipping agent sent me a telegram this morning. Eva's prospective shipper, Alan Noble, died night before last."

"Alan Noble?" Jack frowned. "The father?"

"Yep."

"That would have been the same night that group attacked the mill?" Jack said. He wanted to ask Nate if he was sure it was the father and not the son, but for discretionary reasons, decided against it.

"Apparently so. The agent thought I'd be interested given that not too long ago, the man came up to see me, curious as to Humboldt's interest in a tract of yellow pine forest in Perry County. Land was owned by the daughter of a Pennsylvania investor who grabbed it up after repeal of the 1866 Land Act. Seems Noble had received a tip Humboldt was prepared to pay above market value to get our hands on it. Noble says he made a quick buy to ensure getting it, but then was given cause to believe that perhaps he'd been hasty." Nate pursed his lips. "I confirmed he'd been had. The man who left this office was not happy."

"And now he's dead," Jack said softly. Interesting.

"But hear this. His son was murdered later that same night."

Well, that answered his unasked question. "Was Alan Noble murdered?"

"Stroke, they think."

"Do they know who killed the son?"

"They've arrested one of his boyfriends." Nate flexed his jaw. "Now do either one of you know how long it's gonna take to get that saw working?"

"They damaged the blades for sure," Jack said. "Lucas took a quick look at the carriage before I left. There's some damage there, but Lucas wasn't sure how bad. I've got a Negro sawyer, who claims he knows that thing inside out."

Nate placed his hands steeple fashion under his chin. "Polly or Floyd?"

"Polly," Jack said. "We're trying to find Floyd. He left while Cranston was still there."

"Polly's full of horseshit most of the time," Nate said.

"He's good, though," Jack said. "That's why you kept him when you bought the mill."

192

Nate grinned at Jack. "You kept him." He looked at Mike Friedo, then back at Jack. "You hired most everybody I have workin' for me down here, and as a result, I've met all Humboldt's quotas, except for last year, and that was because of the storm. Now you listen to me good. The reason, and the only reason, Humboldt invested in that outdated mill on the Biloxi three years ago was the existence of that modified gang saw. It is considered a unique jewel. I want it fixed, and I want it fixed before I have to inform Humboldt it's broke. Do you understand?" He looked hard at Jack. "So far, your value to me still outweighs the damage that follows you around. Don't become a liability to me."

Chapter Thirty-seven

Jack stood on the Leaf River's north, or more geographically correct, east bank, not far from where he'd landed his flat boat. Warm, heavy air had sapped energy from his tired limbs. Once longleaf prevailed along this ancient stream, where now the forest floor sparkled from the sunlight, piercing second-growth, deciduous forest interspersed with young loblolly and slash pine. Some distance away longleaf still dominated, but the sellable pine along Mississippi's interior waterways had been harvested since colonial days. Leaves crunched beneath his work boots and a rare, cool breeze rustled the lush foliage of the oak and gum that had replaced the towering pine.

Nate Stephens had been curious about that land Humboldt allegedly wanted, and his curiosity had led Jack through Perry County on his return to the Coast. Mike he'd sent on home.

Miss Louise Adcock, a spinster near sixty now, had owned a narrow five-thousand acre tract of yellow pine forest stretching roughly five miles from west to east and a smidgeon over a mile and a half wide, north to south; its northwest corner began six miles southeast of the rapidly growing lumber center of Hattiesburg. Carters Creek cut north-south across the tract. There was no real mystery as to the perceived value of the land, except other lumbermen had passed it by as too costly for today's market. Miss Adcock's father paid a buck and a quarter an acre for it back in 1878. Her asking price for Alan Noble had been five per acre. Noble, fool that he apparently believed himself to be afterwards, had paid her price. Valuable yes, but not that valuable, at least not for its timber.

More curious still was what Jack found in the Perry County

plat book regarding what bordered the south and east corner of the tract. That was an old five-hundred acre homestead purchased by one Douglas King when he moved his family from Georgia to the Augusta, Mississippi, area in the early 1830s. According to the county record, the present owner was Penny King, and Jack recalled that Hugh King deeded the family farm to his baby girl at her birth, while retaining a life estate. Good lord, the man had been proud of that kid.

The Leaf River cut through the heart of the property, dividing the farm in two, and from what Jack was told growing up, the early King pioneers made a good income from a ferry they built at the point the old Augusta-Jackson Road crossed the river.

To the south, the river followed its age-old path through forest and disappeared around a wide bend that curved east, then north again, for more than a watery mile. Jack studied the river bank with a practiced eye. The old road was gone now, so was the ferry, but remnants of the highway could still be seen on this side of the river. That's how, floating downstream, he'd found this relatively shallow spot. Before the Indian path became a road, and long before the ferry, animals and men forded here. The Leaf was not an inconsequential river by any stretch of the imagination.

Chapter Thirty-eight

"There were no personal items on him, Mrs. Noble. Do you know how much money he had with him?" Charlie Nixon was standing behind his desk, because she refused to sit. She did not mean to be difficult, but the stays pushed up and hurt her breast when she sat. She asked him to sit, but he wouldn't.

"I have no idea," she answered, "but Harold always carried a significant amount of cash. What about his watch? His keys?"

Officer Nixon shook his head. "I checked every pocket myself."

"Was he wearing his jacket?"

"He was fully clothed."

"So you and Chief Craig believe a thief took everything?"

"We believe the killer took everything, yes."

Penny rued the chief's absence, but at least this man appeared cooperative up to a point. "If David Pascal killed my husband in a jealous rage, why would he have robbed him?"

"The chief asked Sheriff Jenkins the same question."

"And did he give him a satisfactory answer?"

"To make it look like a robbery. In case you're wondering, that was not a satisfactory answer. Smacks of premeditation vice a crime of passion."

Penny leaned slightly forward. "You all don't believe David Pascal did it, do you?"

"I can't say. The chief might could if you'd like to wait. I know he wants to talk to you."

She frowned at the young officer. "For how long do you think I'd have to wait, and what does he wish to talk to me about?"

"I have no idea for how long, and the topic is Florence Noble."

196

"Her death, you mean?"

"I believe so."

Believe so her left hind foot. "Where are Alan's and Harold's bodies?"

"The coroner had them as of late morning. I believe he's now sent your husband's to the livery. Your father-in-law is gonna take longer."

"I want Harold's body home, Officer Nixon," she said, her voice breaking, "but I also want to check the place where he was murdered."

He stared at her one long moment. "We'll get him home for you, but why do you want to check the murder site?"

"I want to make sure nothing was left there."

"I checked the room thoroughly. There is nothing there."

"Before or after the Sheriff?"

"Before."

"So Jenkins took nothing out of the room?"

"He took your husband's body, but whoever took whatever it is you're looking for"—Penny braced, because she was so obviously looking for something—"is the person who more than likely killed your husband."

"Which is my point. I might notice something amiss."

"Something related to the killer, you mean."

"Yes."

"There is nothing to indicate anyone else was ever there, Mrs. Noble. If we were of a mind to prove the absurd, we could confidently argue he cut his own jugular." Nixon shrugged. "But for the lack of a murder weapon, which also wasn't there."

Penny sighed in resignation. "Officer Nixon, I'm not sure if this means anything, but my husband's uncle, Jonathan Noble, was supposed to have returned to Mobile the night my husband died."

Nixon didn't say a word, but she had his attention.

"He was at Noble Corporation early this morning informing the company supervisors that Alan and Harold were dead, and that was after visiting my home. I've already checked the train schedule. It's possible he could have made it back, but I do not believe he ever left Biloxi."

Chapter Thirty-nine

Lyle Jenkins ended his investigation seven years ago because he was her grandmother's man. Chief Craig didn't tell her that an hour later when she and Charlie Nixon returned to the jail from the fire station, where the livery forwarded Harold's body. But what Tobias Craig didn't say spoke louder than what he did. Years ago, Jack Gibson had said the same thing. At that time, Lyle Jenkins' partiality in bringing her father's killer to justice hadn't mattered to the ten-year-old child she had been. The Harrison County sheriff was a good man, and his determination to support her family by seeing James Waymon Gibson hanged was the right thing to do.

The chief of police hadn't brought up Florence's death either, so she asked. He told her that he wasn't quite ready to address that subject with her. She wondered why, but left it at that.

And speaking of suspicions and suspects...

Jon Noble was back at the house when she returned home. He asked, of course, if he might stay, at least until his brother and nephew were buried. Besides, he added, Chief Craig wanted to talk to him in the morning. She gave him his usual guest room, then retired early, but she'd heard him up and about later. First, she thought, in Alan's bedroom, searching, and for sure later she heard him try the hallway door to Harold's room next to her, but she'd locked it. Shortly after, she heard him on the stairs, and she rose, lit a candle, and stepped into the dark hall, venturing no farther than the top of the stairs. Below there was enough light cast into the foyer for her to know he was in Alan's office. She blew out the candle, to ensure he wouldn't see, and was about to start down the stairs, when the light below went out and she heard him close the office door. She turned and hurried back to her room. There she locked herself in, then leaned with her ear against the door and listened until she was certain he'd returned to his room.

Safe in her dark bedroom, she felt her way to Harold's door and entered. She suspected Jon was looking for the simple way into Alan's safe. That meant he was searching for the key and the cipher. Everything in this house, at least at present, was hers and the duplicitous Jon Noble had no business accessing or knowing what was or was not in that safe.

Penny pushed the bottom drawer of Harold's dresser shut, then turned to the bedside table on the other side of his bed, the side he didn't sleep on. The matching side tables each had a single drawer, and the one closest to where he had laid his head was the first place she looked. So far, she'd found nothing to help Tobias Craig, and she figured Lyle Jenkins desired no help. She couldn't get past the thought, however, that David Pascal could use some help. And so she looked for she knew not what. She couldn't sleep anyway with Jon Noble roaming through the house at will.

Inside the other night table, she found a stack of letters. She pulled them out—they were untied—and spread them across Harold's neatly-made bed. There were over twenty letters. Fourteen of them, as it turned out, were detailed missives from his cousin Edith in Mobile, and the remaining six, all brief, had come from younger male cousins in Mobile or Montgomery. The letters spanned years and proved nothing more than courteous correspondence between relatives with references to summer visits and debutante balls, gossip about aunts and uncles and other cousins, favored or not. Then the correspondence had stopped. There was nothing more current than ten years ago. It was odd that none of the cousins had written their sorrow over the loss of his mother. But perhaps they had, and Harold had not kept the sympathy notes. Perhaps he'd refused to even open them.

When she was done, the clock on the mantel declared the time to be two in the morning. She knew the hour was past that, and she scooted off the high mattress to wind the thing. She didn't know the time to set it, but sought the comfort of its ticking.

A floorboard groaned on her way to the fireplace. She looked down, then continued to the clock.

Now the methodical tick-tock filled the room, advancing the inaccurate time, and her mind recollected words Harold had said to her the night he died, something to the effect of Lorraine's soul living beneath the floorboards. Penny no longer heard the clock, but focused on where she stepped. Occasionally a joist groaned, and she stooped to check the board, over and over, until she took to crawling on hands and knees, exploring the polished floor of yellow pine covering Harold's room. Against the wall where the huge black walnut Renaissance bed sat, she found the fruit of what Harold had planted. The loose board started just shy of the bedpost and ran under the night stand containing his relatives' letters, then extended eight more feet to near the right corner of the room. The board's far edge ran along the wall beneath the floor molding. It was easy to raise once the night table was out of the way, then slip back into place under the molding, no evidence of its maneuverability obvious to anyone but a keen observer crawling around the floor and looking for dirty little secrets hidden between the joists of a hate-filled house.

I have decided to take my life. I loved Malcolm Hawkins. I want everyone to know that. He came here from New Orleans. I know everything about him. He used to talk to me for hours. He had a mother and a sister and two younger brothers. He loved boiled okra and jambalaya, the muddy Gulf and the pine forests. He hated the big city. That's why he left. His eyes were green and his hands were strong. When he touched me, I felt alive. He knew so much, and he taught me. I'll never love another like I loved him.

He was almost twenty, five years older than me, and he was mulatto. Mother found that extremely distasteful in itself, his skin being darker. She saw us kissing out by the carriage house. He was very much a man's man to look at him. Handsome and muscular from working at the cannery. Mother said he came to her and wanted money or he'd tell about me. But he told me she came to him and offered him money to leave. He wouldn't take it. He told me so. I guess she thought his leaving would cure me of my strangeness. She understands so little about how I am. Mother says he took the money and wanted more. She's lying. I know he wouldn't have done that. He loved me as much as I loved him.

When Malcolm didn't come to me for two straight Wednesdays, I knew something was wrong. I read in Father's newspaper yesterday that a body had washed ashore at Point Cadet near the pier at the canning factory. That was a week ago, so today I went to the factory and found some men who knew what happened. Authorities told them he'd slipped off the quay and drowned, but I think the authorities lied. I won't go to the sheriff, though. I don't trust him. I know in my heart Mother gave the money Malcolm wouldn't take to someone else to kill him, because he wouldn't go away.

Tonight she brought a prostitute home. The woman's name was Sally. She was close to Mother's age. Mother said she was very experienced and would teach me how to be a man. Mother said if I didn't stay with the woman, she would tell Father what I had been doing with Malcolm. Mother stayed in the room and watched what this woman did to me. She watched everything. She said it was to make sure I cooperated, but I think watching excited her. Mama whipped me with the belt when Sally failed to arouse me. Sally said that might help. It didn't. I cried instead and the whore finally left. Mother said I was a pathetic excuse for a man. I could climax with Malcolm. I wonder if she would have liked to watch that? I bet she would have if I hadn't been her son. And she says I'm sick. I hate her. I want her to die.

"What," Penny said aloud, "kind of person was that woman?"

The clock stopped ticking, and Penny braced as the hair along her spine stood on end. Evil sucked the warmth from the room along with the soothing comfort of the gaslight. Simultaneously, the door between her and Harold's rooms slammed shut, and Penny jumped, clutching the letter and the bodice of her nightgown with one hand as she turned in the inky blackness to confront something she could not see. Unbidden, a whimper rose in her throat, and she slid off the bed and stood, rattled and blind. Heart in her throat, no longer daring to move, not even to breathe, she fought down the urge to scream for Jon. She waited, then trembled from cold that creeped from her heart to seep into her bones. Eyes still on the dark expanse separating her from the door to her bedroom, she reached awkwardly behind her with her free hand. Failing in her objective to find the nightstand, she turned and floundered before she finally touched the stand and found the matches in the drawer. Her shaking hand collided with the coal oil lamp, toppling its heavy chimney. It crashed to the floor, but solid as it was, she sensed it didn't shatter. She struck the match, whirled, and cast her eyes toward the distant door. The portal was barely to be seen in the dark, but she discerned it was indeed closed. She turned back to the lamp, found the wick...

The room glowed in the soft light which caught and reflected Penny's warm breath misting in the air. She straightened and dropped the hand clutching the bodice of her gown, bringing it and the crushed letter to her side. A sudden blast of frigid wind ripped the letter from her fingers with a violent tug and sent it flying into the open flame of the lamp, which fed upon it, manifesting into a fiery pillar that floated up. Penny cried out, and swatted the burning paper. The dying embers half-fell, half-floated to the floor where Penny finished stomping the fire out. Scarcely a written word remained, and none not browned or brittle to the touch.

The door to her room squeaked open, and Harold's room warmed. Penny looked down at the ashes, then touched them to make sure they were cool. Shaken, she made her way to the wall sconce and lit the room. She pushed her door wide and turned up the flame in her room. She checked both rooms. Nothing was amiss. Both doors to the hall were still locked.

Penny blew out the coal oil lamp, then replaced the unbroken chimney. She left the gaslight burning in both rooms and did not fall asleep until first light swathed the yard and deep recesses of the house in misty gray.

Chapter Forty

"Chief."

Toby Craig looked up from his desk to find Charlie Nixon, half hanging through the door he'd just swung wide.

"Somebody here wants to ask you about that body we fished out of the Back Bay last night. Also says there was some goin's-on at the jail this mornin' when he got there."

"Let me guess. David Pascal hanged himself last night."

"I didn't think you'd be real surprised."

"I'm surprised he lasted for even a night, much less four." Toby pushed away from his desk and rose. "So, who's out there?"

From the front of the room, Jack Gibson listened to their conversation. Now he watched the deputy step back and Toby Craig's formidable body fill the doorway at the back of the room. The man laughed.

"Well, well, little Jimmy, ain't you a sight. I was sure Lyle would send a deputy when that news broke. You're not working for him, are you?"

Jack started toward the back. "You know better than that, Marshal, but I can't say he won't eventually send somebody."

Craig stuck out a hand. "You still with Humboldt?" he asked, then motioned Jack into his office. "Sit down and tell me what you heard at the jail."

"I went to check on a prisoner I'd sent down to Lyle Jenkins a few nights ago. No one was really interested in talking to me about him, seems some fella named Pascal went and hanged himself in his cell about seven this morning."

"With what?"

Jack frowned. "Didn't think I was interested enough to ask."

Toby leaned back in his swivel chair and cursed the ceiling. "Rope probably," he said, his voice dripping with sarcasm. "They'll say he asked for it."

"Like I said, I didn't think I was interested enough to ask, but I am now."

"You heard about the Nobles, father and son?"

Jack's heart thumped a little harder. "I know they're dead."

"David Pascal was the son's boyfriend. Lyle Jenkins says he killed Harold Noble, Pascal said he didn't."

"You think he was framed?"

"Conveniently set up is more like it."

Jack so wanted Craig to elaborate on that, but decided it was not in his best interest to do so.

Toby looked thoughtfully at Jack. "I see a lot of potential here for your old enemy."

"By design?"

"Don't know, but if she didn't plan it, I'm sure she'll do her best to take advantage." Toby pushed away from his desk and focused fully on Jack. "Now, you're thinkin' you can identify that body Charlie and me pulled out of the water last evenin'?"

Jack smiled at him. "Lyle Jenkins seems to think I can."

Chapter Forty-one

*O*utside, distant thunder permeated the quiet stillness of the house. Gracie was in the cookhouse out back, cleaning up. She should be mostly done now. Jane was somewhere in the house, working quietly. The guests were gone, except Jon, and Penny wasn't sure of his whereabouts. They'd buried Harold today next to Florence, who lay on the other side of Alan's plot from Lorraine. Penny had buried Harold as far away from his mother as she could. Alan's body, which would be laid to rest between his two wives, had yet to be released. She feared Jon intended to stay in Biloxi until the results of the autopsy were reported and his brother buried.

Penny glanced out the parlor window. To the southwest, an angry sky blended seamlessly with the churning Gulf. Drapes and curtains had begun their dance with the strengthening wind, and she moved through the house, shutting west-facing windows, then started for the stairs. In the foyer, the wind howled, leaving her uneasy, and she surrendered to the need to jump over the space from the end of the Aubusson carpet to the first footer on the stairs, skipping that place where Lorraine Noble had most likely come to rest.

The onrushing storm had darkened the entire house by the time she reached the upstairs landing, leaving the hall a murky cavern etched with the likenesses of Noble family members. Lorraine Noble did not lurk among these. Her portrait was at the end of the hall downstairs, where Florence had moved it when she became the new Mrs. Noble.

From the wide French door leading onto the upstairs portico that looked down on the side yard, Penny took in the purple sky.

Lightning pierced the richness of it, brilliant against the mixed hues of gray and violet. A gust of wind tore at the massive live oak at the corner of the house, churning its leaves to a roar and sending them flying. The wind didn't faze its massive limbs, however, which crawled like pythons near the upstairs porch, then twisted their moss-covered bodies through the well-tended gardens below. Another gust battled her for control of the double doors, but she forced them shut, then listened to the protest of groaning panes. Lightning struck close and singed the air, followed by thunder that shook the house. The rain came in huge drops, which splattered the panes and blurred the violence whipping the tree beyond the door. The drops became so heavy they cloaked the vision of the tree's flailing crown in a curtain of mist and sparkling water. Penny loved nature's awe and stood watching, her nose short of actually pressing against the glass. The wind swelled to a cry that pained her head and ears and eyes and Penny glanced over her shoulder, down the darkling hall, then turned full, heart pounding, to look at an altered space. Her skin crawled. The hall was there, but different, and her warm breath misted in cold air. "I could have never laid him next to you," she whispered.

The swelling cry evolved from anguish to hate, then palpable threat. Penny choked on the unseen danger and pivoted to the French doors and the safety of the balcony, but the refuge she sought was yards away and racing from her with each passing second.

Malice whispered along her neck, and cold burrowed into her bones. She was trembling when a frigid fingertip touched her below the ear. She cried out and turned to face the horror at the same moment she reached back—

The cold brass of the doorknob caressed her palm, downstairs someone called her name. She spun back to the doors, now where they should be. Outside the storm still raged, but inside the hall had warmed. She turned the knob. The door flew in and banged against the interior wall. Penny stepped onto the balcony and let the rain, its scent, and its softness bathe her face and subdue her wild hair. Then Jonathan was there, pulling her back inside and pushing the door closed.

"Lack the sense to come out of the rain, Penny?"

Not her preferred explanation. She wiped the raindrops from her eyes and looked at him, also drenched, then around him and down the dim hall.

He looked with her. "What?"

She shook her head. "Nothing. You didn't beat the rain, I see."

"Unfortunately, no. Do you miss him? Does that explain this bizarre behavior?"

She raised her chin. "Most of my memories in this house are good ones." She needn't tell him the few bad ones more than off-set the good.

"That's ironic, considering what I know of the night Alan died."

She wanted to ask what he knew of the night Harold died, but opted for prudence. "I qualified my statement."

"Does the good outweighing the bad go for Harold, too?"

"We were friends. Harold was always honest with me after we wed."

"Harold was no more honest with you after you wed than before." Jon frowned and waved his arm, taking in, she surmised, the house. "And you, did you plan for all this?"

"You're implying what?"

"Ah, I didn't mean to offend, but marriage is always a bargain. Quite often there are terms in the fine print the signers don't see. You've come out much better in the bargain, at least for the moment. Don't waste yourself grieving for Harold."

"I beg your—"

"Where's the loan document?"

She blinked at him. "I'm sorry?"

"The contract between Alan and your grandmother. Where is it?"

She opened her mouth to speak, closed it, then said, "I would imagine it's in the safe."

"No, it's not. Nor is it in any other place where it should have been inside this house. I've been searching for it the past three days."

"You've been in the safe?"

"Yes."

"How?"

He laughed. "With the key and cipher, of course."

"Where did you get a key?"

"Suffice it to say I have a key. Where is yours?"

"I don't have one, but Stuart was expressing interest in that document the morning following Alan's death." She cocked her head. "Does that interest you?"

"It would, if I were not already aware of his and Eva's interest."

She stepped around him and started for her room down the hall. "I don't know where Alan put it," she threw over her shoulder, then gasped when he caught her arm and spun her to face him.

"It should have been in the safe, Penny."

She wrenched her arm free. "Perhaps he moved it to the corporate office."

"I've checked. Is there any way your grandmother could have gotten her hands on it?"

"I made it clear to Stuart he was to stay out of Alan's things."

At her door, she turned full on Jonathan, who was close on her heel. "Should the thing turn up, it's mine."

"What is yours and what is mine is open to speculation at this point."

"Speculation?"

"You might want to consider working with me, darling niece, or risk losing everything."

"I don't believe for an instant that you'd consider working with me unless you know you haven't got a leg to stand on."

A slow smile moved over his lips. "I want that contract."

"I don't have it, and I find the ease with which you have apparently gotten into Alan's safe disturbing."

"I've known about that safe for the past fifteen years. The cipher is on the back of the painting covering it, lower left-hand corner."

"And the key?" she asked.

"Two. Alan had one, and Harold had one."

Her heart was beating in her chest. A bunny, she thought, in the coils of a snake. "And you have?"

"Harold's."

"And where did you get it?"

"From the top drawer of his dresser."

She wanted to ask how he found it, because as of two nights ago, when she searched Harold's room, it wasn't in the dresser, nothing had been but his ties, which she had routinely retrieved and tied for him. In fact, she'd never seen any key in there. Harold kept his keys on his person.

"How long do you plan to stay in Biloxi," she asked frostily.

"Certainly until I know under what circumstances Alan died and then, hopefully, to lay him to rest." He smiled. "I might be here from now on."

Chapter Forty-two

"You sure I don't need to go out and find Floyd, Polly?"

"Hell no you don't, Mista Jack. Thing woulda been workin' two days ago, but fo' dat piston lockin' up. Cain't blame dat on da saw, sho' cain't. Dat fool Floyd couldn't do no mo' dan me."

Jack was not compelled at that moment to point out that the piston was a major part of the steam engine that was the damn saw. Besides, he was only pulling Polly's leg.

Jack shouted back to the boiler man, who responded it was at 150.

"Water out?"

"Yessuh."

Lucas, standing across from him, gave the pulley a short turn and nodded to Jack.

"Start it up slow, then."

And slow he did. The piston moved as did the carriage gears and the blades of the modified gang saw. Jack, stripped to the waist and hot as the dickens, watched for a moment as did the rest of the evening crew. "Open it up," he cried, and the deafening engine roared into action, piston pounding.

Lucas Frazier grinned at Jack, who jumped down from the platform and yelled at two of the men to feed it. A log filled the carriage and the carriage moved forward.

Jack picked up his shirt from atop a stack of two-by-fours and mopped his forehead. A proud Polly Thom sidled over and joined him. He'd fixed the damaged carriage gears and replaced two original blades, which had to be modified before they could be replaced on the saw. The carriage returned, the crew rolled the log, and the carriage sent the log back to the saw for another cut.

211

He, Polly, and Lucas watched a few minutes as crew and saw whittled that log into pieces of lumber, then Jack slapped Polly on the back, gave a thumbs up to the engine operator, who'd spent the better part of the afternoon switching out the piston, and turned to Lucas and hollered, "You're fully operational. Now can we fill our quota? 'Cause if we can't, Nate is gonna fire my ass."

Lucas had leaned toward him, forehead wrinkled in an effort to hear above the engine and the whir of the saw. He nodded in response, then yelled. "Yep, but I still wanna put one man on guard outside. Don't want any more surprises."

Jack's experience of late was that lone guards ended up dead or hurt, but a full crew of twenty-five men, deafened by a saw-mill's racket, wouldn't hear a group of marauders hell-bent to sabotage operations until they were inside the structure. Despite good ol' Arly sittin' pretty up in the Marion County jail claimin' Eva Markiston was the planner behind the Piotona turpentine explosion, and her faithful henchman Clem having been fished out dead from the Back Bay, he couldn't rule out retaliation by the woman, though another act of aggression against Humboldt would, at this point, add to her problems, not relieve them. That pointed to Jack as the next target, not Humboldt. The lone watch should be safe.

Chapter Forty-three

"What was your relationship with your father-in-law, Mrs. Noble?" Tobias Craig asked from behind his desk.

Carrington Farrah of Farrah, Husbands, and Smith Attorneys at Law straightened in the chair beside Penny. "What is the relevancy of that question, Craig? He was her husband's father."

"We're trying to find out what happened at the Nobles' house, Mr. Farrah."

"His doctor says Alan Noble died of a stroke."

"The county coroner hasn't finished his report."

Alan's doctor and the county coroner were one and the same. That would have been amusing were Penny not so worried.

"Toby, I insist you tell me exactly what my client is suspected of as regards the death of her father-in-law."

The police chief studied the lawyer. Penny figured he wanted to say something off-color and probably would if she weren't present. Something to the effect that Alan's over-worked libido had been directly responsible for his stroke, and that had been Penny's design.

Craig's gaze shifted to her, and her stomach quaked. "I told you what happened the night he died."

"But have you told me everything that happened that night?"

"No," she said, and steeled herself. "And I doubt I ever will."

"Penny—"

But Chief Craig held up a hand, stifling Carrington Farrah's impending admonishment. "That doesn't matter right now. What is important is that your mother-in-law's doctor tells me he diagnosed Florence Noble with a gastric ailment that resulted in bleeding ulcers. She died of internal bleeding and dehydration.

213

He now believes the gastric ailment may have been purposefully induced by poison."

Penny's heartbeat quickened.

"Since your dead father-in-law was found in your room, in a telling state of undress, one might conclude that the death of his wife would have been a welcomed event for the both of you."

Penny steeled herself to the man's glare. "Florence Noble was sick for five days. She died a slow, miserable death. I wouldn't wish that on Sherman himself"—she glanced away—"well, maybe Sherman." She drew in a deep breath and met Toby Craig's eye. "If I were going to kill her, I'd have shot her."

Mr. Farrah sat forward in his chair. "For the love of heaven, Penny, don't say things like that."

"Did her husband appear grieved by her death?"

"Don't answer that," Mr. Farrah said.

She turned to the lawyer. "But, he—"

"Not another word."

"I have nothing to hide."

"Yes, you do, but you don't know it, and prudence is not one of your virtues. Don't say anything else." Carrington Farrah focused on Craig. "Are you opening an investigation into the cause of death for Florence Noble?"

"We're suspicious, Carrington."

Mr. Farrah rose. "Then find some evidence. I'll not have my client brow-beaten and insulted because of 'suspicions,' Toby."

Penny abhorred the familiarity between these two men. Accusing and defending her of plotting murder should be more formal.

"I was hoping to find evidence through"—Craig nodded at her—"Mrs. Noble here."

Penny grabbed the arms of the chair and pulled herself forward, but Carrington Farrah moved to restrain her. "Do not say anything, Penny. This man is not your friend."

She blinked at the family's lawyer. "He's the city marshal, and he's trying to find out if—"

"He's trying to screw your grandmother." Mr. Farrah looked

over his shoulder at Craig, who remained sitting. "He couldn't do it in bed, so he's looking for another way."

Penny felt the color drain from her face. A strange concept, because she couldn't believe she had any color left at this point.

"Let's go, my dear." Farrah looked at Chief Craig. "My client has recently buried her husband. She would appreciate some consideration."

"Does she need consideration for her mother-in-law?"

Carrington Farrah opened his mouth to say something, but must have thought better of it. He reached for Penny's elbow and she rose.

Her stomach burned this morning, and she couldn't remember when she'd last eaten. She had no appetite. Farrah turned her to the door. He was a tall, handsome man, in his forties, his sideburns tipped with gray. He was beginning to display a bit of a paunch. Still, he was the pretty, arrogant, and quite capable sort, who would appeal to Evangeline Markiston. He had taken over as Eva's attorney when hers, an original partner in the firm, died six years ago.

"I'm not done with her, Carrington."

Farrah didn't stop or turn around. "Let us know when you've got something other than suspicions."

"Do you want me to inform you when I get the judicial order for an exhumation?" Chief Craig called from the back of the room.

Carrington Farrah let loose a knowing laugh. "Please do, if for no other reason than I'd be curious to learn how you managed it. I might need to use the same trick one day."

Farrah grabbed the doorknob leading from the building, and Penny looked back. Tobias Craig stood in the doorway to his office. He looked at Penny. "Don't leave town, Mrs. Noble."

"I won't."

When the door closed behind them, Penny looked up at Carrington Farrah.

"This doesn't look good, Penny," he said, still holding to her elbow and guiding her down the steps and away from Biloxi's town hall. "He's implying you and Alan Noble conspired to kill Florence."

"I feared that when he requested I come down here."

"And?"

"If Alan plotted to murder Florence, I know nothing of it."

Mr. Farrah nodded to a passerby, then walked Penny down Main Street to her grandmother's carriage, north of Washington Street. "How long had you and Alan been intimate?"

She pulled her elbow from his demanding grasp. "We weren't."

"Your grandmother suspects the two of you were sleeping together."

Penny grasped the front wheel of the carriage. "Grandmother is angry at me. That's why she's saying those awful things."

"I wouldn't know. What I do know is that Alan Noble was found nude and quite dead in your bedroom around five in the morning just days after he buried his wife, who died under what is now considered suspicious circumstances." He helped her into the open coach. "Eva, in retrospect, says you and Alan had become quite chummy over the course of your marriage to Harold."

Penny fidgeted with her skirt in an effort to sit comfortably. That was to little avail. Her stomach and aching head and sore breast refused her any real comfort. Carrington Farrah climbed in the other side of the carriage. "What did happen that night?"

"He was in Harold's room. I don't know why. I had fallen to sleep reading, but woke when he opened the door. I rose, but before I could get to him, he fell into me. He grabbed my night-gown, it was inadvertent, he was falling. That's how it was torn. He knocked me down and I hit my head on the bed. The blow knocked me out. When I woke up he was dead."

Farrah flicked the reins and pulled out onto the street. "You intend to stick to that story?"

Penny raised her chin. "Yes."

She gazed in the direction of the distant water three very long city blocks away. The day was pleasant, and a salty Gulf breeze caressed the corridors of streets making up the city. The Noble house fronted on Main Street, but they'd turn east on Water Street, then enter in the back from Perrella Street.

"And the champagne?"

"He drank it. That's probably why he was sick."

"Out of two flutes?"

She looked at Farrah. "He was eccentric." She was being flippant, but she felt awful, and she had no intention of confessing to this man what happened that horrible night.

"At which point did you or he remove his smoking jacket."

She looked at him. "I didn't do it."

"I'm your lawyer. Anything you tell me will be kept in confidence."

"Except for what you tell my grandmother."

"We're talking about more than suspicion of murder, Penny. We're talking about suspicion of an affair. It will make great fodder for the gossipmongers along our fair Coast."

"There's little I can do about that but weather it. The man did"—she turned to him and tilted her head to one side—"die in my bedroom."

"And Harold's death?"

"I know nothing about why Harold was killed."

"I'm inclined to believe you there."

She studied Carrington Farrah's handsome profile. "Alan told me that Stuart visited him on the day he died."

"To ask him to extend payment of the loan. I know he refused. Do you know if Harold was agreeable to extending the loan?"

"I do not, but Alan expressed concern that Harold was talking directly to Grandmother."

"About?"

"He didn't say, but my best guess is either me or that loan."

Chapter Forty-four

"The undergarments are part of the problem. Get yourself in bed and stay there for a few days until it heals. I don't see how you're able to fit yourself into that corset with that abscess the way it is."

Penny held the left side of her body still. She had for days. Harold's funeral behind her as well as that awful interview with Chief Craig this morning, she'd relented and come to Dr. Clark, an ill-advised journey, he told her, when he saw the wound. He was all the way in Mississippi City. She should have sent for him to come to her.

"I'm going home after I leave here and doing as you say." Careful, she placed her left arm in her lap, close to the aching breast, and looked at the sharp blue eyes of the man who had delivered her into this world. Her mother's doctor...her grandmother's doctor. He'd been her father's doctor, too.

"If one were poisoned, Dr. Clark, what would the symptoms be?"

"That would depend on the poison."

No feigned surprise. She had suspected, as Florence's illness progressed, that he and Dr. Fritz considered something amiss.

"Something that might work slowly? Arsenic?"

"If I were going to murder someone, it would be my poison of choice—if I intended to get away with the crime that is, in which case the poison would be administered slowly. Penny, Florence's death was not slow."

She frowned. "She was sick five days."

"Discreet use of arsenic would be carried out over years. What Florence was given"—he sat forward in his chair when her

218

eyes widened—"if she were indeed poisoned, was one or two comparatively large doses over a couple of days. That or her ulcers, which Dr. Fritz informed me had been causing her discomfort these past two months, when subjected to the agent, killed her."

"So you think she was poisoned?"

He leaned back in his chair. "I'm not at liberty to discuss this with you. The one thing I am sure of is she was very sick and Peter Fritz believes that's a distinct possibility."

Meaning he was the reason for Toby Craig's remark about exhuming Florence's body.

"And you?"

"I support Peter regarding the exhumation, but that's for a judge to decide."

A decision to be based on testimony provided by a doctor in this case, no doubt. "I've had a rather bizarre two weeks."

"True, and that abscess is affecting you now, but I know how sick you were."

"An autopsy—"

"You're still alive." He smiled at his joke, and she smiled in return.

"On Florence—"

"Might well put you on trial for conspiracy to commit murder."

"I had nothing to do with her death."

"I have known you all your life, so I am inclined to believe you, but my prejudiced opinion is irrelevant. If I had to suggest a killer, my best guess would be Alan Noble. And you might not be aware of this, but your own grandmother pointed out to Dr. Reed yesterday morning that Alan is dead, justice served, and it's best to let sleeping dogs lie."

Jon Noble had expressed the exact sentiment after Florence's funeral.

"Have you discussed this with my grandmother?" she asked.

"I have not, but your grandmother's thoughts on the subject are relayed to me every morning via your brother-in-law. Your

219

grandmother has taken quite an interest in the deaths of Mrs. Noble and both Mr. Nobles for reasons, I'm sure, we both understand. But neither Dr. Fritz nor Chief Craig is going to let this matter lie, I fear, and given my role during Mrs. Noble's sickness I do not intend to discuss the issue further with either you or your grandmother."

Penny squeezed her arm tighter against her side. Now that she had her doctor's permission, she longed for the sanctity of her bedroom and a nightgown.

Hadrian Clark, tall, but slightly stooped, rose from behind his desk. He was well into his sixties, he had to be, but he'd managed to hold on to a head of wavy hair, snow white, and he had always had a pleasant smile with straight teeth. He was clean-shaven.

"What's going on in that house, girl?"

She twitched her lips. "Nothing is happening in that house now. All the participants are gone."

"Alan's brother is still there?"

"Yes."

"And you are still alive."

She stared at him a moment, then laughed. "An ominous observation, doctor. Are you proposing me or Jonathan as the next victim?"

Dr. Clark swallowed and moved around to the front of the desk, where he held out his hand. She placed her right one in it, and he pulled her to her feet. "What happened to that breast?"

"It was an accident. Alan scratched me when he fell. Why will no one believe me?"

"Because I know it's a human bite and an infected one at that."

Chapter Forty-five

Dr. Clark hadn't confronted her regarding what she was hiding, just let her know he knew enough. She hoped he didn't convey whatever his beliefs were to Mark. Oh, she'd love to be a fly on the wall in their office.

She lifted the veil, pulled the hat from her head, and set it on the dining room table near the back door of the huge Victorian on Main Street. She turned and looked at her mother, who'd followed her through the door, then took stock of herself in the mirror over the buffet. This was her home now, shared only with her guest, Jonathan Noble, and her live-in servant Jane Griggs.

She played with a sweat-dampened coil of red hair, then pushed a stray tendril behind her ear. Dressed as she was in widow's weeds, she was thankful to be out of the heat and in the cool dimness of the house. Even in July and August, this part of the house remained cooler than the rest.

"You don't look well, sweetheart. Why were you out?"

Penny had been disappointed to find Clarissa Frederick in one of four oak rockers on the back porch, drinking, Penny suspected, gin from a flask. "I've been to see Dr. Clark."

"What did he say?"

"I need to rest."

"You have had a trying time. Have you eaten?"

Penny picked up her hat, then stirred creamed corn in a dish on the buffet. She covered it with a linen cloth and moved out of the dining room into the hall.

"Gracie is laying out leftovers from the wake," her mother called, still following. "We weren't sure when you'd return. You must keep your servants better informed."

Her mother's slur was slight, but Penny heard and hurried down the hall, away from the slur and the scent of alcohol on the woman's breath. She didn't believe she would ever drink again. "I've got to get out of this dress, Mama, and sponge down before I pass out."

"It's almost ready. Your grandmother should be here any minute."

Two steps up, Penny looked over the handrail at her Mother. "Grandmother is coming here?"

"Yes, honey, she wants to talk to you."

"About?"

"I don't know. You know what a fiddle-brain I am when it comes to business."

Pickled-brain described her better, and Penny silently admonished herself. But her mother's half-formed thoughts, which only aroused curiosity and for which the woman, with increasing frequency, had no idea why she voiced them, were particularly irritating today. Her mother passed her on the stairs, and now tugged on her to follow.

"We need to hurry, so lunch doesn't get cold."

She didn't want to keep Eva Markiston waiting, she meant. Penny didn't feel the same urgency. Still, the woman was her grandmother, a powerful dowager, and she shouldn't let Eva's ruthless behavior affect her own good manners.

In the bedroom, her mother turned Penny's back to her and adeptly started unbuttoning the dress. "Where is the other one?"

"In the wardrobe," Penny answered, then peeled the dress off her arms. Her undergarments were soaked.

"I'll get a—"

A quick knock and the door opened. Eva stood there, regal in black, her white hair expertly coiffed. She looked cool and comfortable despite the long black sleeves.

"Oh, Mama," Clarissa said, "come in. Penny wanted to change into something cooler."

Penny watched her grandmother quietly close the door. "You look terrible," Eva said.

Penny pulled the camisole over her head, tossed it aside, then stepped out of her petticoat. "Thank you, Grandmother. You are the fourth person who has pointed that out this morning."

Her mother poured water from the pitcher into a bowl and rinsed out a rag.

"You're coping well?"

"Yes ma'am."

Clarissa raised the rag to the back of Penny's neck and shoulders. Goodness, it felt good.

"You need"—Eva crossed to the bed and sat at its foot—"to show more grief, my dear."

Penny glanced at her grandmother. "I do grieve for them, Grandmother. All of them, but in my own way."

"Harold was murdered, Penny. You need to remember that, and Alan died in your bedroom under mysterious circumstances."

"He died of a stroke. It was Florence who died under mysterious circumstances."

"Perhaps the presence of his naked body in your bedroom is the mystery. Influential persons have been drawn into this."

Penny frowned.

"Judge Puknay is one of them."

"Your man, I believe. How has he been drawn in?"

"Biloxi's chief of police wants to do an autopsy on Florence's body. Toby Craig most certainly is not my man."

Without a doubt, Mr. Farrah's reiteration of their earlier meeting with the police chief had forced this ad hoc luncheon.

Penny took the cotton dress Clarissa held out to her and pulled it over her head. Her mother began buttoning it up, then pressed her palm against Penny's back. "Do you have a fever?"

"I am hot, as are we all." Penny refocused on her grandmother. "I had nothing to do with Florence's death."

"What was Alan doing in your bedroom?"

"He was sick."

"Was he trying to seduce you?"

Penny shot her grandmother a withering look. "He was dying and needed help." Behind her, Clarissa kept buttoning her up.

"Do you know Jonathan's plans?" her grandmother asked.

"I do not, Grandmother, do you?"

Clarissa stilled, and Eva smiled, then stood to tower over Penny. "Where's the promissory note?"

"I don't know. Do you think he has it?"

The woman studied her long and hard, then said, "I was hoping you could tell me."

Penny wanted to laugh, but a sixth sense warned her not to. "He also asked me where it is. I don't know what Alan did with it, and I've had little time to concern myself with the matter." Her mother patted her shoulder, indicating she was done, and Penny moved to step around her grandmother. She'd regained some appetite and wanted to eat. Eva blocked her path. "He's a threat to you."

"Jonathan?"

"Yes."

"You mean he's a threat to you, if he has that note."

"That, too. But it's yet to be hammered out who is the true heir."

"Could we sort this out on a full stomach?"

Despite the flippancy of her words, she'd spoken respectfully, but Eva's eyes hardened anyway, true testimony to the tight smile that shaped her lips.

"You will, of course, come home now."

Penny glanced at the cracked mirror over her dressing table. If only she could. "I am home, Grandmother."

Behind her, Clarissa said, "You're only seventeen, and you're ill. And you don't need to be alone in this house with a male guest."

Penny looked over her shoulder at her mother. "If it's a matter of propriety, Mother, you are welcome to stay until Jonathan leaves."

"Jonathan isn't going to leave," Eva Markiston said. "Not until the courts have decided the outcome of this mess. That could take months, and I don't have months. And by then, you may well have been eliminated."

"You think he's going to kill me?"

"Someone is killing off Nobles."

"Jonathan is more of a Noble than I am. Besides, Alan's death was natural."

Penny again tried to skirt her grandmother. This time the woman didn't stop her, but turned with her. "Two people standing between Jonathan Noble and control of Alan Noble's company are dead in one night. You're all that's left in his way. He doesn't even have to kill you. He'll do his best to see you hanged for complicity in Florence Noble's murder, or he'll discredit you for your nasty affair with Alan. Everyone will think of you as a black widow. Is that what you want?"

"And moving home will change that?"

"In Mississippi City we have our own circle of friends. You are isolated here in Biloxi."

Penny had stopped at the bedroom door, and Eva took a step toward her.

"There's so much we could do with Noble Corporation."

"'We,' Grandmother?"

"King and Gibson." When Penny continued to stare at her, the woman waved her hand in front of her face. "You and I and Stuart, if I must say it."

Penny pulled the door wide. "First the inheritance must be sorted out. Then I'll listen to your —"

Penny felt Eva's hand on her left arm, then fire sliced her underarm when the woman spun her around. Penny bit her lip and tried to hide the pain. Apparently she succeeded.

"I don't have that kind of time. I'm not going to lose the family business."

Penny yanked her scorching arm free. "You should have considered that before you used it as collateral in this bizarre mess."

"Is this your idea of a payback for Mark?"

"Adel was right about Mark. You did me a favor there. It doesn't change the fact that you care nothing for me or my feelings, nor will you ever if I allow Noble Corporation to fall into your clutches. Now, this is my house. My servants have prepared lunch for the three of us in my dining room. I would be happy for you to join me. Then I will be pleased to send you back to your house, alone."

Head high, higher still if one considered the plumed hat on her head, Eva Markiston walked out of the room. Moments later, a wide-eyed Clarissa Frederick blinked at Penny when the closing of the back door echoed through the downstairs hall.

Clarissa stayed for lunch, and food tasted better to Penny than it had in days.

Chapter Forty-six

"Do you think she knows where it is?" Stuart asked.

"Jonathan thinks so." Bereft of her bustle, Eva flopped in the chair behind her desk and toyed with the lapel on her dressing gown. "The only thing I'm relatively sure of at this point is he doesn't have it or he wouldn't have made us the deal he just did."

Stuart raked his hand over his face. "He's being too accommodating, and why would he want the first option on that cutover plot up in Perry County?"

"And why do we care? We'd have sold it anyway once the timber is off. He's agreed to the pre-forgiveness note. Paid in full. We're not going to get a better deal, and I am personally relieved."

"Penny's not gonna foreclose on us."

"She won't foreclose on you, Stuart, but she'll drive me out. And once I'm out of the way, she'll interfere in operations." She found Stuart's eye, then nodded. "You know that as well as I."

"Once she's wed to him, you've lost all hope of gaining control of Noble Corporation."

"At worst, we'll be where we were before Alan's death, but without the outstanding loan. At best, Penny will have some influence on the board, something she'd have never had with Alan or Harold. Now, we need to convince Penny of the advantages of marrying Jonathan Noble."

Chapter Forty-seven

"**W**e appreciate your attendance this morning," Marcella Lewis said to Penny and turned to include the chattering groups of retreating women. "Do we not, ladies?"

"Of course," one responded. "Very much."

Tallulah Wayne, whose response was noncommittal, certainly was not appreciative. Few of the other women even bothered to turn her way.

"Particularly given your circumstances," Prudence McKnight said.

Prudence was a name Penny found easy to remember, particularly when the woman pointed out that Penny was anything but prudent by attending this meeting so soon after the deaths of her husband and in-laws. She'd buried Harold only four days ago. Her appearance was met with shocked expressions by all. With the exception of Marcella and the unflappable matron, Angelina Ladner, none of the eight women offered her more than a nod when she walked through the Lewises' door. No doubt the disasters at the Noble House had led to the assumption of an alternative plan for the play troupe, which Marcella would have enacted this morning had Penny not appeared with a proper update of the effort, forcing Marcella to keep her plans for a coup to herself. So, Penny brought the Coast Arts Association up to date, ignoring its members' silent censure, both to defy her grandmother's warning and to lend credence to her own determination to make a life for herself among the Noble family's elitist friends.

She did a credible job presenting the program to the group, if she did say so herself. Florence's notes were well organized, and an hour with the Masons yesterday followed by the reserving of rooms at the Magnolia Hotel brought Florence's preparations up to date. Penny had even sent off a telegram to the New York-based troupe, whose general manager, Phillip Baker, replied with a confirmation telegram to the remaining Mrs. Noble.

"It is comforting to know the show will go on," Marcella said, looking down her nose at Penny.

"Not only will, but must," Penny said to Marcella, "given the reservation fee for rooms at the hotel is non-refundable." A not insignificant sum, and without the Noble donation to the association, the treasury would feel the pinch. They didn't want to lose that money...or future donations. Penny picked up her reticule, thanked Marcella for hosting the meeting, and followed two other upstanding ladies, talking exclusively to each other, through the door.

Grace saved her in the form of Angelina Ladner, who touched her arm and thanked her for her service and dedication to Florence. "Call on me, should you need any help," the woman said. Ahead of Penny and Mrs. Ladner, members turned and looked at the stately matron, who did not appear to notice their interest at all.

Keeping busy made coping easier, and having this first step in her only tribute to Florence Noble underway, Penny was ready to focus on Noble Corporation. She made an appointment to meet with Mr. Gates the following morning at nine.

Penny started writing acknowledgements after lunch, almost thirty for Alan alone, then others she combined with Harold's, even Florence's, whose acknowledgements she'd yet to finish.

In the late afternoon, the sky clouded and the house darkened. Though the equinox had come and gone, summer ignored its passing and clung to Mississippi as it did most every October. Today, the sigh of the wind and the growl of thunder filled Penny with trepidation. It wasn't the storm, but the anticipated change within the house itself, and she considered riding it out in a rocker on the back porch.

Gracie floated quietly through the rooms, lighting gaslights and the elaborate coal oil lamps. Penny looked up, but finding the woman ignored her, she glanced away. Not so the light-skinned Jane, who stood near the parlor door watching and waiting. Jane cast Penny a smile. Penny smiled in return. Gracie turned and watched them both with dark, non-committal eyes. Penny forced herself calm. The storm blew around them to the northeast.

Penny dined alone on roast and peas. At nine, Gracie took her leave with little fanfare and stepped into the brooding night, filled with the sound of distant thunder, but no rain. After offering Penny a cup of chocolate, which she declined, Jane retired to her room in the back. An hour later, alone with the oppressive quiet, Penny stacked her completed acknowledgments on Florence's secretary, then startled when a chill wind wailed from the fireplace, gathered the letters, and spewed them across the carpet. Penny, uneasy, glanced around the room. She considered leaving the letters scattered until morning, but told herself she was being silly. She gathered her letters, restacked them on the desk, and with thumping heart, turned the valves of the three wall sconces, lowering one light to mere glow. The other two she shut off completely, then hurried out. She stopped at the safety of the threshold and forced herself to look back into the dim room. In the hall, she pulled the door shut behind her with a click and started for her bedroom. She wouldn't sleep there, but in Harold's room. Though she tried, she hadn't actually slept in her bed since the night Alan died.

Penny jumped when the door joining her bedroom to Harold's flew open. She'd been laying out her nightgown. "Pack a bag," Jonathan Noble told her.

"I beg your pardon?"

"You're going home."

She narrowed her eyes. "You've been talking to my grandmother, haven't you? Well, I am home."

"You're sick. I haven't the time to take care of you and at best, our cohabiting in this house is inappropriate, particularly in the wake of your liaison with Alan."

Tense with righteous anger, Penny returned to the drawer of

her highboy. "I had no liaison with Alan. And if you're so concerned with appearances, you go live with Grandmother."

His fingers bit into her upper right arm, and she let out a little squeak as he spun her away from the dresser and into the wall. "Pack a bag," he ground out. "I'm taking you to your parents' house, right now."

Stomach queasy, heart pounding, Penny stared into Jon's dark eyes. "Let me go," she spat.

He glared at her a moment, squeezed her arm until it hurt — she thanked heaven it wasn't her left arm — then pushed her again and let her go. "Pack now or I will bodily throw you in the carriage myself. This is something for you to work out with Eva."

She rubbed her arm. "Let's go," she said, starting around him. "I'm not packing anything, because I'll be back as soon as I've spoken with Grandmother."

Chapter Forty-eight

"This is getting to be too much," Stuart Frederick said.

Eva held up the hypodermic, then rolled up her sleeve. She inserted the needle just below the inside of her elbow. "I've used the stuff for years. There's nothing to worry about."

"You use a small amount, when you're depressed, you say. You've been increasing Penny's dosage every six hours."

"I assure you, I know what I'm doing. She'll be all right, but for being dependent on my will."

"She was already sick with something. You could kill her."

"Oh, pshaw. Last night you worried you'd hit her too hard." Eva pulled her sleeve back down. "You reminded Adel to send a cable from Nashville?"

"Yes."

"Clarissa?"

"Had gin for breakfast. She's probably sleeping by now. I hope Adel can wake her so they can make their switch."

Eva placed her needle back inside its pine case. "Everything will be fine, Stuart."

Stuart turned and looked at the woman. "Fine?"

She laughed. "Fine as regards the blow to her jaw."

"I hope to hell it's not broken. Wouldn't she make a lovely bride then?"

"It's not broken. I checked."

He turned back to the sun-speckled garden. "We're using the wrong tactic with her."

"I don't have to worry about tactics with her. I'm not going to settle her in Alan Noble's house, then have her betray me when this windfall finds her."

232

Stuart faced her again. Eva sat nonchalantly in her chair, a smirk on her lips. "Who betrayed whom, Eva?"

"Do you think that little ninny would have agreed to give up Mark Reed to ensure King and Gibson a shipping line?"

Stuart turned away. "Yes, and hasn't that worked out marvelously."

She shrugged, and anger washed over Stuart. "This is reckless. The authorities have been talking to Penny. She's a suspect in a possible murder, and now you've kidnapped her."

"In a few days, Penny will be begging to do my bidding. She will marry Jonathan Noble. The companies will be combined. I'll have my shipper and my loan paid in full. You and Jonathan should work well together, don't you think? And both of you will get along well with Thomas Gates. He's a very agreeable man. And if he proves less so, you will assume his position within Noble Corporation."

Stuart stared at her, and she leaned back in the swivel chair. "Yes, I thought that might make you feel better."

"Noble Corporation has a board of investors, Eva. It's not going to be easy ousting Thomas Gates."

"Then hopefully we won't have to. I'm sure Jon will help us decide."

Stuart rolled his eyes. "Jonathan is not going to help with anything. You're giving him the only thing he wants, no strings attached."

"We'll have our shipper. Next year, our buyers will provide the shipping. We've just got to get our foot in the door."

"Have you considered what he really wants with Penny? What he's always wanted from the beginning?"

"He wants to go into the canning business, Stuart, the *canning* business. The same thing that so enamored the Reeds about Penny. The same thing their reckless son jeopardized when he fell prey to Adel's charms."

Chapter Forty-nine

"Fella here wants to see you," Charlie Nixon said to Toby, then stepped aside for Thomas Gates, executive vice president for operations at Noble Corporation.

He was middle-aged, balding, tall, and by Toby's standards, a bit on the scrawny side, but a soft-spoken man, who, based on Toby's previous conversations with him, knew his job. Truth was, Toby wasn't sure what the title entailed, but he gathered the man had been Alan Noble's right arm. Toby had interviewed him a week ago as part of his unofficial investigation following the murder of Harold Noble. Toby rose and stuck out his hand.

"Got an issue I'd like to discuss with you, if I could," Gates said, taking the hand.

"Is this about Harold Noble's death or Alan's?"

"Both, indirectly."

Toby nodded to a ladder-back chair in the corner, which Gates pulled closer to the desk. "Penny Noble stopped by the office three days ago. She arranged to meet with me at nine Wednesday. Her goal was to start learning about the business. Mrs. Noble did not make her Wednesday morning meeting with me, nor did I hear from her. Jonathan Noble, however, has been at the office every day since his brother died."

"Isn't that to be expected?"

"Normally, and but for the nonappearance of Mrs. Noble, I would begrudgingly cope." He cleared his throat. "But I've been part of Noble Corporation for almost thirty years. I came on before Horace Noble, the patriarch, passed from us. Neither he, nor Alan, wanted Jonathan involved in the day-to-day operations of Noble Corporation proper. As a young man, he was a gambler and a womanizer. He was undependable at work and, as I understand it, at home, and was sometimes in trouble with authorities. Once as a teenager and again in his early twenties, he was arrested for manslaughter. In both cases he argued self-defense and was acquitted.

"The father left management of the shipping branch of the company to Jonathan in deference...or under duress...to Jon's mother, Horace's second wife, of whom the man was exceedingly fond. His marriage to her brought Noble Corporation the shipping company in Mobile that the dear lady's grandfather established well before the War. Though Jon heads the department, he remains subordinate to the Noble board, a wealthy and savvy group of investors. The old man hoped this ploy would keep both Jonathan and Noble Shipping on the straight and narrow."

"And has it?"

"In a sense, but only because much of the autonomy originally intended for Jon was usurped by his brother and drawn under the purview of the board proper. Jon has chafed for a long time under this arrangement."

"How did...?" Toby had only a rudimentary idea of how businesses worked and this one seemed a little more complicated than the local general store.

"Jon tended to overextend his assets. More and more control was required to keep the department out of trouble. He often accused the board of overextending him, but reviews indicated that with better management, there would have been no problems. Sometimes, Noble Corporation's demands resulted in strained scheduling for Noble Shipping, but Jon's primary complaint was funds, meaning Noble Corporation was slow in paying shipping charges. Such abuses are not unusual in cases where the subsidiary is part of the larger company. Jonathan felt more put out than most because it is a family business." Gates squirmed in his seat. "I do know that Alan was concerned by Jonathan's recent animosity regarding Noble Corporation's failure to reimburse Noble Shipping, and Alan had warned me to be on the lookout for some sort of retaliation on the part of his younger brother."

Toby drew in a breath, and Thomas Gates held up a hand. "No, Chief Craig, I know what you're thinking. I am not accusing Jonathan of plotting murder against his brother. What I am worried about is the young widow Noble. She indicated a strong interest in Noble Corporation. Between me, you, and the light post outside, the bylaws of Noble Corporation, as written, forbid Jonathan Noble to sit on that board. But, bylaws may not hold up in court. Right now, Mrs. Noble is the heir to the company, and I am concerned as to her whereabouts."

"You've been to her home?"

"Late Wednesday morning after she missed our meeting. I wished to avoid meeting Jonathan, who you may know is staying there. The servant said she had taken ill suddenly and was recuperating at her parents' home in Mississippi City."

"Did you go to Mississippi City?"

"I sent a note yesterday. About two hours ago, I received this." He pulled a piece of paper from the inside of his jacket and laid it on the desk in front of Toby. "From Carrington Farrah, Mrs. Markiston's attorney."

It was a power of attorney granting Eva Markiston temporary operational control of, Toby squinted, a whole series of properties and authorities were listed, but what it boiled down to was Noble Corporation as a whole as well as the Nobles' personal properties.

Toby looked at Thomas Gates, who was studying him with the same doubt in his eye that Toby felt in his gut. "Does Jon Noble know about this?"

"He does, and does not seem disturbed in the least. The power of attorney was accompanied with a note, which stated I was hereby advised to address all matters pertinent to Mrs. Noble with Mrs. Markiston."

"You'd have been okay, but for that power of attorney," Carrington Farrah said.

"That was Jonathan's idea. The board has him hamstrung."

"The thing reeks of wrongdoing."

"You witnessed it," Eva said.

"I trusted you."

She laughed. "Never. Like me, you didn't think we'd be caught."

Carrington scowled. "Where is Penny?"

Eva whirled from where she had stopped her pacing and glanced at Stuart Frederick, then her lawyer.

"She's in Baltimore with her mother."

Carrington looked at Stuart, who rolled his eyes.

"When," Carrington ground out, "will they be back?"

Eva seemed to be thinking about her answer, so Stuart said, "The end of the week."

"Well, Toby Craig wants to see her. He actually used the words 'foul play' to me, and considering he told her not to leave town, you need to come up with something more acceptable in regards to her location."

Eva narrowed her eyes at the directive. "What are the chances of Florence's body being exhumed?"

"Growing. For Penny's sake, be careful."

"Damn Tobias Craig to hell."

"He's not letting go of Harold Noble's death either."

Stuart turned to the windows looking out on the garden in back of the house. Across the way, Charlotte tossed out a pan of dishwater. It was a lovely morning—or should have been. What flowers summer's heat hadn't killed still bloomed.

"If I remember correctly...Stuart"—reluctantly, Stuart turned and looked at the lawyer—"Craig was at the scene of Harold's murder when the sheriff arrived."

Eva stepped away from her desk, placing herself between Stuart and Carrington. "And if memory serves, everything in that room had been removed. It was a robbery."

Stuart caught Carrington's eye and grimaced. "Yes, by a distraught, jealous lover. Craig's no fool."

"No doubt," Carrington said, "Toby knows what happened to Harold and why. Wish someone would tell me."

Fists clenched, Eva stepped roughly toward Carrington. "He

does not know the entire story, nor do we, so he can't prove anything."

"He can go to a U.S. marshal, who could come in and investigate the recent suicide in Lyle Jenkins' jail."

"Bah. Craig would spit on a federal before he'd work with one," Eva said and resumed her pacing.

Stuart watched her, step by determined step. "Jonathan still has control of shipping."

"And I still can't get my timber to the yard," she spat.

"We could afford shipping, though, couldn't we, but for a burned-out turpentine still?"

Carrington groaned. "And the whereabouts of the promissory note to Alan Noble?"

Stuart shook his head. Not for the first time since he'd signed that thing, at Eva's direction, he felt like an idiot.

"Could Jonathan have it?"

"We are relatively certain Jonathan does not have it," Eva said.

"The executor could have it," Stuart said, disinterested.

Carrington laughed. "Harold was Alan's executor, and for your information, Harold didn't have a will. It's all moot, anyway. Penny will get everything if we can keep her out of jail. I'm sure she'll forgive the loan."

Stuart snorted, and Carrington eyed him. When Stuart said nothing more, Carrington walked to the hat table near the door and picked up his black Homburg. "Was it always your plan to trap Alan Noble into this agreement, then eliminate the entire Noble family?"

"Go to hell, Carrington," Eva said.

"I fear you wouldn't be away from me for long."

"All I've done is taken advantage of an opportunity."

Hat in hand, the lawyer turned once again to Eva. "As long as you're not making opportunities, dear lady. Penny needs to be here taking charge of Noble Corporation. If she is in Maryland, get her home."

He disappeared out the door, and Eva turned to Stuart.

"Well?" he asked.

"When will Adel and Clarissa be back?"

"Seven days, per your instruction."

"Send them a telegram. Tell them Penny will be married in four, and they need to start back now."

"Do you intend to inform the groom of the change in date?"

"He won't have a problem."

"Dammit, Eva, isn't the man making you the least bit suspicious? After he marries Penny, he'll have everything. Wouldn't it be better to keep Penny?"

She laughed. "And deal with what we have created the rest of our lives? Better he takes her off our hands. Besides, if we double-cross him now, we'll lose our shipping."

"Will the bride be ready in four days?"

"Yes, we'll just have to increase the dosage on the treatment."

"She's sick —"

Eva whirled. "For the love of god, Stuart, we've come too far to back off now."

Chapter Fifty

Tobias Craig reached for the doorknob, but didn't grasp it before it pulled away and Charlie, who started at the sight of him, stepped out the door and onto the shade-covered veranda that stretched around Alan Noble's Biloxi home.

"Did you need to come in, boss?"

"Not unless there's something you want to show me."

"I didn't find anything." Charlie stepped full onto the porch and pulled the door shut behind him.

"Well, tell me this, did you find anything that indicated something might have happened to the young Mrs. Noble?" Toby turned toward the steps, but Charlie stopped.

"According to that servant, Jane Griggs, she heard Penny Noble go upstairs to bed Tuesday night. She was gone the next morning, her bed still made, her clothes still here. Eva Markiston sent word early that morning that Mrs. Noble had gotten ill during the night and returned to Mississippi City and planned to remain there indefinitely."

The same story Thomas Gates had relayed to him. "Did you ask the Griggs girl if she found that peculiar?"

"You know how those people are, boss. They mind their own business. At least they pretend to. But that older woman, Gracie, the housekeeper, said Jonathan Noble spends the time he's not out searching the house for something. Went through all the desks, then the bedrooms upstairs. Said he finally stripped the beds and searched under the mattresses. I don't think she would have brought it up, except that it gave her a lot of extra work and knocked her nose out of joint."

"Did he find what he was looking for?"

"She doesn't know."

Toby took a step down and stopped. "Which one of them cooks?"

"Gracie, now, but according to her, Alan Noble fired the cook around the same time his wife got sick." Charlie smiled. "Her name is Dot Sachs. I knew you'd want to know."

Toby nodded. "Interestin' he fired her."

"From your fishin'," Charlie said, "I'm assumin' you didn't talk to Mrs. Noble either."

"According to her grandmother, who wanted to personally assure me that her granddaughter had not flagrantly ignored my 'advice' she not leave town, simply acquiesced to her family's wishes that she get away for a few days with her mother, she is in Maryland, but will be back in four days. So much for bein' ill."

"Did her grandmother say anything about the widow Noble remarrying?"

Toby, one foot down a riser, the second still on the porch, stopped short. Charlie was gazing at him with a grin that was growing wider by the heartbeat.

"I take it she didn't?"

"What the hell are you tryin' to say?" Toby asked.

"According to the older servant, Gracie, Jonathan Noble is marrying Penny Noble the end of this week."

"And you couldn't have told me that at the start?"

"I figured the grandmother told you."

"Well, she didn't. Her husband hasn't been dead two weeks, and Jon Noble's old enough to be her father. Not to mention, they're related."

Charlie stepped down and around him. "Not by blood, and don't take society's misdemeanors out on me, Chief. I'm only relaying what I've been told, like any good detective would."

"And why didn't Eva Markiston"—he followed Charlie down the steps—"tell me that when she went out of her way to talk to me today?"

Toby walked side by side with Charlie down the shaded brick walk leading from the front porch of the house to Main Street.

"My guess," Charlie said, "would be that she's a contemptuous, self-assuming matriarch who felt it beneath her to even have to speak to you in the first place."

The sidewalk ended with the shade near the surrey Toby had taken to the Frederick house. Charlie climbed onboard. Toby was steaming, and not from the October heat. He was more than happy to let Charlie drive.

"Of course," Charlie continued, "she probably didn't want to waste time dealing with how she knew you'd react and all the questions you'd start askin'." Charlie flipped the reins and the city's old workhorse started off, pulling the carriage behind it. "Now answer me this. What's the advantage of that girl marrying Jonathan Noble?"

"It consolidates power. I imagine the idea is Eva Markiston's. That gal is gonna do what she's told."

"Noble would have to be in agreement."

"And he would be, don't you think? Especially if he's thinkin' she's gonna inherit everything. Could you get that nag moving a little faster, dammit. Stir up a little breeze."

Charlie clicked his tongue at the beast, and they did pick up a little speed, but not much. They turned east onto the well-worn Biloxi-Pass Christian road paralleling the L & N Railroad tracks, then took a left on Perrella and another left on Washington. At Main Street, having circled the block, Charlie turned north and headed back to the town hall.

"Boss, you'd think one day that Markiston woman would put someone she couldn't control in these positions."

"Oh, I'd bet she has," Toby said and shot Charlie a knowing look. "But those mistakes she would correct."

Chapter Fifty-one

Dot Sachs' eyes widened, and she lifted her hand and pointed a thick index finger at Toby. "Miz Florence hired me six yeahs ago. She ain't neba got sick eatin' my cookin', but Mr. Alan fahd me, him say, fo' 'zactly dat. Didn't hab no business runnin' me off. Wouldn't a 'appened if she weren't laid up in da bed." The colored woman, her face gleaming with sweat, lifted the cover to the pot on her wood stove and stirred. Steam and the smell of cooking collards filled the dim room, lit only by a greasy, east-facing window. "Fat ol' man," Toby heard her say under her breath. Again, Dot turned on him, this time brandishing her wooden spoon like a weapon. "If'n it be my cookin' makin' 'em sick, how come dat ol' hog 'imse'f didn't die? Et evahthin' I put on 'is table fo' all dem yeahs."

Dot lumbered toward the rough sideboard, the biggest piece of furniture in the detached kitchen out back of her house. There was no breezeway attaching the two, but the small kitchen had a high, open ceiling, and a covered porch, and it had been built, for-ever and a day ago no doubt, off the ground. The unpainted floor vibrated when she walked. Dot Sachs hadn't missed a meal in a long time, either.

"Actually, Alan Noble did die," Toby said and immediately regretted his words. Dot turned with the grace of a bull elephant and just as mad. "Not from my cookin' he din't!"

Not unless overeating really did kill a person as quickly as angering the cook. Toby held up a hand. "No, Aunt Dot, not from your cookin'. But he died from something and so did Harold No—"

"Him wuz stabbed."

243

"Yes'm, he was." Actually his throat was cut, but Toby would leave it at stabbed. He yanked the handkerchief from his back pocket and wiped sweat from his forehead. Damn, it was hot in this cramped space, and he looked out the rather wide, low door to the porch, then the shade-mottled yard beyond. "But my point is there's been a lot of dead folk in the Noble home lately, and I wanted to ask you some questions—"

"'Bout pois'nin'?"

He twisted back around and had to wait once again for his eyes to adjust to the dark room. The woman was so black in her own right the kitchen had swallowed her up. Ah, there she was, looking at him. "Yes," he said, "but could we talk outside? I'm 'bout to burn up in here."

"Water well on da side ober der"—she indicated with a nod. "Spring fed. Like ice in da winnah. Cup's on a chain." She was stirrin' that pot again and his mouth watered. "You wantin' some dinna?"

He did, but he shouldn't. "No, I'd—"

"You 'fraid a' my cookin'?"

At the door now, he stooped to see back inside the cabin. She was at the stove, stirrin', grinnin', and still aglistenin'.

"Make me a helpin'," he said.

"You actually served the meals?"

"Breakfas' mostly. Usually, dems din't eat a noon meal. Durin' da week, dinnahtime be at night since da men folk wuz at wawk all day. Lots a' times Miz Florence, an' later Miz Penny, et out, ladies' luncheons an' such. But der be times when Miz Florence would 'av 'er lady frenz to 'er house, an' I'd make a big lunch, but mosta time Miz Florence an' Miz Penny 'ad what wuz lef' from da night befo'. Always 'ad Sunday dinna afta church, dough. Sat'day be my day off. Jane wuz der dat day."

"When was her day off?"

"Monday. Gracie was off Sat'day like me."

"Mrs. Noble never cooked?"

"She did, so'd Miz Penny. Sometime on Sat'day. Da only time

dey really bovvered me wuz da holidays or birfdays when dey'd 'av somethin' special dey'd wanna make. If eba I 'ad me a han-kerin' to poison one of 'em, dem times wuz it.

"What time did you leave in the evenings?"

"Seben to seben wuz my workday, but gettin' Mr. Alan fed breakfas' befo' he left fo' work wuz mo' impo'tan' dan when I gots done nights."

Long work hours, but Toby understood the Nobles to be generous with their servants' pay. "Who cleaned up?"

"I cleaned my kitchen an' pots an' pans. Jane an' Gracie did da china dishes afta. I wanted my kitchen ready when I gots back next mawnin'. One or two times, when Jane be new an' din't know no betta, I come in to fine one ob my pans wif bu'nt milk still on da stobe. Miz Florence, an' latah Miz Penny, like choc'late befo' dey go to bed." She nodded to his plate. "You done?"

"Yes'm. Thank you. Best collards I've had in a long time."

"You gotta wife?"

"Nope."

"Need a cook?"

He smiled. "Can't afford you. Wish I could." With his hand-kerchief he wiped juice from the oil cloth covering the crate that had served as their table. He rose from the ladder-back chair, which Dot had taken from the porch, and briefly languished in a breeze that cooled his sweat-soaked neck and rustled the yellow-ing leaves of the pecan under which they'd eaten. Apparently Dot ate out here a lot. He picked up the chair and followed her back to the cookhouse.

"So why do you think he fired you?"

She set down the wooden bucket in which she'd placed their dirty dishes, wiped her hands on her soiled apron, then pursed her lips. "I'm thinkin', Mista Craig, 'im jes' wanted me outa dat 'ouse."

Chapter Fifty-two

"**W**as this Grandmother's idea or yours?" Penny asked.

"I suggested the union. Your grandmother took responsibility for convincing you," Jonathan said. "This is not how I intended things in the beginning. I'm sorry things went astray, but in the end, things will work out for both of us, you'll see. Trust me."

She leaned forward on the settee, where she sat next to him. "Do you know how she coerced me into agreeing to this wedding?"

The man studied her a long moment. "There'll be no problem keeping you supplied."

"You son of a bitch," she said loud enough for everyone to hear. Adel, standing in the middle of the room with pitiful Mark, glanced at Eva.

"Enough, Penelope." Eva leaned over her shoulder. "Unless you'd like to go to bed without your medicine tonight," she whispered.

Nausea washed over Penny. Her dress was clean, her bottom raw. Her wounded breast hurt, but was healing, slowly. She glared at Jonathan Noble and said no more. Eva straightened and must have signaled Adel, because after a moment, Adel and Mark left the room.

Stuart stood behind the couch, her grandmother crouched at her side. Jonathan, silent, kept his place. "Your mother," Eva said softly, "is upstairs, sleeping. Drunk. She cannot help you, and if you dare try and invoke her, I promise you will find this past week you spent under my care heaven compared to the hell I will force you to endure. Tomorrow you will smile and say 'I do' to Jonathan. Then you will kiss him like you love him, and I will turn you over to his care, in which, I am certain, you will be infinitely happier. It is not prudent to call one's husband a son of a bitch. Do you understand me?"

Penny did nothing.

"Look at me!"

She shifted her eyes to take in her grandmother.

"Say yes, Grandmother."

"Yes, Grandmother."

"Now say thank you for all I've done for you."

Penny stared at her.

"Say it," she hissed.

"Stop it!" Stuart barked, "or I'll invoke her damn mother."

Eva's eyes widened in surprise and Jon said, "That really is enough, Eva."

"She has to learn—"

"I think she's aware," Jon said, rising.

"Fine. As of tomorrow she'll be your responsibility."

Penny wished herself dead.

"Things could have gone so much easier for you if you'd only agreed in the beginning," Eva said.

Penny did not blink. After, she thought. She could die *after* she killed Eva Markiston.

Jonathan reached down and took her hand. "These things can be easily managed."

She pulled her hand from his. She thought of Florence Noble in his arms. A sickly little redhead was the last thing this man wanted to care for. The only thing that would keep him from killing her in the next year would be her grandmother killing him first. Then she'd be worse off than dead. Penny convulsed with nausea, and Jonathan hurriedly followed Stuart from the room. Eva pushed the ancient brass spittoon in front of her. Penny kicked it away and threw up on the carpet.

Her grandmother sat beside her, so that when Penny straightened, her head bumped the woman. Eva put an arm around her shoulders and pulled her close. "Listen closely, Penelope, dear. Tomorrow we will go to that little church your mother insisted on, and you will marry Jonathan Noble or you will literally descend into a living hell. I have your power of attorney." Penny started to shake her head, but her grandmother laid her head against Penny's and made her stop. "You signed it. Carrington witnessed it. You simply don't recall. You are sick and incapable of responsibly governing your own affairs. I've already talked to Judge Puknay. With little effort, I could have you committed to the state asylum up at Jackson, where you will rot, lolling in this self-inflicted addiction you indulged yourself with."

Penny's heart hammered in her head, but she said nothing. Her grandmother curled a wisp of Penny's hair around her index finger, then blew gently on the back of Penny's neck.

"You are beginning to sweat. I will escort you to your room," she said, her hand on Penny's arm as they left the room. The two men waited in the hall. "Penny is tired," she told Stuart. "It's time for her medicine." Penny heard the smile in the woman's voice, but she didn't see it. She didn't look at any one of them, but turned to the stairs. "She'll wake tomorrow," Eva continued, "ready for her wedding."

Chapter Fifty-three

"I'll put a poultice on it to draw the infection out," Mark said. "You've a fever, too."

Clarissa sat on the settee next to Penny. "I wanted to postpone the wedding, but your grandmother insists not, and it will be best to have it done, then you can rest, and we can deal...." Clarissa Frederick's eyes slid to Mark, sitting on Penny's other side. For a moment, his eyes met her mother's, then returned to the pustule in the bend of her arm. The one made by her grandmother's hypodermic. Absently, her mother brushed the gauze covering Penny's wrist. Mark's eyes followed, and after a moment, he said, "Are you all right this morning, Penny?"

"All right?"

He eyed her wrist, then found her face. "Your grandmother says you've been distraught."

Clarissa sobbed, then rose and turned her back on them. Penny looked at her mother five feet away, then toyed with the lace sleeve meant to cover her wrist. "She told you I tried to kill myself, didn't she?"

Clarissa turned and looked at her, then covered her mouth with her hand and moved toward the door.

"She did," Mark said softly.

His long tapered fingers were warm and strong. Gently he wrapped the poultice with a clean cloth. "That is no way to solve your problems."

"Why would I kill myself, Mark?"

"Eva says you've been distraught since I..."

"Jilted me?" Penny laughed. "Why, Mark, you've done what I thought no one would be able to do again."

249

"And what is that?" Though by his tone he knew what she was going to say.

"You made me laugh."

"Then why did you do it?"

"I didn't try—"

"It's the addiction," her mother wailed, stepping back toward them.

Mark found Penny's eyes. "Dr. Clark and I have been wondering for some time what ailed you. This heavy addiction you've developed—"

She grabbed his arm. "I didn't develop this addiction. My grandmother forced it on me, and only this past week." At least, she thought it had only been a week.

He stared at her, and for the first time in days and days, hope cried out to her.

"How," he asked, "did she force morphine on you?"

Penny held up both wrists. "She tied me to the bed—"

"Oh, good god, Penny, enough," her mother said. "Do not say such awful things about your grandmother."

Penny turned to her mother. "I told you. It's true, Mama! And Stuart..." Clarissa, hands over her ears, started for the door. "Stuart," she yelled, opening it.

Hands shaking, Penny sucked in a breath and twisted her head back to Mark Reed, still by her side. "I'm telling the truth."

Stuart came in, took one look at Mark, and asked, "What are you doing in here?"

"Your wife asked me to look at Penny's arm."

Stuart glared at Clarissa. "I told you not to let anyone in."

Clarissa wrinkled her brow. "It's Mark, Stuart. Penny's arm is infected."

"We already know that."

Penny nudged Mark and reached for the gauze-covered wrist exposed by the rolled-up sleeve. Stuart turned from his admonition of Clarissa, took a quick step forward, and took Penny's hand in a firm, but gentle hold. "Stop it, Penny," he said. She snarled, struggling in his hold and forcing Mark to rise. Stuart looked at Mark. "We've finally got the bleeding stopped. The cuts weren't deep, but they are messy. We're not going to unwrap them."

Mark nodded.

"I'm telling you the truth," she cried to Mark. Stuart clasped her to him. That was too much for her to bear, and she arched her back against him and screamed, "Let me go!"

Clarissa twisted her fingers together, then waved her hands, crying fully now. "Penny, please stop this and calm down. You're embarrassing Mark and humiliating yourself."

Penny ground her teeth so hard her jaw hurt. Stuart lessened his hold, and Mark started for the door. "Help me," she said. "You can't possibly believe I want to marry. My husband has been dead only a couple of weeks."

"Your husband rejected you," Stuart said, maintaining his hold on Penny but forcing his words toward his son-in-law.

Mark hesitated, and Penny saw his throat work when he swallowed.

"Mark," Stuart said, "you know she blames Eva for breaking the two of you up. Withdrawal has started. Jonathan is willing to take her—and yes, business did drive his decision, but, at least he's going to provide for her."

"I'll check the poultice after the ceremony," Mark said to Stuart, then found Penny's eyes. "I'm sorry, Penny, but I can't believe a grandmother would do this to her granddaughter. She's strong-willed, yes, but what you allege is sick."

Chapter Fifty-four

Her grandmother studied her face, watching her with gray-green eyes that dared Penny to defy her now. The woman's lips, lacking the fullness and the pink blush that had marked them only a few years ago, smirked.

"Are you feeling fidgety, dear? Nerves would be my guess." She smiled knowingly, pleased, it seemed, with the irony embedded in her lie and reached out to gently stroke Penelope's cheek. "You look pale. Nauseated?" She drew in a breath in dismay, so faux in its inception that Penny's gut tightened and she cramped. "We'll give you more medicine after the ceremony."

To ensure her compliance and subsequent entrance into life in a new hell.

"You do understand?" her grandmother said. When Penny said nothing. The horrible old woman's nostrils flared. "Answer me."

Penelope stared.

"Answer her, Penny," her stepfather said from behind her. On her right, Penny caught a movement from her mother.

Her grandmother's hand—her manicured hand—clamped on Penny's shoulder. Penny cocked her head and looked at the offensive hand. "Answer me, Penelope, right now."

Penny's eyes again found her grandmother's.

That offensive hand squeezed her shoulder, her right shoulder, the one which her festering right arm was attached to. Her arm hurt, and nausea-induced saliva pooled beneath Penny's tongue. Penny spat.

Clarissa cried out, and immediately the pressure on Penny's arm ceased. Behind her, Stuart cursed. Penny heard him move, then felt his hand on her shoulder, staying her from whatever step he thought she might take next.

Evangeline Markiston had stepped back, face bowed and hand covering the spot where Penny's spit landed on her left cheek. Eva looked up, eyes hard, face tense. She glared at Penny, then in a move so fast it was hardly discernable, she slung her right palm into Penny's face.

Penny didn't make a sound, but couldn't prevent her head being turned by the stinging blow. Eva struck again. This time, with her other hand fisted, she hit Penny hard on the right cheek.

Stuart was trying to get between them, struggling to ward off Eva's fists. Penny's nose took a blow, jarring her entire head. She tasted blood on her lips.

"Stop it, Mother. Stop it!" Clarissa joined the fray, trying to pull Penny away. Stuart pushed Eva back. "Oh, dear god," her mother whined. "She's got blood right on the front of her dress."

Stuart held Eva. "Stop it. She's going to get married in five minutes. You can't send her out there beat up."

"Dammit, Clarissa, you and your stupid *church* wedding!" The woman jerked out of Stuart's grasp. "The nasty little bitch!"

Stuart stood tense between Penny and her grandmother, ready to ward off another onslaught. Clarissa was already at the door to the oratory, swinging it open. "Adel?" She stepped across the threshold and turned her head in the direction of the sanctuary. She called again for Adel. Louder. Penny held her hand over her nose. The bleeding had stopped, but her fingers were sticky, and her ears were ringing. She saw her mother raise her hand to someone, then move back into the room, looking at Eva, who was fidgeting, calmer now, swiping at her cheek with a handkerchief. Stuart hadn't moved from where he stood between the offended Eva and the battered Penny. Eva glared at him. "No one has ever dared spit on me."

Adel was at the door. She started in, but Clarissa grabbed Penny's arm and dragged her around Stuart and Eva to the portal.

"Oh no," Adel said. "What did she do?"

"Nosebleed," Clarissa said, pushing Penny toward her sister. "Take her into the sacristy and find a bowl of water. We need to get the blood out of her dress as best we can."

Adel raised Penny's chin, and she chuckled. "She's mussed her hair, too. What in the world is going on in here, Mama?"

"Hush and do as I say. Hurry."

Adel hooked her arm through Penny's and led her across the hall. "Fighting with Grandmother finally came to blows. When will you ever learn that life is better if you don't?"

Penny, her body shaking—she thought more from anger and reaction to the attack than from need to feed the addiction—stepped into the small room. There was a mirror there. "Do something with your hair. I'll find some water."

Adel closed the door. Penny, heart racing, looked at it. She reached for the knob. Now her heart pounded in her chest, throbbed in her head. She opened the door. The hall was empty. Across the way was the hall leading to the meeting room, to her left the closed door leading to the room that kept her masters. She could hear her mother's anxious voice inside, then Stuart's. Penny looked to the right and the back door of the church. That's the one she took.

She smelled freedom in the taste of her blood, in the sour refuse wafting from the alley. She ran a block and a half, and she found the old black man, fresh from a delivery and about to start on his way.

"I'll give you this ring if you'll take me," she said to counter his initial surprise. She glanced back from where she'd come. She couldn't see the church from here, and at present, no one there could see her. Her entire body was shaking, part terror at the thought of capture, part excitement at the prospect of escape, and she wanted to rail at the poor fellow, make him aware of her desperation, but she resisted.

The old Negro looked at her now with a greater degree of understanding. What a sight she must be with her hair messed up and the delicate pearl embellishments on the bodice of her pale green dress spotted with blood. It occurred to her she had blood on her face, too. They'd be searching for her by now. She'd managed to foil this wedding, and her grandmother would be furious. God only knew what her fate would be at Eva's mercy.

He glanced at the ring. Then took her hand, and studied it. "Let me see it."

She reached for the seat and started scrambling up. "I'll take it off my finger when you have me where I want to go. It's not far."

"And where dat be, 'zactly, one mo' time?"

Chapter Fifty-five

"**D**oes Jack Gibson still live here?" Penny looked around the worn woman, who she assumed was the landlady. In the dining room beyond, Penny heard the clatter of plates and flatware against one another, and the intermittent voice of a hardy man. They'd just started eating dinner or they'd be talking more. Penny's gaze darted back to the woman. "I must find him."

"Are you hurt?"

The woman stood much taller than Penny and was proving to be a slow-acting, defensive sentinel between Penny and the men in the room beyond. Penny twisted her fingers together and shifted on her feet. "Why do you ask?"

"There's blood on your"—again the woman's eyes moved over her—"dress. And on your face."

Penny bent her head and looked down at the pearl-studded bodice. Yes, there was blood. That's why Adel had left her alone, to get water, to get it out before the ceremony. Penny laughed, short and soft, then returned her attention to the questioning face of the woman. "Praise the good lord, there is." Penny owed so much to those two drops of blood and her grandmother's slap and the spit she'd mustered the courage to bestow on the whore mother. "I need to find Jack Gibson. If he's no longer living here, do you know where he's moved to?"

"It's lunch time, the men are eating."

Penny's racing heart beat faster. "He's here?" And she started to step—

The woman blocked her path, and Penny looked up.

"You don't look well."

"I'm not well. I need to see him. Tell him Penny King. He'll want to see me." She bridled. "He'll even stop his lunch to see me."

The woman snorted. "Out of curiosity, if nothing else." The woman gave her hands one final wipe on her apron and turned to the dining room. "You wait right here."

Penny swallowed and again shifted her weight. She looked at the bloodstains on the bodice and touched them. She needed to wash her face. She touched her nose. There, she felt the dried blood around her left nostril. She noticed her fingers, still stinging from having twisted them. Yes, there was blood there, too, dried. Lots of it actually. It was a miracle there wasn't more. She frowned and pulled the skirt out in front of her and looked down its front. Small drops of blood had dribbled down her dress all the way to the hem.

A chair scraped against the floor in the room at the end of the hall. Penny brought her head up and let the dress fall back into place. A number of men in her line of sight turned her way. As they did, so did others. She could hear Jack's voice now. One of them laughed at something another said. She could hear the woman. The woman protecting Jack. She couldn't hear what she said. She didn't care. She wondered what was going on in Jack's life now.

His body filled the lighted doorway at the end of the hall, and the plunking of his work boots against the hardwood floor filled her ears. His eyes were fixed on her. Amused curiosity marked his face. He stopped in front of her, quirked his mouth, and cocked his head. "What in the world is happening here, Penny?"

Her heart raced faster than ever, and it was heavy, very heavy, too heavy in fact, for her chest. "Have you a sweetheart?" she blurted out.

He frowned at her.

She swallowed. Her mouth was dry. "Do you have anyone you care about? Anyone you're courting?"

Another shadow darkened the dim entry hall, and Penny looked around Jack. The woman filled the door. For certain she was too old for Jack. Still.... "Is she the one?"

Jack turned to look when she spoke. Behind the woman the men kept talking, disinterested now.

"Take her in the parlor if you want to, Jack," the woman said.

Jack looked back at Penny. "Is she the one what?"

"Your sweetheart?"

He took her by the elbow and turned her to the left and into a lovely, large room with a huge hook rug. Penny turned to him when he let her go to close the door. She was breathing hard, and she swore her tongue was beginning to swell. It was dim in the room, despite the light sifting through the lace-draped windows. It was noon and a hot October sun was beating straight down on the double-story boarding house, like minutes ago it had been pounding down on her, hunkered beneath the seat of that wagon.

"Jacob is in the wagon." She grabbed Jack's forearm. He looked at her hand.

"Who is Jacob?"

"Uncle Jacob. He needs money. He wouldn't take my ring. I need to give him something, Jack. He's such a kind old man, and he came out of his way to bring me here, and I—"

"Sweet Jesus, Penny, shut up." He was already headed to the window. "You've said more words to me in the last minute than I've heard you say in years." He pulled back the lace sheers. He was so calm, looked so cool in work britches and white shirt. A clean white shirt. His face was clean, too. Clean-shaven. He'd have washed up and changed shirts before sitting at whatever-her-name-was' dinner table.

"There's no one out there."

He had to be. She told him to wait. She told him she'd get him some pay if he wouldn't take her ring. Ah, but he'd said that was all right. She remembered now. He didn't want pay, but she was going to get him some anyway. She remembered. She wanted to pay him. But he'd left.

Jack straightened and looked back to her, so she went to the window, too. Yes, he was gone. He'd left her here with Jack. Poor old soul wanted to be rid of her before he got in trouble carrying something like her around in his vegetable wagon.

"What do you want me to do now?" Jack said.

She let go of the sheer. "You've an intended?"

He shook his head. "I'm fond of whores, that's about it."

She felt her skin prickle. "You're still meeting Adel?"

His mouth fell open, but only slightly, then he laughed. "I know lots of whores. But your sister was the only one of her class. And no, I like my whores unattached."

"There's no one special then?"

"For the love of Saint Peter, Penny, no."

"I won't stand in the way of your liaisons."

His brow knit.

She took a quick step toward him. Again she touched his arm. Again he looked at her offending hand. She dropped it. "You won't have to touch me if you don't want to." Tears stung her dry, burning eyes, and she blinked, then looked away. "I'm used to that."

"What are you talking about Penny?"

She caught her breath at his tone. She couldn't anger him. Couldn't, not now, and he was staring at her as if he thought her mad. He waved a hand toward her, taking her in head to foot.

"You show up here, beaten and bloody in a formal dress you look like you've brawled in..."

She laughed at that, at the way he said it, more like Jack, now. Yes, she'd brawled of sorts. Brawled with her grandmother, and won, at least initially, without throwing a punch.

"...rambling on like a madwoman."

Madwoman. That sobered her. She looked away, toward the window. Perhaps she was mad. Mad for the growing need of that horrible drug. That dependency, which she detested, which now caused her heart to sink and her stinging eyes to tear anew.

"You have missed your wedding, haven't you, Penelope dear?" he said, his voice high with faux sweetness. "Jonathan Noble. Your uncle of sorts. Shocked the hell out of the whole Coast." He laughed. "All but me that is."

She held her head high, and un-fisting her sweating palms, looked him in the eye. "Yes, left him standing at the altar."

He looked over her blood-stained dress. "Against your grand-mother's wishes?"

"Yes."

"I take it your grandmother doesn't look as bad as you do, or you wouldn't be needing me to help you out of this predicament."

Penny sucked in a breath. "My grandmother is in fine health and form, I can assure you."

He lifted a hand to the back of his neck and started away from the window. "Penny, you are a wealthy widow. She can't force—"

Penny stiffened and pivoted with him as he walked away from her. "She has ways. You have no idea how ruthless she is."

He jerked his gaze to hers. "You don't know who you are talking to, honey."

Heart pounding at her temples, she stepped stiffly to him. "Oh yes, I do, and I've learned more in the last month than you can imagine. I stand by my words. You have no idea."

He laughed, in contempt it seemed. "And what do you want me to do?"

"Marry me."

She was no longer a madwoman. She'd grown two heads and, freakish monster that she must appear to his eyes, she stepped boldly toward him. "I have everything you need to get King and Gibson back, but she has me whipped as I am now. I can't do this alone."

"What about your groom?"

"He's working with her to get everything I have. I'll turn it all over to you if you'll help me destroy her. We can do it in writing if you want. Marry me, please, but we must be quick about it."

Chapter Fifty-six

The first rays of afternoon sun now streamed through the lace curtains covering the windows. The parlor was suddenly stifling, and Jack thought, for the space of a heartbeat, he might suffocate. "Have you lost your mind?" he said finally.

"No," Penny said, "I've had it stolen from me."

Her blue eyes looked odd. There was too much blue, too much iris—too little pupil, shrunk now to a pinprick. He thought he'd noticed something about them in the hall, but had dismissed the abnormality as a trick of dim lighting. But it was bright in the parlor, and those strange eyes bothered her. He could tell by the way she kept blinking. Tears, perhaps, but he didn't think so, not any longer. And the way she was talking. Penny never talked like that. She had always been quiet...and shy. And she hated his guts.

"What are you using?"

"Morphine. I'm addicted to morphine." Her voice gave way to a sob.

"How in the world did—"

"We don't have time for this, Jack. Suffice it to say I will return our fathers' company to you, and I will help you destroy Evangeline Markiston. In return, you are saddling yourself with an addict."

"You inherited everything?"

"That could prove a bit dicey. Jon Noble planned to marry me to secure his claim to Noble Corporation, so I know he believes that's a good possibility, but it doesn't matter. Within Alan Noble's personal estate is a significant loan to King and Gibson, which when called due will bring the company to its knees."

"You've seen this contract?"

"I *have* the promissory note, Jack."

He looked her up and down. "Where? Noble's lawyer should have a document like that. It belongs in his company's papers."

"I hid it. I told you, it was a private contract. I removed it from Alan's safe. The sum given to King and Gibson was excessively generous. Alan's investors would not have agreed to it."

"What are the terms for calling it in?"

"Payment in full, at noon, on the first of November."

"How much?"

"Ten thousand dollars."

"When was it made?"

"May."

"That's only six months, Penny. Why would Stuart Frederick and your grandmother have agreed to that?"

"There was an addendum. If I were pregnant by the first of November, the loan was to be forgiven."

Some people had, in Jack's opinion, more money than good sense.

"But there was no possibility of a child, Jack."

Jack narrowed his eyes, wanting to ask, but figuring it really didn't matter at this point if Penny felt the contract had been a swindle.

"I'm not making this up."

Could anyone possibly make something like this up? "What was put up for collateral?"

"I was to marry Harold Noble, which I did. Grandmother put up King and Gibson and a tract of land up in Perry County."

"How big a tract?"

"Three thousand acres."

Jack frowned. "I'm not convinced King and Gibson is worth that much, and I'm positive the land isn't, not for timber anyway. Why you?"

"That is strange. Jonathan told me not too long ago that he suggested me to Harold. Harold always told me Alan handpicked me, but Alan said I was Harold's choice. So, I don't know 'why me.' I do know Alan wanted a grandson."

"Where is the contract?"

She shook her head. "Marry me first."

"Will Eva be able to pay the loan?"

"She doesn't have the money, and thanks to you she can't earn it. She claims to have my power of attorney, so she could conceivably exploit Noble Corporation, but I don't think Jon Noble will let that happen."

Not unless he wanted to save her ass, but with Penny running out on him, he doubted that would be the case. "You can remove the power of attorney—"

"No!"

Jack studied her face—it made no sense for her to be lying. Penny had always been honest to a fault. She sometimes erred on the side of forthrightness, and when it came to marrying, the last person on earth she'd have wanted to marry was him. Jonathan Noble's claim to Noble Corporation had to be at risk, and Jack wondered how much the man would pay to get Penny back.

She was watching him, her big blue eyes still bright and glistening, her red hair in curly disarray around her sunburned and bloody face. Determined little Penny. Eva had really done something to send this girl to the enemy.

She took a step toward him and lifted her—

"What do you remember of the night your father was killed?" he said before she could touch him. She stopped short and after a moment, dropped her hand. Desperate and vulnerable was good.

"A sound woke me. Two pops, like firecrackers. Then it was quiet. I started to go back to sleep, then I heard Grandmother yelling, and Mama started screaming. I was scared and wanted to go downstairs, but when I opened the door, Grandmother was on the landing, pushing Adel back down the hall. She shoved her into my room and told us to stay put. I asked Adel what was wrong. She didn't know, and Jack, I really don't think she did. The shots woke her like they did me. We got in my bed, and I fell back to sleep. I don't know if she did. I didn't know Daddy was dead till morning."

"Do you remember seeing my father that night?"

"He arrived right before I was sent up to bed."

"Do you recall him leaving?"

"No, and I didn't hear them arguing either. You asked me that years ago. The gunshots woke me, but I didn't know what they were at the time."

"What time was it?"

"Adel told me later it was after midnight. What do you want from me, Jack?"

"I want to prove Eva killed your father."

She threw a hand out in front of her. "If you'll marry me, I'll help you prove she did, whether she's guilty or not."

Her whole body was shaking, and not from fear and certainly not from cold this hideously hot October day. She had the shakes.

"Do you have a fix?"

She frowned at him. "Marry you, that was my plan. Haven't you been listening?"

"I meant another dose of morphine with you, Penny."

Violently she shook her head. "I don't want another dose."

But she needed one.

"You aren't going to marry me, are you?"

Chapter Fifty-seven

Jack stuck his head back inside Kate's dining room. They were on dessert. Peach cobbler, dammit.

"Bo?"

The man raised his tawny head.

"Your mom still got that closed carriage?"

Bo Davidson nodded. "Yep, you need it?"

"Could I borrow it a few days?"

Bo pushed his empty dish away from him. "I imagine. She always liked you better'n she liked me even."

Beside Bo, Will Hutchins snickered and Nick Componi, sitting with his back to the hall door, looked over his shoulder at Jack. "I think everybody's mom liked Jack better than they did their own boys."

"That's cause I always took my dirty plates to the sink." Jack found Kate's eyes. "Isn't that so, Kate?"

"Certainly not today." She reached over Bo's shoulder and picked up his dirty dish. "You going to finish your lunch?" she asked Jack.

He looked to his place near the head of the table. His plate was gone.

"I've got it covered in the kitchen."

He found her eyes. "Could I talk to you a minute?"

Jack considered crossing Bernard Bayou on the Lorraine ferry then keep heading north, but the county line was too far that direction, so he opted to head west on the Pass Christian Road for the relative safety of Hancock County. He and Penny could marry in anonymity, then they'd head north up the Bay St.

Louis-Kiln Road to the Jourdan River Community. Humboldt had leased timber tracts up that way, and Jack was familiar with the lay of the land. What he wanted was to stash her with his aunt in Lumberton while he sought legal counsel.

He'd told Kate they were marrying, and he'd told her they were heading for Alabama. Then he'd smiled at her, and the woman had smiled back. He wasn't going to tell anyone where they were going, and he knew Kate understood, a precaution if Evangeline Markiston proved able to trace Penny to his boarding-house, which was a long shot in itself. First someone would have to have seen Penny get into the wagon with old Uncle Jacob, then Eva would have to find the man, then she'd have to persuade him to tell her where he'd taken the girl—that could prove easy enough once the authorities started accusing the old codger of kidnapping. Jack shuddered. He hoped the old man poured his guts out at that point, because he sure didn't need to be protecting Penny at the risk of his own life, and it could come to that.

Then Uncle Jacob might have hightailed it right back to the church to offer what he knew for a price. Jack didn't think that had happened. They'd be here by now.

Kate had managed to come up with a pair of Michael's old britches. Her teenager had outgrown them. She also pulled a white cotton shirt out of her sewing. Michael had put a corner tear in it two nights ago. The defect was on the right shoulder. Small, but fixable, though Kate seemed content to have come up with a reason not to even try. She told Penny she'd launder the wedding dress, it was a beautiful thing. Penny told her to burn it. Kate blinked at her, and Jack knew she wouldn't do that.

Other than the bitter remark about the wedding dress, Penny was gracious in thanking Kate, right down to Penny's new shoes. Those had also belonged to Michael several years ago. Kate had been saving them for her eleven-year-old, Boyd. Penny disguised, Jack grabbed his frock coat, and they were on the run.

Eva turned from her pacing when Stuart opened the door to her office. "Was Hadrian there?"

266

"He was not," Stuart answered.

She slapped her satin-covered lap. "Well, where the hell was he?"

"His housekeeper said he was on a house call."

"Had she seen her?"

"Said no."

On the settee, Clarissa hiccupped, then took another swallow of gin. "Why do you think she's gone to Hadrian?"

"Because," Eva said, her voice even, "she's sick, and she was trying to convince Mark earlier that I did this to her, don't you recall, darling? Besides, she'll need a doctor to get more morphine."

Clarissa looked at Stuart. "You said she had some disreputable person in Biloxi, someone Harold introduced her to, who supplied her."

Eva looked at Stuart, who shook his head.

Clarissa twisted on the seat. "Well if that's not so, how did Penny become addicted to morphine so suddenly?"

"She wasn't happy in her marriage," Eva said. "She was looking for amusement."

"I"—again Clarissa hiccupped, and Stuart would have found his wife humorous if he didn't have the missing Penny on his mind. "I cannot believe this of her," Clarissa managed.

"Well, do, daughter, because it's happened. She has the fate of not only King and Gibson in her hands, but that of Noble Corporation to boot. Why do you think I was in such a hurry to have her safely ensconced in marriage with a man who knows the business?" Eva narrowed her eyes on Stuart. "Thomas Gates, Noble Corporation?"

"I doubt she'd run there given Jon is in the office every day."

"Nevertheless, the building should be watched. I doubt she knows where the man lives."

Stuart sure as hell didn't know either, and he didn't care. "I'll take care of it."

Clarissa started to cry, and Stuart took her empty glass. "It's barely noon."

"She's upset about Penny, Stuart."

He looked into the condescending eyes of Eva, who smiled at him, then he looked at Clarissa.

"She needs to go to bed," Eva said.

"Of course, Mama." Clarissa rose from where she sat. "I'm still exhausted from the trip back."

"Can you manage?" Stuart asked her.

"Yes. Stay and talk with Mama. We need to find my baby."

Eva watched Clarissa stumble out the door, then ground out, "I'll kill her baby once I get my hands on her."

"You may have already done that."

Eva glared at him, then turned her back and walked to the chair behind her desk.

"How long before she'll need more morphine?"

"I gave her a shot at nine. I wanted to be sure she'd be all right through the ceremony."

"And we gave her a shot at three this morning. Every six hours. Yesterday it was every eight." His nostrils flared. "You've done a good job on her."

"Thank you, and don't act as if you're innocent."

"I warned you against this."

"I'm not in the least sorry for the path I took, Stuart, only for Adel's bungling things at the end."

Adel's bungling his ass. "She'd have never wed him. She'd have stood in front of that preacher and said no, or said nothing at all."

"At which time I'd have spoken for her."

"Listen to me, Eva. She would have never married him." He made a half pivot. "Do you know who all was in that church this morning? The people Clarissa invited? At least two were friends of Hugh. Someone would have listened to her."

She glared. "We need to find her. There will only be you, me, Jon, and Jim Puknay present at the next ceremony."

Stuart sighed in disgust. Perhaps the woman really didn't understand she'd failed.

"There are not that many people she could run to. Do you think she'd come back to Mark?"

"I wouldn't. She could go to Tobias Craig."

Eva laughed at that. "Craig is trying to prove she was in league with Alan in murdering Florence. She won't go to him."

"Adel?"

"Not Adel and not her mother," Eva snapped back. "Don't be a fool. She'll never trust either one of them again. Adel betrayed her, and her mother is a weak, sniveling drunk. She'd come to you before Clarissa."

She would never come to him again. He knew that and so did Eva.

"She'll need morphine soon enough, and she doesn't know the underbelly of Biloxi to find it. That's another reason I'm betting on Hadrian. She needs a doctor."

Chapter Fifty-eight

Jack and Penny arrived in Pass Christian before two, and Jack stowed the carriage at the livery. They caught the train. They'd timed it perfectly, by pure luck. Not having to wait for the ferry to cross the bay probably cut an hour from their trip.

A small Methodist church stood within two blocks of the depot at the corner of Main and Second Streets and within viewing distance of the courthouse. Two lots east of the church was a single-story, wood-framed dress shop, pristine and painfully white in the mid-afternoon sun. Finding the shop was fortuitous. Jack didn't want to marry a woman dressed in boys' clothing. He wanted her in a dress, blue he requested when he led her, reticent, inside the merchant's door. She didn't want to waste time with a dress, but he was sure it would only take a moment. He was wrong about that, as men so often are, it seems, when it comes to such matters. Getting the license didn't take nearly as long.

He paid Mrs. Montague, the shopkeeper, extra to help Penny with her hair. Kate had already washed off the blood crusting around her nostril and the corner of her mouth. Her lip was swollen and there was a bruise on her cheek, but Jack held his head high and ignored Mrs. Montague's withering glance and picked out a little hat for the blue dress Penny chose.

There'd been two dresses to choose from. His favorite was a pale blue, with puffed-up, short sleeves, which made the thing a good choice because it was so doggone hot. The other was more the color of the ocean at St. Andrews, east of Pensacola over in Florida. Teal, the proprietress called it, and she said the color was good for Penny, though both he and Mrs. Montague agreed it didn't fit Penny's coloring as nicely as the pale blue he favored. But Penny wanted long sleeves. She wasn't chilled, though he considered she could be having chills in addition to the sweating she was suffering, and he felt only frustration with her when she insisted on the long-sleeved dress.

Mrs. Montague tacked in the sides and pinned the hem—all done swiftly for two bits. And when they left that shop at a quarter to four, Penny King Noble was a lovely petite young woman, who made a respectable bride if no one questioned her fidgeting and her slightly pummeled face.

*L*yle Jenkins rubbed his hand over his jaw. "I need help on this."

"I've got one officer and no money to hire any more," Toby Craig said. "You put a deputy at the Noble House and the office building. I'll put my man at Dr. Clark's place."

"Fine," Jenkins said and pushed the chair back so hard when he rose that it almost toppled. He stomped to the door and yanked it open. He glared at Charlie, who was about to enter, then strode forward, forcing Charlie out of the way. For a moment, Charlie watched the man's back, then he came inside and pushed the door shut with a clatter.

"What did he want?" Charlie asked.

Toby folded his arms over his chest and leaned back against the jamb of his office door. "Seems Penny Noble left her expectant fiancé waiting at the church about three hours ago."

Charlie hung his slouch hat on the peg by the door. "No kiddin'?"

"Ain't no joke, and that's a fact."

"And the groom is trying to find her."

"Him and the rest of the family. The good Sheriff Jenkins just informed me that Miss Penny has a serious morphine habit."

Charlie narrowed his eyes on Toby, then took a seat. "Do you believe that?"

"I wouldn't have guessed, no, but Jenkins swears that's the case. Given that, they seem to think she'll be looking for a doctor.

Eva Markiston says that doctor of choice is gonna be Hadrian Clark, but you and I both know she's an acquaintance of Peter Fritz. I want you to go talk to him. Let him know, in no uncertain terms, that if Penny Noble approaches him, he is to inform us immediately. Then go stake out Hadrian Clark's place. He's been that gal's doctor her whole life. I don't know that he'll tell us if she shows up, no matter how much we threaten."

Chapter Fifty-nine

"Where are we going now?" Penny asked.

"I've got to get you somewhere comfortable."

Jack helped her into the wagon he'd rented at the livery. The hand she placed in his was sweating. She'd consistently wiped her forehead and dabbed at her upper lip with a handkerchief throughout the short ceremony, performed by a surprised elderly preacher with his equally elderly wife standing by as witness. The preacher signed and dated the license, and Jack watched the man record the ceremony in the church record. Jack signed his name. Penny, despite her shaking hands, signed hers.

"You need more morphine," he said as they left the church.

"No."

"You can't just stop taking it."

"Of course I can."

He'd seen people who used the stuff and couldn't find a fix. It was awful. The shock to her system could prove fatal.

"How long have you been using?"

"Eight days."

He looked at her, antsy on the seat beside him. Eight days. Harold Noble had been murdered just over two weeks ago, mere hours after his father, and the "grieving" widow had been marrying Jon Noble after a "prolonged" mourning period. Jack clicked his tongue, and the horse picked up its gait. That timeline would be enough to make any lawman stop and take notice. But then Eva had friends in high places, and Harold had some pretty rough associates.

They were out of town now, on a roughly graded road in a wagon with no springs. He longed for that carriage left behind in

Pass Christian, but there wasn't one to be had at the livery in the Bay. Penny was rocking forward and holding her stomach. "Jack," she said, "I don't think you're gonna find me much comfort anywhere tonight."

Chapter Sixty

"According to Eva, she's been using morphine for a while," Mark Reed confirmed for Hadrian Clark. Dr. Clark looked at Toby, sitting in a worn gothic armchair in front of the doctor's desk.

Dr. Clark's office was dark and stuffy, lit by floor-to-ceiling windows that looked east over a dusk-shrouded yard. A hodge-podge of furniture filled the room on the first floor of his towering three-story home a block off Beach Boulevard in Mississippi City. Here, Toby was out of his jurisdiction, but his presence was at Jenkins' request. Either way, Toby didn't care. Nor did Hadrian Clark seem to mind the imposition. Toby figured the young Dr. Reed didn't grasp the discrepancy.

Toby turned from where he had twisted to listen to Reed. "What do you think, Dr. Clark?"

"Penny came in to see me after her husband's funeral. She had an abscess on her breast. She was running a fever and was in pain. Because of that, I had occasion to inspect her torso, including her arms. There was nothing there. No sores, no needle marks. She gave no indication of dependency on anything."

"Yet a little more than a week later she's dependent on morphine?" Toby asked.

"Her grandmother has used morphine for years," Clark told him.

Dr. Reed stepped forward and grabbed the back of the wing chair flanking Toby's. "Eva confessed to me she'd introduced Penny to the drug. She mentioned Penny's pain because of the breast ailment. She claims she had no idea Penny would abuse the drug as she did."

"You just said her grandmother told you she's been using the stuff for a while."

Reed shrugged. "I'm not sure what Eva meant by 'a while'."

Hadrian Clark appeared to assess Dr. Reed, then said to Toby, "You know Penny had recently suffered from a stomach ailment."

"The same one which both you and Dr. Fritz originally believed killed Florence Noble?"

"Initially we considered that, but Peter always considered her ulcers the culprit. We're all having different thoughts now."

"You know Alan Noble fired his cook of eight years after Florence Noble became ill?" Toby said.

"I didn't know that," Dr. Clark answered.

"Cook says if Mrs. Noble was poisoned she wasn't the one who did it. It's possible Alan Noble may have fired her to ease his poisoning his wife."

"Did Alan Noble cook?" Reed asked.

Toby looked over his shoulder at the younger man. "I doubt it. I just thought her leaving might give him easier access to the food, but if you're suggesting the younger Mrs. Noble was also being poisoned, then perhaps I should consider an accomplice or a different idea altogether."

Hadrian Clark looked up at Eva Markiston's grandson by marriage. "Thank you, Mark."

The younger man's eyes widened slightly. Then he dropped his hands, nodded, and left the room. Toby was as surprised by the doc's dismissal of Reed as apparently Reed had been.

The good doctor shifted his swivel chair and rested his arms on his desk. "Anything I say will make it back to Eva Markiston. He's fallen under her spell, a fate I myself suffered many years ago. But in answer to your question regarding Penny's possibly being poisoned, the answer is yes. Penny suffered from fatigue, bloody diarrhea and cramping."

"Any idea who would be doing it?"

Dr. Clark held up a hand. "I am Penny's doctor. I could venture a guess as to who might compel her to use morphine, but I know little about what goes...or went on in the Noble household. You might want to talk to Peter Fritz. As you know, he believes Penny could be complicit in Florence Noble's death. I cannot believe she was, but I'm not positive."

Toby grabbed the arm of the chair and started to pull himself out of it, then stopped. "One more thing, Doc. That sore on Penny Noble's breast. What did you make of it?"

Chapter Sixty-one

Jack and Penny reached The Kiln at dusk, and he turned them northwest onto the Kiln-Nicholson Road. There was no way they would reach the railroad stop at Nicholson tonight, and even if Penny were healthy, he wouldn't travel this country road in the dark. He rarely traveled roads at night, even ones he was as familiar with as this one. They were a good twenty miles out, maybe more, and the land undulated like the Gulf in a hurricane. A mile past The Kiln, he turned east onto an ungraded logging trail, which led to an old homesteader's cabin, hastily assembled in anticipation of a title, more hastily transferred by quitclaim deed to Humboldt, the actual purchaser. The rough cabin was used as a line cabin, hidden away in a sea of longleaf pine. Penny was cramping terribly now, and she'd thrown up once. Twenty minutes later, Mars Bullock gave up the cabin for a nearby storeroom.

Jack had hired Mars almost three years ago to foreman a job over in Perry County. He was a colored man and an experienced logger, a skill not particularly common among those of his color, but there were some, and the number was growing. Jack had set him out here a month ago to scout the streams in anticipation of cutting this section in the fall. Mars was also a good person, who'd taken one look at the sick girl and offered his cabin before Jack could ask, and he'd even dared to leave his makeshift quarters and approach Jack in the wee hours of that night when Penny's cries from the cramping had disturbed his rest. At three o'clock that morning, an exhausted Jack had inquired about the nearest doctor and asked him to fetch the man. Penny was quiet by that time, more comatose than coherent, her body spent, but her pulse racing so fast he feared her heart would burst. This coup he was pulling off against Evangeline Markiston was gonna backfire in his face if Penny went and died on him tonight.

"Someone would have to be helping her by now. She'd be screaming. That or she's found someone to supply her craving."

"One of your friends," Stuart said dryly, and Eva looked at him from where she stood near the fireplace. She hadn't sat for hours. She'd been pacing. Pacing so much she'd become a distraction, and Stuart could taste his hatred of her.

"Screaming, Grandmother?" Adel said. "That hardly sounds like recreational use of the drug."

Eva started her pacing again. "What prompted you to leave her in that room?" she asked Adel.

"Your bloodying her wedding dress. No one told me how much she opposed marrying Jonathan, and I certainly had no idea you'd forced a full-blown addiction on her."

Eva stopped short. "Who told you that?"

Adel rolled her eyes, then sat on the settee. "No one had to tell me anything. I'm not stupid, and I know Penny. She wouldn't willingly use that stuff. She detested the fact you used it. If you wanted me to do a top-notch job helping you keep her, you should have kept me better informed."

"She didn't think you'd approve." Stuart sat next to Adel. He didn't bother to look at Eva. He was tired, and he was sick of the woman. And he was in too deep to crawl back out.

"I wouldn't have," Adel answered and shot her grandmother a quick smirk.

"Your disapproval has never stopped you before."

"And it probably"—Adel covered her yawn with a fist—"wouldn't have this time either, however, I could have at least recommended against it."

Finally Eva sat behind her desk. "Take heart," she said, "even if we have lost Noble Corporation, we can assume King and Gibson is safe."

Stuart blew out a breath. "Can we? Truth is, we don't know

where that promissory note is, and if Jonathan has it, we're done for."

"You're panicking, Stuart. Jonathan doesn't have it. I told you before, if he had it, he would never have agreed to marry Penny."

"The hell he wouldn't. He's always wanted her for some undisclosed reason and you've never bothered to find out what. Now he needs Penny to solidify his claim to Noble Corporation. Did you think to offer him Penny for the note?"

"He doesn't have it."

Stuart snorted. "Let's hope not, because having lost Penny you can bet he'll want to cash it in."

Chapter Sixty-two

Jack was back inside. She didn't see him, she heard him. Penny didn't care to open her eyes. She was too weak to move, too exhausted to sleep. And she hurt. Her head hurt, her chest, the injured breast, the infected arm.

She felt his touch on her wrist. "I'm still alive." She thought he might have heard her. She wasn't sure. Legally he should be able to get his hands on everything he needed to wrest King and Gibson from Eva, but he didn't know where the promissory note was.

Nausea hit her anew, and she pulled her knees to her chest. There would be court battles if she died. Not only would Eva challenge his claim to King and Gibson, but an even bigger battle loomed from Jonathan regarding Noble Corporation. Not that Jack was interested in Noble Corporation. Still, a gift horse was a gift horse. As much as she wanted to die at this exact moment, she had to live in order...

She gagged. Jack sat beside her and helped hold her head over the cot. Again, she retched. For a moment she thought she'd choke on bile, and Jack forced her head lower. How many times had he done this tonight?

And the diarrhea? Her bowel movements had been liquid from the start of withdrawal, but for the past several hours she'd been unable to sit on a slop jar. Somehow Jack had managed to keep her reasonably clean. She was naked, but didn't care about that this time. She knew no shame.

Chills wracked her body. Again Jack was moving, wiping her face, checking her bottom, rolling her back and pulling the covers under her chin. He was talking to her. His voice both irritated and distracted her. She needed to concentrate if she were to survive.

The pain dulled, but only because she was losing feeling. Her breathing came harder, too, and when she cramped, she thought she couldn't draw the next breath. At those moments, she didn't care. Then merciful darkness would take her, but with the next cramp, she'd wake again.

"Jack?" She groped in the dark room. He grabbed her hand.

"I sent Mars for a doctor," he said.

Her heart sped up, so ominous—she felt it, felt it thumping, fighting to free itself from the confines of her withered body. "Why?"

He didn't answer. Maybe he hadn't heard. But he was there. He held her hand. She didn't hold his, she had no strength in her fingers. She wanted to squeeze his fingers and couldn't. "Why?"

His lips brushed her ear. "You're very sick."

He was scared, she heard it in his voice. She fought to open her eyes. "No morphine, Jack."

"We'll do what he says."

"No." She'd have screamed the word if she could have, but she feared she'd done little more than mouth it, so she shook her head violently so he understood.

He caught her head and told her to be still. She was dizzy.

"It's in Harold's room."

"What's in his room?"

"Beneath the floor underneath the night chest by his bed."

"What?"

"The promissory note."

"At the Nobles' house?"

She forced her lids open. "Yes." A coal oil lamp cast a dim light. He was a shadow sitting next to her on the bed. "Now you don't have to save me."

He didn't move or speak.

"Let me die."

He squeezed her hand. "If I were going to let you die, I'd have already put an end to this nightmare, for both of us."

She recalled Dr. Clark's words and laughed, though she doubted Jack recognized the sound. "I can't do this again. Not ever. If I can't get off this stuff tonight I'd rather be dead."

"This can be done in moderation. You don't have to kill—"

"If you shoot more of that stuff in me, you won't be any better than she is. Promise."

And he promised.

Chapter Sixty-three

Dr. Mason studied the raw skin on Penny's wrists and told Jack to hold the lantern higher. The doc had unwrapped the dressings, which Jack noted hours ago when he helped Penny out of that pretty little dress. Kate had mentioned the wrists before they left Happy Hallow, but not the infected spot on the inside of her elbow, though he'd noticed that, too, earlier. Dr. Mason said it had been treated recently, but still looked bad. During the doctor's exam, Penny didn't open her eyes. She was going through a lengthening quiet spell, and Jack feared she was giving up.

Gently, the doctor pulled Mars' white shirt back over her head, covering her nakedness, then placed her arms one at a time beneath the covers. He patted the shrouded hand closest to him and rose out of the ladder-back chair Jack vacated when the man arrived more than two hours ago. He opened the door. Outside, first light peeked between the flattened crowns of old longleaf pine, and he motioned Jack onto the narrow porch.

"Where did that girl come from?" the doctor asked when the door shut.

"New Orleans."

"You brought her across a state line?"

"Yes."

"What's your relationship to her?"

Jack didn't like the way this stern old man was looking at him, his movements laced with self-righteous anger and disapproval.

"She's my wife."

"How did she get those abrasions on her wrists?"

"I don't know."

"The hell you don't. If I asked you to show me a marriage license, could you?"

"I could."

"A recent one, I'd bet."

There was no reason to show the man the license. Legal or not, Dr. Edward Mason believed he'd forced Penny to come with him against her will.

"I want to see that license, and I want to know the girl's age."

"The girl is eighteen, and I'm not showing you the license." It sounded as shady as this whole situation appeared. Jack wasn't precisely sure of her age. Hell, he didn't even know Adel's birthday, but he was close enough, and he wasn't going to divulge Penny's name to this man. He'd already told him his, and that was bad enough. Law enforcement in Hancock county might or might not be aware of the young Mrs. Noble's disappearance in Mississippi City, but Jack was pretty sure it wasn't common knowledge among the majority of folks, and the longer it stayed secret the better it was for both him and Penny.

"When is the last time she had the morphine?"

"I believe yesterday morning, but I don't know for sure."

The doctor studied him with something kin to a sneer on his thin lips. "You didn't administer it then?"

"I did not."

Jack was looking at him directly, daring the man to accuse him outright of kidnapping and rape, and that's what the man was thinking. Finally, the doctor averted his eyes. "What else has she been given?"

"Nothing that I know of."

"Her blood pressure is dangerously high, but not as high as it was when I got here." He nodded to the door. "I don't think your trying to get her off the drug like this was a smart idea. A human heart can keep up a pace like that for only so long. That gal's still very sick, but I'm noticing some stabilization in the heartbeat since I arrived, what"—he pulled a pocket watch out of a wrinkled vest—"two hours ago." He returned the watch to its vest pocket. "You should have told that big Nigra I needed to bring morphine. I'm still thinkin' I'll send him for some"—Jack bit his tongue—"but given how far she's come, and how weak she is, coupled with whatever unknown ailment is working in combination with this, I think it's best she weather it on through." Again he found Jack's eyes. "I imagine we're going to find it is an even greater threat than her addiction to the drug."

Jack didn't like the way he used the word "we're" as if the doc considered Jack's purpose in this was to cover up who knew what the mysterious element was.

Well, no matter how odious the doctor's implication—and Jack would probably be thinking the same thing the doc was thinking had he come upon a similar situation—this was the only doctor he had at the moment.

"She told me she'd been using the drug for eight days."

"Only a week?"

Jack nodded.

"I doubt that girl weighs more than eighty pounds. A fortnight ago, I'll grant you, and you probably know this better than me," he said, his voice dripping with accusation, "she probably weighed more, but given the withdrawal symptoms I'm seeing with her, someone has pumped a lot of morphine into her. That smacks of control. Her bottom is raw from lying in her own excrement"—the man clenched his teeth—"and the bindings used on her wrists are obviously the results of coercion. As far as I'm concerned, Mr. Gibson, that's a crime worthy of execution."

"And I agree with you, Doctor, and I can tell you something else. If I had so little concern for that girl's life as to do such a thing, I wouldn't have sent for you during the night."

"My opinion of what warrants the death penalty, sir, and what the State of Mississippi allows are two different things. You'd have sent for me if you feared the latter, or if the girl is of some value to you alive."

Jack wasn't going to stand out here and argue with this person. The situation looked bad for him, and he was smart enough to know it.

"How about that bite mark on her breast? I guess you didn't do that either, did you?"

By the dim lantern light, he'd seen a dark spot on her breast, but had been concentrating too hard on keeping her from drowning in bile to worry about unrelated injuries. "That's a bite mark?"

"A human bite mark. Nasty. It brought blood, I suspect, and infection and a lot of bruising. A real bastard inflicted it."

"Well, I might be a real bastard, Doc, but I didn't do that. Is it healing all right?"

"Seems to be." The man pulled his coat closed with one hand. The dawn was cool.

"What should I do for her?"

"If you're talking about the withdrawal, that's in God's hands now. Otherwise, you could take her back home where she belongs."

And probably certain death. "Thanks for coming, Dr. Mason."

Jack handed the man payment and then some. The "then some" Mason handed back. Fine. He'd hardly handed the man enough for the overage to be regarded a bribe. He wondered about the intelligence of well-educated people sometime. Of course, the man was honest to a fault—a fault that would have gotten him killed, if Jack had been the kind of man to do what the good doctor had accused him of. He heard the doctor's retreating footsteps down the two groaning steps, then a jingle of harness as the man drove away in his neat little open carriage. Jack closed the cabin door.

"Hey, Copper Lee?" Jack touched Penny's shoulder and sighed in relief when she opened her eyes. The outer reaches of the room lay swathed in gray, Penny remained pale-gold in the glow of the lamp.

"He doesn't want—"

"He's gone. Says you're sick." Jack managed to grin at her. She didn't even crack a smile.

"Am I going to die?"

"I'm not going to let you die, but we've got to go. I imagine your good doctor's next stop will be Bay St. Louis and the sheriff's office, and that will be all too soon after he divests himself of his carriage and saddles his horse."

Chapter Sixty-four

Jack told Mars he was taking Penny to her home in New Orleans, only because he figured Mars was gonna be questioned, and as long as he didn't ask Mars to lie, he knew the man wouldn't try. Mars was a damn lousy liar, and New Orleans meshed with what he'd told Dr. Mason.

Then Jack started the wagon bouncing back down that rough logging road, Penny in the back dressed in her relatively clean boys' clothing. He turned west on the McNeill-Kiln Road, figuring they were between four and five hours, given wagon travel, from the train that would take them to Lumberton and the relative safety of Marion County.

Truth was, Jack might be able to convince a local county sheriff he was doing right by Penny, and she really was his legal wife, not some rich girl he'd kidnapped, then forced under duress into sex or marriage. But he couldn't risk, even for a night while the authorities sorted things out, her falling back into the hands of her "loving family."

The withdrawal symptoms could persist for days, the doc had told him early on. Jack looked up through the towering pines flanking the road. The sky was blue, the sun climbing, mottling the straw covering the now relatively smooth road under them. He looked back. Her eyes were closed, and he hoped she slept. He breathed in the clean scent of yellow pine and gave thanks to his God in Heaven for bringing them through that terrible night into this beautiful day. He told himself they would make the noon train. Good Lord willin' and nobody closin' in behind them, they should be in Lumberton by two in the afternoon.

⊰·⊱

"*I*'m sorry to bring this on you," Jack said, standing when his Aunt Millie entered her bright front room.

She waved for him to sit back down. "I can't believe that's Hugh King's baby in there. His mother was a redhead. At least I'm told she was in her younger days. It was gray by the time I knew her, but she was petite like that." The woman looked at him and sat, and Jack retook his seat.

"I'm thinking no one will know to look for her here."

"I doubt Evangeline Markiston even remembers I exist, and if she does, she certainly doesn't know I'm in Lumberton."

"I'll get back as quick as I can." He studied the older woman. She was almost five years older than his mother would have been. That would put her around fifty now. She looked older, but she was old for her age. The War had done that, Sherman's soldiers in Meridian. Jack didn't know the whole story of what happened that night, but he knew enough to hazard a guess. Then Uncle Malcolm had been killed up in Tennessee, near the Alabama line. They'd been young when the promise of their life together had ended. Aunt Millie had made a comeback of sorts, but she never remarried.

"She could stay sick for a while," he said.

"I'm used to taking care of the sick, honey."

He bowed his head and wished the sun weren't where it was right now, but the cool of that front-porch swing was thought, not fact. In the evenings it was exceedingly pleasant on Aunt Millie's front porch. He jerked his head up and looked her in the eye. "Last night I didn't think she'd be here today." He rubbed the back of his neck. "I haven't felt that helpless since the day Daddy was executed."

Millie leaned across and took the hand that lay in his lap. "She's sleeping now."

"Hope she wakes up. Doctor who saw her last night says her heart could just stop. When the cramps come, she might cry out. They don't come too often now, but they do still come. Your neighbors—"

"Only have one. Thompsons moved over to Red Lick two

290

weeks ago. Josh and Todd Berry on the other side work at the mill. Doubt she could holler loud enough to bother them anyway. They're both deaf as cottonmouths. Too many years listening to a buzz saw."

She could scream pretty damn bad when the pains hit her. He'd had no problem at all getting Mars to take off for the doctor last night. Poor man was ready to get out of there, milling around out front, worried about "that little girl" Jack had brought to his place. Mars was a tenderhearted soul, though you'd never believe it to look at his formidable body swathed in the blackest of skin.

"I'll see Clive Morgan and get back as fast as I can."

Millie glanced at the clock on the mantel. "Trains haven't been on schedule for the past month, so I doubt you'll get there before he goes home for the day."

"I wanna stop and see Nate in Piotona anyway before I head up. If I don't see Clive tonight, I'll do it tomorrow morning. Depending on what he tells me, I'm planning on being back tomorrow evening."

"You trust him?"

"Yep. His firm represents Humboldt here in the state. He's a graduate of the University of Mississippi." He smiled. "And his daddy rode with the Fourteenth."

Relief relaxed her eyes and her hands, and she smiled. "I guess we can't do better than that, can we? But I want you to eat before you go. You'll not make it to his office today, and that would be the only reason for you to leave my house hungry."

Chapter Sixty-five

Clive Morgan waved Jack into his office and nodded to one of the two upholstered wing chairs in front of his desk. One full day in Hattiesburg had become three. The first day, Clive sent an investigator out of New Orleans to work on the Coast. That man arrived in Hattiesburg today, report in hand, while Jack and Clive were at lunch. Jack and Clive parted ways two hours ago agreeing to meet back at Clive's office at three, giving the lawyer time to peruse his investigator's information.

"You are officially married in the eyes of Mississippi." Clive waved another yellow piece of paper. "My man reports that the Harrison County sheriff, as well as Jackson County's, are searching for the girl. He doesn't have any details on what they're saying they think might have happened to her, only that she's disappeared and her family is distraught."

He bet they were.

"He did say they're unofficially raiding the dope dens and whorehouses looking for her."

"That's because Eva suspects that's where she's gone for relief. The alternative would be returning to her grandmother. Eva is probably scared she's dead by now."

Clive laid the report on his desk. "Given all this, my advice is to pack her up as soon as she's able to travel and move right back into the Noble home. Alan Noble preceded his son in death, and Harold didn't leave a will. That leaves his widow to inherit. The status of the senior Noble's will is a mess. His executor is dead, and Jonathan Noble is talking to his brother's lawyers. That's why you need to get back there. Jonathan, who I believe is the ditched groom" — Clive eyed Jack, who nodded — "is living in the house. I've had a court order drawn up. I'll have it signed by a judge for the sheriff to evict him before y'all get back."

Jack's stomach twisted at the thought of Jon Noble having free reign in that house with the promissory note squirreled away upstairs.

"Noble's going to be your biggest legal threat. Right now, Carrington Farrah is the Markiston-Frederick lawyer. He is, by default, Penny Noble's. It appears to my man down there that Farrah is looking out for your wife's interest."

"Penny said Eva has her power of attorney."

Clive made a note. "Did she give it to her?"

"She says she didn't. How do we change lawyers?"

"I'll notify Carrington's firm tomorrow that Penny Gibson is switching counsel."

"That will be a shock to them."

"I imagine the switch'll knock Mr. Farrah right on his ass, but he'll fight it, at least till he actually sees Penny alive." He handed Jack a document. "I've scheduled a hearing before the chancery court"—he found Jack's eye—"Harrison County in Biloxi. Sign here. And date it...tomorrow morning at nine...directing Jonathan Noble to cease further participation in Noble Corporation operations pending review of ownership, which is believed to be you."

Jack blew out a breath. His good buddy Jon was gonna like that. Antsy now, Jack started to rise, but Clive held up a finger.

"There's something else I need to talk to you about." He folded his hands together atop the table and leaned forward. "You do know Alan Noble died in his daughter-in-law's bedroom." Clive frowned. "I can tell by the stupid look on your face you did not. He died just a few days after his wife was buried."

"I knew that part."

"He was found on the floor, nude, near his discarded silk smoking jacket. What has she told you about that night?"

The steak Jack had for lunch weighed heavy in his stomach. "We haven't had occasion to discuss it."

"Maybe you should. Biloxi's marshal isn't done with this. The indiscretions revealed by Alan Noble's death prompted him to question Penny about the wife's death. He wants to exhume the woman's body, but can't get a judge to sign off on it. Rumor has it Eva Markiston is standing in the way. Penny's marrying you could cause a change in the woman's grandmotherly heart, and given all that Jonathan Noble has to lose now that he's lost his bride, I'm willing to bet he's gonna do everything he can to have Florence Noble's body exhumed. You do know if the coroner finds that Florence Noble was murdered, your Miss Penny could be in real trouble?"

"I can see that."

"Throw in Harold Noble's murder that same night"—Clive blew out a breath—"Hell, this little bride of yours might well prove to be the grim reaper incarnate."

Chapter Sixty-six

Jack knocked. Penny bid him enter the room where he'd left her sleeping four days earlier. The doubts conjured by Clive's revelations concerning Alan Noble dissipated when she stepped from the window. Despite being pale and looking smaller than he remembered, she no longer looked like death warmed over. The vivacious red hair and brilliant blue eyes, muted by her illness, gave her an intrinsic vulnerability, and he felt an urge to protect. Damn, the little red-headed witch was pretty. He guessed she always had been. He'd just never noticed. Good god, how had he managed to get himself a wife, and what was he to do about her and him?

"I was getting worried," she said.

"I sent a telegram."

"That was two days ago."

The sun streaming through the sheer window curtains reflected off her curls, whose gentle wisps framed the cluster of freckles decorating the bridge of her nose.

"Feelin' better?" he asked.

"Much."

"You look better." He leaned forward and drew an exaggerated breath. "You smell better, too."

She didn't say anything, and he considered he'd embarrassed her. "Aunt Millie says the cramps still come."

"From time to time." She wore a dress of blue cotton, long-sleeved. She'd insisted on that, Aunt Millie told him. He didn't figure he needed to explain why, because his aunt added that the place inside Penny's elbow was healing nicely, and the scabbed wrists were better.

"Your Aunt Millie said you went to Hattiesburg to see a lawyer." Penny took a seat on the neatly made bed, bright with a crocheted coverlet and a patterned quilt folded at its foot. A familiar pot-belly stove stood in a corner, another of winter's accoutrements that made him hot just to look at it. Still, this was a fine house, boasting five rooms and a cookhouse out back. For twelve years, Aunt Millie had kept books for the old Tingston Lumber Company, which began its history on Red Creek making staves for barrels during the Spanish era. It was a small business and had made the post-War transition well. In the end, though, its owners grew ancient and technology outstripped its capabilities. The firm closed down five years ago, and Aunt Millie had given up bookkeeping for honey. She also prepared other canned goods for the local markets. The house was long paid for, secured by his maternal grandfather's modest estate after his death thirteen years ago.

Jack sat in the rocker near Penny's bed. He imagined Aunt Millie had spent some time occupying this very seat over the past four days, waiting by Penny's side while the girl suffered through the final stages of withdrawal.

"Clive Morgan is now our attorney. He confirmed our marriage is legal."

"I can scarcely remember marrying you."

"Unless you want this marriage annulled real quick, don't admit that to anyone other than me."

Something akin to panic filled her eyes. "They can't annul it, can they?"

"Not without a battle. Your family would have to declare you incompetent or prove I coerced you into marriage."

"Grandmother might try and claim the addiction—"

"No doubt she'll claim you were under the influence, but you're not using drugs now. For all purposes you are of sound mind and, despite your age, by virtue of your marriage to Harold Noble, according to Clive, an emancipated woman."

A look of pleasant curiosity replaced that of worry, but she didn't question him on what exactly that meant. Maybe she had it figured out, and he wondered if she factored in the fact she'd now given herself into marriage with him, forfeiting that short-lived status. He cocked his head and studied her. Tough, that's what she was, and she'd proved her mettle. She would prove her mettle when confronting him, too, should it come to that. Jack flexed his jaw. "Your new lawyer has moved Jonathan Noble out of your house, but he's still a threat. You're the only thing standing in the way of his getting Noble Corporation."

"He would have gotten rid of me one way or another if I'd married him."

"Maybe, but now he has few other options and those lie with the courts, which, according to Clive, should be on your side."

"There's some doubt?"

And it came back to him then, the hills they'd yet to take.

"We've got a problem, you and I. That being the death of Florence Noble."

"Ah," she said as if she suddenly remembered the woman's demise, and he frowned.

"Did you have anything to do with her dying?"

"No."

"Did Alan Noble?"

"I don't know."

"He died —"

"In my room. I am aware." She rose from where she sat, and Jack stood, too, chomping at the bit to discover why she and a fat old man.... He shook his head to clear it and forced his voice harder. "When did you plan to tell me you and he were lovers and that you were suspected of murdering your mother-in-law?"

Her eyes widened. "And why, pray tell, would I have told you such ridiculous things? Alan and I were not lovers, and yes, I was questioned regarding Florence's death, but I played no role. Neither incident was weighing heavy on my mind the day I sought you out, nor, come to think of it, would a long-winded confession have worked in my favor. I was, for Pete's sake, begging you to marry me. Perhaps you should have asked."

"I didn't know to ask."

297

"And I didn't think about it mattering. I offered you King and Gibson in return for your help, not promise you a virtuous little bride and undying love. We have a pact and a purpose, or at least I thought we did."

He grimaced. "We do, but I need to keep you out of jail long enough to secure my claim to your dead husband's estate."

Chapter Sixty-seven

"Well, Carrington, why haven't you put a stop to this constant interference?" Eva Markiston asked the moment she laid eyes on her lawyer.

Carrington Farrah stopped short at the threshold of Eva's office. "Are you referring to Toby Craig or Jonathan Noble? Or maybe someone else has come to mind?"

Stuart, standing by the window, looked at him.

"Craig," Eva said. "I've got Jonathan under control."

"No, you do not. Maybe if you'd managed to marry Penny to him. Truth is he needed her more than she needed him."

"I need her with or without Jon. Her marrying him merely eliminated the coming battle and secured our claim."

"Jonathan Noble was always a bad idea," Stuart said from where he stood near the window. "Eventually he'd have stabbed us in the back."

"You think I don't know about the Jonathan Nobles in this world, Stuart? The key is to stab first."

Hands clasped behind him, Stuart angled toward her and Farrah. "The man knows you pretty well, too."

Eva sneered at her son-in-law, and a silent communication passed between them.

Carrington knew them both, too. They might as well have screamed their aborted plan to the world. "Well, neither one of you have her," he said, "and without her, you and Jonathan Noble are useless to one another."

"I'll be the judge of that," Eva said.

"Sit down," he told her, and she bristled. Eva was a beautiful specimen of the "mature" woman. She was also overbearing,

299

overly confident, and had too much power for her limited business acumen. She was in severe financial straits, and despite his having warned her for years, she'd never accepted simply settling back and "doing right." Instead she'd come up with yet another ruthless ploy to get what she wanted, when she wanted. This one, for the first time in his long memory, had backfired on her. He shuddered to think of the things he suspected this woman might have done that he was not privy to. God knows some of the things he did know about, even helped cover up, were bad enough.

"You really need to sit," he said.

She raised her chin, but still didn't sit.

"What's happened?"

Carrington's gaze darted to the window and Stuart Frederick, the hammer in the hands of the gloved fist. He had Stuart's attention, at least. Carrington shifted his eyes back to the gloved fist. "Penny's power of attorney has been vacated, and Jon Noble was served a court order this morning informing him to cease and desist all business transactions pending the results of an inquiry to determine ownership of Noble Corporation."

Eva pushed off the desk. "Determine ownership my ass! He's behind this. He's taking advantage of Penny's disappearance to get control of the company."

"First off," Carrington said, "Jonathan Noble's claim is very strong. This is still a male-dominated society. Without Penny, he's next in line, but he had nothing to do with the order. A chancery court judge signed it. Jon Noble has also been ordered to vacate his brother's house."

Eva's nostrils flared, but Stuart had joined their circle, eyes sharp.

"Who," he started, "requested—"

"Then it's Jonathan's loss," Eva said, "at least for the moment."

Carrington straightened in front of her and gave her a look he hoped came across as patronizing, because that's how he felt. On his left, Stuart shifted his weight. "Was it Penny who requested the stay against Jonathan?"

Eva's breath caught, and she splayed a hand across her chest. "Oh, god, yes, she's alive?"

"Penny didn't make the request."

Eva cursed at the same moment Stuart asked who did.

"James John Gibson."

This time Stuart cursed. Eva, confusion in her eyes, stared at Carrington. "And what," she said finally, "does he think he's doing?"

Stuart turned and made his way back to the window. Then he laughed.

"Well, if nothing else," Carrington said, "he's got a good lawyer who knows what he's doing." He met Eva's glare. "He's begun proceedings to take control of his company."

"His company?"

Stuart turned on her. "For the love of god, Eva, think!"

Mouth open, eyes wide, Eva turned to her son-in-law.

"Penny has married Jack Gibson."

Chapter Sixty-eight

"What do you think of it?" Jack hollered to be heard over the planer.

They were standing at least twelve feet away from the thing, the toe of her boot and the hem of her dress covered in saw dust. She hadn't heard him approach, no surprise there, and when she looked up she found he was facing her.

"I..."

He shook his head and took her elbow to lead her outside the rambling structure that was Humboldt's planing facility at its Biloxi River mill. Out of the corner of her eye, she saw one of Jack's men step away from the planer carriage and start after them. There was a band saw here, too, and a unique gang saw. Humboldt's Biloxi River mill was an impressive facility.

It was mid-afternoon of a beautiful October day. They'd left Lumberton this morning via Red Creek, on a flatboat owned by a man named Neil, who Jack had apparently known forever and a day. During that leg of the journey, she counted fourteen white-tails peering at the travelers between the trunks of second-growth deciduous forest, old now in its own right, which shaded the waterway until the sun got high and changed the brick red of the water to red-orange. Penny felt better, physically, than she had in weeks, and she relished each winding curve of the waterway, the birds, the fresh air, Jack's pointing out a lone beast rummaging through brush and scrub, flora different from the pristine, straw-covered floor of the longleaf forest that preceded it. She recognized the difference, because she'd seen her share of longleaf forests, and she was aware of the history of this place though she'd never traveled Red Creek.

302

Neil landed at the Perkiston community, and Jack hired a man with a wagon to carry them down the Perkiston-McNeil Road to the Biloxi River where he hired the ferry owner's son to take them to the Humboldt sawmill north of Handsboro. Operations were underway by the time they arrived, and Jack made quick introductions between the operations of one piece of noisy equipment or another, holding her hand while his workers slapped him on the back and offered him a sip from a pint one or another pulled from a back pocket or a stash behind a stack of wood. What Jack really thought of being congratulated, Penny wasn't sure, but he smiled and nodded, and thanked the men and partook of their brew. He even offered her a swig and grinned when she declined. A quick tour followed, and though he was gracious in explaining operations to her, the tour and briefings, presented by a man Jack introduced as Lucas Frazier, were directed primarily at Jack.

"Sorry," he said, a short distance outside the building. "Trying to hold a conversation in there is nigh impossible."

"I hadn't thought about you having so much responsibility when I dragged you into all this."

"Yeah, well there's a time for thought and sometimes not. The key to good operations is having the sense to put the right people in the right place. I've done that here."

"You'll soon have King and Gibson to take up your time."

"I've yet to see that promissory note."

Her stomach burned, and she turned from him. "It's there."

"If no one else has found it."

"I certainly wouldn't have come to you if I didn't think we could pull this off."

"And where would you have gone?" he asked softly.

She studied him, and he raised a brow. "Admit it, you were desperate for a safe harbor."

"You think I considered you safe?"

"Relatively. You dangled the one thing under my nose you knew I wouldn't refuse."

She bridled with mock pride. "Beautiful, enticing me?"

"Yeah, you and the promise of a wedding night I'm sure I'll never forget."

"And don't leave out my surprise attribute of whoring murderess." She leaned closer to him, because that fella Lucas Frazier was almost upon them. "The note is real."

"I—"

"Jack," Lucas said. Jack turned, and inside the building, the racket came to another temporary halt.

"I almost forgot. One of those Nobles came here looking for you on Friday."

Penny's heart pounded in her ears. "Jonathan," she forced out and stepped closer to Jack, who glanced at her. "How did he know?"

"Kate sent him, I reckon," Lucas told her.

Jack's foreman didn't appear to find it odd that she asked, so Penny forced herself to be calm.

"What did you tell him?" Jack asked.

"Told him you was up in Piotona with Stephens. That's what I thought." He grinned at Penny. "Didn't know you'd run off and got married."

Penny scooted closer to Jack. "What did—"

But Jack was already shushing her. Lucas' gaze shifted to her, then back to Jack.

"Didn't say what he wanted, only that he wanted to talk to you."

"Thanks, Lucas. I'll take care of it."

Jack turned to her as Lucas strode away.

"He followed me," she choked out.

Jack took her forearms in a firm hold. "I don't know that he did."

"Friday," she said and moved closer to him. Her head was starting to throb. "That was the day after I escaped. He must have known I came to you."

"Maybe."

"But how?"

"Your Uncle Jacob?"

"He wouldn't talk."

"I wouldn't be too sure."

She jerked her head up. "Unless they hurt or threatened him," she squeaked out.

"Penny, as of Friday, the Harrison and Jackson County sheriffs were still searching for you. If Jon Noble knew you were with me, he didn't share that information with anyone else."

"There's nothing to say he would. Oh god, Jack."

He rubbed her arms, but she moved to step into him. He let her, then pressed her body against his hard one. "It doesn't matter now, anyway. Day after tomorrow I intend for us to move back into the Nobles' house. Everyone is going to know where you are."

"And tonight?"

He rubbed her back. Ear against his chest, she heard his heart beating calmly, then the hollow echo of his response. "Kate's."

"But—"

"You'll be safe there. A lot safer than in the Nobles' house with me gone, and I've got to feel some things out tomorrow."

Chapter Sixty-nine

Clive Morgan looked away from the Alan Noble-Eva Markiston promissory note on the table, picked up his cup, and took a sip. "I like this stuff."

"So does Nate." Jack nodded to the note. "What do you think?"

"I think Eva Markiston and her son-in-law have a very large loan outstanding from Noble's estate. It does survive him. The thing was witnessed by William Pickering, Noble's attorney, who no doubt drafted it, which begs the question where was theirs? They were insane to sign this thing. Your nemesis had no recourse but repay the loan — unless her granddaughter forgave it."

"Or she got her hands on it and destroyed it."

"What did she and Frederick have going?"

"If what Penny is telling me is correct, Eva had visions of selling in Europe, bypassing the broker."

Clive snorted. "Well, this serves to validate what your bride told you. King and Gibson was getting desperate."

Jack sat back when the waiter put a plate of jambalaya in front of him. Clive did likewise, making sure the document was out of the way. Then he asked for more coffee.

"Look," Clive said, "I've been talking to Noble Corporation's lawyers. There are two of 'em, and they've been around a long time. Stuffy old fogies, but they confirm what Penny told you about Jon. Have you been over there yet?"

Jack shook his head. "I'm goin' after this."

"As of the day he died, Alan Noble owned forty percent of a very lucrative business. Jon Noble owned fifteen. The remaining forty five percent was divided up between seven other men, two holding twenty and twelve percent respectively, the other five lesser amounts with no one man holding more than five percent. When the patriarch, Horace Noble died, he owned sixty percent of the company. Never had his holdings fallen below fifty-one percent. Neither had Alan's until last year."

Jack met Clive's eyes.

"Alan Noble did a lot of finagling over the last decade to maneuver his brother's shipping department under corporate control. He sold shares, bought favors, and, the lawyers said, made some bad business moves, took risks, that sort of thing. He still had charge of the company, but his hold was slipping, and Jon, who was ever a thorn in his side, was very much aware.

"All the stockholders did was invest money, make lots more, and show up for monthly meetings followed by expensive lunches. They loved doing business with the man, and they're not looking forward to change. According to the lawyers, there's always been enough conflict between the corporation and its shipping arm that the present members of the Noble Corporation board do not want Jon Noble sitting on, much less heading, the board. In his younger days, he was always in trouble with Mobile authorities. He liked hanging out at the docks with his 'associates.' He killed a man in a knife fight when he was nineteen and a second not long after. Horace, the daddy, balled his fists at that point, and the boy made an effort to straighten up, but the lawyers say it was never a night-and-day turnaround. They are emphatic that he is not in line to inherit the corporation or the estate. Harold was the heir. In lieu of him, his spouse should inherit. Right now you are an unknown entity and the lesser of two evils. You might end up a very wealthy man."

Jack swallowed the jambalaya in his mouth and kept his eyes on Clive. "But for Penny, right?"

"Have you talked to her about the night Alan Noble died?"

"I asked if they were lovers. She said no. She also said she had nothing to do with Florence Noble's death. She's not being real forthcoming, Clive, so I didn't press the issue. I wanted to get my hands on the promissory note first."

The lawyer took another sip of Remy Taloose's coffee. "That's it, huh? Well, let me put it to you this way. Without Penny, your claim to the Noble estate, corporation, house, promissory note, everything is in jeopardy, especially if she's found guilty of murder or conspiracy to commit murder. Jonathan Noble will find himself a good lawyer—hell, maybe even those stuffy old fogies or me if you don't change your one-track attitude—and he's gonna lay claim to the family empire, the board willing or not."

"I'm not focused on King and Gibson, Clive. I didn't want to push her. Toby Craig got his permission to exhume Florence Noble's body, I take it?"

"Fritz, the coroner, already has the body. And there's something else you need to know. Humboldt directed me to approach Stuart Frederick with an offer for King and Gibson."

Heart in his throat, Jack stared at Clive. "You—"

"Not me. Nate. You apparently said something to him regarding Eva Markiston's financial distress. You knew Humboldt had been interested in the Wolf River mill for the past two years."

"I've offered Nate encouragement to get it."

"Well, Nate now knows you're in a position to get it yourself, and I figure he realizes if he doesn't act fast, Humboldt is going to lose it to you. You talk too much. Nate's just doing his job."

"Dammit."

"You're okay for right now. Rest assured Humboldt's offer did not meet the ten thousand required for the Markiston woman to pay off this note. Of course, we didn't know how much to offer."

"That company isn't worth ten thousand dollars."

"I know it, but if King and Gibson has any other assets it can liquidate, that won't keep Stuart from selling short of what he owes you before the first."

"Can we—"

"No grounds. That loan isn't due till the first. My advice is to sit tight. Frederick refused to even discuss the matter. From what you're telling me, I imagine that bad decision came from his mother-in-law. She's still holding out hope for Penny's arrest."

"That's part of it." Jack tapped the promissory note with his index finger. "She doesn't even realize her real problem, which is my having this note."

Chapter Seventy

Tobias Craig's brogans clopped on the wooden steps leading up to the police station's side entry. The stairs squeaked, and the sound made him grit his teeth. His head had started to hurt when he turned the corner at Washington after leaving Peter Fritz, the county coroner. Lord he was glad he didn't have that job. He tore the hat from his head and reached for the doorknob.

Jenkins informed him yesterday they'd called off the search for Penny King. She was alive, somewhere, but if Jenkins knew the details, and why the hell wouldn't the county sheriff, he hadn't explained it to Toby. Of most interest was the sudden lack of opposition to the exhumation of Florence Noble's body. Toby shut the door, a little too hard.

"Yo, boss," Charlie Nixon said, "Penny King is back in town."

Toby sighed, then made his way over to the water barrel and pulled the dipper from its nail on the wall. "Biloxi or Mississippi City?"

"Handsboro. She's movin' back into her house in Biloxi to-morrow. Her husband's bringing her home."

"Well, hell. Talk about the biggest pile of horse-shittin' waste of time and taxpayer money. Jon Noble found her, I take it?"

"Nope."

"Well, who the hell—"

"Afternoon, Marshal."

Toby, the dipper still in his hand, looked up to see Jack Gibson in his office door.

"You're the one bringing this gossip? Been to the jail?"

Jack shrugged. "I haven't been to the jail, and I am the one spreading good news."

"Well assumin' Harold Noble hasn't risen from the grave, what damn fool married the little twit?" He glanced at Charlie, who sat at his desk with his mouth open.

"Well, tell me, dammit!"

Charlie looked at Jack and said, "Chief's kinda slow today. Been a rough week."

Toby glowered at Charlie.

"That damn fool would be me," Jack said.

Toby furrowed his brow, then turned on his heel and hung the dipper back on the nail. He looked at the window, stroked his precious mustache, both sides, lord it was a fine mustache, and pivoted on Jack. "Did you just say you married Penny King?"

"Yep."

"Mm hmm." He looked back at the window, then laughed and said, "Looks like that little gal isn't as big a twit as I thought. I bet Eva Markiston could kill an alligator with her bare hands about now."

"Three days ago I couldn't find a judge to even look at an order to do the exhumation, much less sign off on one. Now I've got Lyle Jenkins and the county prosecutor breathing down my neck to make an arrest."

"The Markiston-Frederick clan has removed the fetters," Jack said to Craig, then braced. "You gonna bring her in?"

"I'm not done with my investigation. Hell, I don't even have an official report back on Alan Noble, much less his wife. The coroner seems to think the missus will be easier. Fritz has got a hair up his ass now, and he's corresponding with some detective out of St. Louis who specializes in poisons, or claims to anyway. I think Doc Fritz just wants to play around with some new gol dang experiments he's heard of. That or he's been readin' too many ten-penny novels. My bet is that fat old buzzard Noble died of a stroke wrestlin' with a sweet young thing who didn't want to wrestle." Toby leaned forward in his chair. It was mid-afternoon, and the room was a tad warm. "Before that gal wed you, Eva wanted her protected. Now she wants her arrested, tried, and convicted, and fast. I understand the reasons behind Eva's bein' upset with her granddaughter marrying you, but why did the girl run in the first place?"

"Eva and Stuart have a large debt due to the Noble estate on the first of November. Penny inherited the note. She is also in line to inherit Alan and Harold Noble's shares in the company—but Eva and Stuart had to keep her out of jail for killing Florence Noble. To accomplish all this to their benefit, they had to get her where they could control her, hence marry her off to Jon Noble. But Penny didn't want to marry Jon Noble, so Eva kidnapped her and hooked her on morphine to force her to do what she wanted."

Toby shook his head. "Got a whiff of that talking to Dr. Clark in Mississippi City. Bad as I thought it was, I didn't figure even Eva Markiston being that ruthless." Craig slapped his desk. "The doc said that girl wasn't a dope user."

"Do you believe her capable of having conspired with her father-in-law to kill Florence Noble?"

Toby studied him as if debating whether he should answer or not. Then he sighed. "Depends on her relationship with Alan Noble, and even that doesn't prove your bride is a murderess, only an adulteress whore. He held up a hand, a moot gesture since Jack had made no reaction to the words. "I'm not saying she's either. She had a knot on her noggin and a ripped night-gown the night Alan Noble died. She'd been drinking and gotten sick. I smelled the alcohol and the vomit. She didn't deny nothin'. Said he came to her room sick himself and her injuries were"— Toby rolled his eyes—"accidental. But I can tell you this, son, she wouldn't be the first woman who denied being raped. Figure they're to blame somehow, and they just don't want people to know it happened."

Chapter Seventy-one

"Take the desk," Thomas Gates told Jack. "If the board gets its wish, that's the way it will be."

"You do know I'm a timberman and have never managed anything beyond felling crews in my life." That wasn't completely true, but it was close enough.

"All the better. Initial speculation is that makes you more amenable to good advice."

Jack grinned. "And you're assuring me, Mr. Gates, that the advice will be good."

"It'll be me giving it, at least initially, so yes."

Jack took the seat behind Alan Noble's desk, Thomas Gates the leather chair in front of it. Gates held up a sheaf of papers. "Bylaws. Thought I'd get you started."

Jack wasn't gonna argue. The welcome had honestly been much better than he expected. He did, however, need to get back to Penny.

"I've set you up a meeting with the corporate attorneys at four."

Clive's old fogies, Jack surmised.

"But I wanted to go over something with you first, something I've apprised them of, but have yet to report officially.

"With the deaths of both the chief executive officer and his presumed heir and the board's anticipation of the widow's assumption of corporate duties, we set up an audit. Such change in status is required in the corporate bylaws." Gates nodded to the bound papers he'd placed in front of Jack. "Jon's been demanding an ad hoc audit for the past six weeks. It's a demand he's made periodically over the years, but he's never been accommo-

313

dated. Noble Corporation has a schedule of audits and there's never been a reason or desire to deviate from it. The things are a pain in the ass. However, over the past several years, Alan Noble's distinction as majority shareholder had slipped. Though he was still the primary stockholder, others on the board were in a better position to challenge his hold, and Jon was gaining some influence, particularly among one old shareholder who had originally been on the now defunct Hampton Shipping Corporation board before the death of Jon's maternal grandfather many years ago." Gates rubbed his forehead. "I tell you this, because it probably explains Jon's persistence as well as Alan's resistance to an audit. We found a discrepancy in the accounts."

Jack frowned. "How large a discrepancy?"

"Actually it was two discrepancies, one last April, and one less than three weeks ago. The first for ten thousand dollars, the one last month for"—he blew out a breath—"twenty-five thousand."

The ten thousand was what Alan Noble had loaned Eva from his "personal" account. That twenty-five thousand no doubt represented his purchase of the Perry County property belonging to the Pennsylvania spinster.

"It appears Alan repaid a portion of the ten thousand dollars to the corporate account in July."

"How much?"

"Thirty-five hundred."

"So he was embezzling—"

"The more accurate term is 'wrongful misappropriation' in that it appears he intended to repay the funds. Regardless, it's thievery. Alan was appropriating capital not his own and using it, we must assume, to make a profit. He would then restore the base sum, pocket the gain in his private account and no one was the wiser.

"Out of curiosity, I reviewed the board minutes for the past three years, ascertained where mention was made by one or more members in regards to Jon's appeal for an audit, then had our accountant pull all the records for that time. He's not finished, but so far he's found nothing. I don't expect he will. If, indeed,

Alan did borrow from the account in the past, and then didn't drop dead before he fixed the discrepancies, there'd be nothing to find. As of today, however, the books are thirty-one thousand, five hundred dollars short. Just between you and me, though, I don't believe Jon Noble's past requests for audits would have happened had he not been confident his older brother was misusing company funds."

"How would Jon have known what Alan was doing unless his brother told him?"

Gates shrugged. "Someone else who was aware of Alan's activities might have said something. But I doubt that. Alan was not stupid. This is an egregious offense to investors, and Alan would not have let anyone know. Jon, however, is not stupid either. He would have seen any financial largess reflected in Alan's lifestyle." Gates shook his head. "Such behavior on Alan's part might have gone back as far as Horace's...uh, their father's day. Something known and admonished within the family itself, making Jon all too aware of his brother's propensity to misappropriate the property of others."

"So what do we do now?"

"The easiest thing to do would be as soon as Noble Corporation's next ship comes in"—Gates smiled with his use of the cliché—"you take the sum from your forty percent profit and return it to the account. That's what Alan would have done." Again, Gates looked at the figures. "But this is a rather large expense, I fear. I wonder—"

"I believe it was land speculation in which he expected a quick turnaround that didn't pan out."

Gates looked at him and Jack explained his thoughts on the Perry County land Alan had foolishly invested in. "We could always try to resell the land for cost, but I don't think we'll find a buyer anytime soon. In a few years, maybe."

"You won't have a few years. You may have to liquidate some other personal assets in the short term. If the money is replaced, that should satisfy the board and prevent any involvement by authorities, something always best to avoid. And, of course, before you repay the money, I will provide you a detailed brief of the accountant's findings."

That wasn't really necessary. Jack believed him. The dates and the sums matched known financial dealings of which Jack was aware.

"Well, well, Jack Gibson, the thief who ran off with my intended, not to mention casting me from my brother's house."

Jack looked up from the documents Thomas Gates had left him. Outside the door of what had been Alan Noble's well-outfitted office stood the apparently unflappable Jon Noble, a smile on his face and a suit on his back, all dressed up for work.

"And, adding insult to injury, has now usurped your long-desired desk." Jack knew that for the week and a half leading up to the court order ousting him three days ago, Jon Noble had appropriated this office space on the corner of Lameuse and Jackson Streets in Biloxi. But after lunching with Clive, Jack had come here and occupied Alan Noble's office. Thomas Gates condoned his coup by handing him the company bylaws. Jack cared little for imports, or offices for that matter, but he wasn't giving up this desk.

Jon leaned a shoulder against the jamb and folded his arms over his chest. "Forgive me if I feel betrayed."

"How does it feel?"

"I never compromised you."

"You failed to compromise me, you mean."

"Touché, an error in judgment."

"In favor of your allies over in Mississippi City, no doubt."

Jon sauntered on into the room. "Yes, well, that association appears to have proven a bust all the way around. So, what's your plan?"

Jack leaned back in the swivel chair. "Like I said, I'm sitting in Alan Noble's chair."

"Hmmpf," Jon said, then smiled. "You know my sister-in-law's body's been exhumed."

"I heard. Eva's working fast."

"Eva's angry. She's working too fast for her own good, but this move certainly serves mine. You do know that if Florence is found to have been murdered, your little gain here is going to be in serious jeopardy, not to mention your bride."

"The gamble's worth it."

"I could offer a safer bet. You willin' to hear me out?"

Jack rested his forearm on the desk. "I'm listening."

"You want King and Gibson. I want Noble Corporation."

"If Penny is hanged for murder, you'll have everything. Why do you need me?"

"I don't have time to wait. You can help expedite things. In return, you get King and Gibson as a sure thing."

Jack studied the man a moment, then nodded. "Shut the door and have a seat."

Chapter Seventy-two

Jack scratched at the stubble on his jaw. He washed out back after eating the supper Kate saved him. He would shave in the morning. He turned from the mirror over the dresser and pulled the bed sheet down. Penny was sleeping next door. Kate told him she'd hustled her to bed after she'd eaten. Poor girl was exhausted and couldn't keep her eyes open waiting for him in the parlor. Kate promised Jack would wake her when he got in, but he wasn't going to. He'd had a long day himself. After lunch with Clive, he secured the promissory note at the bank, had his impromptu meetings with Craig, Gates, and Jon Noble, then met in the late afternoon with the Noble Corporation attorneys, the old fogies Clive called them. They confirmed what Clive, and later, Jon Noble had told him. Frail and doddering old lawyers at first glance, they proved pillars of corporate and inheritance law.

In regards to Noble Corporation, they'd structured Horace Noble's bequest to ensure the safekeeping of his company while protecting the limited interests of his younger son, as long as the latter cooperated. If ever Jon reverted to the irresponsible behavior of his youth and threatened Noble Corporation proper, he was to be cut loose and the shipping arm pulled beneath the company umbrella. Alan and the board had already managed the latter with share finagling.

Jon, however, claimed Alan's most recent plans were, with his son's concurrence, to take the shipping away from him and give it to Harold. Whatever, Jon Noble was going to have a hell of a time getting what he wanted, but he knew that. Besides, by Jon's estimation, the two stuffy lawyers would be gone to glory in the short term and their junior partners could prove more

318

amenable to his needs. Family was family, after all, and Noble Corporation was a family business.

Even Jack could see that. Penny wasn't blood, and if she were proven guilty of murder, her claim would be void. Even those stuffy "old fogies" agreed her conviction would cause a serious problem for the wishes of the lately-departed Horace Noble. Jack blew out a breath. He hadn't brought up the thirty-one thousand plus dollars he owed Noble Corporation. That he needed to talk to Clive about first.

Jack dimmed the coal oil lamp on the unadorned table next to the bed, then raised the shade covering the open window. He could smell fall in the moonless night if not feel its chill. The door to the room next to his opened and Penny stepped through, eyes bright and coppery hair in appealing disarray. He moved closer to her. She smelled of sleep-swept skin, sweetened with a hint of toilet water he'd long associated with his Aunt Millie. It was the one thing that alleviated her desirability, which even the service-able nightgown and robe that she had to hold up to keep from tripping on it failed to do. "Pink's not your color," he said.

"Did you find it?"

"I'd have woken you if I hadn't." He tugged on her arm and pulled her into the room.

"I tried to wait up. Where have you been?"

"At Noble Corporation studying bylaws. Have a seat," he said leading her toward the bed. She sat at the foot, though he offered her the pillowed head. He took it instead.

"And what did your lawyer say?"

"He said if Stuart Frederick doesn't come up with ten thou-sand dollars in ten days we can foreclose, assuming you're not in jail for murder." He looked her in the eye. "Florence Noble's body has been exhumed, Penny. What are they going to find?"

"I think they'll find she was poisoned. How were things at the house?"

He pursed his lips, but he didn't push. "That Gracie Cooley woman said someone was back in the house overnight looking for something. She suspects Jon has a key. She said he was going through rooms all week prior to his eviction. She's glad we're coming back because she's tired of cleaning up after him."

"Did Jane not hear him in the house at night?"

"She says no. I made a point of asking Grace her opinion about that. She says she's probably telling the truth since her room is in back, off the dining room. Now," he said, and leaned forward a bit, "this thing about Alan and Florence Noble?"

An oh-sweet-Jesus look crossed her face, and he sat back up straight.

"You said you thought they'd find Florence Noble was poisoned. Why?"

"He was so angry and hurt, and he fired the cook!"

"He was angry at his wife?"

"There was some land they duped him into buying. At least he thought they tricked him. All three of them. Jonathan, Harold, and Florence. I think they did, too."

"Was that the land in Perry County?"

"Yes, you know about it?"

"Alan Noble went up to Piotona a few days before he died. Asked my supervisor about it. He had been led to believe —"

"Humboldt wanted it. That's right."

"The prosecutor is going to focus on Alan's nude body in your bedroom just days after he buried his wife, not land he was tricked into buying by a double-dealing spouse. You're sure there was nothing between you two, not any indication he might be interested in you? Tell me the truth, I'm not going to judge you."

"There was nothing, not until the night he died. He became rather vulgar, made some tasteless remarks about siring his own grandson, and then he dropped dead. That's it."

He lifted his chin and said softly, "Did he rape you?"

"His intent was seduction, that's why the champagne bottle."

"An empty champagne bottle."

She rose from her spot and started for the door. "Look, Jack, no matter what I claim, I look guilty in the eyes of the law, in the eyes of society, and in your eyes, too, I'm sure. I've decided to weather it."

"You might weather society, and I'm not sure yet that I give a darn, but I'm not a threat. You might want to consider talking to your new lawyer, because the problem is gonna be weathering the *law*."

"'Not sure you care?'" She reached for the doorknob. "You and *your* new lawyer could prove quite a threat to me in your own right."

"You listen to me, honey. You get convicted of murder and I'm out everything. So don't try to conceal the sordid facts by saying you no longer trust me."

She blinked with his words, then dropped her hand from the knob. "You know him, don't you?"

Jack's heartbeat quickened.

"You called him Jon earlier. Just Jon. It was less your exclusive use of his given name than how you said it. It wasn't me he was looking for at the Biloxi mill last week. It really was you."

Well hell, he'd done a damn poor job of felling that tree, and he couldn't just set it back up again. He rose from the bed.

"Afraid so, darlin'. I've known him since you married Harold. He came to me. He always comes to me. Back then he tried to bribe me to deny Eva shipping on the Humboldt trunks. I was never in a position to do that, but Humboldt was already squeezing. She was deep in their debt, and they wanted the Wolf River mill. Alan's loan saved her. According to Jon, Eva and Alan were about to cost his shipping branch a lot of money. He says Alan's ploy was to make him look bad in front of the board. Things flip-flopped when Alan and Harold Noble died, and he figured working with Eva was better than against."

"So you knew he planned on marrying me."

"Kate heard the gossip, she told me. I didn't think much about it actually other than it was in pretty poor taste since you'd just buried your husband. I couldn't help but wonder what your daddy would have said. I didn't know you were opposed to marrying him. Where you stood in all this never came up. And you were anything but careful by coming to me. Now I find I was equally reckless in taking you. The only thing I'm sure of is that you made a good choice in me. Verdict is still out as to whether I was wise in the decision I made."

She swung the door wide. "I've kept my promise to you."

"And I've kept mine. Trouble is we're a long way from finished here."

Chapter Seventy-three

"**I** don't want to live there."

Jack looked up from the shell-covered Biloxi-Pass Christian Road. They headed east in Effie Davidson's carriage. "Because of the deaths?"

"Yes. We should get our own place."

"A honeymoon cottage, you mean?"

"No," she snapped. "I'd rather the boarding house to that horrid mansion."

The long stretch of highway, bereft of most everything on the north but pine and massive live-oak since they'd left Handsboro late that morning, was giving way to signs of civilization, and Penny sat back in unveiled annoyance when he turned the carriage south on Caillavet. He planned to pick up that portion of Front Street where easements had been acquired. From the point where Caillavet joined Front at the water, Front would continue eastward, unbroken, until it terminated at the watery entrance to the Back Bay. Jack considered his choice more scenic than the Pass Christian Road. It was also a slower, more circuitous route to the Nobles' House on Main Street.

The ragged shore-line was dotted here and there with wooden piers, some newly built, or rebuilt, and some dilapidated, more flotsam than piers. All were extensions of dirt paths crossing the road and leading to beach-front homes, many impressive, built on knolls and stilts and flanked on all sides by huge verandas. The Nobles' house, one of the more impressive ones, was not on the water, but Jack wanted that house. He gently jiggled the reins, urging the slowing horse faster. "Is that the reason you kept me up all night bouncing around in that room?"

323

"Partly."

"And what's the other part?"

"The fear of unexpected visitors."

"If you were scared, you could have stayed in my room with me."

"Have you ever considered it was your being so close that bothered my sleep?"

"That can be interpreted two ways, Mrs. Gibson."

Her eyes widened. "Well, the correct interpretation is your friendship with Jon Noble."

"First off, Jon Noble and I are not friends. Secondly, you are glad I know him, you just don't realize it. What you really wish is that you didn't know that I know him."

She said something unladylike under her breath.

"I still don't see what all this has to do with our honeymoon bungalow you have suggested, because you'll still have me under the same roof with you, so tell me the truth."

She closed her eyes. "There's something wrong in that house."

"Bad memories or a guilty conscience?" He'd tried to keep his tone light, but part of him did wonder. He knew something was bothering her, but given her recent ordeals he would have never guessed the house.

"I don't have a guilty conscience."

"The memories then?" he said, less jocular now.

"That wouldn't keep me from living there."

"We could fire the last two servants."

"It's not them."

"What is it?"

"I don't know."

"Can you explain it?"

She looked at him, then turned away. "If I could explain it, I'd know, wouldn't I?"

"There's a difference in explaining something and being willing to explain it. What happened between you and Alan Noble the night he died, for instance."

Beside him she gave a derisive snort. He thought she might

have rolled her eyes, too, but he didn't see. She turned in her seat and looked again at the road in front of them. To their right, between a thinned layer of shortleaf pine, he could see the waters of the Gulf glinting in the noonday sun. Twenty yards farther up was a wagon road leading to the water's edge. He took the road. Penny glanced at him, but said nothing. When he'd cleared the trees at the dirt shore and lighted from the carriage to offer her a hand, she took it without comment and let him help her down into the pine straw and grass. He didn't let go of her hand, but pulled her closer to the water.

"Listen, Copper Lee, possession is nine-tenths of the law. One of the reasons our lawyer made the effort to kick Jon out of Alan Noble's house was to get you back in it. The other problem is we are house poor until the courts settle this matter. I just broke my last gold eagle ransoming the carriage from the livery in Pass Christian."

"You still have a job?"

"I get paid the end of the month. I've spent my entire September pay getting married to you." That wasn't true, but he had spent money he didn't normally spend...and the subterfuge supported his case.

"We could sell Jon Noble's ring."

"You need to return Jon Noble's ring."

"I'll return it by courier. I don't want to ever see his face again." She hadn't looked at him when she spoke, but at the placid Gulf. It was hot. Beads of sweat had formed on her brow. They were beneath the pine shade, but that damn long-sleeved dress looked hot. He, on the other hand, had removed his jacket when they got in the carriage. He still wore his long-sleeve shirt. He wished he could remove it and suggest she do likewise with that dress, and they'd run out naked and frolic in the muddy water. It was probably still as warm as a bathtub, but cooler than the air suffocating them. He wouldn't have had to suggest that twice to the little girl she'd been. When it came to getting naked and playing in muddy water, Penny was always quicker than Adel.

She stepped away from him and stared out at the water a good stone's throw away. "The water reflects the sky. From the way the sun is shining on it, you can't even tell how ugly brown it really is."

Inwardly he cursed. "Penny?"

Her back was to him. She looked small and vulnerable...and stubborn. Her head turned halfway so he could see her profile and his groin tightened.

"Let's sit a minute and observe the false beauty of the Gulf."

She cocked her head and studied the water. "Is all beauty false, do you think?"

He was just wondering that himself. He sat in pine straw next to where she stood and coaxed her down beside him. "I think the answer would depend on what one considered beautiful."

"And what do you consider beauty to be?"

"I don't consider it. I know it when I see it. And I didn't come out here to be philosophical."

She turned then and looked at him, laughter in her eyes and a smile on her lips, and she laughed. Yes, *she* was beautiful.

"I don't think I've heard you laugh in years."

She looked away and rested her arms on drawn-up knees. "I've laughed in the intervening seven years. You just haven't been around at happy times."

"Or maybe my presence subdued those happy moments."

"Or maybe you only appear at troubled times, like King Arthur when England needs him most."

"I don't think he's been back yet, Penny."

"Of course he has, just in a different form."

He leaned back on his elbows and enjoyed an intermittent breeze. "You've been reading too much Scott."

"Thomas Moore. Scott is too cumbersome for my taste." She turned and looked at him. "So, why did you pull off the road?"

"To talk you into the house. I have never in my life lived in a house like the Nobles'. I'm looking forward to it. "

"You don't have to talk me into the house. I can't refuse to go there with you, can I?"

He pushed himself up, then purposefully bumped her shoulder with his. "All right, I wanted to give you the delusion it's your choice."

"If it makes you feel less guilty about foisting on me something you know I do not want, I will agree that for pragmatic reasons, we have no other choice right now but to live there."

They passed Main Street where the Noble house stood. The smell of cut grass replaced that of brackish water. A short block later, Jack turned the carriage north on Perrella and five hundred feet farther, just shy of Water Street, he turned the carriage onto the oak-shaded drive of Alan Noble's elegant home, surrounded by Florence's manicured yard. Despite the early afternoon heat, Penny shuddered beneath the tree-domed drive.

"Start on in," Jack said when he helped her down outside the carriage shed. "They're expectin' you. I'll find that boy Roland, and get him to return Miss Effie's carriage, then I'll be in."

Penny rounded the kitchen. The yard was deserted and quiet, the windows of the three-story Victorian dark as obsidian, and she couldn't help but wonder what watched from within. She stopped and looked over her shoulder. A gentle breeze brushed her cheek and she started forward again. Regardless of what else lurked inside, Gracie and Jane would both be stirring.

Penny stepped onto the first of four wide steps leading up to the veranda at the back of the house. The board groaned, and the scrape of a chair on wood echoed the step's protest. The racket was worse for the fright it caused than the unpleasant sound it made, and Penny jerked her head up. A large Negro, hat in hand, stood on the porch looking down on her.

"Miz Gibson," the man said with a nod.

"Yes?"

"You 'member me, ma'am? I be Mars. Mars Bullock, we met da night you wed Mista Jack."

She stared at him. Her palm hurt from her grip on the handrail. She relaxed her hold. "The Humboldt shack in Hancock County," she said softly.

A smile lit the man's face. "Yo' sho' seem like you'z feelin' better den las' I seen you."

"Much better. I never properly thanked you for giving up your home that night."

"Happy to do it. Happy to. Yo' needed a place to curl up, ain't no doubt 'bout it."

Gracie pulled the back door open, looked at Mars, then Penny. "He been waitin' on one a you fo' da pas' two hours. Says Mr. Gibson sent fo' 'im."

Penny restarted her ascent. "Have you eaten?"

"No, ma'am, I —"

"We ain't fed him. Didn't know what he's doin' 'ere. Looks like a field nigga to me."

"Jack, he sent fo' me, Miz Gibson. Messenger come at dinna time yesta'day."

"He didn't say anything to me," Penny said, "but you go on now and get yourself something to eat in the cookhouse."

"Gumbo's ready," Jane called, and Penny looked down the covered breezeway to the cookhouse. The girl stood there, her head stuck out the cookhouse door. "I'll make 'im a bowl, Miz Penny."

Penny tilted her head Jane's direction, bidding the man go.

"You wash," Gracie snapped. "Pump's back da cookhouse."

"Yes'm, Miz Gracie, reckon I know to wash up." He smashed his flop hat back on his head, and with a sassy smile at Gracie and a wink for Penny, he bounded down the steps like a ten-year-old boy, and Penny smiled. He'd probably spent a day and a half on one water and roadway after another and hadn't taken time to eat the entire trip.

"Yo new husban' mighta tol' us he was comin'," Gracie said. "Looks uncouf to me an' big enough to eat you outa house an' home."

"He's a good man, Gracie, and I think we can afford to feed him."

Chapter Seventy-four

"Why is he here?" Penny asked and tossed down the king of clubs. She hadn't wanted to, but she was out of options. She smirked when Jack reached for the draw pile.

He narrowed his eyes, gave the king a second glance.... "Who?"

"Mars, and if it plays, you have to pick it up."

"I know the rules." He drew from the draw pile.

"Doesn't mean you play by them."

He situated his new card in his hand and discarded the trey of diamonds.

"I give you kings, and you toss me threes." She picked it up. "Rummy."

He cursed. Oh lord—she laughed out loud—he was holding near a hundred points. He leaned back in his chair and started canceling what he held against what he'd played.

"You still haven't caught me."

Yes, he was winning, but she was catching up, primarily because they played alike. Uncle Jimmy had liked to hold big cards. She used to watch him and her daddy play when she'd been little. Hugh King would eye Jim Gibson, grin, then whisper in Penny's ear. "He's holding a handful, Copper Lee, whatcha wanna bet?"

She didn't bet. Her daddy was right. Sometimes it paid off for Uncle Jim, sometimes he got stuck holdin'. Playing rummy with Jack tonight, she missed them both.

"You didn't answer me," she said.

He tossed in his cards. "Subtract forty. He's here to protect my investment."

329

She frowned. "Me?"

"Suffice it to say you're the key to it."

"I'm not an investment. I'm a windfall."

"You're a high-risk gamble, and I've bet my whole pot, what little there was, on you." He gathered the deck and started shuffling. "What I don't understand is why Harold wanted you in the first place."

"Jon suggested me as an appropriate wife."

"To Harold or Alan?"

"Harold. Harold approached Alan, who approached Stuart."

"Well, then, do you know any reason why you'd be of greater value to Harold dead than alive?"

He watched her when he said it. Not a blink. She did have the discretion to look him in the eye. "Why did you say that?" she asked.

"Do you know the answer?"

"As to why you said it or why you think they thought me more valuable dead than alive."

"The second one, and who is 'they'? I specifically said Harold."

"I don't know the answer to either of your questions, but Alan, nonspecifically, said 'they'."

"What exactly was Alan referring to and when?"

She picked up the top card in the draw pile and situated it in her hand. "I recall that he made vague reference to 'their' having been up to something for a while and me being key to it. I feared he was accusing me, but now I think it was a warning. That was the night he died. He was drunk."

"He was drunk when—"

"This was earlier in the evening. He came home drunk that night."

"Were you drunk?"

She looked up from her cards. "No."

"So, you interpret that to mean 'they' were trying to kill you?"

She tossed out the two of clubs, then hastily shifted the cards in her hand. "Not until you said what you did about Harold."

"Hit you like a bolt of lightning, huh?"

"More like the striking and extinguishing of a match. I'd never thought of Harold wanting me to die. Play."

He drew the five of diamonds and discarded it on top of the deuce of clubs. "And when were you going to bring up with me what Alan said?"

"Why does it matter? 'They' are all dead."

"Jonathan Noble isn't."

"An acquaintance of yours."

"And that, by default, makes me part of 'they'?"

"I hadn't thought of it that way." She drew and discarded the four of spades. He picked it up and played it with the five and six of spades. She looked at the cards on the table, then at him. "I don't care about the Nobles, Jack. All I care about is Grandmother and King and Gibson, and it's all I think you should care about, too."

"You do, huh?"

She nodded, and he grimaced. "Well, like it or not, I have to be concerned with you, and I think I know the answer as to why Alan was so upset about that Perry County land he was duped into buying. He needed to turn a quick profit to cover the loan he'd made to Eva."

He told her about Alan Noble's taking from the till and the subsequent threat of an audit. She played, then stopped looking at her cards and listened, finally laying her hand face down on the table.

"He'd already repaid thirty-five hundred of the original ten thousand dollars he took for your grandmother," Jack continued. "But Jon's demand for an audit was gaining purchase, and Alan was under the gun. He'd painted himself into a hole when Jon started fidgeting with the shipping schedules. Alan had assumed Noble's purchase of Blake Shipping would accommodate Noble Corporation's meeting its domestic responsibilities, thereby supplying Alan his regular income from Brazil, but Jon allowed obligations for Blake Shipping into the contract for the sale, purposefully delaying shipment on goods Alan needed to make up his shortfall within the time required. Jon maintained it was to meet Eva's requirements. Having gotten himself in a bind, trying to get Jon in a bind, Alan risked a fortune on that land buy. He calculated that a quick turnaround on the Perry County land would provide him enough to cover the shortfall and justify both abuses."

"Only to find out Jonathan, with the help of his own wife and son, had duped him."

"Not only duped him. His baby brother had finally managed to maneuver him into a serious situation. He'd have lost the company and might have gone to jail. Which brings me back around to you."

Her eyes found his.

"You are linked to both companies. If we hold on to King and Gibson, we stand to get Noble Corporation as a bonus prize."

"But now we've got that shortfall —"

"Yes, but that's not really relevant to my argument. My point is this link between you and Noble Corporation is new. It wasn't there when Alan approached Stuart seven months ago. That connection would have never come about except that now Alan and Harold are both dead."

She picked up her hand, then drew a card.

"It was my play," he said.

"Sorry." She replaced the card on top of the draw pile.

"So, understanding there was no connection between you and Noble Corporation at the time Alan Noble approached your grandmother for your hand, what was the reason the Nobles wanted you?"

He picked up the card, the ace of spades, her watching him all the while. "I want that card," she told him.

He grinned. "I know you do. To collect it, no doubt." He discarded it. "Can't pick it up, can you?"

She huffed, but she didn't pick it up. She met his eyes. "I'll get it in a bit. And in answer to your other question, I don't know why they wanted me. But tell me, Jimmy Jack, what will you do when *you* find out I'm more valuable to you dead than alive?"

332

Chapter Seventy-five

Jack rapped once on the door between her room and his and asked if she were decent. He opened it when she answered that she was and handed her the flannel nightgown he'd found on his bed.

"From what you've told me, I've gotten the impression you and Harold were not intimate. Am I right?"

She blinked at him.

"There's a reason for my question."

"I'm sure there is, but what is it?"

He studied her a long moment trying to read her mind, then gave up and said, "Now that we've put forth the theory Harold may have wanted to kill you, we might be able to confirm the answer by whether or not he was sleeping with you."

"Meaning men don't kill women they're intimate with?"

"I would think in some such cases murder would be even more likely, but what I'm getting at is I personally would find it difficult to feign passion for a woman whose death I was actually plotting."

"But one can have relations with some —"

"Penny, I'm aware of all that, believe me. But will you please just answer the question."

"No."

"No?"

She turned away. "No, we were not intimate. Whenever I broached the subject he would get hostile, even violent." She stopped herself, wanting to say more, he thought, but not sure she should. Finally, she blurted, "I found something in —"

A violent gust of wind rattled the glass panels of the closed

333

window and set the curtains of the open one nearest her bed to billowing, knocking over a small vase. Penny jumped as the vase hit the floor and broke, and she turned to him, hand at her throat. "What was that?" she forced out.

Jack shook his head and stepped around the broken vase and closed the window. "A gust of wind." He knelt on one knee and started picking up pieces of glass. "What did you find?" he prodded and looked up when she didn't answer.

She stood braced against the dresser, her eyes darting furtively around the room, her clenched knuckles white.

"Penny?"

Her breathing was heavy, but she did look at him.

"You said you found something. What?"

She started shaking her head rapidly, then pushing herself from the dresser, she squatted and started helping him pick up the glass. Immediately, she cut herself.

He cursed and grabbed her hand wanting to stop her frantic movements as much as the flow of blood. She yanked her hand away and stood. "It's all right." She disappeared into his room without a backward glance. He found her there at his wash bowl, a bloody rag folded over the edge, her injured hand suspended over the basin while she pressed the cut with the other. She looked at him. "Fingers bleed so badly."

He came and stood over her. "It's a bad cut. That's why it's bleeding so badly." He took a clean washrag and pressed it on her hand. "What has you spooked?"

"The suddenness of it, the noise."

"What did you find?"

"I'm sorry?"

"You said you found something."

"Oh, a note. Something Harold wrote. His mother didn't approve of his..."

"Lifestyle?" Jack finished for her.

"Yes. They apparently didn't get along after he got older."

"And his father?"

She gave a nervous laugh and stepped away from him. "I've

told you Alan thinks Harold was part of the plot to dupe him into buying that land. What kind of son would do that?" She eyed Jack. "What kind of father would believe such of his son?"

"I understand what you mean."

"I think his parents' disapproval had something to do with his hostility toward me."

"But didn't he ask his father's help in marrying you?"

"He wanted a place in the company. He got that in return for marrying."

She was flighty now, nervous, anxious. She would not, or could not, be still. Jack rubbed the back of his neck and followed her with his eyes. "Did he ever hurt you...physically, I mean?"

"Only once, and he apologized after. He went to some length to control himself, I think."

Jack nodded, then held out his hand. She placed the uninjured one in his. He squeezed her fingers, then took her other hand and removed the rag. "The bleeding's stopped." Without warning, she stepped into him with a sob. Dismayed by the sob, yet pleasantly surprised by the warmth of her body next to his, he wrapped both arms around her and held her tight. There were no tears, just that one sob. He wanted to ask if she'd like to stay in here with him tonight, but by now an erection had forced itself against his thigh, and he reminded himself of his own doubts about her role in all that had happened. He thought of her feelings, too, as well as his own. It wasn't a good idea. Momentarily, he pushed her back to arm's length. Her eyes were brimming, but there was no expectancy there. Perhaps she understood, or maybe she had doubts of her own. He bent and gave her a chaste kiss. She did not respond, except for the unspoken question in her bright eyes. "You have no idea what it is for a man to exercise control," he said. "You're witnessing it now." He guided her back through the door to her own room. "You might not always be so fortunate with me. Goodnight, Penny."

She watched the door shut and pondered his words with a flutter of excitement, then dismissed them. She'd known Jack all her life. She raised the wick in the lamp beside her bed, stacked the pillows behind her head, and opened her English gothic. She wasn't about to close her eyes and go to sleep in this room.

*J*ack adjusted his britches as he made his way to the carpet-bag he'd dropped on the bed hours ago. He hadn't brought much from Happy Hollow, and that girl Jane, at Penny's direction, had only started packing up Harold's things this afternoon. Nevertheless, there was room in the dresser, and he took advantage of it. Occasionally, he'd glance at the light beneath the door standing sentry between himself and his bride. Finally he checked on her, and finding her asleep, he extinguished her light.

Back in his room, he picked up the plat map Nate Stephens gave him over two weeks ago when he'd sent him down the Leaf to scout out the Perry County property Alan Noble was embroiled in and tossed it on top of Harold's desk. In the desk's middle drawer, he found a pencil, a compass, and a pad of paper, its top sheet annotated with numbers, notes, and scribbles, their meanings no doubt lost with Harold Noble. Jack picked up the pad, placed his map neatly in the bottom of the drawer, placed the pad back on top of it, and closed the drawer.

*P*enny shuddered beneath the sheets, and a wail swelled the darkness, drawing her from fitful slumber. She sat up with a small cry, the sound echoed only by her pounding heart.

A nightmare, though she did not recall dreaming. She turned to where she knew the nightstand to be. Her light...."

Someone, or something, was knocking at her hall door. She drew her knees to her breasts, then turned her head. There was no tell-tale light from next door. She called Jack's name. then stiffened. The knocking had assumed a cadence, each rap echoing on the heel of the last, circling the walls of her room, surrounding her.

Silence. For untold heartbeats it reigned over an impenetrable void. Deaf and blind, Penny breathed. Frigid air stung her nostrils.

She straightened her legs and raised the covers, ready...

The door to the hall crashed against the wall of her room. In front of her a gray portal swirled, and the all-but-forgotten wail crashed through the mist on the tail of a gale that tore at her hair and gown. She raised her hands to protect her face from the bedcovers tormented by the cursed wind.

She screamed, then screamed again, and fighting the covers, she twisted....

The room was warm, the blankets calm. To her left, light streamed into her room from Jack's.

He was beside her. "What the hell!"

She whimpered and reached for him, and he grasped her to him.

"Penny," she heard him say above his heartbeat in her ear. "What the devil is wrong?"

"You were either dreaming or..."

"Or what? I've lost my sanity? You heard the pounding?"

"What you heard was me running into your door."

"I'm talking about before I screamed. It was a horrible racket. It started at the hall door and went around the room. The air shuddered with it. Dear god, the echo"—she covered each ear with a respective fist—"was worse than the pounding. There is no way you didn't hear it. Mrs. Ansley way next door could have heard it, and she's about deaf."

"Jane? How about Mars and Roland in back of the carriage house? Do you see them here wringing their hands?"

She hugged herself.

"It wasn't real. Look." They were in his room, and he pulled her to the threshold of hers. She wouldn't step inside, he didn't try to make her. He crossed her dark room alone and unlocked the door leading into the hall. Yes, he told her, it was still locked. He pulled it wide. Light from the passageway flooded the room. His hall door, next to it, had been open the whole time, not to mention the hall sconces, though low, were burning and burned still.

"There is no way the opening of that door led to a misty hole," he told her. "You were dreaming."

"And what about my light? It's out. I left it on."

"I checked on you not five minutes before this happened and found you sleeping, so I blew it out."

She shook her head. "That door opened."

"How did it do that?"

She breathed through her nostrils. "It opened into hell, and I do not begin to know the powers of hell."

"You said the wind was frigid." He started back her way. "Hell has frozen over, you think?" He crossed the threshold back into his room, then shut the door to hers.

"Lock it," she said.

"Obviously that does no good."

"What happened was real."

"Copper Lee, it was a nightmare."

"It happened the night Alan died." She looked at the door leading to her room, then moved farther into his. "I haven't slept in there since that night, and I shouldn't have been in there tonight. Whatever killed him is in there."

"I thought you were what was in there the night he died?"

*H*er eyes, brilliant with tears, widened. "Yes," she cried, nodding her head up and down in agreement. "Yes, I was in there, but I wasn't the only thing. Something else came in." She jabbed the air over his shoulder with her index finger. "It came in through that same locked door leading to the hall, just like it did a few minutes ago. That was Lorraine's bedroom. This one was Alan's. Florence refused to take Lorraine's old room, despite it being the nicest bedroom in the house, and she and Alan switched to a new suite down the hall soon after they wed."

Jack felt the hair stand up on the back of his neck, and he stepped away from her bedroom door. Dammit, this was insane.

"Did Alan Noble rape you?" he barked out harshly.

She fell back as he drove forward.

"You were beaten and bloodied. Was it him who bit you?"

338

He saw her reach for her breast, then she dropped her hand.

"I told you what happened. What I didn't tell you was he saw what came through that door that opened into hell."

Jack narrowed his eyes on her. "Bullshit, Penny!"

"I lied," she screamed. "I *was* drunk."

Jack froze.

"He forced his way into my room. He had the key. It was his house, after all. He had champagne and two glasses, and he was nude beneath his jacket, which he wore unbelted. I could see every inch of the nasty man when he barged his way in. I didn't want the champagne. I wouldn't drink it, so he forced me back onto the bed and throttled me, then pulled my hair back and pushed the bottle into my mouth. He upended it and forced me to drink. I thought I'd drown. I vomited, but he didn't care. He tore my nightgown down and groped my body. I was barely conscious until he bit me. That woke me up. Then he poured champagne on the wound, and he laughed. To cauterize it, he said. I fought him when he said he was going to do the same to my other breast, and that's when he switched his attention from my breasts. He was on top of me when the door slammed open. He saw what was there, what entered. His face twisted, then he fell full force on top of me. His head hit mine, knocking me out. He was still on top of me when I came to hours later, but he hadn't raped me. He died before he could. I was still sick. It was hard to get him off me, but I managed to push him onto the floor, then I passed out again. I came to the second time maybe half an hour before Chief Craig arrived to tell me Harold was dead. Of course, he wanted to talk to Alan. I had to tell him he was dead, too."

She calmed as she told the story. He had no doubt she'd told the truth, at least as she remembered it. He wished she had been more honest from the start, but realized there probably weren't that many people she'd have confessed that story to, nor for that matter, many other normal people who would have repeated it. She looked at him, closed her eyes, and looked away. He pulled her to him, then led her to the settee on the back wall of Harold's room, found a blanket, and wrapped her in it.

"He dropped dead," she said. "Just like I told you."

He still didn't believe the door to hell had opened up, but he believed she did. Hallucinations brought on by stress and alcohol. To her it had all been terrifyingly real.

She drew in a long breath and pulled the blanket tighter. "Harold had gone out," she said, her voice now normal. "He was rarely home at night anyway. I was worried about Alan. We'd just buried Florence, and he was estranged from his brother and his son. I joined him in the front room and made him a brandy. That was his usual after-dinner drink, but he said it was a whiskey night. So I drank his brandy for him, and he drank my chocolate, which I didn't want, then I poured us both a whiskey, because he so wanted me to. And I did drink with him, but only a sip. As I said before, he became lewd, so I excused myself and went to bed."

"And he followed you up."

"About an hour later I'd guess. I was asleep when I heard Harold's door click. I never imagined such a thing happening to me."

Jack sat next to her. Autumn's first chill had kissed this night, and he surrendered to the temptation to draw her warmth close.

"It sounds like Alan had a stroke. You were probably imagin-ing—"

"Imagining?"

"Seeing things in your drunken stupor."

"Have you ever seen things in a drunken stupor, Jack?"

"Well, I'm not sure because there've been times I've failed to remember what I saw when I was drunk."

"That is not the same, and you know it."

Jack reached for her hand and was relieved when she let him take it. "And you saw nothing but the portal to hell?"

"I *heard* it crash against the wall. I *felt* the cold, I *saw* the open door!"

"You were so drunk, by your own admission, you might not have even closed the door, much less locked it."

"Darn it, Jack, I'm not drunk tonight. And the night Alan

died, the door was closed and locked when I tried to get out hours later when Chief Craig arrived, and it was locked tonight, you know that."

"Yes it was, but I never saw it open, Penny."

Chapter Seventy-six

"**I** haven't seen you in a suit since Daddy's funeral," Penny said.

"I wore one for my dad's, but I believe you missed that one."

She averted her eyes, then swung her legs over the side of the settee in his room where she'd insisted on sleeping, despite his offering the bed. "You look nice."

Jack sat beside her. "Thank you."

"None of us were there for you."

"There were people there for me, Penny, and you were ten. I didn't expect to see you, even if circumstances had been different."

Adel hadn't been there either. Laying his daddy to rest was a small, private ceremony up in Marion County, and this morning he wasn't compelled to wallow in the memory.

"I haven't forgotten what I promised when I asked you to marry me."

Well, yes, there was still that. Penny rose, quite pretty in the nightgown he'd returned to her the night before. She glanced at the door to her room, and he stood. "Come on, I've come this far, I'll go into hell with you. Otherwise I figure you'll be in your nightclothes all day."

He opened the door, then walked across the thick carpet and opened the curtains. Light flooded the room. He looked to where she stood at the threshold. "It's a nice room, Penny."

She followed him in. "I'm okay now."

"Demons don't stalk during the day?"

"It's a ghost."

"So, haints don't haunt when someone is with you?"

She shot him a jaundiced look, and he smiled. "Gather up what you need. I'll get Mars and Gracie up here today. You move into my room. I'll take this one."

She breathed in, then out. "You've been warned."

"Yes, I have, and I am not afraid."

She moved to her wardrobe. "I guess you should tell Chief Craig that Alan attacked me, but I would appreciate your not telling him about the doorway to hell."

"You need to talk to Chief Craig yourself, but only after talking to Clive."

She was shaking her head before he even finished. "I can't repeat that to those men. I didn't even tell you all the disgusting and degrading things that man said and did to me..."

He took her hand. "Listen to me. Odds are Florence Noble was poisoned, everyone thinks so, even you. Your grandmother's pet sheriff and the county prosecutor want the police chief to arrest you. If he doesn't, I think Lyle Jenkins will. Clive and Craig need to hear from your own lips what happened. Who will protect you from your grandmother in Jenkins' jail?"

"Does Chief Craig have a jail?"

"One old pigsty of a cell, but the jailer in Mississippi City has a wife and for that reason, the county puts women prisoners, when it has one, there."

She turned away, trying to take her hand with her.

"I'll be there," he said.

She gave a tiny smile in thanks, and he released her hand. Dress in hand, she closed the wardrobe.

"During your discussions with Jonathan have you had the opportunity to discuss Florence's death?" she asked.

"Only from the impact it might have on your inheritance. As you can figure by now, he wants you convicted, and he thinks I'd be better off partnering with him, not you."

"And what did you say?"

"I told him I wasn't convinced he held the winning hand."

"But now you're beginning to think you might be married to a crazy woman."

"That was not what I was going to say, Penny."

She studied him, her eyes welling tears. She opened her mouth to speak, then gave her head a little shake and turned toward her door.

He reached out to stop her, but she resisted when he tried to pull her to him. She freed herself. "When I came to you last week, I considered myself a dead woman. All I cared about was destroying Grandmother."

"And now you're sorry you came to me?"

"No, that's not what I'm sorry for. I don't want you to feel I'm more trouble than I'm worth."

"And I'll betray you, too."

"Or just resent me."

"I knew I was walking into a hornet's nest by marrying you, and you know I knew that."

"At the time I was desperate, with nothing left to live for. I didn't give enough concern to your feelings."

"I'm a grown man, and I understand a lot of things."

"No matter the outcome, you're saddled with a wife, Jack. What if you meet someone?"

"I do believe you qualified the terms to our agreement. I also believe you've just realized you conceded a little too much in the deal. What if you meet someone?"

"I'm not looking for anyone."

"Neither am I. And remember, you made that concession to me. I never agreed one way or the other."

Stuart stepped through the French door onto the bricked patio, its moss carpet dusted with fallen leaves. Eva sat in one of the wrought-iron chairs beneath the shade of the winding limbs of a single live oak. Carrington Farrah sat next to her.

"Anything?" Stuart asked.

Carrington rose and stuck out his hand, which Stuart took. "Their lawyer says she will not talk to either one of you. Gibson has put a restraining order on you both. You're to stay away from her."

Stuart looked at Eva. "We need to take the Humboldt offer. With the Perry County timber we might have enough to pay off the loan and avoid bankruptcy."

"We don't even know that Jack has the note. I'm not losing my grandfather's company because you're panicking."

"Of course he has it, or he wouldn't have married her."

"He would have married her for Noble Corporation."

"You can say anything you want about the man, but he is not an opportunist. He hates your guts though. He married Penny to take King and Gibson away from you, and he's gonna do it. So it can go to Humboldt or it can go to your self-made nemesis, but you'd better act fast. You're running out of time."

"That would mean Penny had the document the whole time."

"Exactly."

"I don't believe it, not after..." She glanced at Carrington. Stuart glared at her a moment, then turned to the lawyer.

"If he has the note, why do you think he hasn't said anything?"

"He doesn't want to spook you is my guess. You can bet he's aware of the Humboldt offer."

"Precisely," Eva hissed. "Don't you two see? You have this backwards. He wants us to think he has the note so we will sell, and I will have lost the company to Humboldt because you"—she narrowed her eyes on Stuart—"panicked."

Stuart said nothing, but turned solemnly to Carrington, who said, "If Gibson has the promissory note, he'll make claim on the first."

Eva fisted her hand. "Dammit, Carrington, the estate is tied up—"

"Noble Corporation is tied up in court, not Alan and Harold's personal estate. That's Penny's. The best chance you have is to stall it by—"

"Having that little bitch arrested for murder."

"Which Toby Craig is now stonewalling," Stuart said.

"Effectively, I might add. That means he's either building a case or he doesn't have one." Carrington looked pointedly at Eva. "Your influence waning, dear lady?"

She gave him a hateful smile. "When this is over and things have settled down, I'm going to kill Penny."

Stuart's gaze passed to Carrington, then back to her. "Shut up, Eva."

"Or make her wish she were dead."

Carrington reached for his hat on the wrought-iron table next to him. "I don't want to hear any more of this."

Eva's laugh filled the chilly garden. "Why not? You've been privy to worse."

"What did you do, Eva, to turn that girl so hard against you?"

"She is exactly like her father. She'd rather destroy the company than listen to me."

"Damn it, Eva," Stuart railed, "She's destroying *you*, and you know why."

Her lips curled. "You agreed to the wedding and the coercion, whether you liked the coercion or not." Her eyes raked him, "Though I think you probably enjoyed that better than you're willing to admit."

Stuart glanced to Carrington, who was staring at him. But for the lawyer's presence, he would have throttled Eva.

"Neither of you are to approach Penny," Carrington said.

Eva graced him with a smile. "I'll have her mother talk to her then." She turned, still smiling, and looked at Stuart. "Considering your atrocious behavior of late, she might move right in with Penny. Keep it up. Clarissa would prove very useful under that roof."

"Jack would see right through it."

"And do you think he has Penny's best interest at heart?" Carrington asked.

Stuart looked at the lawyer. "He hasn't threatened her life in front of an officer of the court to the best of my knowledge."

"Hmmm. Adel, perhaps, is a more reliable agent." Eva's smile was smug. "But who do you think she should approach, Stuart dear, Penny or Jack?"

Chapter Seventy-seven

"Leave it. I don't want it in my room."

"Yo' sho'? Goes wif da furniture, don't it?" Mars touched the wood frame of the mirror. "Real nice. Shame 'bout dat crack."

Gracie stopped sweeping where the dresser had been and looked at the mirror, then Penny. "Wasn't der yesta'day."

Penny pulled the small drawer from her bedside table. "No, it wasn't. That happened during the night." She turned to Gracie and silently dared her to ask how. The Negress returned her gaze for the space of a heartbeat, then looked at the loquacious Mars, who had grown silent. Penny moved and pulled the dead plant from the corner near her bed. "You forgot to water it while I was gone?"

"Watered it good every day, but it was determined to die," Gracie said.

Mars grinned. "Missed you, Miz Penny."

Penny touched a brown frond, and it fell into the pot. It was such a pretty plant when her mother gave it to her not long after she wed Harold.

"I'll take it to da back poach," Mars said. "Cut it back an' plant it in da yahd. Dem plants dey grow good outside, 'specially heah where it don't get so cold in da winnah'time. Might come back."

Gracie shrugged. "Not gonna come back if'n no life lef' in it."

"Might be der's still some," Mars said, then lifted three of Penny's still full drawers and started for the room next door. "Ain't gonna know till we try. Won't hurt nuffin' to try."

"Hmmpf," Gracie groused. "Sho' won't hurt me if'n it's you diggin' da hole."

"I'll dig it. Sho' will. Jest sho' me where."

Penny picked up a hat box in each hand and started after him. "We'll find a good place to plant it, Mars. Near the house."

"Yes'm," he said, looking over his shoulder. "You an' ol' Jack gots a nice yahd out der. Gonna want sun. Dem kinda plants, dey sho do like sun."

Maybe that's why it died. Maybe it was its diet of chocolate.

"Der's a haint heah, ain't der?

Penny almost dropped the boxes. "You can sense it?"

He laughed. "No ma'am, I don't sense nuffin', but I can tell by da tremble in yo' lips an' da way you peeks ober yo' shoulda at me an' Miz Gracie dat yo is spooked. Mirror in da hall be cracked, too. I knows somebody might can he'p."

"The play, I assume?" Penny asked Angelina Ladner, as she ushered the woman through the entry and into Florence Noble's parlor.

"In a manner of speaking. I used the ladies' decision to cancel as a reason to visit."

"Oh?"

"Even I agree that under the circumstances the Masons might be inclined to deny you use of the opera house. That would prove awkward, and I absolutely refused to support someone else taking chair of the event. You and Florence worked too hard to be cast aside, and I do not care what the circumstances. But truth is I doubt the owners would have dealt with you, and that will be the case until the events surrounding Florence's death are resolved." Mrs. Ladner rolled her eyes. "If only she'd stayed buried."

There would have still been Alan's naked corpse in her bedroom.

Penny offered Mrs. Ladner a place on the settee in front of the cold fireplace, then pushed the heavy drapes aside before taking the seat next to one of Biloxi's most charming and influential matrons. Even with the drapes open, the room required the light from the gas sconces around the walls. A fire would have been nice to chase away the late-morning chill clinging to this south-facing room. It was nearly the end of October and now, finally, fall had made a call, probably a brief one, on the Mississippi Gulf Coast. Jane knocked, then entered with the coffee service.

"I asked Jane to make us chocolate," Penny said to her guest, then thanked the girl. Penny filled the two cups, and Mrs. Ladner took a sip.

"Always a treat. The entire Coast does so hope that source does not dry up as a result of Alan's passing."

"My new husband has taken a special interest in the chocolate business." That was not precisely true, but Jack was showing interest in Noble Corporation in general.

"It is my understanding the young man's trade is timber, as was his father's and yours before him."

"True," Penny said with a nod, "which leaves him a lot to learn about imports."

"An odd combination."

Penny made a point of finding the woman's eyes, and Mrs. Ladner smiled. "I knew your father from the time he was in his teens. His father was a very dear friend, who once provided a service to my husband and me that we could never repay. We saw Hugh only on occasion after Albert died, and I am sorry we lost contact over the years. I was dismayed by his untimely death and regret not taking the time to see more of him. And you, my dear, are, I believe, the only grandchild of a precious friend?"

"Yes."

Penny's paternal grandparents produced five babies, but only her father survived the first year. But Penny suspected the long-ago event to which Mrs. Ladner referred happened when Albert King was still a young, unattached adventurer.

"So, bad tidings regarding the play troupe aside, you may have guessed that your recent nuptials are what brought me to your home this morning."

Though everyone who cared would know by now she'd married Jack, few knew the circumstances behind their impromptu wedding. Worse yet, Angelina Ladner had been one of the few non-family members invited to Penny's wedding to Jon Noble. Penny looked into the cool gray eyes of the dowager, and Mrs. Ladner lifted her elegant chin, waiting.

"It was one of those ad hoc moments," Penny said, "when one sees clearly what one must do."

Mrs. Ladner cocked a brow. "Given the history between your family and that of the man you wed, ad hoc is an understatement. A daring tactical foray would describe your sudden conquest better. I was in the church, you know, waiting with Jonathan Noble for the appearance of his bride. Jon is a handsome man, but too old for one so young. Given Harold had been buried only two weeks, any fool could guess you were not ready to remarry — even if you hadn't run. Then you married anyway." The woman looked away a moment, then back to Penny, stiff at her side. "Be careful, my dear. Desperation has been known to breed recklessness. My wedding wish for you is that your desperate act proves as satisfying as the one I made fifty-four years ago."

"Will you tell me what that was?"

The woman patted her hand. "No. That's a story I shared with only one person — though your grandfather played a role in it — that debt I referred to earlier. I lost my true love five years ago, but we were terribly happy for almost five decades."

Penny looked to the fire. "Mrs. Lad —"

"Angelina, please, and you are a woman after my own heart. But my wish is nothing more than an old woman's blessing for a happy ending. I can only imagine your desperation at the time, but I do not know your young man, or what drove him to participate in your flight, though Noble Corporation is quite a plum. That's not to lessen you, my dear, but I know Jack Gibson's history with your sister and his father's alleged role in the death of yours."

"Alleged?"

"My late husband and I sat through that trial. Every day of it. My albatross, you might say. So much of what convicted James Waymon Gibson was hearsay and circumstantial — my darling's words. He was a retired lawyer. That doesn't mean Gibson didn't do it, but it put reasonable doubt in this old woman's mind, if it didn't those of the jurors. Vengeance for a teenage boy could well become justice to a young man who believes he never gained it."

Hot tears burned Penny's eyes, and she turned away. Uncle Jimmy. It was the first time in her life that anyone, other than Jack, had suggested to her face that an injustice might have occurred seven years earlier. No, Chief Craig had implied likewise, though Penny had made an extra effort to ignore his innuendo.

Penny recalled her mother went to the trial off and on over the ten days of the proceedings. Eva Markiston was there every day.

"Angelina" — Penny smiled and sucked in a breath — "thank you for your concern and your blessing. They are, I believe, appropriate for mine and Jack's circumstances."

At the door minutes later, Angelina looked over Penny's shoulder and found Gracie at the far end of the hall. "I imagine my boy Roy is in your kitchen."

Gracie nodded. "I'll send 'im out front."

"Tell him to hurry. Looks like we've rain to beat home." She winked at Penny. "I'll see you Friday week for lunch."

"I'm looking forward to it."

The door clicked shut, and Penny turned back into the dark central hall. So much to think about, for better or for worse, but think she must. When she'd begun this journey with Jack, she had but one goal in mind, to destroy Eva Markiston by wresting King and Gibson from her and returning it to her grandmother's enemy. She'd given no thought to her own future. Penny stepped back into the parlor. Today, if not joy, there was at least life without physical suffering, the escape discovered in a good book, tasty food and sweet chocolate, all of which might be no more than the afterglow of her tactical victories over the morphine and resulting improved health. She thought of Jack's comment this morning upstairs. And what of Jack Gibson himself?

She closed the door to Florence Noble's quiet hideaway, then opened up the valve to the gas sconce closest to the door. The

351

added light had not been needed when she and Angelina left this room two minutes ago. Odd, but this parlor was always dark.

The heavy velvet curtains, which she'd opened upon the arrival of Angelina Ladner, were drawn again. How had she missed passing Gracie, who she'd seen in the hallway?

Light from the coal oil lamps reflected in the gleaming surface of the dark library desk. Black walnut, Jack had told her. He'd spent a good half hour after supper last night leading her through the lower story, identifying the wood used to build the furniture. Mostly mahogany, cherry, and black walnut—quality stuff, he told her, much of it built before the War.

She pulled Florence's notes from where she knew them to be and leafed through the pages, looking for the troupe's itinerary, from which she could glean their present location. She needed to send Mr. Baker a telegram to cancel the engagement. He would keep the partial payment.

Ah, they would be in Philadelphia on Wednesday. Penny pulled out Florence's chair to the desk, sat, then opened a drawer in search of paper. Thunder rumbled to the south, and she raised the wick on the coal oil lamp. Brighter colors would lighten this room. The dark paneling could be painted. It was, after all, her parlor now, and she didn't plan on holding any encounters with the...

Instinctively she knew she'd just tempted fate. Outside, she heard the wind pummel the trees, and at Penny's back, the marble fireplace groaned in tandem with the gust. A shiver raced through her and with it a compelling need to get out of this room. She pushed the papers to the back of the desk and started to rise. She sensed she was too late before she really was.

The sconces dimmed and flickered, and her gut quaked. Then the horrid wail that had preceded Alan's death and savaged last night's sleep peeled down the chimney and crossed the hearth, drawing its icy fingers along the length of her spine. Behind her something crashed, and Penny spun in her seat to face what was there.

Florence's heirloom coffee service she'd left sitting on the table in front of the settee lay shattered across the hearth, and Penny wanted to weep at the waste of a thing so old and precious. Then a frigid whisper kissed her cheek and set her teeth to chattering. With trembling arms, she pushed away from the desk, then rose warily from her chair.

Heart thudding in her chest, Penny gauged the distance to the hall door and stepped away from the desk. She jumped at a movement caught in the corner of her eye, spun, and found her reflection, uncomfortably close, watching her from inside the tall pier glass mirror on the adjacent wall. Florence's primping mirror.

Magic mirror on my wall...

Penny brought a shaky hand to the base of her throat, then laughed softly at herself. Her image did the same, *then* jumped at her, smashing its face against the glass, flattening its nose and mouth into a grotesque mask. Penny fell back with a cry and landed on her bottom. When the misty image charged again, Penny closed her eyes and pushed back on her heels before trying to find her feet, listening all the while for the shattering of glass that would mean the thing had broken through and was in the room with her. She opened her eyes when she backed into the fireplace stand, which toppled with a horrendous racket, that finally drew a scream from Penny as well as her image in the mirror, which kept screaming, its mouth wide and glistening, a savage beast howling at a nonexistent moon.

Penny covered her ears in a failed attempt to shut out the sound, then she twisted and tried to push herself up. But now something sat on her and pushed her flat, hindering her breathing and constricting her clothing. She clawed the oriental carpet, and managed to get to her hands and knees. In the mirror, the altered image of herself had ceased its mocking screams and watched Penny struggle. It, too, was on all fours. It did not struggle, but appeared preparing to pounce.

The air stilled as if a portal had shut, and Penny, no longer weighed down, rose, gulping in great breaths of air. She closed her eyes and tried to force herself calm.

She opened her eyes. On the hearth, she spied the broken coffee service, then the toppled fireplace tools. That much, at least, had been real. She picked up the poker and, steeling herself, turned to face the mirror.

She eased closer to her image, pristine and sharp, but for the dimness of the room. She reached out a hand and flattened her palm against the cool, smooth surface of the glass, and the pale girl in the mirror did the same. Penny relaxed. It had all been in her—

An ear-splitting screech shattered the stillness and the hand inside the looking glass punched through, breaking the glass and grabbing her wrist. It yanked, and Penny's hand entered the shattered glass.

A scream, her own, echoed off the walls. She dropped the poker. The door to the parlor swung open. Her image released her, and Penny fell to the floor. Then Gracie was by her side, wrapping her wrist in a white kerchief and calling for Jane to hurry and get that man Mars out on the back porch. Gracie's voice was loud and clear, her caramel skin and red dress were vivid, and the room was warm and calm.

Chapter Seventy-eight

"Penny has serious problems. I am aware of them. I'm assuming you are, too."

Jack was certain he was more aware of Penny's problems, and their root cause, than this snot of a man Roland fetched from Mississippi City, as long ago, it seems, as two damn hours. Only after he'd returned with the doctor had the Noble's yard boy come for him, and the poor kid apologized all the way home for not being able to answer Jack's questions as to how Penny was injured and how bad she was. Roland also apologized, repeatedly, for not bringing the "real" doctor as Gracie instructed him to. Hadrian Clark was not in the office, Mark Reed was.

Mars, guarding the comings and goings like a sentry, met Jack on the back porch. She'd cut a wrist, Mars told him, but he didn't know how, and Miss Penny was alone when the injury occurred.

Halfway down the hall, Jack almost collided with Gracie, hurrying out back with a bundle of bloodstained towels. "She be all right now," the Negress told him without missing a step. Finally, at the foot of the stairs, Mark Reed waylaid him and demanded they talk. Torn between seeing Penny and finding out what happened, and how bad it was, Jack led Penny's once-forever-love to Alan Noble's office, where they now stood facing each other eye to eye. Jack narrowed his on the man.

"What are you saying, Mark?"

"She tried to take her own life."

"She told you that?"

"Of course she denied it."

"Then why do you think it?"

"Penny has betrayed herself and her family. She feels she has no reason to live."

Penny? The same girl who told him just this morning that she not only wanted to live, but wanted to enjoy life. Jack heaved in a breath and strolled to Alan Noble's private stash he'd found inside the credenza behind the desk. He poured himself a shot. He even mustered the good manners to offer Mark one. The man declined, and Jack shrugged. Maybe he had more work today. Maybe he was a teetotaler. But Jack figured, plain and simple, Mark Reed didn't want to drink with him. That was fine by Jack. He let loose a short laugh. "Are you telling me she's showing remorse at having married me?"

"I think she regrets marrying you. I understand you may now be in a position to take King and Gibson from the family."

Jack threw back his head and downed the shot. "Might be, but the idea was hers, not mine."

"So you do intend to do it?"

Jack shrugged. "Would you please tell me what happened here today?"

"She cut her wrist. She's already tried that once. You've seen her wrists."

"You mean the rope burns?"

Mark stilled, then he raised his chin. "Whatever. But today is more definitive. She said she broke the mirror in her office while cleaning it. But the cut's too deep. It nicked a tendon pretty good, not to mention the artery. If not for your man Mars' application of pressure, she would have lost a good deal of blood by the time I got here." Mark studied Jack long and hard, then said finally, "I can't understand why she came to you."

Jack tried to ignore the perusal and poured himself another shot of bourbon. He couldn't ignore the comment. "Because she wants to take King and Gibson away from her grandmother, and she knew I'd help her do it."

"She didn't want to marry Jonathan Noble."

"That, too, but mostly it was her grandmother's devastating interference in her life."

"Penny wed you under the influence of morphine. Her grand-mother was trying to ensure Penny's security as well as protect the interests of King and Gibson when she proposed Penny's marriage to Jon Noble. I know it was a business match, not love, but Penny was so depressed and so dependent on the morphine, she couldn't see it was for the best. Her behavior in marrying you proves it."

"You got the last part right, except Eva was protecting her own interest in King and Gibson. She played Penny wrong and now she's on the brink of losing it all."

"Clarissa and Adel do not believe Penny would do such a thing to the family without you manipulating her weaknesses. You're behind this."

"You, Dr. Reed, are the latest in a long line of Markiston dupes. Penny's morphine habit developed after Harold Noble's death, in her parents' house under the tender ministrations of her grandmother. Since I assume you have ten fingers and ten toes, you can use them to count the days between Harold's funeral and the intended Noble-Noble wedding. Eleven days. Within that timeframe, Eva Markiston forced the addiction on her grand-daughter, insurance that Penny would do her will, which was to ensure Eva didn't lose the lumber company. For Jon Noble, mar-rying Penny removed any legal battles he'd have to wage, and possibly lose, to inherit Noble Corporation. Now, I have no in-tention of dignifying your accusations with details of what Eva was trying to accomplish by Penny's union with Jon Noble. You consider yourself smart, you figure it out. Before you can do that, however, you need to get your head out of Eva Markiston's ass."

Mark's face reddened. "You are a crude man, Gibson. I've always wondered what Adel saw in you."

"You just said it. Crude. That's what she saw, and that's what she wanted. A base man."

"Thank the lord she outgrew it."

Jack snorted and poured himself another drink.

"What are you up to with Jonathan Noble?" Mark asked.

"Up to? Eva must be worried, but I don't see what difference it makes to her. Her chips were in the pot, and she's lost every hand so far. She's about out of anything to ante up."

"All that company means to you is vengeance."

"Wrong. Having that company will provide me vengeance, but it was Hugh and my father's company."

"It was Eva's grandfather's."

"It was Hugh King's great-grandfather's. It belonged to Eva's grandfather for two years during the War after a thief convinced the world his cousin, Hugh, the true heir, was killed in action. The court found for Hugh, and he and James Gibson picked up the thread of a paper memory and made it real again. Eva did nothing but manipulate her way in by prostituting her daughter to Hugh. Adel she prostituted to you."

Mark's snarl preceded his punch by only a heartbeat. Pain exploded in Jack's left jaw, and he saw stars. He stepped awkwardly back, then found his balance. Mark stood in front of him breathing hard, fists still balled.

Jack narrowed his eyes on the man, then rubbed his jaw. "She's your wife. I'll give you that one," he said, turning to set the shot glass on the credenza. Then arm back, he spun and ploughed his fist into Mark's pretty face. Pain numbed his hand. Mark stumbled backward into the small cabriolet side table next to the settee, toppling the table and breaking the vase on top of it. Still off balance, he fell on the upended table, smashing it, then rolled awkwardly onto his butt, arms and legs flailing. "That one was for *my* wife."

Mark grabbed the arm of the settee and started to pull himself up. He was jerky, but ready to continue the fray, that much Jack saw in his movements. On his feet, he looked Jack up and down, then appeared caught off guard by the blood running from his nose. A lot of blood, and that gave the man pause.

"Let it be," Jack said.

"If you do manage to take the company, the only thing"— Mark bent his head back, then pulled a handkerchief out of his pocket—"the only thing standing between you and full control of King and Gibson is Penny," he said with some difficulty. He straightened, and blood dripped on his tweed jacket. He swiped at it with the handkerchief.

"More speculation from the Markiston-Frederick camp?"

"I know you're working with Jon Noble." Mark sounded stuffy and cleared his throat, a nasty sound, then spat blood and phlegm onto the carpet near the hearth. "He says you were in east Biloxi the night Harold Noble died. I told Penny that little detail a few minutes ago."

Jack balled his sweating palms, and Mark Reed laughed.

"Surely you didn't expect him to remain discreet after you double-crossed him."

"If you're done with your asinine insinuations I want to go upstairs and attend to my wife, and I want you to get the hell out of my house and stay out of it." Jack looked at the soiled carpet. "You call me crude? You're downright nasty."

Mark turned and picked up his bag at the end of the settee. He'd actually fallen over it. "That would be convenient for you," he said, then blew a bloody bubble out his nose. "But I intend to check on my patient until she tells me differently."

"That'll be the next time she sees you."

"Penny won't let me go easily."

Jack's heart skipped a beat. "You don't think? You reckon she's been holdin' out hope all this time you'd come to your senses and discover what a fool you were? Well, you haven't changed a bit. You're still a fool." Jack took a menacing step his way. Mark braced. At least the bastard didn't run. "Or is this renewed affection for Penny part of another twisted plot dreamed up by Eva to woo Penny back into the fold?"

"I might very well have rushed into marrying Adel, Gibson, but I can tell you this, any relationship I have with Penny has to do with my feelings for her and nothing to do with Eva."

Jack flexed his fingers. "You're too late."

"I don't think so." He turned away, then spun at the door. "Penny's had stomach problems for a couple of months now. Three weeks ago, Dr. Clark confided in Eva that he considered it possible Penny had been poisoned."

"You're trying to say someone in this house was poisoning her?"

"*Was*, Gibson? I know what you're up to, and I know who you're working with. If anything happens to her there will be an autopsy."

"You're a real hero. I'm sure Penny will be comforted."

Chapter Seventy-nine

So, was the slug fishing or did he know for a fact Penny was in danger at the Noble house? Jack took the stairs two at a time. Shoot, until they returned a few days ago, Penny hadn't been in this house for two weeks. Jack wished he knew how much of Mark Reed's guesswork the man had shared with her.

He tapped on the door of Harold's old room, then entered. The gas lamp centered over the room cast a recessive glow outward. East-facing, the room was dim and chilly this afternoon.

She was on her chaise draped with an afghan, a coal-oil lamp burning brightly on the table beside her. She marked her spot and laid her book in her lap. When they were all younger, Adel teased her for being a bookworm.

He sat on the foot of the chaise and reached for the tome. *Mystery on Hanover Moor*. "Good?" he asked.

"It shows potential."

"Scary?"

"I think it will be," she said and cocked her head before reaching out to touch his face. He pulled back. "Mark hit you?" she asked.

"I don't think you need scary, and I hit him back."

"That was the racket I heard a few minutes ago?"

He nodded and leafed through the book.

"What did you break?"

"Pretty Mark's nose, I think. Not nearly as costly as the mess you made." Gently he returned the book to her lap, then took her bandaged wrist. A little blood had seeped through the dressings. "What happened?"

"I broke a mirror—"

"I just took a look at it, that gargantuan thing mounted on the wall in Florence's office. How?"

She sat there as if waiting for him to explain what had happened, so he turned her hand over and studied the unblemished knuckles. "There's a hole in the glass. Looks like you hit it with your fist, but that would have broken your hand for sure."

She pulled her hand from his, then flexed her fingers. "I didn't punch the mirror, Jack."

"Did you hit it with the poker?"

"Gracie suggested I did that, didn't she?"

"She heard you scream, and when she opened the door you were in front of the mirror bleeding. The mirror was smashed, as was the Irish coffee service that had apparently belonged to Florence Noble's grandmother."

"Jack?" She touched his arm to draw his attention. She didn't need to. "Did I have the poker?"

"Gracie said you dropped it when she came in the door. The entire stand had been knocked over."

She tightened her lips and sighed. "I backed into it."

"Tell me what happened."

"If..." She sighed and picked up her book. "I *must* have broke it with the poker."

He took her book. "Then cut your wrist?"

"A piece could have flown up and —"

"It didn't, Penny."

Her jaw tightened, and she looked at her book in his hands. "Please give me my book."

"Pretty Mark said the cut was too deep. He thinks it was intentional."

"You and I both know that Mark Reed is an idiot."

"My sentiments exactly, but for different reasons."

"I doubt that."

"I'm not talking to him now. I'm talking to you. I want to know if you cut your wrist intentionally."

Her eyes widened. "Why would you think I'd do that? Didn't we discuss our happy life together just this morning?"

362

"Which might have been the catalyst."

She swallowed. "Perhaps I misinterpreted your intent earlier, but I took your words as a veiled promise."

For a moment, he studied her. A 'promise' she'd said. "Did you get angry at yourself?"

She frowned. "This is beginning to sound like Mark's convoluted analysis that I hate myself. Only in your case it would mean that the thought someone actually cared about unworthy me would compel me to take my life."

He tried to stifle his smile.

She flailed an arm. "You find that amusing!"

He grabbed her hand. He had caused her distress with his little grin, and he hadn't meant to. "The thought of you deciding to take your own life because you hated yourself is amusing. No one who knows you would believe that."

She moved her legs over the edge of the chaise and stood.

"I feel no remorse for marrying you."

"For what then?"

"For nothing."

"When do you intend to tell me what went on behind your bedroom door?"

She turned slightly from where she stood, silhouetted against the waning afternoon light. What a striking woman she'd become.

"I told you last night."

"Your bedroom at home, sweetheart. Your mother and stepfather's house."

"You know what happened. Grandmother hooked me on morphine."

"Tell me how it happened."

She rolled her eyes to the ceiling. "Jon forced me to go home to talk to them. When I got there, I was told I would marry Jon for the good of all. I refused and started to leave the house. Stuart hit me. Knocked me out. When I woke up I was tied to my bed. I couldn't stop her giving me the morphine."

"What else?"

"Why do you think there is something else?" she asked and turned her back to him. From where he sat, he could see the limb of a huge live oak, broad enough for him to walk along should he desire. He rose off the settee.

"What do you intend to do, keep it bottled up inside until you go mad?"

"Mad, Jack?"

"I think your body has endured too much physical strain and it's having an effect on your mind."

She turned back with his words, her eyes glistening in the afternoon light. "The aftereffect of the dependency, you think?"

He guessed it could be that. "Or too many knocks on the noggin."

"If you put me in an insane asylum, what happens to King and Gibson?"

"Assuming we manage to hold on to our claim, I guess it goes to me."

"Eva won't get it back?"

"Over my dead body."

"So the asylum would benefit you alone?"

He shrugged. "I reckon so."

"You know so."

She sauntered away from the window and started, slowly, to circle him. "Mark says you're still in love with Adel. He says you're in partnership with Jonathan Noble and you plan on disposing of me and the two of you divvying up Noble Corporation."

"A suspicion you've already raised with me, but I assure you Jon Noble has no intention of divvying up anything. All I want is King and Gibson."

"But I come with the deal."

"You and, as it turns out, Noble Corporation."

She smiled, still circling. "Neither of which you wanted."

He turned with her now, keeping his eyes fixed on her. "But I'm willing to take both."

"I'm sure you find the corporation more desirable."

"I'm sure you don't know what you're talking about."

She stopped suddenly, almost back to the window. "Did you kill Harold for him?"

His chest constricted. "I did not. I was in Biloxi that night, supposedly to meet Jon for a discussion in that very hotel room. It was Stuart who 'supposedly' stumbled upon Harold's body in the room. I can only assume that was who Harold thought he was meeting."

Her brow furrowed. "Do you think Stuart killed Harold?"

"Nope. I think Stuart expected to find him dead when he got there."

"He must have seen you. How else would Mark —"

"Because Jon, Eva, and Stuart planned it. Lyle Jenkins was already in Biloxi that night, too. I was supposed to be caught red-handed in that room with your husband's dead body, but the only person who saw me in Biloxi that night was Jon. I was never in that room."

"Are you still dealing with Jonathan?" she said at last.

"Only so far as benefits you and me. That's what I meant yesterday when I said you were glad I knew him."

"But didn't realize it." She averted her eyes, then nodded.

"Mark Reed wants you back. Are you going to leave me for him?"

A knowing smile shaped her lips. She was looking at him now. Again, she started moving in that circle. "I find you infinitely more exciting...and dangerous. Mark's dull and stupid."

"I'd guess you were about 'dangered' out. Too many novels?" Turning with her, he added, "He says he cares for you. Maybe he does. Are you sure about me?"

"He was there, Jack," she said, the whisper of her voice echoed by the rustle of satin. "I asked for his help the day I was to wed Jonathan. He didn't believe a word I said. I came to you. You were the one who helped me. I don't need the pathetic regrets of Mark Reed."

"You made me a promise I couldn't refuse."

"I didn't think for old times' sake would work."

"What I'd do for Hugh King's daughter might surprise you."

He swore her eyes softened, but she said nothing and though she made a brief misstep, she didn't stop her incessant circling.

"Are you trying to make me dizzy?"

"I'm trying to make sure I have your attention." She stopped at the door separating their two bedrooms. "I didn't try to kill myself, and you're not putting me in an asylum."

"A challenge, sweetheart?"

"A warning."

With a quick step forward, he grabbed her arm, then crushed her to him. She whimpered when he covered her lips with his. "I'm shivering in my polished brogans," he whispered against her lips, then he let her go.

Daunted, though she hid it well, she straightened her shoulders, then reached for the knob and pushed the door wide.

"We got the rooms switched today."

"I noticed."

With a wide sweep of her arm, she motioned him into her old room next door. "Per your request, the one with the portal to hell is now yours."

"Are you sure you wish to cast me in there? Whatever lurks within might get me, then you'll be all alone."

"I don't think it wants you, Jack."

Chapter Eighty

It grabbed her, she told him. Jack had refused to go into his room until she did. The image in the mirror reached out and grabbed her, then tried to pull her in. That's how she'd cut her wrist...or how her wrist got cut. Now, alone, in Florence Noble's parlor, he bent down in front of the mirror and studied the damage. Behind the asymmetrical break, he could see the mirror's wooden back. No damage, no dent, not even a splinter. The hole was limited to a relatively clean, fist-sized opening in the glass itself with fissures radiating from it. Circular, if one had to come up with a shape for it. Odd the thick, heavy glass could have broken in such a way, even if she had taken the poker to it.

Gracie walked into the room, fresh water in her bucket. An hour ago the carpet had been stained with Penny's blood. Grace had gotten most of it out. He dreaded telling the poor woman about Mark Reed's mess in Alan's office.

"Where did you find pieces of glass?" he asked her.

"Splinters all around da room." She walked to the trash can on the other side of the desk, picked it up, and handed it to him. Then she pointed out several landing places, best she could remember. One shard had flown nearly as far as the fireplace. He looked back at the hole, then glanced at himself in the mirror. In the looking glass, the room behind him looked ominous and un-friendly—his heart beat faster—downright hostile as a matter-of-fact. He pivoted and faced the space directly. It looked gently back at him, friendly and in perfect order thanks to the woman scrubbing at his feet. He reached for the knob, told her to cover the mirror and to leave the door open; he'd have Mars and Roland remove the thing tomorrow.

Chapter Eighty-one

Jonathan Noble knocked once, walked into what was now Jack's downtown office, and took a seat in the chair opposite Jack.

"Word is, your young bride is a prime candidate for the State Lunatic Asylum."

"I wouldn't place much stock in Mark Reed's determination of attempted suicide."

Jon chuckled. "Could be a useful rumor. That and her hearing things that go bump in the night."

That last was servants' gossip, not Mark Reed, and annoyance washed over Jack. "Could have been you saddled with her."

"And she'd be asylum-bound for sure, and you wouldn't be sitting at my desk. Are you who broke Reed's nose?"

"Probably, unless he's picked a fight with someone else he thinks is in love with his wife."

Jon grinned. "Well, that could be any number of people, couldn't it?"

"If you say so. I try to keep out of touch these days." Jack couldn't help but wonder if Jon counted himself among Adel's fellas. The last rumor he'd heard, and this he'd gotten from Kate, who'd gotten it from her washer woman, because gossip ran rampant among the Negroes over in Handsboro and Mississippi City, too, was that Adel had developed a taste for the older men in Eva's circle. Wealthy men, preferably married, making discretion a priority, and Jack weighed the possibility of Madam Eva having resorted to blackmail in an attempt to save the business.

"That aside, I'm glad you stopped in."

Jon cocked an eyebrow.

"Mark Reed's daddy left here about an hour ago. He wanted to talk to me about that piece of property over on the Escatawpa. He's still interested in a canning factory there."

Jonathan pursed his lips and leaned back in the chair. "So?"

"Got me to thinking why a girl like Penny drew the interest of a group of wealthy merchants like you Nobles."

"We wealthy merchants see the value in diversification."

Jack nodded. "You're admitting to an interest in canning?"

"Possibly."

"How about expansion of the shipping arm?"

Jon shrugged. "Could make a sound port of entry."

"Doubtful." Jack leaned back in his chair. "You know when I moved into Harold's old bedroom, I found a desk. In that desk was a pad of paper, and on that pad were some numbers that at first look didn't mean much to me. But working with plat maps of county sections and townships the way I do, it occurred to me those numbers looked like coordinates...and coordinates local to the areas I've been working most of my life. Curious by then, I pulled out that pad and compared those coordinates to a plat map I just happened to have handy. Now it has occurred to me that either some members of the Noble family really do intend to go into the timber business or there's something else driving their ambitions." He smiled at Jon. "What are your thoughts on Perry County, slow-rising grades, and the Leaf River?"

Jon's nonchalance was eclipsed by his glare. Jack relaxed in his chair. "Seems your interest in Penny goes back a ways and predates her association with Noble Corporation proper. I do believe you've been holding out on me, *friend*."

Edwina Picard was a light-skinned Negress with green eyes and dark hair wrapped in a cotton kerchief. She was young, probably still in her teens, and she was, Jack knew, relatively new to the Frederick household. Jack wiped his brow with a white, cotton handkerchief. A chill had greeted him when he opened the back door this morning, but it was early afternoon now and hot.

The girl took what he offered, looked one direction down the porch, then the other. He considered leading her away from the house so that no one saw them, but he doubted she'd go. She didn't know him well, but for sure she'd been warned about him since that day he'd busted in on her.

"All I knows is she come home right afta 'er husband's fun'ral. We didn't see 'er. She stayed up in 'er room. Da one she were in 'fo she lef'. I don't know 'bout dat 'cause I din't wawk heah den. All I knows is what I'z tol'. Only folk I eben seen go in der was Miz Markiston an' Miss Penny's stepdaddy."

"You never went into the room to clean it? Never emptied a chamber pot? Never collected any laundry?"

The girl waved a finger. "Oooh, funny 'bout dat laundry. Miz Markiston would bring dem sheets out an' take new ones back in. Dat's why I wuz thinkin' dat woman be sick wif somethin' tur'ble an' dey din't want nobody to know it. Almost up an' quit. But da pay heah be too good."

"You paid to keep yo' mouf shut, Eddie."

Jack spun around. Charlotte Hines stood glaring at them from the shaded west corner of the porch, the side the cookhouse sat on and where the breezeway led from the house. Charlotte did know him.

"You take dat man's money an' lose yo' job. He payin' you enuff till you fin' anover?"

Edwina shook her head rapidly.

"Git yo'sef back to wawk, girl, an' don't you be talkin' stuff to any mo' people come to you wif money in dem's hands wantin' to know what goes on in dis house."

Edwina disappeared through the French doors leading into what he knew to be the Frederick dining room, leaving him to face the stout and ornery Charlotte. "You git yo' white ass to da cookhouse," she said to him. "Der be somethin' I need to say to you skulkin' 'round heah like dis."

She was gone, back around the corner of the porch. After a moment he followed. She was waiting for him when he entered the kitchen door. It was hot in here. It was always hot in here and a thousand other cookhouses throughout Mississippi, and the place smelled of food-soaked wood. He figured there was corn-bread in the oven, right now.

"Dey kep' dat girl in 'er ol' room fo' ten days." She raised an eyebrow. "Did Edwina tell you da do'h be locked?"

"She didn't. So they locked her in?"

Charlotte shook her head. "No, dey locked evah'body else out. Dat girl couldn't get to da do'h if'n she wanted to, an' I'm sho' she pro'bly did if'n 'er could think. She was tied to da bed."

He'd known that from the start.

"She was tied stawk naked to dat bed, Jack Gibson, an' she was gagged dat one time I saw 'em goin' in late at night."

Jack's stomach sickened. These disturbing revelations he hadn't suspected.

Charlotte sneered. "Dat haw'ble ol' woman went in an' outa dat room, towin' Miss Penny's stepdaddy wif 'er, wif one a dem needles. Got 'er on dope is what dey did. Don't know what else dey did to 'er. Girl soiled herself. Had to burn da mattress afta. Miss Penny always be so clean. Took so many bafs, eben when she were a lit'l bitty thing, I was scared 'er gonna get sick. "

"That night you spoke of, you were allowed in there?"

"No, suh, I weren't allowed in 'der. Dey didn't want nobody knowin' what dey be doin'. I was puttin' laundry in da cu'board. Late workin' der was so much to git done. Dey didn't see me watchin'."

"Where was Miss Clarissa?"

Charlotte snorted. "She and Miz Adel gone up nawf. Wouldn't made no diff'rence anyhow. Anytime Mrs. Markiston wants Miz Clarissa outa 'er business, she jus' gibs 'er a bottle a booze an' tells 'er to start drinkin'. Miz Clarissa is happy to do 'dat. She got back in time fo' da weddin'." Charlotte grinned. "Dat didn't happen thanks to you."

Hardly thanks to him.

"Night she git back she say she wanted to see 'er girl, but Miz Eva tell 'er to leave Miz Penny alone, 'cause dey finally had 'er agreed to marry dat man Noble an' dey din't want Miz Clarissa upsettin' 'er. I knows," she said, when Jack started to interrupt, "cause I heard 'em talkin' at suppa. She jes' looked at 'er mama, an' Miz Eva stare at 'er wif dat warnin' she gib wif 'er eyes"—Charlotte mimicked by narrowing her own—"an' Miz Clarissa didn't say anotha wawd, cept to git 'er way 'bout a chu'ch weddin'. Gib 'er dat bone to shut 'er up, I think."

"Did Miss Adel know what was happening?"

Charlotte studied him for a long moment. "Miz Adel she do 'er grandma's biddin' like she tol' to. But I thinks she likes to do it. You know 'er well as me."

Better.

"Don't know how much she knew when she lef' fo' up nawf, but I think she know'd da day of da weddin' 'er baby sista didn't want to marry dat man. If she know'd how dey got 'er to go along, I don't know, but I doubt she cared."

The only way Adel couldn't have known was if she hadn't even bothered to see and talk to Penny. Certainly she knew what Eva was capable of. Aware or not, Adel hadn't given a damn.

"Do you think Mr. Frederick raped Penny?" he asked.

A pained expression crossed Charlotte's face. "I ain't got no way a knowin' dat, Jack Gibson. She don't know?"

He wasn't going to tell her that Penny wouldn't—

"Won't tell you, will she? You wouldn't a waltzed into dis lion's den to fin' out if'n she would."

No, Penny hadn't elaborated much, which might well indicate that's exactly what had happened behind those closed bedroom doors. "Thought I'd try and find out whatever I could," he said and pulled out the five dollar note he'd been fingering in his pocket. He offered it to Charlotte. She stared at it. "Take it."

She folded her arms under her breasts. "I don't want yo' damn money. I been workin' in dis house fo' nineteen yeahs. Hired by Hugh King when he come to Mis'sippi City. I ain't neba had no need to tell secrets on folk dat keep me fed, but now I recall da man who gib me a job an' how he doted on 'is li'l daughtah. I don't feel no guilt 'bout tellin' you da trash dat happened in dis house, an' I didn't tell you fo' money."

He returned the note to his pocket. "Hugh King is long dead, and his little red-headed daughter lives in my house now, not this one. If you're thinkin' of a new job" — he looked back toward the exit door — "or if you find you *need* a new job, you come to me." He turned to the door.

"Mr. Jack?"

He pivoted.

"Seben yeahs ago dey was fightin' in dis house, too. Lots a fightin'. I can't prove nuffin', min' you. If I could, I'da come to you long time ago. I tol' da shurff Miz Eva an' Hugh King had ha'sh wawds. Had gone on fo' weeks, eben months, but got real, real bad da week dey say yo daddy kilt 'im."

"Did you ever hear my father and Hugh King arguing?"

"Yep, but mostly 'bout how to handle a problem dey bo'f agreed on. Not da problem 'erse'f. I tol' da shurff I didn't b'lieve yo' daddy kilt Mr. King. Him gib me dat same look Miz Eva gibs folk she ain't happy wif, like I should jes' shut my mouf an' keep it shut."

The long afternoons had grown shorter, but there was still plenty of daylight this time of day. Most men here in Handsboro had closed their offices and gone home. Stuart Frederick hadn't. Jack figured he didn't want to go home.

He didn't knock and was pleasantly surprised to feel the door to King and Gibson open when he turned the knob and pushed. He went in, then kept moving, headed to Stuart Frederick's office in the back. Not a fancy thing. It never had been, even when it had belonged to Jimmy Gibson. Jack pushed the half-closed door open. The man was there, as Jack expected he'd be, papers strewn over the large, battered desk, which also harbored a stack of files in one corner. Frederick sat behind the desk, a half-full bottle of whiskey in front of him. He had rolled his white shirt sleeves up to his elbows, and he held a shot glass in one hand. He took one look at Jack and downed it.

"Back for your daddy's desk?" he said. "You're a wee bit early."

"You're late. You should have left long ago."

Frederick released a guttural sound and leaned forward in his squeaking swivel chair to pour himself another shot. "I should have never shown up. I'll give you the house if you'll take the women who live there."

"I have a woman, thanks."

The man downed his shot and leaned back. "But do you have the one you want?"

"Penny is the reason I'm here."

Frederick watched him expectantly .

"I want your version of what went on behind her bedroom door during her most recent visit home."

"She told you about the coercion? I feared she might. Didn't figure you'd come to me though."

"I'd like to beat the shit out of you, you sick son of a bitch. Can you figure that?"

That wiped the sneer off the bastard's face.

"I didn't touch her."

"That's not what I conclude."

"Penny didn't tell you I did it"—the words struck Jack right in his gut and sucked his breath away—"because that'd be a lie, and that girl is incapable of lying. That's part of her weakness." He looked away. "At least I thought it was. She lied about having the promissory note, didn't she?"

Jack didn't respond. He was too invested now in Frederick's comment about who did what.

Frederick must have seen something in Jack's eyes, because he added hastily, "She wouldn't have lied about me, dammit."

"If you didn't rape her, then who did? Jon Noble?"

Frederick shot him a baffled look, hesitated, then said, "So, she hasn't told you what happened?"

"No, but you sure as hell are fixin' to."

"Eva did it with a dildo."

Nausea swept Jack, and he thought he might actually throw up. "What?"

Stuart Frederick drew in a stuttered breath. "Eva said it was security in case of a court battle. She claimed we had to be able to prove Penny's marriage to Harold Noble was consummated for Penny to inherit." He turned, not meeting Jack's eyes. "In a couple of months we'll enter the nineties. Who would believe such a test would be directed by the courts in this day and age?"

"You," Jack said harshly.

"No, not me, not that bitch either! It was about control. I had to witness the deed. Me being a man, and her stepfather, added to Penny's degradation. Degradation is what my mother-in-law thought would mold her to our will." The man swallowed. "Of all the people in that household, Penny was the most loyal to the family and by default to the company. She would have done what was right to protect King and Gibson if for no other reason than her father. Eva took that loyalty and abused it to the breaking point with Adel and Mark, then destroyed it trying to force her to marry Jon Noble."

"Damn your black soul, Frederick. Why did you go along with the woman?"

"Why does anyone? Why the hell would anyone go along with her?"

The promise of wealth and power. Blackmail. Eva probably had something on him.

"Besides, I didn't know how smart Penny was either."

Jack turned toward the door, but stopped. "You sit back on your ass and help her kill off anyone who stands in her way. Have you ever given any thought to just killing *her* off?"

"I found myself on the inside at a full table, with a warm bed, and a beautiful woman to share it with, and Eva is ruthless when it comes to getting and keeping what she wants. She wanted me for King and Gibson...for Clarissa."

Disgust washed over Jack. "For herself, you mean. She could manipulate you."

"*Control* me, you bastard. Control me." He glared at Jack long and hard. "She couldn't control Hugh King." Stuart leaned back and snorted. "Once I didn't mind being controlled. Now, too late, I don't know where the bitch has my secrets hidden."

Chapter Eighty-two

"Mr. Jack," Mars said.

Jack stopped short. He'd been heading around the detached kitchen from the carriage house on his way to the back porch, the house, and his wife, when the big colored headed him off, purpose in his step and an apology in his tone.

"What's wrong?"

Mars had wadded his flop hat and was passing it from hand to hand. "Nuffin', Jack, nuffin's wrong, 'cept I sent fo' somebody to come heah. My cousin an' 'er brotha's boy. He lib wif 'er. Dey be from Manchac on da nawf sho'."

Pontchartrain's North Shore. "Are they looking for a job?"

Mars let loose a little laugh. "No, suh, not 'zactly. Well, she be inside wawkin' right now, in a manna o' speakin'."

Jack frowned. "She's already here, in my house?"

"Yes, suh. I'z hopin' you be late. Miz Penny thinkin' you might not...well, might be fo' da bes' you done come home now."

"Where *is* Miss Penny?"

"She in der. Dey done met."

Jack straightened and steadied his gaze on the big Negro. "What's goin' on, Mars?"

"I'm a thinkin' you gots yo'sef a haint in dat 'ouse. Miz Penny, she think so, too. My cousin Wealthy, she 'as da sight."

"Wealthy, huh?"

"Dat be her name."

Jack shook his head and stepped around Mars. Probably got the idea for her name from the profits she earned from fools.

Wealthy Maignon was of mixed blood, no small part of

376

which was white, but enough Negro to be considered Negro both socially and legally. Jack bet there was some Indian in her, too. One of the smaller, local tribes that no longer existed. She was beautiful and exotic, dressed in a unique mix of bright, colorful clothing that in style was nothing more than a summer work shift favored by slaves of a bygone era, something they would have worn in Africa or the Caribbean, and decorated by aprons and a simple shawl of some bright pink tint that would hurt one's eyes in bright sunshine. Everything she wore screamed color. And jewelry. Gold hoops hung from her earlobes and touched silken, honey-colored cheeks. Her brown eyes watched him kiss a wide-eyed Penny on the cheek. "Caught ya, didn't I?" he said to Penny, then watched Wealthy Maignon's lips curl into a smile. He nodded curtly to the woman, then to the teenage boy who stood at her side.

"This is—"

"Wealthy Maignon, and her nephew Beau," Jack finished for Penny. Despite his irritation, he took the woman's hand when she offered it.

"You believe me a charlatan, Mr. Gibson," she said in a voice as lovely as she was, soft and breathless and accented with cultured Creole with its hint of French.

"I put more stock in ghosts than in those who admit to communicating with them."

"Wise, but I assure you some of us are legitimate."

She exuded a fresh, rain-water scent, muted, less invasive than perfume or toilet water, as if the scent emanated naturally from her skin. The woman raised an eyebrow, then nodded in acknowledgement. "Thank you," she said. "I find your essence attractive as well."

He hazarded a glimpse at Penny, who was watching him curiously, and he felt his face flush, an experience he couldn't recall since he was a boy.

"Only a tiny drop of the Indian blood remains. Caribbean. Diluted now for nearly two centuries. My great-great-grandmother was from Senegal, my grandmother a quadroon. The name Maignon is French Huguenot and my grandmother took it from a man she admired. Whether or not he was her father, I do not know, but he took good care of her." The woman shrugged. "He may have been only a lover. He was not my mother's father that much I know. I am the youngest of four sons and seven daughters"—her almond-shaped eyes smiled—"and you, *monsieur*, have an evil spirit in your house."

"Which anyone who has been listening to local gos—"

"Don't say anything," Penny cautioned with a gentle touch to his arm. He looked at her. "She lives on the D'Iberville River north of New Orleans. She knows nothing of what went on here. Mars sent for her two days ago, and I purposefully asked him to tell her nothing for the very reason you fear."

"Penny, for Saint Peter's—"

"You trust Mars, don't you?"

"Yes"—he turned and found Mars watching and listening. Jack blew out a breath. "That still doesn't mean... How much?"

Penny wet her lips.

"Fifty dollars," Wealthy answered, "plus travel."

Jack sucked in a breath and turned to Penny. Their money was tied up in court. "And you got this sum from—"

She shushed him with a wave of her hand. "I had a little left in a household fund, and I've paid her, so let her earn her money."

It was a hell of a lot of earning as far as he was concerned.

Penny took his hand. "Please, Jack."

"Was me thought of dis, Jack," Mars said. "Don't you be blamin' Miz Penny."

Jack thought the world of Mars, but he sure the devil didn't figure him for more than human, and he couldn't help but wonder how big a cut of that fifty bucks he was getting.

"None," Wealthy said.

Jack held out his hands palm up. "Say nothing more. Just do whatever it is you do. Do we need a table?"

She smiled. "I am not a minstrel-show poseur who peers in crystal balls and entertains people by having them sit in a circle holding hands in the dark."

"Yeah, well, they are the rage among the wealthy, which"— he glanced at Penny—"we apparently are."

"Look," the woman said and took his arm, turning him to the mirror midway down the central hall. He grimaced at the image of his double self. Like a growing number in his house, this particular looking glass was cracked. Two of Wealthy Maignon, then Beau, appeared in the glass behind the two of him. One Penny each moved to the side of either Jack.

That looking glass was a thing from children's nightmares.

In the mirror, he saw Wealthy Maignon turn her head and look at him. He did likewise and found her real self. "I feel the restless thing." She looked around, then stepped confidently around him and into Florence Noble's parlor on the right. "It is a woman," she said softly in that beautiful, French-laced accent of hers. "She is angry I am here."

"Do you know who she is?"

"Someone who died a violent death here." Wealthy was looking at him as she spoke those words. "Do *you* know who she is?"

"I don't believe any of this."

She smiled. "You don't want to believe any of this."

"Assuming I did want to believe this, does she believe her death to be murder?"

"She was murdered before she was ready to go." Wealthy hugged herself, then turned to Penny, who hesitated outside the door. "Her animosity is great. You feel her, too."

Penny started to speak, then didn't.

"You are the present object of her hate," the older woman said. "There have been others. In life she loved to hate."

Penny shot Jack a furtive glance.

"Why would she hate Penny?" Jack asked. Then again, maybe he really didn't want to know.

Wealthy held out a hand to Penny. "Come to me."

Jack turned to watch his bride, watching him. "Go on," he said.

Penny thrust her chin and moved past him and took the Negress' hand. Wealthy touched her cheek. Penny allowed the intimacy, nervous he thought, and he quelled the desire to stand beside her.

"She hates her because this young woman knows about her, knows what she did," Wealthy said.

For what Wealthy Maignon's opinion was worth.

The woman snapped her eyes on him. "You are disappointed."

Jack thought he knew what Florence Noble had done and honestly, that did not warrant the hate supposedly emanating from the creature sharing this house. "I'd hoped for something more justifiable."

"I do not know the passions driving your questions, Mr. Gibson, but the passions driving your evil spirit are pride and deceit. It acknowledges no wrongdoing, but hates the one who can expose its trespass. Now, I wish to wander about the house."

"You are welcome to, but would you like refreshment first?"

"The thing's presence sours my stomach." She turned to her nephew. "Beau, perhaps?"

"No," the young man said. "I'll go with you."

Well, hell, Jack had every intention of going with her, too.

"There should be a center," the woman said. "A place where the thing is strongest."

A chill raced up Jack's spine. Penny touched his hand, and he looked down at her. "Let her be. Let's see what she comes up with."

"I will tell you what I feel," the woman said. "Then Beau and I must go. The presence is strong and malevolent."

𝒯he two rooms were the ones Jack might have guessed if he believed in such nonsense, the bedroom he now occupied and Penny's...uh, Florence's parlor.

"The thing is dangerous," Wealthy told them as she left with Mars and Beau. "And it is growing more powerful. It feeds off fear." She looked at Penny. "Show no fear, and you can fight it." It could not really hurt Penny, she said, but it could cause her to hurt herself. The woman's eyes had widened when Jack told her about the mirror in the study "grabbing" Penny and the resulting cut wrist. The woman hadn't "seen" that—nor had Mars told her of the incident, obviously, which made Jack feel a little better about his man's participation in this bamboozle.

When Penny had asked Wealthy how to get rid of it, she told them to find a priest, though in her opinion, that solution was questionable. The thing could force its way back through the veil of death when least expected. A door had been opened recently, and Wealthy couldn't close it. They should not stay in this place, she said, and Jack inwardly cursed. How were they supposed to abandon a house like this one? "Just go," the woman had said in response to his unvoiced question.

"She's smart," Jack pointed out to Penny after the entourage departed. "She could have read all about Florence's and Alan's deaths in the papers and put it all together."

"She doesn't read, Jack."

Jack considered Wealthy's diction, her vocabulary, her composure. He didn't believe that either. "Are you sure Mars didn't tell her?"

"You know him better than I do."

Jack handed her a glass of water. He opted for whiskey. She handed him the water back. "I'd like wine."

He blinked at her. She sat on the settee. "And what of the cracked mirrors?" she asked.

"The house is settling."

"Settling? Is that something on the order of earthquakes? And the cracks are in mirrors, not on the walls."

He gave her a glass of wine.

"You think I'm doing it?" she coaxed.

He didn't respond immediately, but shortly said, "She says Florence was murdered. The coroner's report will tell you how well that fifty dollars was spent. You could have waited."

"It's not Florence."

"Then who is it?"

"Lorraine Noble, Harold's mother. I thought you understood that. I told you my bedroom had been hers."

381

"I didn't make that connection. I assumed it was someone who had a personal relationship with you. You didn't know this other woman, did you?"

"No, she got in weeks ago, during a séance. She visited Florence for days before she died. Florence was terrified of her."

"Did Florence tell you she saw her?"

"Yes, and Florence did know her."

"And here I was thinking the woman would tell us Florence wasn't murdered."

"I didn't ask her here to prove I didn't kill Florence." Her eyes filled with tears, and his stomach quaked.

"I'm trying to prove to you I'm sane. You think it was the drug, but I wasn't on the morphine as of the night Alan died, the night she came through the door."

He sat beside her. "There was something else."

"I'm sorry?"

"Dr. Mason thought there was something more than the morphine in your system the night you almost died."

"Our wedding night?" She looked away. "I was sick off and on last summer."

"Mark Reed says Dr. Clark suspects you were being poisoned."

"Dr. Clark thought it was something I ate or a stomach ailment..."

Jack was shaking his head, and Penny didn't bother to finish, the distress on her face palpable. "Oh, Jack, do you really want to be right about this? I can leave this house if there's an evil spirit, but what's left of my mind is going with me wherever I go."

Chapter Eighty-three

Penny stepped out of the carriage house. Mars, right behind her, said he reckoned he'd find Roland in the cookhouse with Jane and started for the rear door of the outbuilding. Penny, instead, walked around it and headed for the dusk-shrouded back porch. This most recent foray out had been to the telegraph office—she'd forgotten to notify Mr. Baker of the cancellation of the play troupe following everything that happened in the wake of Angelina Ladner's departure three days before. She'd spent most of the day out, poor Mars with her every step of the way, and despite the fact Jack might actually worry as to her whereabouts, she hoped he'd beat her home. She dreaded going back inside that house.

Shadow oppressed the narrow alley between the kitchen and the well house, but beyond, day's waning light highlighted the steps leading to the back porch. She gave the encroaching darkness no thought until she cleared the corner of the well house and someone stepped...

She jerked to the side, then fell back against the wall of the cookhouse. Around the corner, Mars charged out the kitchen door and onto the breezeway leading to the house. From the corner of her eye, she saw him land gracefully by her side. He'd jumped the breezeway railing. Then he carefully pushed Penny behind him and loomed over Mark Reed, who started.

"What you skulkin' 'round heah fo', Doc?" Mars challenged.

Mark looked around the black man. "I'm sorry I frightened you, Penny. I wanted to talk to you before you went inside."

Considering his last visit, and he still sported two black eyes, Penny was surprised the man had come anywhere near the house.

"It's all right, Mars."

The big colored frowned at Mark. "How'd you git heah?"

Penny considered Mark didn't feel he had to answer, but when Mars refused to move, Mark nodded behind him and said, "My carriage is up on Water Street, one block over." Again Mark looked at Penny. "I didn't want Gibson to know I'm here." Mars folded his arms across his chest, and Mark said to Penny, "I need to talk to you."

Penny touched Mars' arm. "Jack broke the doctor's nose during his last visit. His fear is understandable."

Mars let loose a little laugh. "Yes'm, I reckon you right."

"Prudence, Penny," Mark said. "Not fear. I don't want any trouble."

"Well, you best be 'fraid a me," the Negro said, "'cause I got strict awders to watch da missus. You jumpin' outa da dark li'ble to get you kilt." He raised a finger and stuck it in Mark's face. "And so you know, Mr. Jack, he's gonna know you wuz heah."

Penny looked up at her defender.

Mark glanced up to the breezeway, where Gracie, Jane, and Roland had gathered. Again he looked around Mars to Penny. "I need to talk to you alone."

Mars drew a long breath, and turned to Penny. "He be okay?"

Penny gave Mars a little smile. "No, but he is harmless."

Mars nodded to the kitchen window. "I'll go sit in der wif Miz Gracie." He bent down to look Mark straight in the eye. "We all can see y'all from der, an' I is gonna be watchin'."

"I followed Adel here," Mark said when the kitchen door closed behind the servants.

Inwardly, Penny cursed. "I don't want to see her."

"She's here to see him."

Penny's heart skipped a beat. "Jack?"

"Yes, Jack."

Penny started to turn. "Is he even home yet?"

Mark stepped in front of her. "Of course, he's here. He let her in. I saw him."

She swallowed. "I see nothing wrong with him letting her in the house. She is my sister, after all."

"My point is, why is she here?"

"Because it's Halloween and all the evil spirits are afoot."

"What is that supposed to mean?"

"It means tomorrow is the first of November."

"And you are going to foreclose on your grandmother and stepfather."

"Indeed I am, unless your wife can talk Jack out of it."

"I don't believe you."

"That we'll foreclose or that Adel is here to convince Jack not to?"

"That you'll foreclose."

"I am sorry to disappoint you, and I'm sorry about Adel." Again Penny tried to get around him. Truth was she wanted to get inside and find out what was going on. "Would you please move," she said and cursed the suspicion Mark had put in her head. Their meeting couldn't have been a preplanned liaison. Jack wouldn't have even known Penny'd be out when he got home.

Mark grabbed her arm, and she stiffened. Immediately he dropped his hand. "I don't want her to know I'm here."

"How often do you follow her, Mark?"

"This is the first time. Your grandmother has..." He stepped back suddenly and tightened his lips.

"Grandmother suggested you follow her?"

He didn't say anything, but she knew the answer. For whatever reason, Eva and Adel were setting a trap. If it were for Mark Reed, she didn't care, but if Jack....

But, of course, Jack was the target. Tomorrow the loan was due, and Mark was of no account to them. Her pounding heart wreaked havoc on her temples, but she resisted the urge to massage them. What did it matter, if he were fool enough to fall prey?

Mark placed his hands behind his back and dipped his handsome head closer. He was dressed in a suit and smelled of some crisp, wood-scented cologne. "Penny," he said gently.

Wary, she drew back.

"You've grown up immensely. Striking, if I might say so. A beautiful, desirable young woman."

"I would think you'd be more interested in retrieving your wife than whispering sweet nothings to me."

"I want to apologize for betraying your love."

"I am no longer bothered by that betrayal. I am, in fact, thankful for it. Now, I'm going inside. If you don't wish to see Adel, you need to leave."

"You must be aware that they've been carrying on this relationship since she wed me."

"I am aware of no such thing." But her hand was shaking when she grasped the stair rail.

"She sees him whenever she can."

Penny started up the stairs. "I wouldn't know."

"I want to divorce her."

Penny jerked her face to his. "Then do so." But she knew he wouldn't, the social stigma was too great. Penny knew the Reed family well enough to know Mark's mother and father would rather him live with an adulteress than disgrace the family with a divorce.

"I cannot, not without grounds."

Penny gurgled out a laugh. "And you wish to use my husband as grounds?"

"I was hop—"

"Well, stop 'hoping' if your plot in any way includes me. Adel sees many men. Pick another."

He narrowed his eyes. "What do you mean, 'many men'?"

For a moment she studied his handsome face. Confused, or simply refusing to see the truth. "Did she tell you it was Jack, Mark?"

"Tell me what you mean by 'many men.' Can you prove that?"

"I can't prove anything," Penny snapped, "but if Adel told you she was sleeping with Jack, it is either wishful thinking on her part or another convoluted plot by my grandmother to cause trouble."

"Why would she want to cause trouble?"

Dear god, could he be so oblivious? "Haven't you figured any of this out yet? Adel seduced and married you at Grandmother's behest. You spat me out like hot soup, then she convinced me to marry Harold Noble. My advice to you is to beat Adel black and blue and keep her away from Evangeline Markiston." She stepped around him, but he seized her arm.

"Jack Gibson will be a rich widower with you gone."

Penny stared at his restricting hand, then found his eyes. "Free to marry the woman he loves when I'm dead, is that what you're afraid of?" She yanked her arm free. "Well, she's married to another, Mr. Reed. If you think Jack's in love with Adel, I'd advise you to start worrying about your own black hide, not mine."

He leaned close and spoke softly. "We could protect each other, Penny. Then we could start again, make things the way we dreamed they would be when we were younger."

𝓕rom the double doors leading into the parlor, Penny watched Jack remove Adel's hand from his shoulder. Then he moved away. Adel didn't smile or tease him with words or even wet her lips with the tip of her tongue as Penny had seen her do with men for years. "But I've missed you, Jack," her sister said, and she spoke the words as if she meant them.

"Ah, good, finally we're getting to the part I've been waiting to hear. Well, darlin', I've been thinkin' a lot about you, too. About us back in the beginning."

There was Adel's smile, the one meant to tease and to tempt. "When our love was new. When we spent hours exploring each other's bodies."

"Sweet," he said. "Innocent." He frowned at her. "Or was I a fool, Adel?"

"Reckless," she said, following him as he moved away.

"Tell Eva I'm being a lot more careful these days, and we will foreclose tomorrow, so tell your stepdaddy to pack up." Jack turned and noticed Penny in the doorway. He acknowledged her with a nod and addressed himself to her. "Seems Carrington Farrah delivered a friendly reminder to Stuart Frederick just this afternoon that the loan from Alan Noble's estate is due in full tomorrow. In response, your sister has graced us with a visit." He shrugged. "I'm assuming that means they don't have the money."

"Indeed, this is a surprise, Adel," Penny said.

Adel gave Penny a smile before starting toward her with hands outstretched. Penny wondered what Eva's faux smile would look like this afternoon, or whether the woman would even be able to muster one.

"My, my Penny, you do look so much happier than last I saw you."

Now she was being hateful. Penny had gathered the courage to look into the hall mirror before poking her head into this room. She'd looked more like the haint she feared materializing than the happy girl she used to be. Of course, her conversation out back with Mark could account for part of that.

Adel seized Penny's biceps and pulled her close to place a kiss at the corner of her mouth. She was pert and pretty, a head taller than Penny. Everything about her was perfect, her hair, her makeup, the purple wool traveling suit with bustle and ruffled blouse. The extravagant hat. She smelled good, too, like gardenia. Once Penny had loved her so. She wanted to be like her, exactly like her. Now she wanted the woman to remove her hands.

Which Adel did not do immediately. "I was telling Jack how astonished we all were, you two deciding to wed."

"One unpleasant surprise followed by another at your house, I imagine," Penny said and shook herself out of Adel's grasp. Penny walked toward Jack and he, thank goodness, started her way. They met in the middle of the large room. Adel followed with a crooked smile on her lips and jest in her eyes.

"Safety in numbers?"

"Why are you here, Adel?" Penny said.

She shrugged, then took a seat in one of the two wing-back chairs situated across from a matching settee. "Grandmother feels family members should at least talk to one another."

"You can tell her the spit she received at my aborted wedding is the last 'word' I ever intend to say to her."

Adel chuckled. "Did you spit on her? Mama said you had. Poor Mama, she was so upset. She couldn't believe you'd done such a nasty thing."

Poor Mama lived in a world apart from the rest of them, swathed in illusion soaked in alcohol. Clarissa Frederick believed what Eva Markiston told her to believe, and she was content with that.

Adel pursed her lips. "Grandmother asked after your health. She hopes your dependency has no long-term repercussions."

"Repercussions," of course, would refer to her alleged suicide attempt, conveyed, no doubt, by Mark.

Jack said, "Tell Eva I'm taking very good care of her."

Penny noted how carefully he crafted the sentence, how he relayed each word.

"She received the writ banning her from approaching Penny. A bit much, don't you think, Jack?"

"I wish I'd had one drawn up against you."

Adel laughed.

"Why didn't Mama come?" Penny asked.

Adel looked askance at Jack, then back. "Mama would have hindered me. I was told you'd be gone, else I'd have brought her."

"If you'd known Penny was going to be here, you wouldn't have come," Jack said tersely. "Now go home."

Penny watched her sister cock her head, then adeptly caress her upper lip with her tongue. "That's not what you said before Penny entered the room." Adel turned her focus to Penny. "Jack wished to speak to me in private."

Penny looked at Jack, and he looked at Adel. "The only personal thing left between you and me, Adel, is Penny, and since the company is in dire straits, there's not even business to discuss."

"Yes," Adel said, "you married well, Jack."

"No one knows better than I why he married me," Penny said.

Adel rose and smiled at Jack. "We'll continue our talk later, then?" She winked at Penny. "The one you interrupted, I mean."

Chapter Eighty-four

"Penny?" Jack said.

Her back was to him. She didn't speak immediately, but apparently waited for Adel to get out the door. Then she turned her head, and he could see her profile. "I told you when you agreed to marry me I would not interfere with your liaisons."

"We've already had this conversation. I never agreed to that bull. And besides, Adel is your enemy and a threat to you. My screwing her under any circumstances would be unforgivable."

"Our enemy, Jack." She pivoted fully. "She *is* your enemy, isn't she?"

"I think she's been my enemy for a long, long time."

Penny laid her reticule and books on the settee. "Mark was out back when Mars and I got home."

"Just now?"

"Yes. He followed Adel here. Grandmother suggested he should."

Jack pondered how long Adel had lain in wait for Penny to leave...and for him to come home.

Penny raised her arms above her head and started pulling pins from the little hat on her head. Done, she cocked her head sideways, removed the hat, and tossed it on top of her books. "Did you like her hat?"

He frowned at her and tried to recall Adel's hat, an elaborate thing that matched her dress. "I recall it was light purple—"

"Lavender. It complemented her dress, which was purple."

"I really didn't pay much attention."

Penny smoothed her hair, then very adeptly ran the tip of her tongue over a lovely upper lip.

"But hats draw your attention, even though you don't think you notice them, do they not?"

"I don't think a hat has ever really drawn my attention."

"Do you really 'think'? I believe I will start buying nice hats."

"You're not wearing a hat now."

She smiled demurely, then reached for her things on the settee. "He says he wants a divorce."

"Who?"

She straightened with a huff. "You implied that I had your attention. Mark, of course."

"I told you the woman had my attention, not the things that sit on her head or words that come out of her mouth."

She looked away, as if in thought, and again did that trick with her tongue. His groin tightened. She turned on him suddenly.

"Can a tongue count for words?" she said.

"There are no words that can substitute for that tongue."

Her eyes softened—his words must have pleased her—then she sucked in a breath. "He intends to name you in his lawsuit."

Jack frowned. She was looking at him as if trying to read his mind. No, she wasn't. She was trying to pull the truth out of him. "He's accusing me of seeing her?"

"Why else would Eva have sent him after her?"

"The only time I've slept with her since she wed was the morning after her marriage, and you are painfully aware of that incident. What else did he say to you?"

"He implied you were a threat to me, that perhaps he and I should work to protect each other."

He laughed. "Against Adel and me, huh?"

She shrugged and started for the door.

Perhaps he shouldn't have laughed. "How much of this poison is seeping under your skin?"

"How much of Adel is still under your skin?" she said over her shoulder.

He started after her. "I told you—"

"It doesn't matter," she cried and whirled on him. "It doesn't matter that you haven't slept with her or that you know she's the enemy, if you can't stop loving her, wanting her."

"And what about you and Mark?" He came to a stop close to her, and she prodded his chest with her index finger.

"I never had the intimate relationship with Mark that you had with Adel. For me, intimacy was something I dreamed about, but never had. My relationship with Mark was girlish illusion. Yours with Adel is real—"

"Was real, dammit. *Was*. It's behind me."

"Fine," she said, her voice high pitched. "All I ask is that if you discover it's not..."

*S*he blinked to clear her vision, or was it her head? Heck no. She wasn't going to surrender like this.

He frowned. "Discover it's not what?"

"I beg your pardon?"

"You were telling me that if I ever discovered something..., then you stopped."

Penny sucked in a fortifying breath, then touched his chest, and she braced because she wasn't sure if he'd push her hand away or leave, or curse or what. As it turned out, he cursed *and* pushed her hand away at the same moment he yanked her to him and pressed his lips to hers. He crushed the straw hat she held, and her books thudded against the floor.

He pushed her back, maintaining his hold.

"Is that all there is?" she asked.

"All there is?"

"To a kiss," she snapped because she really did wonder why he was being so obtuse.

"Response helps."

"Response to what?" she cried.

"Part your lips."

She did, but only because she meant to say something that forever after she could not recall. His tongue filled her mouth and for a moment she balked, but he pressed his encircling arm to the small of her back, forcing her breasts against his chest. Tentatively, she touched her tongue to his. He groaned, and she circled her arms around his neck.

He broke their kiss and pushed her back just enough that he could see her face. "Was that more exciting?"

"Yes," she said, "and did I arouse you, too?"

A slow grin curled his lips. "Where the devil do you learn the words you use?"

"Reading," she answered, and laid her head against his chest and listened to his heartbeat.

His arm circled her shoulder and pressed her closer. "You read books that discuss sexual arousal?"

"I'm a twice-married woman, Jack. No one monitors my reading material any longer."

"And is that where you learn your seduction techniques, because if you told me the truth, your first husband didn't teach you anything, and I know for a fact you haven't learned much from your second husband."

"From Adel, late at night. She loved to talk about men and sex. That's what arouses you. Memories."

"She talked about our—"

"After she was older. After our fathers were gone and you'd left for the Piney Woods. Mostly she talked in general. Her men had faces, but she offered no names." She smiled at the impact of what she'd foolishly confessed and pulled out of his arms. "It's the memory of Adel's technique that arouses you."

He stayed where he was when she turned away. Then he said to her back. "Honey, you are nothing like Adel."

She felt the color leave her cheeks, but faced him anyway. "Is that an insult or a compliment?"

"It's not a bad thing, Penny"—and he sounded almost apologetic—"the last thing you want is to remind me of Adel."

Again, she wasn't sure if she'd been slighted, but he caught her arm when she started to turn away. "You're like Penny," he said. "Unique unto yourself and, until you brought it up, I never thought to compare."

"And now that you've thought?"

⇥•⇤

*H*e considered not answering. His thoughts, after all, were his own, and he'd learned in his twenty-four years not to compare one woman to another in either's presence. But he'd also learned what women needed. He pursed his lips. "Adel was easier," he told her, and smiled when he said it, because it was so true. "Much, much easier."

His smile drew one from her, and he kissed her, gently this time and again wrapped her in his arms. Thank goodness she did not ask in what way. That's because she thought she knew. But Adel was easier in every way. Easier to love, easier to hate, to leave, to 'arouse.' The woman had ceased to be a challenge at all.

He kissed Penny's neck, then dipped his head and kissed her toile-covered breast. Again he found her lips, his hands her slender hips, and he pressed her pelvis against his erection. Pliant, she curved against him. He thought of her abuse at the hands of Alan Noble and of her subsequent violation at the hands of her grandmother, and his gut twisted with the horror that she might never...

Then he recalled the young woman who'd stubbornly risked her young life to purge an addiction from her body, then rallied to the fray. No, Penny wasn't timid nor was she permanently damaged. At least, not so much so that she wouldn't attempt intimacy

"Are you sure you're ready for this, Copper Lee?" he whispered against her ear heartbeats later.

"Yes, but it changes everything."

He stooped to pick her up. "And that means what?"

She breathed against his neck, then kissed him below the ear. His pelvis warmed.

"I will insist there be no other women."

He lauged in relief, and mounted the steps with ease. Harold's bedroom door was open when he reached it, and he laid her on her bed, then locked the door. It was late afternoon, the room hazy in the afterglow of the day's retreat. He caught her watching him, and he returned to the bed where he leaned over and kissed

394

her. Anxious to practice her new skill, it seemed, she parted her lips and pulled him down. His erection swelled. He broke the kiss and asked, "Can I undress you?"

She frowned. "You don't normally ask, do you?"

"No," he said and reached for the buttons on her bodice. "It's usually understood, but given the way you've been treated recently, I thought it prudent to prepare you for what comes next."

"To put me at ease?"

"As best I can."

She studied his face and he hers, and he saw when understanding dawned, when she realized he knew what had happened in that bedroom on Texas street.

"The only thought in my head right now, Jack Gibson, is being in this room with you. So, would you undress me, please?"

She smiled, coaxing one from him. "You little minx." He tossed his white shirt over the chair behind him and trembled at the touch of her fingertips on his chest, his stomach, and his navel.

"You are a handsome man, Jack."

When he could endure no more of her teasing caresses, he caught her exploring hand and kissed her, and she kissed him back.

In the fading light, the room shrank to him and her, Penny's hair aflame in the golden light, her ivory skin dappled with shadow, her eyes bright. His palms brushed the lace ruffles covering her breasts, and he kissed her again. Her free hand touched his upper thigh, then the buttons of his britches.

"I was gonna do that," he whispered against her lips.

"That's all right," she echoed. "You've been distracted." Awkwardly, she freed a button, while he struggled with the bodice of her dress.

She stilled when she was done, which gave him some respite, and when he'd finished with her buttons, he rolled her over.

Undressing a woman was always difficult and finally he felt forced to guide her off the bed and stand her up. He pulled the dress over her head, and she turned her back to him, then looked over her shoulder with a coquettish grin. Her hair was falling in places, framing her face with curls. The skin along her shoulder and neck was pale as cream...he kissed her nape...and as smooth. "Turn around."

She turned to him in her cotton eyelet chemise and petticoat, gracing him with a tempting view of scantily covered breasts. She released a soft breath when he reached for the top button of her chemise, and moments later he pushed it apart to expose her breasts. He had the quickness of thought to find her eyes, and he kissed her before he touched the site of Alan Noble's bite. She gasped when he suckled her.

He had her back on the bed, him beside her tearing off his boots and britches. She tried to tackle her petticoat and pantaloons, but he pushed her back to the mattress and finished undressing her slowly, keeping eye contact with her and stealing only quick glances at the pale flesh he longed to lose himself in.

He kissed her nose. "You've gotten freckles today."

"Do you hate them?"

He answered with a kiss on her lips. "I love everything about your body." He moved to neck and breasts, hardening when she traced her fingers down his spine...and he traced his up her inner thigh.

She grasped him to her with a small cry that surprised her. Now, she knew the fascination sex held for Adel. Jack pushed her back onto the quilts and straddled her. A lock of hair fell across his forehead, and his lips curled. "You are a beautiful woman, Penny, and I want you now like I've never wanted anything before in my life."

Penny coaxed him forward. His lips found hers when he filled her, but then he stilled and found her eyes. When he opened his mouth to speak, she placed an index finger over his lips. "I'm all right," she whispered.

"But I'm not done yet," he said.

"Oh, good, because I'm enjoying this."

He grinned at her and started to move.

Shortly after, his eyes locked on her face, his body stilled, then stiffened, and he cried out with ragged breaths. When his ardor cooled, his eyes still roaming over her face, he whispered *damn,* and he closed his eyes and collapsed beside her.

She pushed up on one elbow. "What's wrong?"

A smile moved over his lips. He turned his head and opened one eye, and smoothing the hair back from her face, he pulled her down beside him and wrapped her tight in his arms. She felt him kiss her head. "I see your face, Penny King Gibson," he said, and she was sure she heard emotion in his voice. "Nothing could be more right."

Chapter Eighty-five

Mark Reed brought the undergarments, still warm, to his face and breathed in. They reeked of sex, of her, and of another.

"What...?"

Adel's eyes dropped to the cotton drawers he held in his hand. "It's almost nine," he growled. "Who have you been with? Did you meet Gibson somewhere?"

She came into the room, but turned to her dresser instead of looking at him. "Perhaps I should move into another room, if you intend on making a habit of violating my personal things."

"Violating your things, hell. I want to know who violated my goddamn wife."

She slammed the drawer and whipped around, something white and, no doubt, soft in her hand. "Keep your voice down."

White. Purity. The damn whoring bitch. His one hand crushing the soiled, stinking pantaloons, he stepped toward her, then threw them in her face. "No, I won't. Your stepfather left and your mother has passed out."

The pantaloons, which she'd slapped away, now rested on the floor. "The servants haven't." She tried to sidestep around him, but he grabbed her arm, then squeezed with all the strength he could muster. She cried out, dipped a shoulder, and tried to pull away. He pushed her back to the bed, then ripped the dressing gown, forcing the garment, which would not give easily, to strap around her arms and shoulders. He hoped the force hurt her and bruised her and cut her. She fought him and whimpered, twisting in his hold, grunting and slapping at his hands, until he slapped her face, and she fell back naked on the bed, her hand covering the mark. He fell on top of her, and forcing her legs apart, he

398

shoved two fingers inside her, wide and wet from her tryst with a lover. He took his fingers and shoved them between her lips. "How does Jack Gibson taste, now, Adel?"

She bit him hard, and he yelped and grabbed her hair. With his brutal yank she released him. "As good as ever, you son of a bitch."

He slapped her again, and she fell back with a moan, arching her back at the same time and twisting to get out from beneath him. He laughed at the virility that swept his body and filled the muscle between his legs. In wide-eyed surprise, her blue eyes locked on his, and he crushed her twisting body beneath him, rising enough so that he could reach the buttons on his pants.

"You think he's better than me, you bitch?"

"I know he's better than you."

His penis surged, but rising to his knees, he abandoned his buttons for his belt. She tried to get away, but he caught her with one hand in her hair while he freed his belt from his pant loops with the other. "You've never had any respect for me, have you, Adel?"

Her lips clenched, his fingers still twisted in her flaxen locks. "How much respect do you think I'd have for a man who dumped my little sister for a moment's pleasure? All I had to do was spread my legs, and I had you. Poor Penny doesn't realize it, but I did her a big favor. You were a fool and an easy one at that."

Oh, he was going to enjoy this. "Roll over."

"Go to hell."

With one hand, he drew the leather belt over his shoulder and brought it across her breasts with brutal force. She screamed out. She reached for the hand still holding her hair. At the same time, she tried to kick him, but he protected his erection with a knee and whipped her again. "Roll your ass over so I can get to it or I will beat every inch of your body black and blue."

How easily she did this time, and he only had to hold her in place for two blows across the silky flesh of her derriere before she surrendered, her face in the pillow, her body twitching with each blow, which he continued until the reddened flesh bled. He considered her bottom numb by then, and he tossed the belt away, freed his aching penis and jerked her to her knees. She was crying, real tears, and he was the happiest man alive when he rammed his cock into her lover's leavings, and she cried out, rising from her supine position and molding her naked back to his chest. She reached back, her arms circling his neck, and brought his forehead against the back of her head. He placed one hand between her legs, holding her to him, stroking her. She cried out and stiffened, gyrating her hips in sequence with his thrusts. Then his mind exploded with his manhood. She fell forward, and he dropped next to her naked body. She curled in a ball and moved her back against his bloody white shirt. He rolled his head on the pillow and closed his eyes. He didn't care if she suffered. In fact, that pleased him. He'd never felt more in control, more like a man.

"Oh my god," she said, "that was the best it's ever been."

Chapter Eighty-six

That policeman who worked for Tobias Craig appeared early the next morning. Mars Bullock came into the dining room where she and Jack were eating breakfast and fetched Jack out back to talk to the man. Jack returned five minutes later to kiss her goodbye. He had to track down Clive Morgan, their lawyer, quick. And, oh yes, he told her, Toby would be by within the hour to arrest her for conspiracy to commit murder. He squeezed her shoulder, and she looked up at him. "He has to arrest you, Penny. He doesn't want to, but if he doesn't, Lyle Jenkins will. Today. This way, Toby can claim you as his prisoner."

"Alan did poison Florence then?" she said quietly, not quite sure she believed it.

"Florence Noble died of natural causes. Alan was poisoned. Belladonna," he said, then disappeared out the back door, leaving her sitting at the dining room table with her mouth open.

That was four hours ago. She'd seen neither hide nor hair of him, but she had now seen the inside of the Harrison County Jail. She'd driven past and around it on Texas Street all her life, but she'd never been inside.

Her cell was eight by eight or thereabouts. The only other one was empty. There was an anteroom beyond the cell block where Lyle Jenkins came and went. Two of his deputies were out there now with Charlie Nixon, who was staying close. Mars was outside the jail, on the porch, but she knew there was no way he could help her in here without getting himself killed. Charlie Nixon had already told him to lie low.

The jailer and his wife lived upstairs. The wife had brought Penny's dinner to her fifteen minutes ago. Fried chicken and creamed potatoes. The meal smelled good, but the only thing Penny realized from it was nausea. She did make some effort to sit and eat, if for no other reason than to please the woman who'd made it, a pleasant, red-faced lady who kept her hair under a printed kerchief. She told Penny she was making sweet potato pie for that evening's dessert, and Penny had nearly cried. Not at the thought of sweet potato pie, but at the thought of still being here at suppertime.

She'd just washed down a forkful of black-eyed peas when she heard the voice she'd been dreading the last three hours. Then came the scraping of a chair against the floor of the room outside and the loud guffaws of Lyle Jenkins. Whether he was laughing at her, about her, or something completely unrelated, didn't change the fact that "yes, her granddaughter was here, and would she like to see her?"

The door swung open and Eva Markiston in all her grandeur swept in. No one would have thought the woman all but destitute. She smiled at Penny. "Well, Penelope, it seems you're in a fine fix."

Penny, head pounding and knees weak, breathed in through her nostrils.

"But, my darling grandchild, do not lose heart. I intend to do everything in my power to keep you from the gallows. I'm told you are mentally disturbed. It's an undocumented fact that you've tried to take your own life once, now Mark tells me you've made a second attempt, and your servants say you see ghosts." Eva looked around the jail block. "Where is your husband?" She laughed. "I wondered how long it would take him to abandon you."

Penny's strained heart beat faster. What if one of Eva's henchmen had waylaid him?

Eva looked her up and down. "What a pretty little blue dress. Your daddy always liked you in blue. You look like you're putting on some weight after that terrible bout with the morphine. Dear Mark told me I'd be pleased to learn that you've beaten your addiction. I wasn't. You do know that it only takes one small dose, and you're completely dependent again? So...." She started to open her reticule, but caught sight of Charlie Nixon, who'd slipped through the door behind the sheriff. "Can I talk to Penny alone?" she demanded of Jenkins.

The sheriff turned to Nixon, who spoke before he could. "No, ma'am. She's a Biloxi police prisoner and she's not to be left alone with anyone." He looked at Jenkins. "This woman has a restraining order against her. She's not to go near Mrs. Gibson. I want her out of here."

The sheriff looked fit to be tied, and Penny wondered how much of Charlie Nixon was bluff and how much was real. "This is my jail, Nixon," the sheriff bellowed. "Has your boss ever laid out for you who the senior law enforcement officer in this county is?"

"That would be you, Sheriff, but she's still my prisoner, and there's still that restraining order. That's the law, so how about you gettin' on with enforcing it?"

Eva, listening to Nixon, actually produced a crooked little smile and turned to face the two men. "He's very amusing, Lyle."

Jenkins swung the jail block door wide. "Get out!"

"No, sir."

Penny's heart was throbbing, and she feared she would lose the jailer's wife's dinner.

"Hays, Ewelle, get him out of here and give me them keys. We gotta git in this cell."

Charlie Nixon stepped farther into the room, then held up a finger to the first man to cross the threshold. "You lay a hand on me, Bob Hays, and I'll beat the hell out of you."

Hays and the man behind him looked to the sheriff. "What's goin' on here, boss?" Hays asked.

"I want this son of a bitch outa here, that's what's goin' on. Ewelle, toss me them keys."

Ewelle didn't toss them, he handed them, then jumped to one side as Charlie Nixon shoved Hays. He almost knocked the man clean through the door, but Hays caught himself on the frame and braced. It was all over then, because Ewelle had Nixon from behind and was shoving, while Hays switched to pulling, with

403

Nixon hollering that they meant that woman harm and Bob sure as hell knew he was doin' wrong.

The door closed, though the commotion outside didn't. Penny had approached the bars, now Eva pivoted and looked down on her, hate in her eyes and a malicious smile on her lips. "There," she said softly. "All done." She took one small step to one side so Jenkins could fit the key in the lock. Eva returned to her reticule. "Get her sleeve up," Eva said, even as Penny was backing away from the huge hulk of a man.

The door crashed open and banged against the wall with a deafening clatter. Jack Gibson strode in, for a moment filling the doorway.

"Get the hell out..." Jenkins clamped his mouth shut when a dapper-looking fellow entered behind Jack, already in the cell shielding Penny from Jenkins, who was now focused on the goings-on behind him. Charlie Nixon followed the dapper-looking man and made a beeline for Eva and clasped her forearm. She made a brief effort to pull away, but Charlie firmly escorted her out the door. At the threshold Toby Craig tipped his hat to her and said, "Good day, Mrs. Markiston." She glared at him, yanked her arm free, and went no farther.

Jenkins looked around the dapper-looking fellow. "What the hell do you think you're doing, Craig?"

The dapper-looking fellow handed Jenkins a writ. "Mrs. Gibson has made bail."

Jenkins snatched it from his hand at the same time Eva tried to reenter. Nixon blocked her way. "How?" the woman screeched. "Judge Puknay—"

"Had a change of heart as regards the setting of bail, Mrs. Markiston. Seems there's some things frighten him even more than you." The dapper-looking man smiled. "By the way, while I was waiting on the writ, I escorted your son-in-law out of King and Gibson's Handsboro office. King and Gibson had until noon. You do know Jack and Penny have foreclosed, do you not? Stuart turned over the keys and the books. Exactly what are you trying to accomplish here?"

The woman was seething mad; Penny could see it, even scrunched up as she was against Jack. She felt him move, and she looked up.

"Are you all right?" he asked softly.

She nodded and her vision blurred. "I didn't know what had happened to you."

He hugged her to him. "You mean you didn't think I was coming."

She sobbed and buried her face against his breast. "I knew you'd come if you could, but I was beginning to fear you wouldn't come in time. I'm sorry."

He squeezed her tighter. "You don't have to be."

*J*ack turned, Penny with him, and came face to face with Lyle Jenkins. The man glared at them a moment, then hollered, "Hays, where the hell is your weapon?"

Toby stayed Robert Hays' hand with his own. Hays had not gone for his gun, though his hand hovered close.

"I can pull my pistol before you can line up that scattergun, buddy," Charlie Nixon called to someone beyond Jack's point of view.

Toby turned to Jenkins. "Puknay has abandoned ship, might be time for you to do likewise, unless you're plannin' on killin' off the entire Biloxi Police Department and"—he nodded at Clive, who stood beside him—"this fine lawyer here."

"I want to know what's goin' on?"

Clive stepped in front of the good sheriff, brushing up against the latter's robust belly and forcing him back a step. "You've got the writ, read it. Let's go, Jack." Clive followed Jack and Penny out of the cell, made a show of looking around, and said, "Mighty sloppy procedures you have here, Jenkins. I do believe you served Mrs. Markiston a writ ordering her away from her granddaughter, yet today you allow the woman to intimidate the incarcerated defendent. You haven't heard the last of this incident."

Chapter Eighty-seven

It was late afternoon by the time they got home to Biloxi. Before leaving Mississippi City, Jack asked their lawyer, Mr. Morgan — today was Penny's first opportunity to meet the man — Toby, and that badger Charlie Nixon to come for dinner. Despite her fatigue, Penny looked forward to an enjoyable evening and perhaps an opportunity to strategize about her defense for murder. After a quick respite and change of clothes, she left her room, pointedly avoided the mirror in the dimly lit hall, and grabbed the stair rail. Halfway down, she called Jack's name, then stopped cold when Jonathan Noble's voice called, "We're in here."

She breathed again when Jack appeared at the door to the large front room and motioned her in. Jonathan rose out of the wing chair flanking the settee when she walked into the room.

"Join us," Jonathan said. "We were just discussing the course of this tangled plot and wondering how we managed to let it get so far out of control."

Penny looked at Jack, who motioned her to a place on the settee. She studied him for the pace of three throbbing heart beats, then walked over and sat. He sat next to her. She looked at Jonathan, who also sat back down. "I'd been told you two were friendly," she said.

"Yes, we go back a long ways, Jack and I."

"To before Humboldt manipulated your grandmother's shipping on the dummy lines," Jack said. Penny placed her hands in her lap and looked at him, watching her. He winked, and she wondered at this bizarre game he was playing.

Jonathan straightened in his seat. "That was my idea. I had to put an end to your grandmother's pressuring Alan to pressure me."

Penny fisted her hands. "So you contrived a plan to end her operations altogether."

"And unfortunately"—Jon flashed Penny a quick smile—"or fortunately as the case may be, set in motion all that followed."

"You killed Harold?"

Jonathan gave Jack a lazy glance, and Penny's heartbeat quickened. "I would not say so, no," Jon said, but Penny had followed his gaze to Jack, who discreetly shook his head at her. She already knew Jack's side of the story.

"Why did you want Harold to marry me?"

"I didn't. I wanted to marry you myself, and would have, but I made the mistake of informing my lover of the plan. Florence would have none of it. She didn't want me married to another. She interfered, first by convincing Harold he could get everything he wanted from his father simply by agreeing to marry, but the deal was, she'd help convince his father only if he agreed to marry you. So he did. She then approached Alan on Harold's behalf. It was Alan who pressed Harold's suit, essentially purchasing you from Eva Markiston."

"But why did you want to marry me to begin with?"

"To expand the interests of Noble Shipping."

Penny furrowed her brow.

"He's talking about overland shipping, Penny," Jack said. "Hugh King's family farm up in Perry County is the key. It, along with the tract Eva put up for collateral, and the tract Jonathan, Harold, and Florence duped Alan into buying, lie along a proposed right of way for a common carrier between Mobile and Memphis."

"A railroad?"

Jack nodded.

"But in the beginning there was only your farm. That's what led me to you," Jon said.

"The ideal spot to build the trestle over the Leaf lies on your family farm," Jack explained.

Penny again faced Jonathan. "Harold knew this?"

"He figured it out. He always wondered why I would have chosen you. Harold was actually smarter than either his father or Florence. They assumed I wanted that Escatawpa property, the significance of which I didn't even appreciate until Alan informed me of his and Tom Gates' interest. Harold didn't figure me for timber or canning. He knew from the start there had to be something potentially much more lucrative, so he investigated. What's missing is what Alan got out of the deal."

"He wanted a grandson."

Jon laughed. "Not exactly. Allow me to explain. Ever since his mother's death, Harold has wanted what he considered his rightful place in the business. Alan, on the other hand, wanted Harold wed. A respectable Harold, married with a family, was sure to be accepted as head of shipping in Mobile. More than anything in the world, Alan wanted me out of Noble Corporation. He could control Harold with the promise or denial of his inheritance, something he could neither promise nor deny me even if he'd wanted to, which he didn't. Dear old Dad did what he considered right by me, then made sure I was out of the running.

"As far as the mythical grandson over which you were so concerned, dear girl...well, a respectable young family worked in favor of Harold's acceptability as heir to the corporation, but a child was really of secondary importance to Alan and of absolutely none to Harold." Jon pursed his lips. "I, on the other hand, might have been pleased to have sired a son...or even a daughter, the only potential problem being that six-year wait for your Perry County property, should the Mississippi legislature ever come around and approve the railroad. It was more than just land. I planned for that trestle to land me a place on the railroad board."

Penny glanced at Jack, who was studying Jon with what might have been fascinated curiosity. Now Jack turned and met her eyes. "Your father left that land for you in a trust," he said.

"I know, but..."

"There's nothing you could have done to expedite matters.

That was the family farm. You could not get title to it until you were twenty-four, nor could your spouse."

"A railroad requires investors and a board, Penny," Jon elaborated, "and unimpeded control of the land. Your widower will have that, your husband won't until your twenty-fourth birthday."

Penny turned and studied Jack, who met her gaze straight on. Then she held her chin high and turned back to Jon. "Did y'all know the terms of the trust when Harold married me?"

"I did. I'm not sure exactly when Harold figured it out, but I know that at the end he had."

"So, you meant to kill me all along."

"That would have depended on the legislature, actually. If it never acted there would have been no need. Harold, on the other hand, suffered immediate regrets at having wed you, and as time went on, you continued to make matters worse, or so he said. You see, you conjured unpleasant memories of his mother."

"How could I have possibly reminded him of that horrid wo—"

The gas sconces flickered, and Penny searched the dim corners of the room.

Jon laughed. "Do you see ghosts, Penny?"

She didn't answer.

"Whatever. In answer to your question, you weren't like her, but he resented your efforts to make a marriage, and he detested the fact that his father compelled him to wed in order to get what he felt was his by right. Your property in Perry County was icing on the cake, and his abetting me in exacerbating his father's financial duress hastened his gaining control of the company.

"Harold planned to kill you the night Alan died. Fate intervened. And as it turned out, someone"—he looked directly at Jack—"killed him first."

Penny refused to let him distract her this time. "Florence—was she part of the plot?"

"Alan thought so, but I'm not sure what she and Harold had concocted. She was jealous of you because of me, but she actually did like you. That doesn't mean a lot, though. I like you, too." He smiled suggestively. "So does, Jack, I imagine."

"Don't listen to him, Penny."

Jon shrugged. "No, don't. But as I was saying, my situation with Alan was growing untenable."

"Wouldn't it have been easier to kill Alan instead of putting this convoluted plot in motion?" Jack said.

"You would think so, yes, but remember I could not sit the Noble Corporation Board. Harold would have inherited, and I'd have been no better off than I was, except he'd be building a common carrier, not I. Besides, the plan wasn't convoluted at the outset. I wanted Penny, Eva wanted shipping. Simple. Then Alan butted in with his sodomite son, his offer of a loan, *and* still the promise of shipping. Eva really should have stuck with me."

Jack reached a short distance and touched the hands knotted in her lap. She met his eyes, then gave him her hand. Jon saw and snickered.

"Why," she asked Jonathan, "after Harold was killed, didn't you ask me to marry you instead of giving me to Grandmother?"

His mouth dropped open, then he clamped it shut. "And if I had, what would you have said?"

"No."

"And that's what I figured. Eva and I came to a mutual agreement. Apparently you'd managed to anger your grandmother."

"I defied her."

Jonathan looked at Jack. "And continued to do so. Now, your new husband, who has hated your family for some years, stands to gain everything, once you're found guilty of murdering Alan."

"I didn't kill Alan."

"You and Alan were the only ones home at dinner that night. Harold had left to meet a friend, and I was in Mobile."

"You weren't in Mobile," Jack said.

Jon glanced at him. "You are correct." Jon refocused on Penny. "Jack saw me in east Biloxi in the late hours of the evening. He's the one who informed me Harold was dead."

"I told you what I was doing there," Jack said when she looked at him.

"The person Harold was meeting was supposedly Stuart." She narrowed her eyes on Jon. "What were you doing there?"

"Waiting on Jack."

"I didn't kill Harold, Penny."

She swallowed hard. The only motive Jack would have had for killing Harold would have been as Jon's hired killer. "Why would I have wanted to kill Alan?" she asked.

"You wouldn't. You had no motive to kill anyone. You didn't know Harold was going to die that night, and I didn't know Alan was going to die. You have no idea how pleasantly surprised I was when I got to the house the next morning and learned Alan was dead and you very much alive." Jon leaned forward in his seat. "I know that, Penny. A jury will not. They will be looking at a beautiful opportunist who manipulated the murder of two men in order to inherit a fortune."

Penny looked at Jack, who sat quietly in his seat, listening to Jon. "Jack?"

Jon smirked. "He won't help you."

Jack looked at her. "What he's saying is that he doesn't think I can help you, but he doesn't believe that either. He wants you to believe it."

"I repeat, he won't help you."

Penny's gut quaked, but she focused on what mattered, not Jon's obfuscation. "Alan was fine after he got home. Jane saw him."

"Do you know how belladonna works, Penny?" Jon asked.

She waited, and he smiled. "Its effects take several hours. Whatever killed him at nine had been fed to him hours earlier."

"You killed Alan and Harold in order to marry me and inherit everything. Nothing else makes sense."

"Now you sound desperate. Of course, something else makes sense. The truth. For the record, Harold's murder is closed. Officially, David Pascal killed him, and I had absolutely nothing to do with Alan's death, but I do know why he died." Jon rose

411

and stopped in front of Penny. "Everything I've told you is the truth." He glanced at Jack, who watched him calmly. "Jack says y'all have guests coming for dinner. I'm sure you have things you'd like to discuss before they arrive. I will see you both in court."

"Wait," she said, and Jon stopped.

"Was it belladonna that Alan used to kill Lorraine?"

"Belladonna was the poison used, but it was Harold, not Alan who administered it. Alan realized that later and covered it up."

"Where would Harold have gotten belladonna?"

"An apothecary? Or someone with knowledge of its effects supplied it to him. It does serve a useful purpose, you know?"

"For what?"

"It's used to treat ulcers, among other things," Jack said.

Penny frowned at Jon. "You're impugning Florence."

"The drug frightened Peter Fritz, but her doctor in Mobile prescribed it routinely. She used it throughout her teen years."

"I don't believe Florence supplied Harold that drug. Did she even know him then? It's more likely she was *your* source."

"And I Harold's confidant? You were with her when she died. I heard what she supposedly said to you. Consider her hallucination a confession of her guilt. It all but confirmed what I have long suspected. And as for Florence's knowing Harold, our families had been friendly for years. At the time of her coming out, Florence was my girl. She was several years older than Harold, too old to be his 'perfect' match, but to Lorraine's horror, she was not too young to catch Alan's roving eye, a fact not missed by Florence's mercenary mother. Lorraine was jealous of Florence, and her dislike catered to insult. Florence and Abigail chaffed from offense. For years growing up, Florence sympathized with her young friend's plight at the hands of his domineering mother. Now she was feeling the witch's wrath. Add to that Florence's ability to manipulate Harold, and perhaps you can forgive this jilted lover's harboring doubts as to her role in Lorraine's death, albeit for her own satisfaction, not Harold's."

He turned abruptly and left the room, pleased with himself,

Penny thought, and his telling of the tale. Jack followed him out, and she wondered if they spoke.

Uneasy, she rose and moved to the chess game she and Jack started two nights before. It seemed like forever ago. She'd been playing quite well.

"He's trying to put doubt in your mind."

She looked up. Jack was watching her from the doorway. "It's doubtful the prosecution even has a good case against you."

"Did you kill Harold?" she asked.

"For him, you mean? I'm not a hired assassin. I told you, I was meant to be caught in the room with Harold's body when Stuart arrived. Jon was working with Stuart and Eva. I didn't trust Jon. I never have. I never went inside that building. Jon killed him."

"How do you know for certain?"

"I wasn't there, if that's what you're asking, but he practically told you so just now. Think about what he said. 'Everything I've told you is the truth.' And it was. It's a lie because of all he left out. Officially Harold's murder is closed, but Jon didn't return to Mobile that night. He was in Biloxi. When I told him Harold was dead, he didn't even suck in a breath. He already knew."

She touched her shining knight. "He has Harold's key to Alan's safe. He told me he found it in Harold's drawer, but Harold always kept his keys with him. I had Alan's key. That's how I was able to get in the safe so fast and remove the promissory note." She pulled out her chair and sat. It had been her move when they quit, night before last.

"That would explain how he has keys to the house." Jack took his seat, looked at the board, then her.

"Is that how he got in tonight?" she asked.

He looked at her across the board. "I let him in."

She dropped her gaze to the board.

"All I wanted was King and Gibson, Penny."

"But now there's so much more for you to want."

Jack watched her move, then took her queen. "Yes there is, sweetheart."

413

Chapter Eighty-eight

Clive and Toby arrived on schedule. Jack knew 'em both well enough to know they were ready to eat. That tenacious Nixon fella had other plans for his evening though. From what Mars told him about the man, Jack owed him a number of meals. Penny asked Toby if Nixon were married. He wasn't. A sweetheart then, perhaps?

Maybe. Toby didn't know.

Jack left Mars in the kitchen with Gracie, whose company he appeared to enjoy more and more despite a pretentious snobbery on her part. Jack knew Gracie was a widow and had two boys at home, both in their teens. Gracie could read and write. So could her boys, she'd told him a couple of days ago. She wanted them to attend Alcorn.

They ate fried catfish and collards and black-eyed peas. Jack had approved the menu before he and Penny sat down to what began as a pleasant breakfast almost twelve hours ago. He'd done the meal approving several times since they moved in, primarily because it gave him more say in what they ate, and the menu had been in a state of flux since Alan Noble fired his cook. They were, in fact, at the mercy of whatever Gracie knew how to cook, and what she and hers had eaten for a lifetime meshed well with what he and his had eaten. Clive, a south-central Mississippi boy, raved over the meal, and Toby always had an appetite.

Jack sat on the settee after dinner holding Penny's hand, while Toby rehashed the death of David Pascal. Clive studied the chessboard. He asked who lost their queen and seemed disappointed it wasn't Jack. Clive was waiting for coffee, that chicory-laden stuff Gracie promised ten minutes ago.

414

Penny was listening to Toby. Though pleasant, she was mostly quiet and had been since Jon left. At length she asked the Biloxi marshal about belladonna. Deadly nightshade, Toby explained, and most of what he knew, he'd learned this past week from Dr. Fritz. It was sweet and, used in excess, deadly with no known antidote, the only chance for survival being immediate regurgitation. It was used medicinally for pain and, as strange as it seemed to Toby, given Florence Noble's condition, ulcers, confirming what John had said earlier. That's why Dr. Fritz suspected the poison. He knew of it, and because of what he knew, he didn't use it on his patients. He also knew Florence had used it as a girl. Before killing its victim, the poison resulted in hallucinations, vomiting, and stole its victim's ability to speak.

Jack turned at the knock on the doorjamb. Mars stood there, purpose etched across his face. "Need to speak at ya'."

At the door, Gracie, coffee service in her hands, scooted around him, and Clive abandoned the chessboard.

Mars led Jack down the hall to the dining room, then out the back door. Descending the steps, he said, "That boy Roland come and got Jane a few minutes ago. Din't think much of it, till he come right back in wifout 'er. I was curious, you know, 'cause I figured he wanted to be wif 'er. So's I went out back. Wandered 'round a li'l bit, den I heard her talkin' wif a man. Dey was back a da carriage house an' was 'bout done wif der talk, cause I had to hurry roun' to da otha side when she started back to da house. I went on roun' back. Man was gone bes' I could tell. Black as pitch back der, but I'd a sensed 'im if'n 'im was still der."

In the glow of the kitchen lights penetrating the window, Jack saw Mars nod to the north. "Figured he took off walkin' up Perrella Street. Sho' nuff, I waited a couple minutes an' a hawse an' carriage drove back down. Bettin' it was 'im."

"Could you tell anything about him?"

"Too dark."

Jack had already started walking to the rear of the kitchen. "Have you asked Jane?"

"Got you fu'st."

415

Jack climbed the stairs and almost collided with Roland coming out. "Who did Jane meet out back just now?"

The boy's friendly demeanor degenerated to fright in the space of a heartbeat, and he looked from Jack to Mars. "I din't—"

"You talk now!" Mars said and moved to stand toe-to-toe with the youth.

"She be all right, Mars. She already back in da 'ouse."

"We're not worried about her, Roland. We want to know who she met," Jack said.

Roland blinked at Mars, then stepped closer to Jack. "Mr. Jon Noble. He asked me to fetch her. Din't see no harm."

Jack slapped him on the shoulder, then moved around him. "You didn't do anything wrong." He stepped through the back door into the warm kitchen at the same time Gracie entered the front from the breezeway. "Where's Jane?"

"Takin' Miss Penny 'er chocolate."

"Mars Bullock," Gracie said, "earn yo' keep an' pump me up some watah so's I can get to washin'."

Mars had earned his keep today, but Jack's gut told him Mars liked doing things for Gracie. As if he read her thoughts, she looked at Jack and smiled.

"Evah night Jane would take Miss Penny her choc'late, den make 'er an' me a cup. Mr. Alan say it be okay. Is it still?"

"Sure," he said slowly. He was missing something important here.

She reached for the sugar tin. Jack stared at it a moment. Sweet. *He drank my chocolate, which I didn't want, and I drank his brandy.* Jack blinked. *Harold planned to kill you the night Alan died.* What had he been thinking? They knew the belladona had been meant for Penny. Harold had to have an accomplice in this house.

Jack straightened, looked at Mars, pumping away, then back to Gracie, who had stopped her progress and was now watching him. Suddenly her eyes widened, her realization validating his worst fears. His heartbeat quickened, and he hurried between them and through the breezeway door. Behind him he heard the dishes clatter, then Gracie barked Mars' name.

❧

Jane handed Penny the cup, then turned with her small platter to glance at the coffee service.

"You can leave the coffee," Penny said, holding up the cup and bringing it to her lips. She needed to tell Jane to quit making it for her. "Thank you for the chocolate."

Jane nodded without looking at her, then started in surprise. Penny, her mouth open, watched Jack take the cup from her hand. Jane began to move around him, but Mars blocked her retreat. Penny shut her mouth.

"Jane's been making you chocolate for so long," Jack said, "I think it would be nice if you let her drink this one." He set the cup on the oval table in front of the settee.

Toby, almost asleep in front of the fire, blinked awake. In the chair across from Penny, Clive Morgan craned his head to get a better bead on what was going on.

Jack nodded to the seat next to Penny. "Sit down, Jane."

"I gotta he'p Gracie in da kitchen."

"I be right heah," Gracie said, stepping around Mars. "Mr. Jack says sit. You sit."

Jane hesitated only a moment, then, head bowed, she sat. Jack, pushed the cup in front of her, and she looked up at him, her eyes wide. "Drink it," he said, his voice soft.

Violently, the girl shook her head. Her eyes were bright with tears, and Penny squirmed in her seat. Jack chopped the air in front of her face, and she stilled.

"Why not?" he asked Jane.

Jane swallowed. "Miss Penny likes lotsa sugah."

"And you don't think you would?"

Jane bowed her head and looked at the clasped hands in her lap. "Don't like choc'late."

"I know that's not so. Now drink this cup."

She shook her head.

"I insist."

Toby had risen. Clive watched. To Penny's right, Mars and Gracie remained rigid. Jack squatted in front of Jane and said,

"Start talkin' or I'm gonna sit on you, and Mars is gonna pour this stuff down your throat."

Jane started crying. Penny could scarcely breathe.

Jack rose. "Mars."

Jane jerked her head up and screamed, "No! It was Mr. Noble. He make me do it."

"Jonathan Noble?"

She nodded.

"How did he make you do it?"

"Said he'd tell 'bout da night Mr. Alan died if I din't."

"You poisoned Alan Noble?" Toby asked.

Jane spun around and looked at Chief Craig. "Mr. Harold, it was him made me do it."

"How?"

"He say I had to. Say'd da ars'nic be takin' too long. He tell me he would run me off if'n I din't do it."

"You were giving Alan Noble arsenic?" Toby asked.

Jane shook her head. "Miss Penny. Puttin' it in 'er choc'late since summer time."

Gracie stepped around Mars. "Mista Harold din't make you do nuffin'. He gib you money to do it." The older woman found Jack's eyes. "She been buyin' dresses ain't fit to work in. New shoes. Pretties she couldn't hab on 'er pay. Things she din't need. I wondered how she be doin' dat. Now I know."

"Tell us what Mr. Harold had you do the night Alan Noble died," Toby said.

"Him wanted me to put da nightshade in Miz Penny's choc'late. Weren't supposed to kill him's daddy."

Penny covered her mouth with her hand. "Alan drank my chocolate that night."

"Dat mornin' when you tell da marshal Mr. Alan was dead and der you wuz alive, I wuz scared he drank yo' choc'late. I thought Mr. Harold'd kill me when he found out what 'appened, but den I foun' out he be dead, too, so I din't worry none. Den tonight, Mr. Jon tell me he know'd what I done."

Clive stepped forward. "How did he know?"

"I imagine Harold told him right before Jon killed him, which was, no doubt, Jon's plan all along in luring Harold there. I was the prize for the Markiston-Frederick clan, who'd sworn fealty in return for framing me. When Harold confessed to his uncle he'd poisoned Penny and won the golden prize—"

"The what?" Toby asked.

"Jack is referring to that King property up in Perry County," Clive clarified.

"At that point," Jack continued, "Jon killed Harold anyway. He went to bed that night believing he'd once again been thwarted by his loving family, but he'd foiled Alan, too, by ruthlessly eliminating Alan's son, who Alan planned to replace Jon at Noble Shipping. Jon came to this house the next morning expecting to find Alan alive and grieving, and Penny dead." Jack looked at Penny. "He said he was pleasantly surprised, remember, to find the opposite to be the case. That was an understatement, because with your husband and his older brother dead his prospects of getting everything, you included, must have looked downright rosy. You were key, and the only way he'd get leverage with you, was through your grandmother. For that he needed the loan document. Eva Markiston suddenly was looking at control of Noble Corporation through Penny. She wasn't going to sacrifice that without good reason."

Penny looked at Jane and asked softly, "And tonight?"

"Answer her," Toby said to the sobbing Jane.

Jane swiped at a tear and looked at Penny. "He say Mr. Jack would be blamed. He say once you an' Mr. Jack out da way, he'd be rich an' gib me lots a money."

Gracie snorted. "He'd a put a knife in yo' gullet mor'n likely."

"Amen to dat," Mars said. "Shut yo' fool mouf fo' good, girl."

Toby took the girl's arm and started to pull her from the settee. "No! I won't do nuffin' like dis again. I promise. It was dem made me do it."

Penny opened her mouth, but Jack stepped between her and the girl. "Toby, I'll send Mars with you."

"Yeah," Toby said, "I'm lookin' forward to seein' Jenkins

again tonight." Toby stepped back into Penny's line of sight, a sobbing Jane in tow. Jack, Mars, and Gracie followed them out.

Clive sat beside her as the group disappeared out the door. Momentarily he looked at his coffee cup, then pushed it away. "Well, Mrs. Gibson, looks like you're off the hook for murdering Alan Noble."

Penny swallowed, then looked at the man. "Mr. Morgan," she asked, "how much was my bail this afternoon?"

He blew out a breath. "Have you talked to Jack?"

"Not about that."

"A thousand dollars."

Tears filled her eyes. "He'd retained you to defend me?"

"Not me, a criminal attorney I recommended."

"How much?"

"A lot."

"Where did he get that kind of money? All our assets are tied up in the courts." She blinked at Clive Morgan. "Except for..."

She swiped at a tear on her cheek. Clive handed her a handkerchief. Goodness, this had been an awful day. "He sold...?" Clive Morgan patted her hand.

"To Humboldt. They've been interested, especially in the mill over on the Wolf, for a long time."

The man rose with a smile for Jack, who stepped inside the room. Penny rose, too, skin tingling and eyes burning. She stepped toward him.

"What were you thinking? You had no way of knowing I wasn't guilty of Alan's murder. King and Gibson was the only thing you had for sure." She held out her hands, palms up. "It's the one thing I promised you that you really wanted."

"You made me an unspoken promise last night, sweetheart, and it eclipsed years of want."

Penny drew in a stuttered breath, then opened her arms as Jack crossed the room and pulled her into his. He held her for a moment, then kissed her, and she clung to him, and they stayed that way until Clive cleared his throat and bid them goodnight.

Chapter Eighty-nine

It was a good night filled with anxiety, overshadowed by anticipation, and sweetened with fulfillment. Jack succumbed to her initial wish that they leave the light on, but later he made love to her in the dark, and she could hear the smile in his voice when afterwards, entwined in each other's arms, he whispered her name and told her how beautiful she was, even in the dark. He lingered in the house until late morning, then left to meet Clive at Humboldt's Handsboro Office. There was more paperwork involved with the hastily structured sale of King and Gibson. Penny asked if there was a way out of the deal since she was now cleared of murder. But Jack said no. His obsession with King and Gibson was over, and she and he would start with something new.

Penny stepped onto the bottom step of the broad entry stairway and lifted the hem of her dark blue evening dress, donned in anticipation of Jack's return. Dusk darkened their entry hall, but for a gas sconce burning dimly near the top landing, and she longed for his return. Alan's death may have been resolved, but Lorraine Noble's haunting had not. Penny looked up the carpeted stairs, hesitated a moment, then started to climb. Below, the front door rattled, then opened, and she breathed out and turned, anxious to see Jack's face, but doubtful given it was the front door.

"Penny."

She cringed at Mark Reed's voice and took two steps back down until she could see him in the front hall, not looking at her, but looking down the hall in the direction of the dining room.

421

"What do you want?" Where was Mars?

He jerked his face up when she spoke. Now he grasped the stair post. "Stuart and your mother just drove up out back, but I wanted to be the one to tell you. I did it. I'm not going to deny it. I was justified, and there's not a jury in this state that will condemn me for it."

Penny's heart, already strained by Mark's appearance, pounded against her breastbone. "What are you talking about?"

He placed a foot on the bottom step.

"Stay where you are! What have you done?"

"I killed them."

She swallowed. "Who?" she asked, then screamed at him when he stood there staring stupidly.

"My wife and your husband."

Head spinning, she took two quick steps down the stairs. "What?"

He straightened, as if anticipating a physical attack, but she stopped her advance. "They were together, in bed, having sex. I followed her." With both hands he ran his fingers through his hair, causing it to stand on end. He was no longer looking at her, but at the wall. "I shot them both."

"Where were they?"

"In bed."

"Where, damn you?" She reached him and slapped his head. "Where are they?"

He looked at her, blinked, then looked away. He was sweating profusely. "They're at that boarding house in Handsboro. The one Gibson stays at."

Nausea swelled Penny's gut. "I don't believe you. I don't believe Jack was with her." She shoved him out of her way and started to run down the hall toward the back of the house to find Mars, to find Roland, to find the carriage, the doctor. A whine escaped her lips, swelled into a sob, and ended in a snarl. Darkness filled the dining room entry, then her mother stepped into the hall with a face so bleak she might have slapped Penny, and Penny knew something terrible had indeed happened.

"Adel," the woman sobbed, then screamed when she saw Mark near the stairwell. She pointed at him, then turned to Stuart coming through the dining room door behind her. "There he is! Dear god in heaven, get him!"

Stuart pushed past Clarissa. Penny fell back against the wall and hugged herself, then her mother grabbed her and held her to her. "The bastard killed her. Killed my baby. Did he plan to kill you, too?"

Penny numbly watched Mark move backwards toward the front door. "She had it coming, Stuart," Mark railed. "You know better than I how much she deserved it."

Stuart held out his hand. "Yes, Mark, I know. Do you still have the gun?"

Mark nodded.

"Give it to me. You're not going to be able to claim justifiable homicide if you kill all..."

Penny thought he would have turned over the gun he took out of his coat pocket, but for Eva Markiston's appearance through the dining room door. Penny braced, but the woman ignored her, then halted when Mark stepped to one side of Stuart and fixed his gaze, along with the muzzle of the pistol, on her. He twisted his lips.

"You're the one who needs to die, you whore mother."

Clarissa turned her back, sweeping Penny around with her, but Penny didn't want to be swept away or protected. She wanted to find Jack, and with a violent twist freed herself from her mother's grasp at the same time Stuart rushed Mark and pushed his gun hand up. His body slammed the younger man into the petticoat table sitting against the hall wall. Mark dropped the gun, Clarissa cried out, and Eva Markiston's hand circled Penny's forearm before she made it through the dining room door. "Get her other arm," Eva spat at Clarissa, who protested as Penny cried to her mother to let her go. Eva repeated her hateful order to her daughter, and sobbing, Clarissa clamped her two hands on Penny's other side. Together she and Eva dragged Penny into the front room and forced her onto the settee.

Stuart had reined in the now sobbing Mark, whom he directed into a wing chair near the back corner of the room. "It'll be all right," he kept repeating to the younger man. "Everything will be all right."

"No, it won't," Clarissa screeched at Stuart, who stood and rolled his eyes, then cast Eva a furtive glance.

"Be quiet, Clarissa," Eva said. "He's simply trying to calm Mark. Sit down."

Penny rose, and Eva slugged her above the left ear with her reticule, a blow hard enough to send Penny to her knees in front of the settee.

Clarissa yelped in protest, then started to rise, but Eva shoved her back, too. "Hush. We don't have much time. You're very upset. I want you to go upstairs and lie down for a while."

"Oh, Mama, I can't rest." She swiped at sudden tears. "I think I'm losing my mind." Suddenly she grabbed for her mother's waist, and Eva pulled her to her feet. "Adel's dead," she whispered into her mother's shoulder.

"I know, sweetheart, and we're all devastated. No one more than I." Eva took Clarissa's face in her hands. "But we'll get through this together. Go rest now."

"Stuart, come with me."

"I need him," Eva said. "We won't be long."

Clarissa looked down at Penny. "Penny should come home."

"We'll see. Now go."

Eva waited until Clarissa left the room, then prodded Penny with the toe of her boot. "Are you all right, Penelope? Behave yourself and we won't have to resort to any more head bashing."

Penny touched her throbbing temple. "Get out of my house."

"Yes," Eva said, making a point of looking around the high-ceilinged room with its rich moldings. "I consider all this a lost asset." She turned back to Penny. "Not to mention the loss of my company. I am very, very angry, and since I have no real recourse short of the death of Jack Gibson and controlling you to recoup anything from this fiasco"—she opened her reticule and pulled out a syringe—"I'm going to take the gamble. Even if I fail to get

424

away with reasserting my authority over you, I will, at least, have vengeance."

Mark rose. "Put that away," he told Eva. She laughed at him.

Penny's world teetered slightly. But for her hatred for her grandmother, she had nothing to cling to, and she swallowed. Could she have been such a fool as to have believed Jack Gibson loved her? That he sacrificed King and Gibson...

But he had. She closed her eyes and sucked in a breath. He had. "What did you do to Mars?" Penny asked.

"The big colored?" her grandmother asked.

"I'm afraid," Mark said to Penny, "that I knocked him out. He was on the back porch when I drove up. He challenged me. But he knew me as your doctor. I told him I needed help with my carriage wheel, and when he bent over to look at the axle, I knocked him out with the carriage stop."

A stone they used when parking carriages near the carriage house. That meant Mars was probably on the other side of the cookhouse. Gracie was preparing supper. She wouldn't find him unless she had occasion to step out back.

"Stuart?" Eva snapped.

He took a seat in the wing chair in front of the fireplace. "I'm not participating. Not this time."

Mark took a step toward Eva, and she turned to Stuart. "Fine. All I ask is that you not allow him to interfere."

"You bitch," Mark said, and started to rush her. Stuart shouted at him, then Mark stopped cold, shock as plain on his face as if someone had punched him. Stuart fell back into his seat. Penny, who'd been focused on Mark and Stuart, blinked and from the corner of her eye saw Eva, who stood at her side, gyrate, in tandem with a cry. Penny raised her head, then covered her mouth to keep her heart from leaping out of it.

Across the room, Stuart Frederick moved as if to stand up, and Jack, still holding Eva's wrist with one hand, steadied the barrel of a large pistol with the other. "Get out of that chair, you son of a bitch, and I'll kill you." Jack's voice was cold and hard. He sounded as if he meant every word.

"He has Mark's gun," Penny said.

"And probably one of his own." Jack pulled back on the hammer. Stuart raised his hands. "I've only got Mark's."

"Let's see it, butt first."

Stuart showed it, butt first. Jack glanced at a dumbfounded Mark Reed and told him to back up and sit down. "Put the gun on the floor," Jack told Stuart, "and kick it toward Penny." Stuart did as he was told and stayed put.

Penny crawled to Mark's gun, then sat back hard on her butt and leaned against the settee. The room was spinning, but she nodded yes when Jack asked if she was okay. Reassured, he shoved his pistol into his waistband and glared at Eva Markiston, who jerked from his grasp and took a rocky step backwards. Penny had never in her life seen the woman cower, but she cowered now. A heartbeat later Jack was crushing Eva's wrist that still held the syringe. Eva grimaced in pain and dropped it to the thick oriental carpet. Jack twisted his free hand into Eva's elaborate coiffure and yanked back. The harridan cried out, more bark than scream. "Can you get up?" he said to Penny.

"Yes." Her voice shook and nausea threatened, but she leaned forward, set her hands against the plush carpet, and pushed herself up. "Mark said he..." Her lips started to tremble.

"He killed Adel," Jack said softly.

Penny's heart plummeted at the realization he had actually been with—

"I know I got you, too," Mark ground out, hate as real as the disbelief in his voice.

Jack focused on him. "The man you killed with Adel was Jonathan Noble."

Shame muted Penny's relief, but she set her guilt aside and allowed relief to fill her. "You were there?"

"I got there shortly after the shooting. Kate sent word to me that Jon was over there. He rented a room from her two days ago under a false name, but he'd been there last month looking for me. I told her who he was when she asked. She learned this afternoon that authorities were looking for him for your attempted murder. I don't even think Jon realized he'd been found out, isolated as he was over there." Jack scanned the room. "Is your mother here?"

Shaking, Penny forced her way to her feet. "She's lying down upstairs."

"Is she the reason you opened the door, dammit, Penny?"

"They came in the back. Mark was..." Penny yelped and rushed her grandmother, who had pulled a small pistol from the pocket of her coat, but Jack was quicker, pushing the woman's arm toward the ceiling, then slamming her into the bookshelves lining the wall of the room. The derringer fell from Eva's hand. Immediately, Penny, Mark's .38 in hand, swung toward Stuart, who remained in his seat, and Penny wondered if he'd lied about carrying a weapon. He was too calm. To his right, on the other side of the room, Mark sat, his white-knuckled hands grasping the arms of the chair.

Pistol at the ready, Penny backed onto the settee and sat, casting furtive glances at the two seated men, then looked at Jack, who yanked back on Eva's hair. Eva, almost as tall as he, arched back with a short cry. He twisted his hand. Her head turned, and she hissed. He pulled harder and the silver locks came undone, as a wide-eyed Clarissa Frederick rushed into the room.

"Watch her," Jack said to Penny, and Penny rose on shaky legs and placed herself between Jack and her grandmother and Clarissa. But Clarissa turned to Stuart and spoke his name like a question. He shrugged in answer.

"You ever approach her again," Jack ground out to Eva, "and I'll break your scrawny neck with my bare hands." He yanked back hard on the hair once more. Eva, her fingers curled, reached for his face, but he twisted away and again shoved her into the shelves. Free from his grasp, and support, she nearly fell.

"Jack, what in god's name are you doing?" Clarissa cried.

"What someone should have done years ago, before she managed to do away with your husbands and prostitute your daughters." Jack yanked Eva away from the shelves and spun her onto the settee. She glared up at him, then smoothed her hair with shaking hands. She was nearing seventy, but arrogance kept her strong. And she was mean. Penny doubted the woman had ever been manhandled in her life.

Jack stepped to one side and retrieved the derringer. His back to the bookshelves, he turned on Clarissa. "She never had to use physical force on you, did she, Clarissa? Just plied you with gin and told you who to fuck."

Clarissa's gaze passed to her mother, then back to Jack, who found the discarded syringe on the carpet. He crushed it beneath his shoe, then squatted and picked up the remains. He held it in front of her. "You knew about Adel's father, didn't you?"

"He beat me."

"I doubt that mattered when your loving mother wed you to him. Married you off to a rich carpetbagger, then killed him when he 'beat' her little girl." Jack threw the hypodermic against Clarissa's breast. "But an overdose of morphine wouldn't work with Hugh King. He dealt with his pain differently. Plus, there was James Gibson. He was less tolerant of your mother's interference than your husband, wasn't he?"

Clarissa blinked, then turned on her mother who was rapidly recomposing herself. The older woman smiled knowingly at her daughter, and Clarissa drew in a breath through her nostrils.

"My beautiful Adel," Clarissa whispered, then turned on Mark. "Why did you do such a thing?"

"Eva told me to follow her. She said she was having an affair with Gibson."

"That was day before yesterday, you fool."

Clarissa's nostrils flared, and she took a step toward the settee and Eva. "You wanted him to kill Adel?"

"I wanted him to kill Jack, you drunken idiot. I sent her over here to him."

"What...you," Clarissa got out, then blinked as if someone had suddenly lit a dark room.

"*You* told Hugh."

Eva Markiston's eyes flashed. "Shut up, Clarissa."

"You said it was Jim who told Hugh about me and Stuart, but it was you who told. All the time it was you. You planned it all." Clarissa splayed her hand over her chest. "And I...oh, god, what did I do!"

Penny's heart was pounding in her throbbing head. "Mama?"

Clarissa didn't look at her, but continued to stare at Eva, and truth slammed into Penny with the force of a falling pine.

"You killed Daddy," Penny said to her mother.

Clarissa turned to her. "He was leaving me and taking you."

"He would have never done that."

"Yes, he would. He found out what I did." Clarissa spun on her mother. "You told me Jim was the one who told him, that Jim wanted to separate us, but it was you who told, not Jim. *You.*"

Eva shrugged.

"You wanted me to kill him."

"An unpleasant surprise. I'd actually planned for Stuart to do it. I thought Hugh would at least have the gumption to fight for you. I was wrong."

Penny turned and looked at Stuart, still quiet in the chair. Heart clamoring, she turned back to her mother.

"You were unfaithful to Daddy?"

Clarissa turned away. "He'd grown inattentive." She covered her face with her hands. "He accused me of being a drunkard." She dropped her hands and turned to Stuart. "Stuart was very attentive. At first."

"You couldn't find a way to give up strong drink, daughter." Eva Markiston raised her chin with a sneer. "Any man prefers a lively woman as opposed to one who falls into a drunken stupor every night."

Clarissa's face twisted into a snarl. "You brought Stuart to me." She took a threatening step Eva's direction. "You encouraged my drinking."

The woman laughed. "Don't you dare blame your weaknesses on me. I manipulated you because you liked it. You enjoyed being passed from one man's bed to another." Eva's voice softened. "I myself have known the pleasure of many men. Why saddle your-self with one? They certainly don't set limitations on themselves. You didn't do anything wrong, Clarissa."

Clarissa stared at the woman. "Adel."

Eva sobered. "Yes, my poor beautiful Adel. Well, she died doing what she loved best, and she lived without one regret." Eva turned her eye on Jack. "Not one."

Jack looked across the room to Mark Reed, who leaned for-ward to hear, hate so patent in his glare the air smelled of it. Jack nodded at him. "Tell it to someone who cares, Eva."

Down the hall, the back door opened. "That should be the police," Jack said, then looked at Penny. "I sent Roland for Toby when I found Mars out back."

Chapter Ninety

"What were they doing out of jail?" Jack asked Toby.

"Farrah had them out an hour after Jenkins locked 'em up. Clarissa Frederick left a note. Women tend to do that, more so than men. Women don't normally shoot themselves in the head, though. That's what made me suspicious maybe Stuart killed them both, but after I talked to him, I don't think so."

Jack handed Toby Craig a shot of whiskey and sat in the wing chair opposite him in front of the fire. The third morning of November had started out chilly, and the temperature had plummeted when he opened the door to the Biloxi police chief and met the man's eye.

"Mark is still in jail?"

"Yep, but he'll get off. Justifiable homicide."

Jack blew out a breath. "What got you involved?"

"Jenkins. He asked me to look at the scene and tell him what I thought, but I think it was Charlie he wanted. I volunteered to come tell you and Penny. That's what he wanted out of me."

"I'd like to tell Penny."

"That's fine with me."

Damn, the funerals. Her mother's, her grandmother's, and Adel's. Adel's would be hardest. It would be hard on him, too, though a lot easier than if he were burying Penny. Funny how quickly things had changed. What he felt with Adel's loss was sorrow, not grief. Maybe he'd never loved her, though he found that hard to believe. Maybe that eighteen-year-old boy hadn't known what love was, or maybe there were different degrees of love. The one thing he knew for certain was that he'd found a woman he loved much, much more.

There was one other thing Jack wanted, and he braced before turning to Toby. "What did her note say?"

Tobias Craig rubbed the back of his neck and smiled. "She admitted she killed Hugh King, and then let her mother frame your daddy. Is that what you wanted to know?"

"Yes. Jenkins let you see that?"

"Stuart had the letter, his insurance against an accusation of double murder. He was the first on the scene. Heard the shot from his office downstairs. The women were in Eva's room. She was in bed, dead. Clarissa was in a chair next to her with one side of her head blown away. The gun was on the floor by the chair." Toby rubbed his hand over his face. "Hugh King's forty-four, son."

Good lord, but that must have made a mess.

"As regards Eva, I think the coroner will verify a morphine overdose."

"Is Jenkins even aware of the letter?"

"I showed it to him after I showed it to Dr. Fritz. It's in evidence now, but you don't need to worry. Clarissa didn't implicate the good sheriff in the framing of Jimmy. Tell the truth, I think he's more guilty of being manipulated than of collusion. At least in that particular case."

"I'd like my daddy's name cleared."

"Me, too. We'll work on it. Ain't never easy for a state to admit it executed an innocent man, but it'll have little choice here."

"You come to any conclusions on Harold Noble's death?"

"Officially, David Pascal did it, but I agree with you, Jon Noble did it." Toby blew out a breath. "Damn, Jack, there's more dead bodies resulting from this mess than what came out of a bunch of blue bellies stumbling into a Confederate ambush."

Jack found Penny in the front room, ashen-faced, and for a moment he feared she'd overheard him and Toby.

"Do you think," she said, "that Alan and I could have had the same hallucination?"

No, he didn't. That statement and one look at the cracked

mirror told him he was mistaken about her overhearing them. But the nightmare that even he now believed lurked within these walls had again shaken her as much as the horror tale he was about to relay to her.

She listened to him, never moving, never speaking, simply watching him as he told her that her mother and grandmother were dead. She'd shook her head gently, and he wasn't sure if she were expressing disbelief or resignation. Either way, she knew he spoke the truth.

"Stuart found the bodies after hearing the gunshot. They were in your grandmother's bedroom. Eva died of an overdose of morphine. She was in bed. Charlotte said she took a sleeping powder before she went to bed last night."

"They think Mama gave her the overdose?"

"She said she did in her note.

"And Mama?"

Jack swallowed. "She shot herself in the head. I know it's hard to imagine —"

"She shot Daddy." Penny turned her wide blue eyes on him and blinked back tears. "I'm trying to remember the last words I said to her. Do you remember?"

"I don't recall you saying anything at all, honey. Not after she admitted what she'd done."

"She killed both our fathers, directly or indirectly, and she never once told either one of us she was sorry."

Nor asked forgiveness. Clarissa's entire focus was on her mother. She'd wanted Eva to tell her she was sorry, Jack thought now. Obviously, Eva hadn't, and that would have been because she wasn't.

"Your grandmother created a monster, sweetheart, and it destroyed her."

"Where's Adel?" Penny said, then mercifully started to cry.

He pulled her into his arms, and she fell against him. "I think she's back on Texas Street." He laid his head on hers and faced the mirror. She faced away. There was another crack, moving away at an angle from the first.

"I don't want to stay in this awful place, Jack."

"We're not going to," he said, watching a third crack creep through the axis of the first two. "We're getting out of here right now."

Epilogue

"Your Aunt Millie told me the Leaf flooded the house sometime after the War, and Uncle Jimmy had Daddy bring my grandmother to Meridian until the house could be repaired."

"*Our* Aunt Millie, and the house never was repaired," Jack said. "That's why we don't see it now."

"Grandma died."

"Yeah, but that was years later. She didn't need to be out here by herself, and your daddy bought her a house in Meridian. Aunt Millie said she didn't want to be on the Coast. I'm not sure why."

Penny snorted. "She probably didn't want to live with Daddy's new family. Aunt Millie told me she looked after her."

"Some. She lived close by. Aunt Millie thought a lot of her. I think your grandmother provided her comfort during those years. Aunt Millie returned to Marion County after she died. There was nothing keeping her in Meridian then." Jack held out his hand and pulled Penny a short distance up the little knoll he was climbing. "She says you favor her."

"She's never said that to me."

"She wouldn't. She says telling people they look like someone doesn't endear you to them if they have their hearts set on looking like somebody else."

"And who do you want to look like?"

"Just me."

"I'm glad you look like you."

He caught her eye. "I'm glad you look like you, too, Copper

435

Lee." He turned away and pointed to a dark green bush a few steps away. It had buds. "Camellia," he said. "My guess is we are close to the old home site."

Penny pulled her wool coat tighter and turned to look down the soggy knoll, between the trunks of hundred-year-old oak and gum, their remaining leaves rich with fall color. Interspersed were the golds and reds of other invasive trees and the always vibrant green of smaller, yet faster-growing pine. Fifteen miles to the east, ancient longleaf still dominated the landscape, but here, along the river, the massive forest had been harvested since before her great-grandfather came from Carolina. Beyond, less than a quarter mile away, sunlight glinted off the presently placid Leaf, which only two weeks ago had swollen out of its banks during heavy fall rains.

"I'd like it built on stilts. If the river flooded this high all those years ago, I wouldn't want to risk it."

"It hasn't since, far as I know."

"As far as you know?" She turned to look at him. "And are stilts a problem, Mr. Gibson? I would think they'd be your forte, of sorts, considering you're a timberman."

"And cheap if the deal ever goes through, but are we sure we'd want a house here?" He nodded to the distant river. "A railroad trestle will mar the view, not to mention the peace and quiet."

She gave him a questioning look and he grimaced. "Look, I say we hold on to this place. If that railroad is ever approved, which is highly speculative, they'll come to us."

"You want to stay at Noble Corporation?"

He laughed. "Noble Corporation is something I'd like to put behind us."

"The shortfall, you mean?"

"Yes. Tom Gates says there are two ships due in this month. The problem is the audit, but he's confident the board doesn't want the authorities involved. He thinks they'll be willing to let us apply those profits to what Alan stole. He says it won't be enough, though. We're gonna have to sell off some stock. Truth is, I think they're gonna want us to break up Alan's forty percent. There are prospective buyers sitting that board. But if we could hold on to maybe ten percent, that would make a nice little income for Piney Woods folk."

"Piney Woods folk?"

He shrugged.

"And the Adcock section?"

"That's something else we need to hold on to. It might take a few years, but that patch of longleaf will pay for itself and then some. It makes no sense to sell it now. Alan paid too much for it, and we won't get the money back."

A chilly wind blew. She turned into his arms, and he held her tight, braced against the momentary onslaught. Not only had fall finally arrived, so had its temperatures, at least on some days.

"You want to go back to Marion County, don't you?"

He looked down at her cuddled against him. "I really do. Nice place my granddaddy built. The cabin's foundation is still solid and the roofline is as straight as the day he built it. It's small, but can be added to. It's still surrounded by longleaf and we'll keep it that way. It hasn't changed much since last you saw it."

She smiled. "So, you want to return to our timber roots?"

He squeezed her tighter. "In a manner of speaking. Granddaddy raised cows and there's always turpentine. But I've been thinking I'd like to work in conservation." His arm still around her shoulder, he jostled her so that she looked up at him.

"Experimentation and rejuvenation. Something has to be done with the cutover land. Daddy said the Piney Woods would never make more than hardscrabble farms. Said God made it timber country and He meant pine to be its cash crop."

"Folks could sure get hungry between harvests."

Jack smiled. "Even with the faster-growing variety." Penny moved around to his side when they started back down the hill.

"There's a lot of study that needs to be done to offset this coming butchery. Life must go on after longleaf."

"And if you do get involved with rejuvenation, will that make you a scientist?"

"I like the term forester."

"Um...positive progress. I think Daddy would have liked that, too. That must explain why fate intervened, and I married a timberman."

He snorted. "None of that had anything to do with why you married me."

"I beg to differ. Timber was the catalyst for our marriage, and it had everything to do with why you married me."

"A beautiful, desperate young girl who needed me was why I married you."

"I bribed you."

"You *begged* me, you said so yourself. And compassionate fella that I am, I agreed." He tapped a finger against the tip of her nose. "Yep, that's what I'm gonna tell our children." He laughed out loud. "My boys are gonna love that!"

Historical Note

Mississippi's timber industry is one to which I am indirectly, yet indelibly linked. Logging Piney Woods' longleaf fed my great-grandfather and his family after they left Murray County, Georgia, in the wake of the War Between the States. Those immediate ancestors were among the logging and mill laborers who worked for a wage and, when Mississippi's longleaf was exhausted, returned to the cutover land and the agrarian economy that had long sustained them and their ancestors. This broke their link, and mine, to Mississippi's timber industry.

The timber industry, of course, continues to this day as do small "hobby" farms; however, the small farming operations like my granddaddy's certainly are not self-sustaining today. But I still have that 120-acre farm on the northern reaches of Simpson County where the last of Mississippi's massive old-growth (and overripe) longleaf was harvested. If left on its own, the land returns to pine (though not longleaf) within a ten-year period. But 120 acres won't support a timber livelihood anymore than it would an independent farm. So my husband and I grow old, enjoy the novelty, and wonder what the kids will do with this old family farm when we're gone.

This lengthy, but I hope entertaining, history brings the reader up to the time of my story. Longleaf's era continued more than four decades after 1890, roughly the year *Requited Harvest* ended. That year is noteworthy for the ratification of Mississippi's current constitution. Its 1869 predecessor, the masterpiece created by Mississippians' Northern betters and Southern sycophants to make Mississippians better Americans was not a popular one. With the end of Reconstruction, most Southern states immediately replaced the despised ruling documents foisted upon them by the hated Republican regimes that framed them. Constitutional conventions, however, are expensive, so Mississippi chose to amend hers and live with it through Redemption, a murky period between Reconstruction and Democrat hegemony. For better or worse, 1890 ushered in a new era for Mississippi.

A hundred and fifty years ago, at the close of the War Between the States, a massive virgin forest of longleaf (yellow) pine stretched, as it had for centuries, from southeastern Virginia to east Texas. Mississippi's Piney Woods stretches from the Alabama line to the Bluff Hills west of the Pearl and Homochitto Rivers and roughly 150 miles north of the Gulf of Mexico into southern Rankin County. Beginning with the Escatawpa and Pascagoula Rivers in the east to the Pearl and Bogue Chitto in the west, it is crisscrossed by creeks, bayous, and rivers that proved of incalculable importance to logging during the colonial and antebellum periods.

At the beginning of the 18th century, authorities in French Louisiana encouraged the timber industry, not only to make their southern colonies self-sufficient, but also to support the more lucrative West Indies sugar enterprise. France's British and later Spanish successors exploited the ancient forest for domestic building material and shipbuilding and were keenly aware of the region's value for production of naval stores (tar, pitch, turpentine). Throughout the colonial period, sawmills popped up along river banks, bayous, and river mouths emptying into the Gulf.

During Mississippi's territorial days, refugees from the poorer regions of Georgia and the Carolinas moved into the Piney Woods. It's important to note that these settlers were not marginalized rejects. Immigrants to the Piney Woods were fiercely independent individuals who sought refuge from a habitat becoming overpopulated with people, government, and ancillary laws demanded by progress. These folks were pastoral by nature, surviving off herding and hunting. Farming was primarily for subsistence. For the most part these folks had the Pine Barrens to themselves. Even cleared, the land was not valuable for farming, and drew little interest from the dominant agrarian class.

—∗∗—

The earliest sawmills were of the pit variety, one man on a trestle above, a second in a pit below, respectively pushing and pulling on a six- to seven-foot saw. Little changed before 1800. There are records of water-powered mills operating on the Coast and in the interior, usually in conjunction with grist and rice mills and cotton gins.

Mississippi's first steam mill is believed to have been built in Pascagoula in 1835. By 1840, ten steam mills were in operation in the part of Hancock County (Handsboro) that became Harrison County in 1843. At that time, Jackson County boasted only two steam mills while Lawrence County in the backwoods laid claim to ten. With advances in the circular saw after 1850 and construction between 1852 and 1857 of the Mobile and Ohio Railroad in the eastern pine belt and the New Orleans, Jackson, and Great Northern Railroad in the west, the number of mills in the Pascagoula district increased sharply. Where a few years before only water mills had operated in the pine belt's interior, now steam mills popped up along the railroads. Though still in its infancy as of 1860, Mississippi lumber was marketed in St. Louis, along the eastern seaboard, in Cuba and Mexico, and in Europe.

Slaves made up the bulk of the manpower in the mills. Loggers tended to be white. I have a theory on why this was the case. Though not unprecedented, there were not many slaves in the Piney Woods. The economy simply didn't support them. In the earliest days, loggers and lumbermen were not necessarily one and the same. Loggers, who may or may not have lived in the Piney Woods, were independent. Wherever they came from, they penetrated the forests via navigable waterways, cut the timber conveniently located along the streams, and "herded" the logs downstream to the nearest mill or the one fetching the best price. Timbermen often sold their logs to other loggers at the stream rather than ferry their logs themselves.

At the mills, the lumbermen bought the logs from the loggers and sawed the raw timber into lumber for resale. The lumbermen used slave labor in the mill because it was cheaper. Some owned slaves, some leased them. Often the laborer or his owner were paid in goods (lumber) rather than wages.

Independent logging continued until well after the War, but by the late 1880s/early 1890s (the time of my story) the big companies were buying or leasing the timberland and employing their own loggers. Independent logging continued, but as the timber contiguous to the streams was cut, and the railroads penetrated farther and farther into the hinterland, it became physically and financially impossible for the independent logger to operate. The bigger companies had the capital to build tram lines and buy locomotives and cars for hauling the timber to the major rail lines and streams. Though independent loggers were still around as of the late '80s, most would have found work with one of the larger firms. Though not an independent "logger," Eva Markiston had failed to take the steps necessary to ensure she could get her timber to her mills. She recklessly left herself vulnerable to a large company that was more than happy to help shut her down.

It's hard to estimate the damage done to Mississippi's timber industry by the War Between the States. Some mills were confiscated or converted in support of the Confederacy, but many survived unscathed. There is evidence that mills at the mouth of the Pearl continued to operate for the duration of the War. Nevertheless, given the Northern blockade of Southern ports, trade was limited. One exception was trade with federally-occupied New Orleans, which was not interfered with. *That* would be the "evidence of continued operation" referenced above and is, furthermore, an indicator that some Yankees (and Scalawag wannabes) were profiting from the trade. Again, that's a history for another book.

Continued operations and survivors notwithstanding, the War had a detrimental effect on Mississippi's burgeoning timber industry, but after the War, the timber industry was one of the first to revive, and it did so almost immediately. This was due in part to the demands of Mexico under the French puppet Maximilian. At the time, lumber in the New Orleans market brought $24-$30 per thousand board feet. That ended in 1867 when the Republic of Mexico executed Maximilian.

Except for New Orleans, Mississippi's promising markets of 1860 found other sources for its lumber between 1861-1865. Though there were limited markets in the Caribbean during the early post-War years, recapturing old markets and finding new ones were imperative.

The antebellum lumber industry on the interior, which had just gained a firm foothold when the conflict began, was all but destroyed by the War, along with the plantation economy that had supported it. The Yankees didn't burn the forests down but they did destroy the mills and the turpentine stills.

In the immediate aftermath of the conflict, lumber shipments north of the Ohio were negligible. The old Northwest's white pine industry was at its peak, and as of 1875, yellow pine was virtually unknown in the great Northern markets.

In the late 1860s, steam-powered circular saw mills began appearing within dummy-line distance of the Illinois Central and Mobile and Ohio railroads, but the markets lay in New Orleans to the south or just north in small Mississippi and Tennessee towns. Though towns like Brookhaven and mills in Copiah and Pike Counties showed promise, lumbering in the interior in 1870 still lagged behind what it had been in 1860. Mississippi needed updated manufacturing facilities, skilled labor, markets, shipping, and capital.

The saving grace came in the mid-1870s from Lafayette Car Shops, Indianapolis Car Foundry Company, Ohio Falls Car Company, and the Missouri Car Foundry Company and their demand for sills (the bottom horizontal layer of a frame). If you're guessing carriages, you're guessing wrong. These folks built railroad cars, and for its strength, availability, and cost, Southern yellow pine fit the need.

By the late '70s, longleaf was competing with white pine on a small scale, but being air-dried, it was heavy, and lumbermen couldn't afford its shipping costs. To alleviate this problem, Southern lumbermen invested in kilns. Kiln-drying produced superior grade lumber and cut its weight from 40,000 pounds to 23,000 pounds per car. This gave Mississippi lumber access to markets north of the Ohio. Still, it would take years to overcome Northern prejudices. Although carpenters found it difficult to handle compared to white pine, the bad name given it by white pine merchants for not taking paint and being quick to decay were bogus, yet embedded in the Northern psyche. Still, it was cheap, selling in some grades in the Midwestern market for $13 per thousand board feet less than white pine. By 1885, yellow pine was the largest single class of freight on the Illinois Central Railroad.

Most importantly, Yankee ingenuity for destruction had exhausted the North's white pine forests.

Double saws, gang saws, and planing saws; improved carriage feeds; and mechanized movement of logs from the mill pond to the saw and from the saw to storage ramps, all being used in the Great Lakes mills in the '70s, did not reach Mississippi until the early '80s. By that time, merchants and exporters had taken the hint and were investing in Mississippi's mills, resulting in expansion to large-scale operations. The W. Denny Company, at the mouth of the Escatawpa River, produced 15,000,000 board feet of lumber in 1870. By the late '80s, employing the latest in sawmill technology, that increased to 55,000,000 board feet annually.

What was happening in the Pascagoula district was equally true of the Pearl River district. By the early '80s, folks who'd made a livelihood from agricultural and pastoral pursuits along the Pearl, Biloxi, Pascagoula, and Escatawpa Rivers and their tributaries had turned to timber for a living. The Pearl River district, which made a phenomenal comeback after the War (in part, because it appears to have never ceased operations), grew between 1880-1890, but not as greatly as did Pascagoula. Timberlands accessible to water were more limited along the Pearl, and the area was meeting stiff competition from interior mills that sprang up along the newly constructed New Orleans and Northeastern Railroad, which cut the Pearl River district in two.

Lumberton, represented in my story as the home of Jack's Aunt Millie, was originally an Indian village. In 1886, the Hinton brothers, John, Robert, and H.P. and their cousin Herbert Camp erected a mill there, and the town grew into a major lumber manufacturing and distribution center, swallowing up the better-established community of Piotona just to its north.

Relative to Pascagoula and the Pearl River district during the '70s and '80s, lumber industry expansion along Bayou Bernard (Handsboro, the location of King and Gibson's primary mill) and the Bay of St. Louis (the site of King and Gibson's Wolf River mill) was insignificant. Here, mill owners continued operations as they had before the War, but were hampered by lack of capital and unable to transition to the large-scale operations necessary for success in the forthcoming lumber boom. The other drawback for those on Bayou Bernard was the depletion of prime timber near the rafting streams.

By the late '80s the Northern timber industry was looking for new trees to cut. The South had the trees, the labor, and a handful of updated mills. The North offered expanded markets and capital to bring the whole operation up to snuff. But the expansion of Southern lumbering during the 1880s was the result of those above-mentioned markets north of the Ohio and in the Midwest, not capital investment on the part of Northern lumbermen. When the trade journals began hawking the potential of Southern timber and its worldwide demand, it wasn't the North's forest industry that initially listened, but Northern and European (particularly British) land speculators hoping for an increase in timber prices. To them it didn't matter if a Northerner's life was forfeit in the South or if the labor and livestock were inferior (as per the prevailing Republican Party propaganda of the day). White pine was about exhausted and yellow pine was cheap and plentiful. Instinct told those savvy investors that the value of Southern timberland was about to go up.

⁂

Much has been said of the depredations to the Southern pine lands in the wake of the War Between the States. Here I intend to speak only of the demise of Mississippi's longleaf. There's much that's clear and much that's not, and I have, admittedly, struggled with how much to include here to orient the reader within the bounds of my tale. Truth is, the redistribution of Mississippi's Pine Barrens (indeed, of the South's Pine Barrens) in the wake of the War Between the States is a subject worthy of a Ph.D. dissertation, as is the aforementioned murky period of Redemption in Mississippi. I'm toying with the role the Redeemers' decision *not* to rewrite Mississippi's constitution in 1877 might have played in the sell-out of Mississippi's pine lands, if any. Repeatedly, names such as W. H. Griggs and James Hill appear in the historical record of transactions and investigations of the fraudulent transfers of huge chunks of Mississippi's Piney Woods to single buyers and corporations, which occurred well after the revolution that drove Governor Adelbert Ames and the Radicals out of Mississippi. But Griggs and Hill were not Redeemers. Griggs was a Union army officer who set up camp in Mississippi immediately after the War. He'd served as a federal postal officer in Jackson in 1852 and was relieved for embezzlement. Hill was a native Negro who served as Mississippi's Secretary of State during the Ames administration and amassed a modest fortune in "land" sales. Men of their ilk wrote the book on "How to Create a Government to Serve the Self-Aggrandizing Few." They were both Radicals. Griggs played a major role in the framing of the 1869 constitution which remained in effect during Redemption. Perhaps that Constitution left too much of the Republican agenda in place and allowed its sycophants to retain positions of influence, if not political power. Political influence can be purchased.

My primary source for this portion of my note is Nollie Hickman's *Mississippi Harvest* (1962). He devotes two chapters of his history to governmental policies regarding the pine belt in Mississippi and more generally the South. It is an excellent overview and an enjoyable read, but Mr. Hickman doesn't begin to scratch the surface of what happened during Reconstruction

446

and its legacy during early Redemption. For the purposes of my novel, there is really only one plot point hinting at the political depredations of that period: the Louisa Adcock property Alan Noble is duped by his family into buying. To delve into the gory details of perverting homestead and other land laws for the transfer of hundreds of thousands of Southern acres into the hands of a few Northern and foreign speculators is best left for the historical note of another novel, or several notes and novels. What follows is an overview of both federal and state land policies. I hope to leave the reader with a general idea of where Mississippi and later Northern timbermen figured in the policies; and finally to touch upon the speculators whose success was made possible by corrupt officials operating within a still more corrupt system.

At the end of The War Between the States, there were two groups who realized the value of the Pine Barrens: the people who emigrated to it as a moth to a flame over a half century earlier and those making up the timber industry, some of whom could claim the same longevity and ancestry. For the first group it was home. Like the indigenous peoples who preceded them, they adapted themselves to the forest and the forest's resources to themselves.

The second group evolved into an infant industrial enterprise in the decade before the War. Though severely impacted by the conflict, this industry was quick to revive. It was less merciful to the forest. Indeed, much of the merchantable timber along the navigable streams was removed in the decades leading up to the War.

When Congress granted Mississippi statehood in 1817, the majority of land in Mississippi belonged to the federal government. This was typical for all new states. Uncle Sam culled what he needed from the vast public domain and put the rest up for sale, offered it for homesteading, or entered it into private ownership through programs such as the Soldiers and Sailors Act as rewards for military service. Some federal lands were passed to the states as sixteenth-section lands, whereby the 16th section of each township was granted for public schools. That act went back to 1785 and under it the federal government transferred 308,000 acres of Mississippi pine land to the state. Another 156,000 acres were donated to Mississippi's four universities and roughly 1,400,000 acres of forested land came to the state indirectly via federal grants to railroads.

Despite the fact that between 1817 and 1850 the price of federal lands ranged from $0.25 to $2 an acre, Uncle Sam still laid claim to 13,000,000 acres of Mississippi, most in the Pine Barrens. The other area of interest during Reconstruction and early Redemption was the Yazoo-Mississippi Delta. The reason Uncle Sam couldn't "give this land away" was because it was unusable. The Pine Barrens' soil was...well, barren, and the Delta was swamp.

In 1850, the federal government enacted the National Swamplands Act to transfer large chunks of land to the states. Of course, there were standards for what actually constituted swamplands. Uncle Sam's goal in dumping land on the states was to improve the land. Read that to mean, under the best case scenario, the state was to improve it to make it fit for farming or, with the federal government's blessing, make it navigable. A navigable stream, of course, is not fit for farming, but it might be considered a boon for trading farm products, right? Or better yet, for moving timber downstream.

Under the Swamplands Act, "sections" were donated as exactly that—entire sections. So when a state chose its swampy area, it got everything in the "section" to which the swamp was part. The trick was to find swamps in sections with a lot of otherwise high, dry land. The states (not just Mississippi here, but every state) ultimately ended up with some of the best if not *the* best land. *And why, pray tell, shouldn't they?* Much of Mississippi's fertile agricultural land passed into private ownership this way, as well as thousands of acres of virgin timberlands in Copiah, Hancock, Marion, Lawrence, and Simpson Counties.

In 1852, the boards of police (today, these are our boards of

supervisors) for these five counties each appointed two commissioners to a board titled the "Commissioners of the Southern
District of Pearl River." This group handled sale and reclamation
of these "swamplands" at a minimum sale price of $0.25 to $0.50
per acre. Over the years, the number of acres which could be
purchased by one individual varied from between 160 acres to
240 acres. In my story, this is how Jack Gibson's grandfather
acquired his farm in Marion County in 1853.

In Harrison County, the so-called swampland granted to the
state had squatters on it. These folks were offered the land at
$0.05 an acre and in return for $32 they could buy a section of
virgin timber. They had to wait another sixty days before purchasing another section; however, as became standard operating
procedure, buyers could purchase the land under another's name.
That individual, for a price, would then draw a quitclaim deed
and transfer the land to the true buyer. Between 1858 and 1860,
timbermen bought up vast tracts along the Wolf and Biloxi Rivers
as well as Black and Red Creeks, and most of the state-owned
swamplands in Harrison County were in private possession by
1865. It doesn't take a whole lot of smarts to figure out that the
timber- and lumbermen were in cahoots with the Commissioners
of the Southern District of Pearl River. I would go so far as to
suggest timber concerns drove identification of which "swamplands" the state identified for its annual grant. One might also
conclude that the federal land agents were aware of the tactic.

Since territorial days, the lumber industry in Mississippi fed
off the public domain, both state and federal. Yes, some land was
privately held, but the majority wasn't. Clear title really wasn't
necessary if neither the US nor the state governments didn't
make an issue of the theft, i.e., if the thieves were prudent enough
to remain off military reserves. But as the timber industry grew
in the 1850s, so did the depredations, and both state and federal
authorities wanted the thieving stopped. They wanted people to
buy the land, not steal the resources off it. Of course, the loggers
and lumbermen didn't want to buy it. Once the trees were off the

land, it was worthless...to everyone. This is important, folks. Without its trees, the bulk of land in the Pine Barrens was worthless to *everyone*. That land, as Jack told Penny in my story, was meant to grow pine trees.

In 1854, with the timber industry growing and depredations increasing along logging streams, special federal agents were (not for the first time) hired to end theft. Ship captains caught moving "federal" logs on navigable streams lost not only their logs but also their boats and equipment. They were fined, then sent to jail. Paying for the stolen timber was not enough. The culprit had to buy the land from whence the logs were cut. Guess that was one way to force a sale.

But how did the federal agents figure out where the logs came from? This was only one problem with the effort. The inhabitants of the Piney Woods weren't of much help to the authorities in identifying violators. They sided with the loggers. In a lot of cases, they probably *were* the loggers. That particular program was scrapped in 1855.

It was also during the '50s that a handful of lumbermen obtained 160-acre tracts of virgin forest under the Soldiers and Sailors Act.

Given the War, I'm not sure how much federal land transferred to private ownership with the Federal Homestead Act of 1862. The 160-acre tract granted under that act, however, was cut in half with the Southern Homestead Act of 1866 and was applicable to the South alone (the "states of the rebellion"). In 1866, the federal government owned 47,700,000 acres of land in the Deep South. In Mississippi most of that was in the Pine Barrens. In an effort to curtail land speculation and encourage homesteads for former slaves, parcels of land were now sold in 80-acre increments. Ex-Confederates were restricted from purchasing the land. Timber speculators bypassed the law, settling individuals on one 80-acre plot after another and amassed large acreages for exploitation. The freedman didn't want it. He could not make squat out of 80 acres of timber and couldn't farm the land after the timber was gone. As early as 1871, then-*Senator*

James Alcorn warned that the Homestead Act of 1866 was ineffective and that the timber along the streams in federally-owned Pine Barrens was decimated. He'd warned of this as governor, he told the Senate, and the federals had taken no action. He stated further that the land beyond the navigable streams wasn't worth a cent.

In 1876, Southern politicians regained home rule. Eager for development, they led the fight to repeal the 1866 Southern Homestead Act. At this point the federals decided to take action against the depredations of the Southern timber industry.

Note two things in the story I'm about to convey. First is Carl Schurz, Rutherford Hayes' Secretary of the Interior. Second is the date when this reaction to depredations of federal timberland took place: 1877.

Carl Schurz was one of those Prussian reformers driven out of Prussia in 1848. Having failed at reforming his country, he crossed the Atlantic and joined in the effort to reform ours. I'm particularly prejudiced against this crowd because in my humble opinion they didn't know what the American republic was all about, but proceeded to play an important part in altering it into what it wasn't. He joined the antislavery movement, but my superficial understanding of the man is that he did so to prevent Negro "contamination" of the nation. The Negro should be free — that fed into the "ideal" — but he needed to be free somewhere else. Schurz was a reformer. That was his thing. If there was nothing in need of reform, he'd find something. Okay, you get my gist, whether I'm right or wrong in my opinion of the man, the point is there were plenty of other Southerners at the time who had similar opinions toward those of his ilk. He had ideas about conservation — and I'm not opposed to his concerns about preservation of the Southern forests; however, whether you love Teddy Roosevelt or not, it was not a federal concern. But then the War was lost and anything the federals now wanted to concern themselves with they could. But my biggest problem with Schurz was his high-handed arrogance in his use of federal power, and I do not care what potential good one might see in such abuse. With every encroachment, a precedent is set and more liberty is lost.

Now, the date. A year before, Mississippi all but ran its Maine-born Radical Republican governor Adelbert Ames, son-in-law to Massachusetts's Benjamin "Beast" Butler, out of the state on a rail. Shortly thereafter, Hayes became president on a compromise that removed the last of the federal occupying forces from the South. The Republican Party was on the defensive. How die-hard a Republican Schurz was I'm not certain. Goodness knows, there was room for reform within that party. He was not a Radical, and he routinely fell out with his fellow Republicans. That could be considered in his favor (again my opinion).

Prussia protected its forests. In Schurz' mind, so should the United States. His subordinate, the Federal Land Commissioner Joseph Williamson, agreed. Their conclusion was that over the past two decades, i.e., since 1857 and the spurt in the Southern timber industry, the federal government had collected only $200,000 at a cost of roughly $46,000 in dealing with timber thieves...and the timber contiguous to all those raft-worthy streams was gone. With the consent of Schurz, Williamson fired his land officers, divided federal lands into districts and assigned special agents to enforce the no-trespassing laws on government property. *Then*, and this is the part that gets my goat, he initiated legal proceedings to punish trespassers or to collect damages for the waste *already* committed. How the devil were they going to collect damages for waste already committed, and by whom? And *from* whom were they going to collect it?

Murray A. Carter, the new special agent for Mississippi, Alabama, Florida, and Louisiana, quickly reported depredations in all those Southern states and then proceeded to seize logs, lumber, and naval stores at the mouth of the Pascagoula and other locations. He placed a federal marshal with a double-barreled shotgun on the drawbridge forming part of the railroad that spanned the entrance to East Pascagoula Bay, effectively bringing to a halt the shipment of forest products by boat.

Ultimately, thirty-seven Mississippi Coast sawmills were shut down, and the livelihood of hundreds of people put in jeopardy.

The huge Griffin Mill at Moss Point claimed its logs had been removed from state lands...and this is the main point. Federal marshals had no way of determining from where the logs had been removed. If Schurz and Williamson had started in March 1877 by firing their agents (where the problem originally lay and had, technically, since 1817) and started real policing from that point, they'd have been in the right, but this heavy-handed use of force went part in parcel with the worst fears of what centralized government meant. Government exists to protect private property. That's why people create it. Technically government should have no property of its own except that needed to function...and granted, Uncle Sam had been trying to get rid of those Pine Barrens for sixty years and couldn't, so why did Schurz jump in with both feet at this point and start acting like failure to write off timber already cut was gonna make a difference? Conservation? Not much you can do to conserve a dead tree.

How about a flagrant display of power? Works for me. Think "hind end of a mule" here, and that's whether he cared about conservation or not. Yes, he had a duty as Secretary of the Interior, but the trees from those logs were already lost. As a reformer who claimed to care about people, he might have shown a little concern about the families of mill workers dependent on the lumber industry.

The Coast's lumber industry remained shut down for three years. Ultimately, most of the litigation was dropped. The one, *questionably*, "positive" thing that came out of this display of tyranny was that people started buying the land...cheap. Still, not enough Southerners had the capital to buy it. Northern lumbermen in the early '80s still weren't sure they wanted to venture into what the Republican party had styled as the jaws of death to cut timber and make lumber. Ah, but the speculators sent agents forth, or already had some here in the form of Southern land agents. These agents were ready and willing, for a price, to pervert homestead laws and ensure that huge chunks of property ended up in the hands of single buyers or corporations. Truth is, large chunks of land in the hands of private enterprise was the only practical way to make use of the Piney Woods. Unfortunately, speculators naturally were part of this process. But they sure the devil should have had to pay a decent price for it. Those people got that land for next to nothing. Good job, Schurz!

In 1877, Mississippi initiated a law limiting the amount of swampland sold to a single buyer to 240 acres, but hopes on the part of Southern congressmen that public lands would quickly pass into private hands were not immediately realized. Then in 1880 *The Northwestern Lumberman* began to field questions regarding the Southern Pine Barrens, and between 1881-1883, almost 2,000,000 acres of Mississippi's Piney Woods disappeared from the public rolls. By the close of 1884, federal and state authorities had stepped back from the sale of forested lands and the federal government had suggested setting aside some portions of its holdings for reserves. In 1886, the *Pascagoula Star* decried the rate at which Mississippi's federal timberlands were passing into the hands of Northern and Eastern capitalists. Pascagoula mill men, who owned little land but obtained their timber from the national domain, were about to find themselves at the mercy of Michigan corporations. Michigan investors were active in the years 1883-1884, Chicago investors joined them by 1884-1886. By 1887, most of Mississippi's public timberlands along the railroad had been purchased and the price was up to $15 an acre—remember, the railroads had both state and federal donations. They eventually sold their timberland to the lumbermen.

In 1887, lumbermen in conjunction with ancillary railroad interests conducted excursions for investors across the South. As a result, the federal government sold 128,000 acres for $1.25 per acre. The purchase was made by individuals and groups. That price was meant to promote small, individual farms. A quick story if I might: Delos A. Blodgett went to Michigan in 1848. In 1878, he built the largest sawmill in that state. In 1882 he started buying federal and state land in Mississippi at $1.25 an acre. By 1906, he owned 721,000 acres of Mississippi longleaf in Jackson, Wayne, Perry, Greene, Marion, and Pearl River Counties. Between 1908 and 1912 he started selling large tracts of timberland to lumbermen at $30-40 an acre. Technically, Blodgett was a lumberman. In fact, he was a timber speculator. There were many like him.

This fear of "monopoly" had Southern legislators concerned. In 1888, Senator E. Walthall of Mississippi introduced a bill in the U.S. Congress to end disposal of the national domain by private entry. Between 1877 and 1890, the federal government had culled its 4,000,000 acres of public Mississippi holdings to under 1,500,000 acres. After 1890, the government donated another 90,000 acres to Mississippi's four universities (roughly 23,000 each). Ole Miss held on to her donation, but the other three sold their land to railroad and timber interests. Anything the railroads had, they also sold to the timber interests.

The balance of the 1,500,000 federal acres passed to private ownership via homesteading.

One last attempt at a homestead act was passed by the state legislature in 1888. Maximum purchase again was 240 acres at $1.25 an acre. Purchasers had to be state citizens; corporations and nonresidents were not allowed. This was an attempt to implement the Jeffersonian ideal of small independent farms, but since most of the land being offered up was unfit for agriculture, the move was a non-starter, and this act was repealed in 1890.

In 1892, the office of Swampland Commissioner was abolished and management of all state lands, less the Choctaw school lands, was turned over to the State Land Commissioner. Buyers were limited to 160 acres in any twelve-month period; non-resident aliens and corporations need not apply.

In the State Land Commissioner's first report to the legislature he informed it that laws designed to limit holdings were ineffective and recommended that the land be surveyed, classified, and sold according to its value. He rebuked those responsible for protection of the timberlands, pointing out they were the very people who betrayed the public's trust. He also recommended solutions for halting depredations against the lands, but what the state came up with as deterrents failed to deter and convictions were rarely forthcoming before unsympathetic juries. The key, in my opinion, was putting a proper price on the value of the land. As of 1896 the state claimed roughly 145,000 acres in the pine belt, roughly half in the three Coast counties, but the commissioner admitted he could not determine how much was actually owned by the state because large acreage had been "improperly" placed on the tax rolls, before being sold, then was disposed of through tax sales. I'm sorry, but that had to be done at the county or county supervisor level and it reeks of malfeasance.

To give the reader an idea of how lumbering was doing at the close of the 19th century: In 1880, the port of Pascagoula reported shipping 60,000,000 board feet of longleaf pine. By 1893, that total had risen to 130,000,000 board feet. By the close of the 19th century, Southern sawmills, virtually unchanged for two hundred and fifty years prior, were some of the biggest in the world, and the turpentiners were living on borrowed time. The locust hordes of lumbermen were chopping down fresh trees before the turpentine "cutters" could get them boxed.

Here I'd like to broach the subject of Jack Gibson's alleged ownership of Deacon French's turpentine distillery in Piotona. Such arrangements during this period were not unprecedented and would have been made at the request of the black man, who would have asked a trusted white man to front for him in the tumultuous years during and after Reconstruction. It was a discretionary tactic employed to protect the owner and his family from perceived threats by the jealous or vindictive, who might have attributed the black man's success to prior alignment with the corrupt Republican hegemony that had recently been overthrown. Such seemingly petty jealousies were not necessarily petty, but might have served the purpose of removing a successful rival from the competition. In my story, this was not the case. Eva Markiston targeted a still she believed belonged to Jack Gibson, and she did so for the sole purpose of hurting Jack Gibson. Of course, she didn't care who else got hurt in the process.

❧❦

This brings the reader up to the time of my novel, but long-leaf's story does not end here. In 1890, there was a lot of virgin timber in the hands of speculators and lots of lumbermen itching to get their hands on it. Many had the capital to do so. For the next forty years, up to the Depression, the industry provided a good livelihood for a lot of regular folk across the South, but in the end, it had slain the goose that laid the golden egg.

Jack's desire to become a "forester," as described in the epilogue, represents this author's desire to end the story on a positive note, at least as far as the flora of the Piney Woods is concerned. His prescience, however, will no doubt be recognized by those familiar with this period as occurring thirty years too early. Though one cannot rule out the concerns of individual inhabitants of the Piney Woods (and that's what I consider Jack), it wasn't until the 1920s that state leaders, still enjoying the lumber boom, would step back and look at the devastation and ask themselves what the hell just happened? At that point they had to face the fact that they'd either turn over vast acreages of cutover lands to outsiders who might "do something" with the mess, or they could fix it. Turning the land over to outsiders might have pushed much of Mississippi's population to either leave the state or suffer the mercies of absentee landlords. Thank the good Lord, the state fixed it, but it didn't happen overnight. Y'all do know that today, timber is Mississippi's number one cash crop, right? Again, a history for another novel.

By the 1930s, this cut-and-run logging had devastated the centuries-old forest and left it no way to recover, at least not without help. Help was hard to come by, not from lack of interest, but because of ignorance about the ecology of the longleaf.

Longleaf is a slow-growing tree. It is also difficult to grow, particularly when foresters, trying to create the best conditions for its rejuvenation, are actually doing the opposite. The key is fire. For untold centuries, fire rejuvenated the longleaf habitat and kept it going. A longleaf grows for years without a seed fall; in fact, heat from fire causes the seed fall. (See, those damn Yankees couldn't have destroyed longleaf with fire even it they'd wanted to.) Because the cones are larger and the seeds heavier, longleaf seedlings don't grow far from the parent trees, thus more than a few trees need to be left after cutting to encourage reseeding. Further, those seeds don't do well in shrub and undergrowth — both features that natural fires keep at bay. [Okay, I give, the Yankees' fires wouldn't have been "natural" fires. Those vandals would have used an accelerant. They used phosphorous on Jackson in 1863.]

All these things forest managers have had to learn over the past century. Of course, an old Piney Woods rancher could, and probably did, tell them about the "fire" thing.

Fire or not, the trees are slow to grow. Loblolly and slash pine, which quickly took over longleaf's habitat, grow fast. Both are good timber and paper mill trees — and folks or companies looking to raise timber for resale saw little future in a tree they couldn't harvest for eighty years.

Perhaps I exaggerate. Truth is, today forest managers are trying to regenerate longleaf, and a longleaf forest can be thinned for "telephone" poles after fifteen years. You may have heard, also, that longleaf fared better than loblolly during Katrina — but it is natural that it would. Fires and hurricanes are part of longleaf's "life" style; that's why God put it where He did.

He didn't make it to survive man, though. That He left to man, and man is trying to right the wrong. It's been hit and miss for the past century, but those forest managers have had more hits than misses lately, and as a Mississippian I'm proud to say that my state has more acreage in rejuvenated longleaf than any other. We are managing longleaf as a commercial, renewable resource. It's a darn fine tree for being an ugly ole pine.

Now a few words on the towns, creeks, and byways traveled by my characters along the Mississippi Gulf Coast and in and out of the Piney Woods. All the towns and creeks are or were real, but it is risky to presume previous existence of a town or hamlet based merely on its being present at the moment. In the last half of the 19th century numerous towns popped up along burgeoning railroad routes that had heretofore not existed. This is particularly true in Mississippi's Piney Woods. Many a little town presently along what is now the Illinois Central or what was the New Orleans-Great Western did not exist before the 1880s or later. Alternately, many towns bypassed by the railroad died out. That is why you can still find Lumberton on a state map, but not Piotona a few miles north. From my Mississippi Railroad Commissioner's 1888 Rand McNally railroad map, I was able to puzzle out the names of back roads such as Columbia-Piotona. Identifying routes by their respective termini persists to this day. The commissioner's map even shows Gulfport, terminus of the proposed Gulf-Ship Island railroad. At the time of my story, both city and railroad were under construction, struggling with funding. Eventually, both came to fruition, but my map predated the actual incorporation of Gulfport by a decade. Nicholson, the location of a mill to which Humboldt was moving lumber early in the story, is now part of the Picayune community. At the request of the citizens of the Hobolochitto community, the name Picayune was chosen for their settlement by celebrity resident Eliza Jane Poitevent Nicholson, the writer popularly known as Pearl Rivers and owner and publisher of the *New Orleans Daily Picayune*. Picayune was incorporated as a township in 1904 and as a city in 1921. So at the time of my story, it's still Nicholson (or Hobolochitto), but it's Nicholson on the Rand-McNally map, and that's where the railroad stop was.

Further, for those of you familiar with the present layout of south Mississippi, but not the evolution of her counties...Lamar, Forrest, Stone, and George Counties did not exist in 1889. That's why no one traverses them in the narrative.

The Carrollton Hotel and Resort in New Orleans where Penny and Harold spent their disappointing honeymoon was a popular resort replete with oak-shaded flower gardens, fine dining, and access to the walkway along the Mississippi River levee, set with rows of china ball trees, at Riverbend. Hotel and resort were demolished in 1896 to make way for a new levee.

Carrollton (uptown New Orleans) began life as the eighteenth-century Macarty plantation on the uppermost part of Bienville's 1719 land grant. The plantation property was eventually sold to developers and in 1833 Charles Zimpel laid out the town lots from which rose the town of Carrollton. The hamlet was linked to a growing New Orleans by a dirt road (today's St. Charles Avenue) and a street car system, one of the earliest railroads in the United States. It's still there, despite now being powered by electricity rather than horse or mule-drawn trams. As of 1870, Carrollton was a thriving suburb of New Orleans with shell-paved streets, sidewalks, gas lighting, its own fire department, and newspapers. It was annexed by the city in 1874, so by the time of Penny and Harold's visit, Carrollton was an integral part of New Orleans.

The streets making up Biloxi, Handsboro, and Mississippi City as well as those linking the hamlets along the Coast are valid. In addition to contemporary street maps, I consulted the 1893 set of Sanborn Fire Insurance Company maps for my layout of Biloxi. This may surprise some of you, but the first official road map in the United States was first published by Rand-McNally in 1903 and lays out Boston, Massachusetts. Government maps highlighting post roads and military maps did exist and had since the beginning of the Republic (and probably well back into colonial times), but regular city street and county road maps did not, as a rule, exist. That certainly didn't prevent individuals from drawing their own maps. I have squirreled away in my files a copy of an 1850s-era map drawn in pencil by John J. McCaughan detailing Railroad Road (now Gulfport's Courthouse Road) trekking north across Bernard Bayou and continuing almost due north spanning Harrison County and terminating at Augusta, then the Perry County seat. The drafter annotated the drawing as the "old road" to Augusta.

Today, all the coastal towns are linked by U.S. Highway 90, also known as Beach Boulevard. In 1888, however, a portion of "Beach Boulevard," which in Biloxi parallels the Gulf, was called Front Street. Additionally, the Beach Boulevard/Front Street expanse was broken by the private ownership of property extending down to the Mississippi Sound itself. Easements had yet to be purchased along the entire Gulf, so enjoying the gulf breeze in carriage rides from Pass Christian to Biloxi Bay was not possible, though as of 1883 one could travel unimpeded from Mississippi City to Porter Avenue. Front Street in Biloxi appears to be unimpeded from, at least, Fayard Avenue to the entrance to the Back Bay as of 1893.

From what I can decipher, the surest straight shot linking all the hamlets was the Biloxi-Pass Christian Road. This route is now known as Pass Road, and today is broken in Gulfport by the U.S. Naval Construction Battalion Center and in Biloxi by Keesler Air Force Base. East of Keesler in Biloxi, old Pass Road is now Howard Avenue.

In 1889, Main Street Handsboro was a section of Pass Road, so it is the route I had Jack and Penny Gibson take after leaving Kate's boarding house in Happy Hollow (east Handsboro) to the Noble house in Biloxi. Jack's detour to the Gulf was by design. He did not have to leave the Biloxi-Pass Christian Road to get to Main Street Biloxi (location of the Noble house).

Biloxi was a thriving little city at the end of the 19th century, as were the other hamlets along the Coast. The seafood canning industry on Biloxi's Back Bay was growing; the timber industry had exploded and continued to thrive until the 1930s. Though much of the area separating the towns—and this includes the environs right outside the city limits—was rural, the towns were well connected by roads, rail, and waterways. Before the end of the century, electricity and telephones were the rage. The Nobles' house used coal oil lamps, but also boasted its own coal gas plant.

In regards to the Biloxi police force, information came sparingly. What I do have I owe to the Local History and Genealogy branch of the Harrison County Library System in Biloxi.

Biloxi had a small police force in 1889 and had had one for a long time prior. Biloxi, even then, was not a young city. Its history, in fact, goes back to 1699 when Pierre Le Moyne, Sieur d'Iberville, founded Fort Maurepas, Old Biloxi (now Ocean Springs), on the east shore of Biloxi Bay. During Queen Anne's War, the French moved its administrative capitol to Mobile (1702) to be closer to their Spanish allies in Pensacola. By 1717 the goodwill between cousins sitting on the respective French and Spanish thrones had soured (War of the Quadruple Alliance) and the French moved the military contingent from Fort Maurepas, along with the administrative capitol of French Louisiana in Mobile, to the western shore of Biloxi Bay, the city's present site. Unfortunately there is little to be found on the police force of a settlement that has been around as long as Biloxi has. This, too, was explained to me by History and Genealogy at the Biloxi Library. Apparently, at some point in the 1980s, a new administration ushered in a house-cleaning initiative, destroying all records determined unnecessary for current operations.

We know, of course, there was a police department prior to the 1980s; its activities are well documented in both print and video (newspaper and television). It's the structure and activities in the "dark ages" before television and in the days of limited newspapers where the problem arises. To make a long story short, I know little about the police force in 1889, but I did find an 1896 newspaper article on city administration in general that identified one chief of police/city marshal and two deputies. I had already created a fictional chief of police with one subordinate in 1889 and figured I was close enough.

Further, a new city hall had been approved as of the time of my story, replete with an office for Biloxi's chief of police along with two prisoners' cells at the rear of the first floor. I have an unverified verbal source (library) that indicates the old town hall also housed the office of the chief of police and if he had prisoner facilities, and he probably did, they would have been in that same building. I found the old "Town Hall" on the Sanborn map, on the east side of Main Street, north of Washington. For the purposes of my plot, I devised a mechanism that places Penny in the county lockup in Mississippi City (the county seat) rather than in the relatively safe hands of Tobias Craig in Biloxi.

The last historical reference I wish to address is money. It's enlightening to look at what our present day monopoly money system has done to the value of the dollar over the last century plus. It is also difficult for me to guess how much money an Eva Markiston would have needed to realize her extravagant dreams for King and Gibson; or how much a lender would be willing to risk on her company and what sort of profit it would expect in return; or how much a powerful Northern company would pay for land it could get for next to nothing by working with criminals in state government exploiting a corrupt federal system. Suffice it to say I remained on the fringes of such details. My story is one of escape fiction, after all, my objective merely to suspend disbelief. Thus having qualified the assumptions I made in the story, that $10,000 Alan Noble appropriated from his corporation and loaned to Eva Markiston was the equivalent of $250,000 in today's money, and the $25,000 he "borrowed" from the company kitty to purchase the land on which he hoped to realize a fast return from Humboldt Timber would be worth a whopping $625,000 today. I guess the biggest assumption I have made and hope to sell you on, is that Noble Corporation was a *very* lucrative enterprise to have that much in liquid funds available—understanding there was not a lot of capital in the South at that time. The only way Alan Noble could have gotten out of trouble with his misappropriation was by a quick turnaround on the land, the demand for which proved a hoax. The only sure standard I have to determine my values is the going price of the timberland at the time (see page 454 in this note) and the rise in land speculation that was ongoing from the 1880s on. Alan took the risk, as Jon suspected he might, because he was already in a bind with the ten-thousand-dollar loan he'd made to Eva. With the flim-flam perpetrated on him by Jon, Alan was in much bigger trouble. He could sell the land, probably at a loss. If he then foreclosed on

King and Gibson and coaxed a good selling price out of Humboldt for that property...*and* if he liquidated his forty percent in Noble Corporation, he might have been able to break even and stay out of jail. Whatever, Jon finally had big brother where he wanted him, a driving point in the story.

The $100 with which Jon Noble attempted to bribe Jack was equivalent to $2,500 today.

I hope I have explained, or at least satisfied your questions arising during the reading journey. Thanks for reading *Requited Harvest*. I hope you enjoyed reading the tale as much as I enjoyed writing it.

If you enjoyed *Requited Harvest* don't miss Charlsie Russell's award-winning first novel

The Devil's Bastard

Natchez on the river, 1793. The Spanish Fleet controls the Mississippi, and the Dons rule their rowdy British and American subjects with a patient hand. The location is strategic, the land fertile, and within two decades, cotton will be king. Into this web of international intrigue, the rich and powerful Elizabeth Boswell welcomes her orphaned grandniece Angelique Veilleux and introduces the impoverished beauty to a world of privilege. But power has enemies and wealth demands a price. Rumors state that Elizabeth's success stems from dalliance with a lustful demon that still prowls her family farm of De Leau outside Natchez.

At the center of this ominous legend is Elizabeth's grandson, the handsome and dangerous Mathias Douglas, who saves Angelique from degradation and death near the end of her journey to Natchez. Mathias is the son of the doomed Julianna, Elizabeth's only daughter. Mathias's father, locals whisper, is Elizabeth's demon.

Despite the dark legend, Angelique cannot quell her feelings for Mathias, for whom she would make any sacrifice. An outcast, Mathias is cruelly tested by Angelique's affection. Determined not to dishonor her, he callously puts her aside. But Elizabeth has other plans and offers him the family farm at De Leau to marry the girl. Soon Angelique finds herself desperately in love with the man who has conquered her body and possessed her soul.

But something in the swamps surrounding De Leau stalks her, and nightmares invade her dreams. What she perceives as Mathias' indifference to the threat leaves Angelique isolated and afraid. She begins to doubt her grandaunt's motives for sending her to De Leau, as well as Mathias' role in Elizabeth's plan. Resolving her doubts means uncovering the secret of Mathias' sire.

From Mathias and Angelique's first meeting to Elizabeth Boswell's revelation at story's end, *The Devil's Bastard* is a splendid read. First and foremost a sensual romance, it is also a well-researched historical with a haunting mystery.

Don't miss Charlsie Russell's second award-winning novel

Wolf Dawson

Ten years after the Confederate Army reported him killed in action, dirt-poor Jeff Dawson returns to Natchez, Mississippi, a wealthy man and purchases White Oak Glen, the once opulent home of the now impoverished Seatons, the aristocratic family that years ago shattered his own.

Burdened with her drunken brother, Tucker, and besieged by greedy relatives, Juliet Seaton struggles to hold on to what remains of her farm. Now she finds her family faced with a new menace in the form of a marauding wolf that slaughters valuable stock and assails the mind of her alcoholic brother. Tucker Seaton warns his sister that the man occupying White Oak Glen is a ghost, who in the form of that vicious wolf seeks to destroy what is left of the Seatons.

An infant when events occurred setting her family against the Dawsons, Juliet appears pitted against a neighbor hell-bent on avenging his sister, who died in childbirth after being violated by a Seaton male. Jeff's grandfather was part Creek Indian.

Local legend states he terrorized unfriendly neighbors with tales of his ability to shape-shift into a deadly wolf. Unidentified persons lynched the colorful old man following the savage killing, apparently by a wolf, of the Seaton who raped Jeff Dawson's sister.

But Juliet finds the handsome Jeff a living, breathing man, hot-blooded, to boot. His seductive touch weakens her resolve and blinds her to the danger he poses. Jeff, however, is no longer compelled to destroy the Seatons, if he ever was; they have destroyed themselves and left the vulnerable Juliet to his mercy — mercy he's quite willing to give, though he's not ready to let the feisty beauty know that.

Into this explosive mix of fear and distrust comes a sadistic killer, and what this fiend kills is not Seaton livestock.

With the countryside ablaze with suspicion directed toward Jeff, he and Juliet overcome mutual distrust and strip away a lost generation's hatred as quickly as the clothes covering their bodies. Old lies give way to new truths, lust to love, and together, the lovers set out to uncover not only a killer, but the identity of the spectral beast haunting the countryside.

Don't miss Charlsie Russell's third award-winning novel

Epico Bayou

In the fall of 1897, a grand old gentleman of Handsboro, Mississippi dies a very wealthy man, and much to the chagrin of Lionel Augustus's siblings, he leaves the bulk of his estate to his estranged bastard son, Clay Boudreaux, and his beloved step-daughter, Olivia Lee. There is but one stipulation to Lionel's will, the two must wed.

For reasons of their own, the two young people agree to marry, sight unseen, but only days after her marriage by proxy to Deputy Sheriff Clay Boudreaux of Galveston County, Texas, Olivia learns her husband has died in a house fire and her extended family intends to contest the terms of the will. Exacerbating her situation, a mysterious stranger, claiming to be the dead Clay, but who her family warns is Clay's older brother Troy, invades Olivia's opulent home and accuses her of hiring Troy to kill Clay...and yet another henchman to eliminate Clay's killer.

Olivia and the handsome stranger both have sound reasons

469

for confusing their roles in the plot to murder Clay Boudreaux, reasons dealing with duty, justice, and survival. Neither is sure of the role the other plays in the Machiavellian plan of Lionel's siblings, nor is it clear if Lionel's brother and sister are the only subversives working to sabotage the terms of Lionel's will. So clear is the present danger, it overshadows the dark secret driving Lionel's bizarre stipulation that Clay and Olivia wed.

Set on the Mississippi Gulf Coast at the close of the nineteenth century, Charlsie Russell's third novel is both a romantic charade and a compelling mystery, pitting the wit and will of one wary lover against the honor and sheer determination of the other, even while the sinister machinations of dangerous foes force them into a grudging alliance.

Though the tangled mystery sets this novel apart from her edgy Gothics, *The Devil's Bastard* and *Wolf Dawson*, Ms. Russell's *Epico Bayou* still features those tried and true elements of suspense, sensual romance, and historical setting that characterize her work. Pure escape. Don't miss this journey!

And if you like what you've read so far, look for

River's Bend

Rafe Stone came back to Mississippi seeking justice and the house irrevocably linked to everything that makes him who he is. But the magnificent structure that began life as a one-room, French-Dominion log cabin and grew into an antebellum showcase south of Natchez has fallen into disrepair and into the hands of a savvy Mississippi City businessman by the name of Josephus Collander. The astute Collander has no use for the tax-draining piece of real estate; moreover, he needs to unburden himself of a recently acquired orphaned niece who, through no fault of her own, is wreaking havoc within his household. The house is not for sale, Collander tells the disappointed Rafe...but he can have it for nothing, if he'll accept it as Delilah Graff's dowry.

Rafe's desperation, coupled with Delilah's beauty, makes the decision, albeit a reckless one, easy. But what secret in the siren's past would cause a seemingly kind and responsible kinsman to barter her to a stranger?

Tragedy, followed by a difficult childhood, has left Delilah jaundiced toward life, bitter toward men, and eager for the independence she is sure is coming. Instead, the financial support her beneficent Uncle Joe promised is suddenly forfeit, and he has called in his markers, compelling her to wed a man she does not know. Worse yet, her uncle doesn't appear to know much about the handsome Rafe Stone either. Adding to her discomfort, this Mr. Stone takes her to Natchez, a city where her name is synonymous with disgrace. There he moves her into a house rumored, over the course of its nearly two hundred years, to have hosted treason, robbery, adultery, and murder. A house still reputed to harbor the specter of a vicious killer.

And who is Rafe Stone, the man to whom she has sworn her troth and under whose roof she sleeps at night? A man who claims to be a stranger to Mississippi, yet knows more about the ominously majestic River's Bend, and its past, than he should? What is his link to the dark legends haunting River's Bend and to the ghost walking its rambling halls? Is he the personification of her nightmare or an unbidden dream come true?

Mystery, suspense, romance, and history, dear reader. Enjoy this look back to the time when the memory of the Old South blossomed into legend.

And if you haven't already read it, make sure to read

Camellia Creek

In September 1865, Lieutenant Colonel, Confederate States Army, Eli Calhoon, returns to his war-ravaged plantation, Camellia Creek, outside Port Gibson in Claiborne County, Mississippi, resolved to begin again. But Mississippi, like the rest of the South, lies prostrate in the wake of a devastating conflict that wasted its population and destroyed what had been, only four years earlier, the third strongest economy in the world. More troubling, the South's recovery is now overseen by a victorious enemy determined that the Southern economy, as well as the South's influence within the Union, will never be revived. For Southerners, getting a spring crop in the field is as far out of reach as is the payment of five years' back taxes Congress demands from the states in Rebellion to pay for the War it waged against them.

Orphaned Alice Shelton, late of Ohio by way of Chicago, has come to Mississippi with her aunt and uncle, Betty and Peter Franklin. Peter is a speculator in search of investment. A veteran of the War, he knows opportunity exists in the defeated South. His preference for a home for his wife, daughter, and niece is the lovely Camellia Creek. In company with the Franklins are Peter's widowed sister-in-law Eustacia and her son, Jonathan, who Peter believes is the perfect match for Alice, heiress to a fortune.

Alice's widowed father, Jacob Shelton, and his two sons were killed in action during the War, fighting for the Union. The losses have left Alice in despair so deep her aunt fears Alice might take her own life.

Seth Parker, Major, United States Marine Corps, has come to Mississippi on orders at the request of a friend and military senior to investigate the murder of a U.S. Treasury agent, which possibly ties in to cotton thefts rampant among the white army officers stationed in Mississippi. The powers that be prefer he find a Southerner to blame, but the senior officer is not so sure. To investigate the death, Seth is given a troop of nine men, all Negro members of Mississippi's Native Guard, for the most part former slaves recruited into the Union Army during the War.

Desperate times call for desperate measures, and in a lawless South, desperate measures are gambles that sometimes pay off. When an indiscretion not of her own making lands the lovely Alice into the hands of a determined Eli Calhoon, he blackmails her into marriage and brings her to Camellia Creek, where she is haunted by Jocelyn LeBlanc, an ill-fated beauty who died under mysterious circumstances decades earlier. In addition to Jocelyn's ghostly presence, the War's aftermath, murder, and jealous greed vex Alice, threatening her newfound desire to live, a desire ignited by the very man who could be plotting to snuff it out.

And don't miss the sequel to *Camellia Creek*

Honor's Banner

As of January 1866, Major Seth Parker, United States Marine Corps, has been in war-ravaged Mississippi two months investigating the murder of Treasury operative Alan Guthrie. Guthrie was in Mississippi only a short time when he was killed, and his reason for being in the area remains a mystery, both to authorities here and, if they are to be believed, to his seniors in Washington.

This is not Parker's first foray into Mississippi's hinterland. He was here in the spring of '63, before Vicksburg fell, but his covert operations at that time led to only fleeting success and a precipitous departure with a bullet in his chest and a battle for his life.

Widowed Rebecca Mackey lost not only her young husband and unborn son to the War, but her father, a brother, and a sister. Now, her sole surviving sibling, Eli Calhoon, ex-CSA, is fighting for his life, the victim of an attack linking him not only to Alan Guthrie's murder, but to a web of intrigue in the U. S. Treasury.

At a time when treason is synonymous with the South and her people convenient scapegoats to disguise the misdeeds of unprincipled men, Becky learns her brother is suspected not only in Guthrie's death, but of continued sedition. Worse, the man who set his sights on Eli Calhoon two months earlier is Seth Parker, the enemy whose life she saved in 1863, a man she is loath to trust, but who might prove her greatest ally.

Honor's Banner is a sequel to Charlsie Russell's *Camellia Creek* and advances the mystery of murdered Treasury agent Alan Guthrie, the catalyst that brought Seth Parker into the lives of unreconstructed rebel Eli Calhoon and his reluctant bride. Rich in the history of the period, it explores the multifaceted narrative of the unwarranted War, state rights, federal violations of the Constitution, and the institutionalization of tyranny by a United States in the hands of fanatics and traitors, a focus largely ignored when discussing Reconstruction today.

About the Author

Charlsie Russell is a retired United States Navy commander turned author. She loves history, and she loves the South. She focuses her writing on historical suspense set in her home state of Mississippi.

After seven years of rejection, she woke up one morning and determined she did not have enough years left on this planet to sit back and hope a New York publisher would one day take a risk on her novels. Thus resolved, she expanded her horizons into the publishing realm with the creation of Loblolly Writer's House.

In addition to writing and publishing, Ms. Russell is a mother, grandmother, and homemaker.

To learn more about Charlsie Russell, visit:

www.charlsierussell.com
www.loblollywritershouse.com

Or visit her blog at:

http://loblollylog.blogspot.com.

Follow her on Twitter @CharlsieRussell, and on Google+ as Charlsie Russell.

www.ingramcontent.com/pod-product-compliance
Lightning Source LLC
Chambersburg PA
CBHW051204120726
47905CB00004B/976